Doctor Blood Moon

Doctor Blood Moon

Jack Walker

Library of Congress Control Number: 2014916559
ISBN: Hardcover   978-1-4990-7099-6
                      Softcover   978-1-4990-7098-9
                      eBook   978-1-4990-7097-2

Rev. date: 09/17/2014

To order additional copies of this book, contact:
Xlibris LLC
1-888-795-4274
www.Xlibris.com
Orders@Xlibris.com
650507

For Patrick and Amy

PART ONE

CHAPTER ONE

Southern Montana, December 1967

It was a bad day to have no socks on. Cold plains wind, threat of rain. The boy liked to stop in the town library to do his homework and listen to tiny Mrs. Pine Leaf talk about books. Not today. He felt embarrassed with no socks and was worried about his mother. So he was running the mile home.

None of his classmates had noticed his bare ankles. Their heads were down because it was test time. He liked test time. But Mrs. Pine Leaf would notice. He had a sweet roll in his backpack for his ma. He pulled it out of the trash bin behind the bakery this morning. He knew how to find food in Lodge Grass. This Crow boy could take care of himself.

The ground west of town was hardpan, scattered rocks, scrub, cuts, culverts. Hard to run on in the December dusk, so he crossed the reservation road south for the soft even turf along Greasy Grass Creek. That was his favorite running route even though it took longer, twisting through the dark cedars hissing in the wind like angry Indian ghosts.

On Thanksgiving up in Crow Agency, Uncle Howard had wished him a happy tenth birthday. When he told that to Mrs. Pine Leaf, she said that would make this month his eleventh December. His legs were getting longer, and he was a good runner. He was proud how far he could run without stopping. Johnny Ryan Blood Moon, in his eleventh year.

He loped among twisted trees, his arms and legs moving in easy rhythm, the world dimly lit by a silver strip of sun at the horizon, defying dark heavy clouds. His thin face cut through the raw wind. His ears and ankles were ice cold. His back under his backpack was sweating. Five minutes he'd be home. The cold was the real reason to run—he couldn't find enough clothes that morning. George never came home, and Ma didn't move when he said good-bye. She usually smiled at least.

Johnny jumped up to the porch of the isolated shack, made up of a main room plus a small room with a closet and a bathroom. Outside was girded by a broken-tooth porch. Above the front door, the roof gaped open to the sky. A cluster of rusty buckets caught the rain.

Out of breath, Johnny pushed open the front door and entered the familiar cloud of whiskey. George was home. He surveyed the dim room. On the right was a familiar sculpture of broken furniture. In the kitchen corner on the left was a black wood-burning stove, the only source of warmth. Johnny slept on a thin mattress near the stove, with his laundry as a pillow. Nola and George, when he was home, slept in the small bedroom in summer and on the other side of the stove in winter. When George wasn't home, Nola Ryan Wind-In-The-Trees Blood Moon, Johnny's Crow-Irish ma, his love, his hero, his seamstress, his songstress, his warmth, his favorite person in the world, she would join him on his mattress. So sad now, her being so sick and weak.

He saw George sitting slumped against the far wall, his stubble chin down on his filthy work shirt. Next to George was the open bedroll where Johnny had last seen his mother. "Hey, George, you awake?" Johnny said.

George twitched, knocking over an empty bottle. He opened an eye and twisted his face.

"Damn, Johnny, 'bout time, boy. Oh, hey. Come here, go in the powder room. Bring all the stuff from the medicine box here. My head hurts awful."

The boy dropped his backpack and jogged into the small bedroom. He emerged with three bottles and a small box, and set them down next to George. "It's all there is. Where's Ma? You okay?"

"Hell no! *Shit* headache. Bad. Your ma's dead. I need you to go back to town and call Howard, tell him that, and tell him come get her"—he roughly rubbed his face—"but first go fill up this here dead soldier from the pail by the door."

George's puffy red eyes were half open now. He held out the empty bottle.

The boy didn't move. "You say . . . what? . . . Ma's dead?"

"'Swhat I said, isn't it?" George's voice went weary. "People die. It's out the back porch, outa her misery. Wrapped up in a sheet. She's all right there till Howard comes to pick it up."

The boy rocked back and forth on his haunches studying George's leather face. There was a weakness in George's eyes he didn't recognize.

"Wharya lookin' at?" George raised his gravel voice and waggled the bottle. "Fill this here up like I said 'fore I whup ya. I know somethin' about cold and dead people from Korea—it happens."

The boy knew the man couldn't stand up much less whup anyone. Tears pooled in his eyes. He gasped once, still breathless from the running.

"Don't you cry now, I told you that." George closed his eyes tight. "You wanna go see, go out back real quick. Don' open the blanket, though.

"Here's old man Red Bird's phone number." He fumbled in his shirt pocket. "Ask him for Howard. He'll go get him. Me and Howard we made a plan. He'll take you in up at Crow." Pause. "Go see your library lady, she'll let you call—she fancies you. Don' tell her any Nola's dead. Don' need no police or nothin'. Wouldn' come anyway like them doctors never came. Just shit Indians out here."

Johnny took the slip of paper.

"Tonight, he should come, Howard should, if he ain't too drunk. It ain't gonna last on the porch long 'fore it starts to smell enough for the animals to come."

The boy stared at the slip of paper. He whispered, "Can I see her?"

"I said you could. Nothin' to see." He closed his eyes again and dropped his voice. "I wrapped her nice as I could. Be quick." George snapped his eyes open as if to heed a distant sound, a George tic.

The boy shuffled to the back porch. As he stepped out, he saw something on his left that looked like a double cord of wood wrapped in a white sheet. He squatted and put his hand where he figured her head was. He saw a dark moist spot there.

"Ma?" he whispered. "*Ma?*"

The silence was overwhelming. He stood, turned, and vomited over the porch railing into the blue-black night.

CHAPTER TWO

Beverly Hills, July 2009

The tall surgeon stared at the flat line on the OR monitor. He raised his bloody gloved hands. "Max! Can't we try one more . . ."

The young doctor peered up at his mentor, Dr. Johnny Blood, and tilted his head. Their gowns were stained with sweat and blood. "Johnny, it's over. The man's dead."

Johnny stepped back. He bowed his head. "I don't understand this. Best writer of the twentieth century. Dead! *On my table!*"

"I'll close up," Max said, stepping up to the corpse, wielding his tools.

Johnny sagged, snapped off his gloves and mask, and threw them at the waste bin. He removed his blue cap and tossed his long, thick, black hair, which sprayed sweat. He knuckled the state-of-the-art heart-lung machine and surveyed the vast, gleaming, most sophisticated cardiac OR in the western United States. Stately broad-shouldered gunmetal and chrome machines blinked and winked uselessly, like stunned generals after a lost battle. The blue-clad staff froze, watching their famous leader struggle for control. This heart transplant theater was his baby. He designed it, funded it, assembled it with his own hands over twenty-five years.

Johnny waved his hand. "All this *crap*, we still can't save Manuel Maria Gomez." He stepped forward and carefully lifted the cloth to peer at the dead man's stone-gray death mask—the face had recently been the color of his own face. He touched the parchment forehead. "Vaya con dios, amigo."

"He did it to himself, Johnny," Max mumbled, working efficiently to close the dead man's chest. "You saw the lungs. He smoked right to the end, never took his meds. St. John's said his son snuck cigarettes into the CCU."

"Geniuses have their own rules, Max."

"Really? Sometimes I get so pissed how patients ignore basic——"

"Gomez is not just any patient! But . . . you're right, he didn't take care of himself." Johnny gazed reverently at the famous face. "Dead. Shit. I just wanted to have one more conversation with him." He resettled the cloth and stepped back. "Unlike most of them, he deserved his Nobel Prize. Deserved better of me."

"He was very sick. Not only the heart was dying."

"I know all that. We didn't have much room. But still, it totally feels like a failure." He stepped back and untied his blue gown. "Now, as my reward, I get nailed by the front office boys, why I admitted him in the first place, why we won't get paid, maybe get sued. I'll be filleted at the Morbidity and Mortality Committee meeting. Is that Monday?"

"Tuesday, next week. Monday we welcome the rookies. Remind me never to get sick in July. Yeah, management will want to hear all about it. Can I cover for you? I get along with Paul and even your friend Poulos."

"Poulos? Lord. Still hates me after all these years. No, he'll want me in the barrel. I hope you'll be there, though, in case I hyperventilate."

"There you go, boss."

Johnny shook his head. "Okay, on to the next of kin. The fun part."

***

Dr. Johnny Blood, the top heart surgeon on the West Coast, was a perfectionist. By his lights, it was a disaster to lose *any* patient, much less his literary hero. He viewed his job as thwarting death—no exceptions. As he pushed through the double doors into the hallway, a wave of nausea rose in his throat. He turned into the Authorized Personnel Only bathroom, gripped the sink, and looked in the mirror. His face was chalk, like Gomez's death mask. He slapped cold water and took several deep breaths. Feeling steadier, he returned to the corridor.

Six foot four, broad shouldered, movie-star handsome, Johnny steamed along the shadowless halls toward surgery guest waiting. His carbon-black eyes, fixed dead ahead, missed the fluttery glances; he was steeling himself to meet the Gomez family. He hoped they would take him for Mexican, maybe go easy on him.

In Hispanic LA, sepia-skinned Johnny passed as Mexican; in Persian Beverly Hills, as Iranian; in other neighborhoods, as Pakistani, Armenian, Jewish, even African American. No one pegged him as "American American," as he liked to say. His story should have made him proud; instead, it weighed on him. A Crow Indian orphan from hardscrabble Montana, he had climbed to the top of world-class UC Cedars Medical Center in Beverly Hills. His patients were the rich and famous; indeed, he was rich and famous himself. And now, this, the most important surgery of his life, a botch.

Striding along, Johnny recalled the anonymous call two weeks ago reporting that Señor Gomez was dying and that no reputable doctor would take his call. Alarmed, Johnny called Gomez's LA agent, a former patient, who agreed to take Johnny to Gomez's Holmby Hills pied-à-terre. On the phone, the agent said that Gomez was trying to finish his second novel about the Mexican drug cartels. He had optioned Gomez's first novel on the subject, but it wasn't going anywhere. "Kind of a tricky theme."

Arriving Sunday morning, the two men were met by several surly brown-skinned men. A young boy with enormous dark eyes lurked in the background. The sun-filled hillside condo was crammed with books and magazines. A bodyguard body-searched the two men. "*Con permiso, Señores.* There have been death threats."

Finally admitted to Gomez's presence, Johnny smelled cigarettes. After introductions, Johnny spoke. "I'll speak in English, Señor Gomez. My Spanish is bad. Our friend here can translate." Gomez nodded once, his famous blue eyes placid. Johnny knew Gomez's English was equally limited.

"I am honored to meet you, Señor," Johnny continued. "I want to help you. I've read all of your books." The agent translated.

The author's eyes sparkled. Encouraged, Johnny said that if he wanted to keep on writing, he would need a new heart. The agent translated, adding that Johnny was the best heart transplant doctor in the country. Gomez shrugged and uttered his only words of the morning, "Por favor, mi hijo. Ayúdeme a acabar mi trabajo. ¡Estos hombres malvados!"

***

Please, my son, help me finish my work. These evil men! Walking along the hospital corridor, Johnny recalled the look of trust in Gomez's eyes. And now, he was dead—under his care. He wouldn't finish his work. The evil men, whoever they were, would live on, to do more evil.

Johnny stopped before the gray door of the guest waiting room. The existential question he'd been stuffing for years rose in his throat: *What on earth have I been doing with my life?*

CHAPTER THREE

As Johnny pushed through the door into the small room, he saw two young boys and several men with dark, darting eyes hunched away from each other. Some fingered cell phones, others hooded cigarettes in spite of posted signs. Only one, a short, gray-haired man wearing a Hawaiian shirt, seemed over thirty. A massive young man in the center of the group appeared to be the alpha. He wore a leather vest and a black watch cap. Tattoos crawled up his powerful arms and neck.

Johnny recognized the smallest boy from his visit to Gomez's condo. The boy scrambled off the floor and stood in front of Johnny with hunched shoulders as if expecting a blow.

Johnny spoke. "Is this the Gomez family?"

The boy answered in a small voice, "Y mi primo también." He waved toward an older boy. "Somos la familia."

"Well . . .," Johnny said, composing himself. "So you and your cousin, you two, are the only family? These other men are . . . ?"

The older cousin spoke, "Amigos, Señor Doctor."

"Just *amigos*? Well, I'm afraid . . . I have bad news."

Johnny directed his words to the young boy. "My name is Dr. John Blood. I'm the surgeon who operated on Señor Gomez. I'm sad to say he died on the operating table. I did everything I possibly could do. He was a very sick man. A very great author, if I may say. A special hero of mine."

After a long moment, the young boy exclaimed, "¿Muerto?"

"Si. Él es muerto," Johnny answered after a beat.

The tattooed alpha stood and strode out of the room, followed by the gray-haired man. Others shuffled behind them. The small boy stood still. Tears spilled down his cheeks.

"Are you the son?" Johnny asked. "¿Habla Inglés?"

The boy sobbed once and thrust forward, sliding on his knees and wrapping his arms around Johnny's legs. His young cousin sprang forward and tried to pull him up. "Juanito. ¡Vamonos!"

"¡Espera!" the boy shouted, violently shaking off his cousin's grip. He looked up at Johnny with puppy eyes. His whisper was full of feeling. "Señor Doctor, did he say anything for me? I am, yes, his son, Juan."

Johnny squatted down. "I'm sorry, Juan. Your father was sedated—unconscious—the whole time when I was with him."

The boy went limp. Then he stood up slowly and leaned into his cousin, his face wet with tears. They shuffled out together arm in arm.

Johnny stood and watched them leave. The boy's tears had stirred him. Juan was the same age as Johnny Ryan Blood Moon when he lost his father in Lodge Grass so many years ago.

***

Johnny stalked along the preternaturally white hallway. As he waited for the elevator to his suite, the raspy voice of Dr. Arthur Poulos ripped through his reverie like a dull dagger. "Dr. Blood!"

Johnny turned to see the vice chief of staff approaching. Poulos was a swarthy toad of a man, his broad dark face twitchy with impatience. Poor health had forced him out of clinical practice years ago, but the powerful chief of staff, Dr. Stanley McRae, persuaded the Medical Executive Committee to appoint Poulos as his full-time vice chief because of his administrative and bad-cop skills.

"If you have a second."

Johnny looked around. They were alone. "Yes, Arthur. What's up?" Johnny knew what was up. He bit his lip.

"We can't afford your largesse," Poulos growled. "I know your bullshit line—ability to pay is not an issue in admissions. But now you're reaching out for these deadbeats!"

"Yes, in the case of Gomez, I did reach out. He's a Nobel Prize winner. Somebody called me, told me he was dying. I was concerned that because of his . . . history, no decent hospital would admit him. He's . . ."

"His *history*? That he doesn't pay his bills and sues every hospital he comes in contact with?"

"He's a great man! Was. I thought I could . . ."

"You're a fool, Johnny! You like reading books, so UC Cedars has to take a financial and publicity hit? Right in the middle of a capital campaign?"

The elevator chimed and opened. Johnny leaned on the door, glaring at Poulos. "Arthur, back off. This man needed my help. Capital campaigns, publicity hits, those things do not concern me."

The door began its angry buzz.

"You want to talk, come on up. I'll be glad to refresh your recollection what it means to be a physician." Poulos turned on his heel.

***

The Los Angeles basin is a stewpot of cities. Beverly Hills is one, and inside Beverly Hills is yet another formidable city: the UC Cedars Medical Center. That it was built with grateful show-business money is apparent by the names on the towers and streets: Lassie, George Burns, Elizabeth Taylor, Marvin Davis, Gracie Allen, on and on. All dead celebrities now, to be sure, but kept alive longer and perhaps made more comfortable by the magic of the UC Cedars staff, the presumptive best in the west. It's part of the ethos of LA—if you make a ton of money making films, you have a priority claim on the absolute best medical care, and that's at UC Cedars. Importantly, your reputation will not suffer by the choice. By choosing UC Cedars (and by writing big checks in the bargain), your brand and reruns have the best chance of living on, whether or not *you* do.

Like his professional reputation, Johnny's suite in the Bell Heart Wing was at the highest point on the UC Cedars campus, a matter of controversy among the medical staff. It had been a condition of the wealthy Wing funder, Wild Will Bell, a special tribute to Johnny for saving his life fifteen years ago. Another Wild Will condition was that Johnny be appointed director of the Heart Institute, jumping him over one Dr. Arthur Poulos, who had coveted the job.

As the elevator rose, Johnny felt his heart sink. It wasn't only Poulos who hated him. Alas, he was respected but not loved at UC Cedars. Ambitious, his face on magazine covers, his suite looking down on everyone—and on top of that, rich, because he'd married Wild Will's widow. He occasionally entertained thoughts of bailing out, going somewhere else, doing something else. But he couldn't imagine what that would be. And he was so busy.

Arriving at the door of his suite, Johnny stared at the stenciled words: John Blood, MD, Director, Heart Institute. He sighed and turned the knob. He was surprised to see his best friend stretched out on the leather sofa reading an old swimsuit issue of *Sports Illustrated*.

Dr. Gus Rogosin, a cardiologist, ran the Beverly Heart Foundation, Johnny's medical group. A down-to-earth Midwesterner, Gus had dark curly hair, a compact body, rugged handsome looks, and a twinkle in his eye under chaotic brows. He was revered in the medical center for his fearless, team-oriented, selfless approach to practice and people.

"Johnny boy,"—Gus lowered the magazine and grinned—"I can't believe these boobs. They gotta be photoshopped."

Johnny scowled and shook his head.

Gus swung his short strong legs to the floor with a thump and looked around. "This suite so reminds me of the Polo Lounge, which I can't afford to go there. So your lovely wife just called. She wants you to call back."

"*Really?* My lovely wife, who grabbed your ass two years ago?"

"Christmas 2006, as I recall. That was a serious party."

"I need to shower before I'm ready for social calls, Gus. Then you can tell me what you're doing in my space, answering my phone, schmoozing with my wife." Johnny slammed the bathroom door behind him.

"Whoa, dude!" Gus shouted. "Time is money! Lakers tip off soon."

***

Johnny soaked his head under the hottest water he could stand, cooking off his frustration. Time is *not* money, goddamn it! He wondered what Lisa wanted. She never called his office.

Johnny cold-rinsed himself and stepped out of the shower. He rubbed gel into his thick black hair and examined his beige body in the mirror. He was buff and sexy enough, healthy as a Crow horse. What a colossal waste. He spun away from the mirror. He realized Gus was right about this place looking like the Polo Lounge—even the bathroom—Lisa's memorial to our one good day in seven years.

He remembered how his colleagues reacted when he married Lisa. He still heard their nattering—Johnny Blood Money and his rich patient-donor-wife. He figured there'd be a celebration when they finally divorced.

He dressed and stepped back into his office. "Sorry, Gus. Bad hair day." He collapsed into his desk chair and rubbed his face.

"Heard about your Gomez," Gus said. "I'm sorry. That's why I'm here. One reason. Lemme ask you, though—does that say Matisse?"

Johnny examined the painting on the wall to his left. "It does. He painted that black-eyed woman over and over."

"I don't know shit about art, but that's probably worth millions." Gus stared at the painting.

"I never look at it, Gus."

Gus shook his head and opened his hands. "Hey, dude, sorry about Gomez. I know you had a thing for him. But everyone knows he was insolvent, no insurance, no nothing. Mortgaged his book rights. Only asset is a bullshit malpractice lawsuit against St. John's, which I hear he's about to lose."

"He was sick." Johnny raised his hands. "Yes, a long shot, and I took it. It's what I do, Gus."

"You really got an anonymous call and went to visit him?"

"What's your point, Gus? If I don't help a guy the stature of Gomez,"—Johnny picked up a pencil—"why be a physician?"

"You'll hear from Poulos."

"He jumped me on my way over here. I'd like to strangle the jerk."

"You're way too much a physician to kill even a schmuck like Arthur."

"Shit, Gus. Is money relevant when you're dealing with a genius? It's like a celebrity body shop here. I'm so *sick* of this place!" Johnny slammed his hand on the desk. The pencil flew toward Gus, who caught it in midair.

"Nice catch." Johnny suppressed a smile. He stood up.

"Thanks." Gus returned the pencil to Johnny's desk. "Dunno, big guy, but I bet they sue. Like they sued St. John's after they saved his fucking life twice. Anyway, so the other reason I'm here, there's a rumor you're thinking about going over to Harbor?"

"Is that ESP? I was thinking exactly that in the elevator after Poulos ambushed me. My crazy old friend over there calls me every so often."

"It's fucking ridiculous. It'd kill our heart group."

Johnny studied Beverly Boulevard out the window. "See those palm trees? They're not native, doing the best they can. Ignored by everyone except the dogs."

Gus crossed his legs and picked lint off his knee. "Fuck the trees, Johnny! Listen to me! Your surgical practice is our profit center. You're the magnet for all those nip-tuck assholes who you may not like, but they can write a check and don't use insurance. No one comes near you."

"Relax, my man. I'm not going to Harbor. I talk to him because I'm still guilty about not helping poor Indians like I set out to do in med school. Lots of poor people over at Harbor."

"Lots of gangbangers too. Some of them not so poor."

"True. But I'm so fed up here. You know I've never felt at home. Except for you and Stanley. Maybe Emilio." He looked out at the milky sky.

"Dude, stop the victim shit. You're a great surgeon. A little aloof sometimes? But the market speaks the truth."

"The market. You cardiologists with your pills and treadmills have taken the market away from us surgeons. Except for heart transplants, which you'll probably figure out how to do in the cath lab."

Johnny flapped a phone slip. "You said Lisa called?"

"Saw the caller ID, we had a nice chat. You're a lucky man."

"I'm a lucky man," Johnny said flatly. He saw Gus's alert look and switched subjects. "So Poulos still trying to screw me. He's such a sad case. You think he'd let it go after a dozen years."

"He's a Greek Jew. Worse than the Irish when it comes to grudges."

"Poulos's Jewish?"

"Jewish mother," Gus said. "That's what I heard."

"Did not know that. Twenty years ago everyone at UC Cedars was Jewish. When the money comes back, if it ever comes back, it'll all be Asian, just watch, like Max Kim, who, by the way, worked his ass off on Gomez. He's good. Thank god for dumb Anglos like you and craven Indians like me who carry the water when the money is crappy."

Gus smiled at Johnny's demographic analysis. "You have anything happy to say, Johnny? And by the way, I'm a Slav, not an Anglo."

"Not really. Still trying to understand what happened on Gomez. Emilio Hand was the anesthesiologist. Old reliable."

"You use Emilio all the time. What's up?"

"Don't know. The body just shut down. The donor heart was fine. It was like trying to put a beating heart into a store mannequin. It's probably silly."

"What's silly? You want me to talk to Emilio?"

"Quietly, if you do. Don't want to upset him or get the M&M people stirred up. Just in case he noticed anything."

"Consider it done."

Gus stood and put his hand on Johnny's shoulder. "Listen, friend, shit happens in this business, okay? Get over it. I'll give you the weekend, then back to your usual upbeat self." He winked and left.

Johnny sat on the sofa and stared at Matisse's dark-eyed woman. He sighed, unsheathed his cell, and touched LISA.

CHAPTER FOUR

Lisa's tone on the phone was corporate. "Johnny, we need to meet with Jack Pettker. He can come up to Benedict Cañon Sunday."

"The lawyer? Yeah, fine, Sunday. Whatever. What time?" They made the arrangement—they'd meet after her weekly golf game at Bel Air Country Club. He touched END and pressed his fist to his cheek.

Lisa styled her Beverly Hills mansion, Benedict Cañon, after the tony street address. Flamboyantly designed by *arriviste* Wild Will Bell, the house was completed just in time for their 1987 marriage. She had no input into the faux French chateau design; indeed, she had little input into anything in those years. After Will passed eleven years later, she commissioned a major interior redesign, softened some of the external features, and stayed on.

After their 2002 wedding, Johnny leased his smaller Bel Air home to a colleague and moved into Lisa's mansion. It was all the same to him—a place to sleep and shower. Over the following six years, the mansion became a cold shell, a place of loneliness and separate entrances into separate quarters, much like their marriage.

***

Johnny first met Jack Pettker when Wild Will funded the Bell Heart Wing. They sat in Lisa's vast sunken living room discussing books, when she swept in, her usual half hour late, offering no apology. She poked at Johnny's manners. "Have you been offered coffee, Jack?"

Lisa's late arrivals annoyed Johnny, who was obsessively on time. "We're fine, Lisa," he said. "Let's just get going." Pettker shuffled papers.

Johnny watched Lisa perch on a wing chair, her blonde curls spilling gracefully over tense shoulders. How stunning she was, still. Her tailored beige suit was accented by a blue silk Liberty scarf. Johnny remembered buying that scarf for her in London.

"So," Lisa said, stone cold, "Jack prepared the trust required by the prenup. I fund it with fifty million. You get a hundred thousand a month and the use of this house. I buy your old Bel Air house outright for five million cash, which, I hope you appreciate, Johnny, is generous in this awful economy. I'll move in as soon as your tenant is out."

"He tells me it'll be this Friday," Johnny said.

"Fine, keep me posted. And we keep everything private, including any past, uh, indiscretions." She glared at Johnny. "No talking to the newspapers. I run a charitable foundation, and I don't need tabloid gossip."

Pettker's voice was flat. "You do understand, Doctor, that when the trust terminates, the principal goes over to the Heart Institute, and this house reverts to Mrs. Bell or her estate?"

Johnny had tuned out. Technicalities unrelated to people bored him, caused him pain. Pettker cleared his throat. Johnny looked over at him. "What? Sorry. Daydreaming." Lisa hissed and shifted in her chair.

Papers sat in tidy stacks on the coffee table. "Want to look at any documents, Doctor?"

"No, no. Sounds fine, actually very generous, Lisa. I'll want my lawyer to look it over, though."

Lisa looked up. "You haven't even talked with Bo yet?"

"No . . . I will." Johnny rubbed his cheek.

"Johnny, please! And by the way, the foundation will continue to pay Tom Schultz to handle the Heart Institute books and your personal finances. I'm concerned your inevitable mess will fall back on me."

"Fine," Johnny said through clenched teeth. "I'll get Bo Rathgeber to call you, Jack,"

"*Soon*, Johnny," Lisa said with velvet impatience. She suddenly stood and hugged her handbag, her face pale. She looked down at Pettker and pointed to Johnny. "Don't let him drag it out." She strode past Johnny to the base of the carpeted stairway, trailing perfume. Johnny watched her perfect butt sway as she climbed up to her bedroom, formerly their marriage suite, soon to be Johnny's alone.

***

Lisa sat on the edge of the bed, folded her hands, and gazed out the north-facing window. Sighing, she pulled a tissue from the bedside table and touched her eyes.

It was a brilliant day. She could see the glistening lap pool thrusting toward the dry brown hills, flanked by the wings of the mansion: the wing on the right where Wild Will died, the wing on the left where Johnny lived as their marriage died. She pulled off the Liberty scarf and buried her face in it, breathing deeply.

She heard a murmur of voices from below. She walked across the vast room to the bedroom door and pushed it closed. Returning to the window, she stood for a moment, seeing nothing, tears spilling. She fell facedown like a cut tree into a mound of pillows on the bed and sobbed. It had to be another woman.

Crying herself out, she rolled over and kicked her shoes off. After a minute, she rose and stumbled into the bathroom. She opened a drawer under the sink and removed a small bottle of whiskey. She took a long pull and returned the bottle to the drawer. After washing her face and spraying her breath, she padded across the bedroom to her walk-in closet. Clearing clothes out of the way, she opened the small safe, reached in, lifted a green cloth, and picked up a small brown envelope. Back on the bed, she carefully extracted the fragile paper with its rude black writing.

Dear Elizabeth. I'm not a leter writer but I just heard Cindy died by Her own hand on last Christmas and I need to tell somone Im so sad about that so Im picking on You. Mother wont care what I feel and mabey You dont ether, Mother is impossible and threw me out but I dont blaim Her no sir don't get me wrong. She's a good woman mostly and I hope shes all right. She tried to keep You and your sister safe and sound Im not always an easy man to live with Im afraid althouh I did try. I hope this isn't just wining but I fort in Korea You know, You saw the medals in the bedroom many times and came back a troubled man, but Your Mother didnt know and I guess I didnt ether until after it came out after I got the job at the steel mill and we had You girls. Anyhow I loved Cindy and I loved You too in spite of evrything. I probly never told you that but I hope You knew. Cindy loved me and Im gessing She never got over my leaving so sudden because I didnt ether. It was Your Mother and but I felt angry when I left and its worst now if Cindy killed Herself because of me leaving, I take the blaim, I assume so. You was so darn pretty, Elizabeth, I use to tell your Mother too pretty for Your own good. I hope your all right. I was sad I culdnt know You better beuz of You Mother protected You being so pretty which I gess I undustood. Its just sad, I know I wuz a bad father. Drank too much which was a big problem but I had a lot of stress. I will not bother You again but I want to tell somone about poor

Cindy and how I felt once. Sorry about the spelling. Your sad
sad father. May 1983 Somewhere Else Not Cal.

***

As Lisa was reading the letter, Johnny sat below in the sunken living room,
talking on the phone with his friend and lawyer Bo. Lisa's stepson, Billy Bell,
cracked open the front door of the mansion and peered in. Johnny saw him
and waved. Billy quietly closed the massive door behind him. Johnny pocketed
his phone and stood to welcome Billy.

"Lisa still here?" Billy asked in a stage whisper.

"Upstairs. Shh." Johnny pointed at the stairway as he stood up. They shook
hands and grimly smiled at each other. "What a nice thing to see you, Billy,"
Johnny whispered. "Let's go to the den so we can talk."

William Terence Bell, Wild Will Bell's only child, was eight years older
than his stepmother, Lisa. Billy had a very big body, a bigger heart, a large bald
dome of a head, and a brilliant mind. His full lips and sheep's eyes projected
calmness. He loved to discuss large, woolly subjects, especially with Johnny
Blood. His rumbling laugh was unconditional and infectious. Johnny was always
happy to see Billy, his one friend who didn't compete with him for anything.

After closing the den door, Billy collapsed into an overstuffed chair and
picked up a hard candy from a crystal bowl. "So! Chief Blood Moon! I saw Jack
Pettker driving away. You okay?"

"Sort of." Johnny tossed his head impatiently. "Let's talk about something
else."

"Okay, well . . . Bruins looked pretty good this year, Doctor," Billy said with
a wry smile. "They should have gone deeper into the tournament."

Johnny shrugged and glanced around. "Another painful subject. That
game was embarrassing. What've you been up to?"

"Not much. Dodgers—love my Dodgers. Doing some writing. Watching my
stepmom fuss about you."

"Writing about?" Johnny ignored the invitation to discuss Lisa.

"Quantum stuff. Multiverses. But I struggle with the math. I'm rusty and
I'm lazy. I think the notion of multiverses is a probability. You shouldn't delay
this divorce, Johnny. It's going to be good for both of you."

"Who's speaking, you or Lisa?"

"She doesn't talk about it. I read her body language. And I see her drinking
more. As for you, I infer from how you've disappeared that you're embarrassed."

"Disappeared?"

"You never failed at anything. You regard this divorce as a major defeat. You don't know what to do with defeat, so you hide in your teepee. You even turned me down on Dodgers opening day." Billy smiled. "I know I'm invading your privacy—your local universe—but that's why you love me. You may have left the reservation, but I don't think the reservation ever left you, Johnny. It's time to join the human race. Take the money and run, get a life, go back to being the best heart guy on earth."

"What money? What do you know about . . . ?"

"I don't know details, but I know my stepmom. I'm guessing she'll take care of you, like she takes care of me."

"Doesn't it bother you that she runs your finances?" Johnny moved to the window and pulled back the drapes.

"Why should it? She's good at it, I'm not," Billy said. "And you're not. You know nothing about money. You're good at surgery."

Johnny tapped a finger on his cheek. "I'm not good at money—that's true. I'm not even good at surgery anymore. Not good at anything."

"Just because of that Mexican author?" Billy shifted his bulk as if to stand. "Please, Johnny. You want something to eat? I could eat something."

"Not now. What kind of a divorce is it where she supervises my life?"

"A divorce most people would kill for." Billy hauled himself out of the chair. It took two tries to stand. "Oh, is Ernest off? I forgot it's Sunday."

"No, he's here. Billy, Jesus!" Johnny suddenly raised his voice. "You've *got* to lose weight, man! You're a walking heart attack."

"I know, I know," Billy mumbled and stepped toward the door.

"You lose fifty pounds, I'll sign the divorce," Johnny said.

Billy swiveled his head. "Seriously? A deal? I like deals."

"No, Billy, not a deal, just our mutual promises." Johnny stood and offered Billy his fist for a knuckle bump.

Billy studied Johnny's fist and shook his head slowly. "Isn't it remarkable that it's taken 13.7 billion years for two creatures to come to this point of such rational interchange?" He bumped Johnny's fist and laughed his deep laugh. "Now where's Ernest?"

CHAPTER FIVE

Johnny arrived early for the M&M Committee meeting Tuesday. As he entered the executive suite, he ran into the chief of staff himself, Stanley McRae, who offered a handshake and a complicated smile. "Johnny, glad to see you. Would you have a minute before you go in there?"

"Sure, Stan. I'm early."

Johnny revered Stan McRae, his longtime mentor. The chief was the eye of the storm in the medical center—rabbinical, serene, fair; a rock of a man in whom one could confide. He never pressed for information; it came to him. Maybe the busiest person in the hospital, he made you feel as if he had all day, as if he'd been longing for quiet time with just you. He had been extended as chief three times and was recently made hospital vice president, a first for a chief of staff. Stan had been flattered, but now he was beyond flattery and wanted out, hoping his final months would be calm and respectful of his long service.

Johnny followed him to his office, passing by the glass wall of the conference room where he could see Arthur Poulos huddled in conversation with others.

Entering McRae's warm, windowless office was a trip back in time. The scarred wooden desk, piled with papers, sat on a faded Asian carpet. On the wall, yellowing commendations and photos spanned fifty years.

McRae was a vigorous and handsome seventy-four. He walked to and from work from his condo in West Hollywood in a town where walking is highly suspect. He wore a bow tie and colorful braces. As he leaned back in his chair, he stroked his neat Sigmund Freud beard. "Close the door there, Johnny, and sit. I'd like to talk about this, uh . . . Gomez situation."

Johnny pushed the door closed and lowered himself into a worn wooden chair. "It knocked me out."

McRae removed his half-glasses and studied them. He spoke precisely. "I heard that. Anything specific?"

"Don't know. The heart was fine, but the body just gave out."

"So *why*?"

"I really don't know, Stan. It never happened to me before. It feels like I've lost it. It makes me want to give it all up."

"Give it all up? Just this one outcome?"

"Plus . . . well, I'm going through a divorce too. That's confidential."

McRae knitted his brows. "I'm sorry. That's not easy."

"No," Johnny said, "it's awful."

After a moment, McRae continued. "Tell me more about Gomez, your relationship. You visited him? I read him years ago. I remember one of the reasons you and I liked each other—we both read novels, and admitted it. And I remember you liked Gomez."

"I did. He was the best."

"So tell me. Did Gomez have any . . . how to phrase this? Is there anything odd in his background that you know of?"

Johnny thought for a second. "Not sure what you mean. Nothing that isn't public I don't think. He filed that lawsuit against St. John's, which seemed out of character. Oh, when I visited him, one of his handlers said he'd received death threats."

"Oh? Because?"

"Didn't say. His last novel was controversial, about Mexican drug gangs."

McRae was watching Johnny closely. "I scanned it. It's quite long. Tendentious. What did you think of it?"

"I read it—didn't particularly like it. Stan, you're not asking these questions to get a book recommendation. What's going on?"

"Sorry, can't quite say. Please trust me."

"Fine. Anyway, the book was a bit of a rant." Johnny paused. "He was quite sick. Max Kim thought I was wasting my time operating."

"Max told me that."

Johnny looked up at McRae. "Right, but I thought I had a shot. If I have a shot, I take it. You know me, Stan."

"I do know you. And we are supposed to take that shot. There was nothing else out of the ordinary?"

"About the operation? Or what? You're being cryptic, Stan."

"Just . . . hoping to anticipate."

"Anticipate? You mean what I'm gonna say in there?" Johnny turned his chin toward the conference room. "Which . . ." Johnny looked at his watch. "I probably should get in there."

"Just be careful."

"What are you worried about?" Johnny asked.

"Arthur. I tried to wall him off from this. But you know Arthur, he insisted. Probably to take another shot at you."

"Shit. Will he ever let it go?"

McRae shifted in his chair. "You and I have been through a lot, Johnny. You have many talents, but you can be rash. And stubborn. Arthur . . . carries grudges. Not a good combination."

"Lord, tell me," Johnny said, "it's been years. For all I care anymore, he can have the damn directorship."

McRae's face tightened. "It was never just about the directorship. He was profoundly jealous of your talent." McRae blew his nose. "This hospital was an Eden once, Johnny, and you were a beautiful young physician full of drive. Lately it's become complicated."

"Arthur accosted me in the corridor right after Gomez died. We had a bit of a squabble."

"Well? I understand you reached out for Gomez. No liquid resources, and he sued St. John's for malpractice. We do have a business to operate."

"I thought I could help him."

McRae sighed. "You know, Johnny, I'm well past retirement age. When I graduated from medical school fifty years ago—seems like yesterday—medicine was a true profession. Physicians were respected, not questioned at every turn. We did great work. There were mistakes, sure, but patients accepted that and absorbed the cost of it. Now, we're villains, targets. Lawyers, regulators . . . medicine's changing, Johnny, not for the better. And of course, the monetary rewards are less, plus this awful financial collapse—so many good senior doctors are unhappy. We need to protect our profession . . ."

"Where're you going with this, Stan?"

McRae fingered his beard. "No idea." He stood up, walked around his desk, and faced the door. "Thanks for your time. Please keep this conversation between us."

"You know I will, Stan." Johnny stood up.

"I do." McRae's eyes drifted up to Johnny's face. "You're an excellent surgeon, Johnny. The best. You've been like my son here. It saddens me to see you losing your spirit."

"Saddens me too." Johnny looked at his Rolex. "We done, Stan? Wouldn't want to be late for my own crucifixion."

McRae smiled. "Just keep a level head with Arthur."

As Johnny moved to the door, they spoke simultaneously, "Good luck." They shook hands.

***

Johnny loathed meetings. He especially loathed administrators poking at his work. But he would keep a level head. Walking into the conference room, he was assaulted by sullen stares. Arthur Poulos slumped low at one end of the long table. He had a brackish, disheveled aspect, projecting disdain. At the center of the polished blond mahogany conference table sat the prim chief of surgery, Dr. Paul Richards, drumming his fingers. Also present were a senior male lawyer from risk management with a yellow pad full of notes, a junior female lawyer, several staff surgeons, a squad of residents, two nurses—and Max Kim, who winked at Johnny.

"Where do you want me, Paul?"

Richards waved at the chair across from him. "We'll be starting in a few minutes, Johnny."

Johnny sat, pulled out his cell, and opened his e-mails. He saw a recent one from Gus Rogosin: "Spoke to Emilio about Gomez. He said he didn't see anything out of order, except that Gomez died. The old story: operation a success, patient dead. :) He had a funny look, but I didn't press him. See you Monday at racquetball."

Richards cleared his throat, and Johnny pocketed his phone. Richards walked Johnny through the surgery. Poulos said nothing. At the end, the senior lawyer nervously cleared his throat. "As you know, Dr. Blood, this meeting is required by state law and medical center rules. I don't see a problem, but given the proclivity of these people to sue, I plan to do a fuller incident report. I understand there's an *LA Times* reporter on this. Can you tell me who you've discussed this matter with? You spoke to the family?"

"I did. It was several men, most of them not family. His young son, Juan, was there. I also spoke with Stan McRae just earlier, and my partner, Gus Rogosin, Friday. I think that's all."

"Anybody outside? Your wife?"

Johnny winced. "Nobody else."

"What did you tell the next-of-kin group? Was anyone with you?"

"I was alone. I told them Gomez died, that I did everything I could. I found myself talking to the boy, maybe ten? He was listening, crying too. The others looked more like they were calculating."

The female lawyer scribbled furiously. Poulos sunk lower in his chair.

***

Weeks later, the lawyers produced an incident report, declaring that there was no medical error. Johnny was startled by two comments: that the transplant team was slow in assembling, and that the cause of death was given as "rejection of donor heart." On the first point, Johnny had explained that he had called a surgeon at St. John's before scrubbing in to clarify points from Gomez's last heart operation. The report made no mention of the call. On the second point, Johnny knew there was no rejection. It was anything but that. But Johnny was in no mood to fight the medical-industrial machine.

Then the mischief started. Someone leaked the report to the *LA Times.* Unnamed sources said that the famous surgeon Dr. John Blood had "lost" Señor Gomez. The story was on the front page above the fold along with a box of statistics showing that UC Cedars had a relatively high incidence of medical error. The statistics were wrong, but by the time the correction was printed, on a back page, the damage had been done. The article said that Dr. McRae was retiring "to spend time with his family"—even though he had no family—and that Vice Chief Poulos was also retiring. Hospital trustees, in the middle of a capital campaign, were livid at the publicity.

Lawyers for the Gomez estate promptly filed a multimillion dollar lawsuit against UC Cedars and Johnny Blood. UC Cedars quickly settled the case, the insurance company paying an extremely large amount to the Gomez estate. From the outside, it appeared that the Gomez "loss" had cast UC Cedars into chaos and that McRae and Poulos had been sacked.

***

In unhappy parallel with Johnny's professional woes, his divorce was proceeding. In mid-August, Johnny and Bo Rathgeber rode the elevator up to Jack Pettker's office high above downtown LA.

"Such sadness, Johnny. My January's devastated." Bo's wife, January, was friendly with Lisa Bell.

"How about me?"

"Of course. But like the man said, a bad divorce is better than a bad marriage. And this isn't that bad of a divorce."

"Easy for you to say. How long will this take?" Johnny asked.

"Not long. Sign a few papers, we're done. Probably be just Lisa and Pettker. Pettker's a notary."

Lisa wasn't there. "She sends her apologies," Pettker said. "Because your Bel Air house was available, she decided to move in today to avoid . . ."

"Me. My presence. Another kick in the gut."

Pettker, flustered, handed documents to Bo. "Lisa signed everything. Bo will show you where to sign. This is hard on Lisa, Johnny, if I may say."

Johnny squinted at Pettker. "Please. Let's just get this done."

***

The following Monday evening Gus Rogosin and Johnny played racquetball as they did most Mondays. The court and gym in the basement of the Bell Heart

Wing had been Wild Will Bell's second special tribute to exercise freak Johnny, icing on Will's munificent gift to UC Cedars and another source of resentment among the hospital staff.

Johnny, losing badly, was playing with unusual abandon. Gus noticed. "Johnny, easy, boy. You're gonna kill yourself." The floor was slick with sweat.

Johnny served, and Gus hit a drop shot into the left corner. Johnny dove for it, winning the point but slipping and landing awkwardly on his left hand. "Ohh, shoot! Goddamn it!"

"What happened—you okay, John? Oh god."

Johnny raised his broken wrist, grimacing. "Point to Dr. Blood!"

The break was severe. He would need an operation—Johnny hated the idea. He trusted just one orthopedic surgeon on earth: his college friend Mike Dillon up the coast in Redwood City. Mike's sports medicine group was the premier orthopedic clinic in the metro Bay Area.

Johnny called Mike to arrange the surgery. Then he called Bo Rathgeber. In the elevator ride down from Pettker's office, Bo had urged Johnny to get away for a few days to Bo's vacation house in Mexico. Johnny, who never took vacations, deflected the idea, but that was before the broken wrist.

Bo answered his own phone. "Rathgeber."

"Bo, Johnny. Is the Cabo house available the week after Labor Day?"

"The Lord be praised! Johnny's taking a vacation!"

"I broke my wrist. Can't work."

"Oh my! I'm sorry. Yes, it's available then. January and I will be there through Labor Day. Maybe we can overlap a night."

CHAPTER SIX

Johnny flew to Cabo San Lucas on Labor Day, wrist in a soft cast, apprehensive about doing *nothing* for two weeks. He was glad he would see Bo and Jan if only for one evening.

Bo and Johnny had been an odd couple at UCLA. Johnny was tall and athletic, affable and girl crazy; Bo from Brooklyn was small and lumpish, private and shy. The son of holocaust survivors, Bo cast a wary eye on the world. He had a dry wit and a penetrating intelligence. He was also a keen listener and knew from childhood that he would become a lawyer.

Bo had met his future wife in freshman year—she was January Corot, a lithe, dark-haired sorority girl from the San Fernando Valley. In junior year, January introduced her boyfriend Bo to Mike Dillon, whose family owned an apartment building on Veteran Avenue. Mike, a premed colleague of Johnny's, lived in the building and was looking for tenants. Mike invited Bo and Johnny to take rooms for senior year.

January was a constant presence at Veteran that year. To complete the friendship circle, she introduced landlord Mike to her psych major friend Ora Collins. Mike and Ora fell madly in love and married right after graduation. Jan and Bo married a year later, after his first year at NYU Law. Jan lured Bo back to California after graduation to join her father's Encino law firm, where Bo eventually became senior partner. Jan became a paralegal and also handled the business side of the firm.

Bo had drawn the best room at Veteran. It was on the top floor and overlooked the federal cemetery and the VA Hospital. He also had the best television set. So Bo's room was the gathering place for January, Johnny, Mike, Ora, and Johnny's serial girlfriends.

At graduation, Johnny dubbed Mike and Ora and Bo and Jan the "Final Four." Johnny stayed single for twenty-three years, until Lisa.

***

Johnny arrived in Cabo as Bo and Jan were packing to leave. They were heading back tomorrow to attend their thirtieth reunion at UCLA. Johnny would skip it, embarrassed by his collapsed marriage.

In the late afternoon, the three friends were sipping drinks on the white stone patio high above sparkling Cabo harbor. Bo was nursing a Diet Coke. January and Johnny were enjoying margaritas. The sun slid through the cobalt sky toward the Pacific Ocean. Johnny licked the salt off the rim of his glass. "What a view. The colors. I always think of my cousin Benny when I see the Pacific."

"Who's Benny?" Bo asked. "I remember Howard, the medicine man."

"Benny was Howard's son. Benny took care of me. He used to show me pictures of sunsets over the Pacific Ocean. Including the girls in bikinis. And he'd always sing the Beach Boys on his guitar. He would've loved this view."

"So Benny's the one who got you off on the wrong foot with women?" Jan asked, an eyebrow high. "You were such a terrible horndog in college."

"January, please be nice to our guest," Bo said, smiling.

"Truth is a complete defense. And Johnny knows I love him," Jan said.

"I love you, too—both of you," Johnny said. "I also love your house here, in spite of the ghosts."

"Lisa and you spent your honeymoon here," Jan said.

"Yes. And we had our first fight here."

"What was that about, if I may ask?"

"Not about sex, if that's what you're fishing for. So her wedding gift was she paid off my Bel Air mortgage. I freaked."

"Why?" Bo asked.

"Lord knows. It felt like a power play, like she wanted . . ."

"To be on top?" Jan asked.

Johnny laughed. "Now you're back to sex."

Jan sipped her drink. "I don't get it. Why did you freak?"

"Beats me." Johnny squirmed uncomfortably. "New subject, Bo, what did you do with your time here?"

"I read. We talked, walked. I like being with my wife. They have great trails here and exercise facilities, but I'm not big on exercise."

"You look pretty fit. How's the heart?" Bo had chest pains five years ago, and Gus had implanted a stent.

"Fine. Your friend Rogosin checks me—I like Rogosin. He just gets the job done—no bullshit, unlike most of you prima donnas." Bo turned toward the house. "Maria's a little slow with dinner, Jan."

"Here they come." Jan stood up.

***

Johnny woke before dawn. When he heard the front door close behind Bo and Jan, he felt a pang of loneliness. He also felt the fuzzy residue of multiple margaritas. He was not a good drinker—famous at UCLA for bingeing after exams or the collapse of a relationship with a young lady.

Giving up on sleep, he pulled on running clothes and picked his way down the cliff trail in the gathering light. He ran along the surf, absorbing the morning. The pungent marine smell and pastel colors were exhilarating. When he returned to the cliff-top house, coffee was in the air.

Later that day, Johnny began to feel the burden of time. He watched his e-mails and soon began to consult on cases by phone. Gus called. "Johnny, what the hell you doing babysitting your patients from a thousand miles? These young doctors think you don't trust them. Let it go."

It was true that Johnny didn't trust other doctors, but he finally more or less "let it go." His last week was his best week. He read a couple of novels and pondered the future. He tried to imagine life without surgery.

***

On the night before his flight home, Johnny sat at the Cabo Casas clubhouse bar nursing a beer. The massive bartender trundled over, polishing a glass. He rapped his knuckles softly on the bar. "Señor Doctor?"

"*No mas,* Jorge. Flying home tomorrow."

"You would like to meet a pretty American lady?"

"What's this? An escort service?"

"No, no, no, Doctor. I lose my job." Jorge rumbled with laughter.

"Well, then what?"

Jorge tilted his head. "Over there, that is a really classy *señorita* who, like you, is alone here from LA."

Johnny looked down the bar and saw an attractive dark-haired woman reading something on her lap. A glass of red wine glistened in front of her. "I'll think about it, Jorge."

Johnny sat still while Jorge moved away. Then he grabbed his beer bottle and walked over to the woman. She looked up, apprehension in her dark eyes.

"'Excuse me. Haven't done this in years. May I sit? You look too busy."

"Well?"

"I'm harmless. Jorge over there,"—Johnny nodded toward the bartender, absorbed in polishing glasses—"he tells me you're by yourself, tells me I'm by myself, we're both from LA. He suggested I come over."

"So it's not your fault?" she said, smiling.

He detected a slight accent. "Oh, no, fully my fault. I used to do this in college, so I completely understand the risks of approaching women in bars. But that was a long time ago. And the bars weren't nearly this nice."

"Well . . . you don't look harmless. Sure, please sit."

"I'll take that as a compliment." Johnny sat and placed his half-empty Corona on the bar. "What part of LA?"

"What happened to your hand? You married? Tell me your name."

"Name's Johnny Blood. And I *am* married. What's your name?"

"Michaela. Where's the wife, Johnny Blood? A pirate name."

"Back in LA. We're getting a divorce," Johnny said. "You?"

"What happened to your hand?"

"Broke my wrist playing racquetball."

"You don't look clumsy." She raised her eyebrows. "So, me, I'm single, Greek, green card person. Reading a film script. Hoping to crack Hollywood. Or at least pay the bills. So that's me." She sighed, lifted the script, bookmarked it with a pencil, and dropped it on the bar with a thud.

Jorge drifted over. "Another *cerveza*, Doctor? Lady? On the house."

"Not me, Jorge," Johnny said. Michaela shook her head. Her warm smile made Johnny wonder if she sent Jorge to fetch him.

"What's the script about?" Johnny asked when Jorge moved off.

"Amazon role. Angelina Jolie sort of thing. But I'm not Angelina Jolie."

Johnny studied her face. She was gorgeous. "You'll do. You're younger."

She smiled. "Thanks. Yeah, Angi's getting so old. Keeps the postproduction people busy. Lots of us waiting around to pick up her leavings, like Brad." Michaela laughed, a cascading waterfall. "So you're a doctor, or is Jorge pimping for you?"

"No, I'm a doctor. A heart doctor." He almost said "surgeon," but the word stuck in his throat.

"A heart doctor going through a divorce? Is that called irony?"

Johnny laughed. "More than you know. You really here alone?"

"That's a personal question. So . . . I was with a production team until a day ago. They let me stay on to finish this script."

"So I'm in your way?"

"I would say I brought it on myself. Sitting in a bar, looking like fair game for a pickup."

"Are you?"

"What kind of question is that?" she asked archly.

"A direct question, I guess." Johnny smiled.

"If you didn't have such a nice smile, I'd spit in your eye."

"Good feedback. Looks like I've lost my touch after all these years."

"No, I wouldn't say that, Johnny Blood. Girls get complicated as they get older. At least . . . their lives do. Tell you what. Before this gets out of hand." She stood and reached into her purse. "Here's my card."

"I didn't get handed cards in college," he said.

"You haven't been around. Girls have cards now. And e-mail addresses. Call me *after* your divorce is final." She offered her hand. She had long shapely fingers and wore no jewelry.

"Leaving? Guess I *have* lost my touch," he said, taking her hand. It was warm and soft.

"No. On the contrary." She wheeled around and stepped off.

He looked down at her card. *Michelle Powell, Actor.*

"Don't forget your script, Michelle." He picked up the thick script and held it out.

She turned back. "Oh, that's embarrassing. Can't forget *that.* Let me have my card back and a pen please."

Johnny complied. She crossed out "Michelle" and wrote "Michaela." "That's pronounced 'Mee-KAY-la.' Michelle is just the screen name." She handed the card back. "Call me if your divorce goes final."

"Michaela? Sure, I can do that."

She winked and walked away with brisk, rhythmic steps. She was tall. He admired the rear view, sighed, and slipped the card into his wallet.

"So, señor, no luck?" A grinning Jorge placed a finger of single malt scotch at Johnny's place.

"No. On the contrary."

"What means 'on the contrary,' Señor Doctor?"

Johnny studied the clear tawny liquid. "I'm hoping it means 'see you later.'" He swirled the scotch and tossed it down in one motion. He stood up and threw an American twenty on the bar. "Thanks for the scotch and for the introduction."

Jorge bowed. "De nada, amigo. Hasta luego."

CHAPTER SEVEN

When Johnny returned to the empty mansion and his hollowed-out medical practice, he felt lost. Having time on his hands in Cabo was one thing; in LA it was quite another. He read books and magazines, ran long distances, went to movies alone. Professionally, he did things he had avoided for years: rounds with interns, research work, attending surgeries as an instructor, presenting at conferences. Johnny had built the Heart Transplant Center from scratch; now there were a half-dozen certified specialists and a small platoon of trained nurses and techs.

Against Mike Dillon's advice, Johnny removed the cast after only eight weeks in favor of a wrap. He had purchased a black-and-red Harley-Davidson motorcycle and was eager to drive it. Except for long trips, his Maserati sat in the garage. The new bike recalled his sorties around New England during medical school days on his battered, beloved motor bike.

Johnny was able to avoid patient crises until December, when a prominent Hollywood producer experienced chest pains and demanded Dr. Blood's involvement in a stent implant procedure, not normally handled by a cardiothoracic surgeon. Johnny felt awkward in the cath lab sitting on a stool between two residents, watching Gus Rogosin handle the procedure.

Johnny and Gus worked out together that evening in the Bell Wing gym. After exercise, they soaked in the Jacuzzi, Johnny holding his wrapped hand high and dry. Gus shouted above the hissing water jets. "Feels good to be back here. How'd you like the cath lab? Soon you'll be back in the OR."

"Maybe not, Gus."

"Huh? Where's *this* coming from? Is this the political crap?"

"No, that's not it." Johnny shrugged. "I just don't feel the *fire*."

"The fire? You're gonna quit doing surgery? To do what? That's like Yo-Yo Ma quitting the cello because he hit a bad note. I heard something about your marriage. Was Lisa with you in Cabo?"

"I went alone. We're getting a divorce," Johnny spoke dully.

"Divorce? What the fuck? Wow! You hear rumors, but I can't believe it. I mean . . . Lisa's amazing!"

"I used to think so."

"So back up, dude. You're thinking of . . . what? Quitting what?"

"Don't know," Johnny said. "Maybe a leave of absence? You need to help me think it through. Publicity, patients, referring physicians. Whatever. I don't know."

"You sound totally fucked up."

"I am. If the fire comes back, then maybe I come back. With two good hands." He tried to smile and failed miserably.

Gus looked at Johnny with soft eyes. "You're just going through some personal stuff."

"It's not 'just' personal stuff, Gus. It's really fucking hard." Johnny felt tears welling up. He dunked his head. When he came to the surface, he shook off the water, cleared his throat, and changed the subject. "So . . . you're sure a wizard in the cath lab."

"I'm good, man. Which reminds me, Johnny boy—a couple of our young docs have the potential to become great heart surgeons. Max Kim for one. He's senior resident now, wants to get transplant certified. Love you to take him under your wing. You're always so off on your own."

"I like Max. I like that he talks back to me. I want to be useful."

"You need to chill out, dude," Gus said. "Got a lot on your plate. Broken hand, can't play racquetball, Bruins suck, broken marriage, surgical practice on hold. Crash and burn for most humans."

"Blessing in disguise. Just watch. But I'll need your help."

"You got it."

***

The divorce became final in January. Johnny's hand was still weak, so he called Mike Dillon one night for a next-day consultation in Redwood City. Mike agreed to squeeze him in.

"Appreciate it, Mike. Can I also buy some of Ora's shrink time?"

"A twofer? I'm sure you can. Hold on." Mike handed Ora the phone.

"Needing to see me, Johnny dear?" Ora asked. "Love it. Come over when you and Mike are done. Your perfect life showing cracks again?"

"Let's just say, sweetheart, you'll earn your money this time."

"I always earn my money, Dr. Blood. Stay over, Johnny. Our kids live out now. And they're doing fine, thank you very much. One day at a time."

"Lovely invitation. Sure, I can crash. One day at a time for all of us."

***

Johnny was happy to see Mike. "What's up with the 49ers?" Mike personally roamed the sidelines of the NFL team and proudly wore a Super Bowl ring from the team's better days. "They won their last two games, no? You're doing something right."

Palpating Johnny's wrist, Mike shook his head. "Eight wins and eight losses. They basically suck." He hung x-rays on the light board. "The bones are healing, see here and here? But I'm concerned the strength isn't returning. Probably neurological? You really nuked this wrist. You should get it looked at, given what you do for a living."

Johnny shrugged. "I don't like any neurologist at UC Cedars. I'd rather not go to anyone at all. But you say so . . . can you recommend a guy in LA?"

Mike pulled out a card and scribbled a name. "Better than all the 'guys' down there. In Pasadena, Huntington. Call her, use my name."

They gossiped until the nurse announced Mike's next patient.

"*Ciao.* If I need heart surgery, I have a chip at UC Cedars?"

Johnny shrugged. "Maybe no more surgery."

"You mean, like never? Because . . . ?"

"Right now the bad hand. But . . . I don't know, midlife crisis? And it's time for the youngsters to step up." Johnny suddenly felt emotional.

"Man," said Mike, frowning, "hate when that day comes for me."

***

After leaving the clinic, Johnny looked around for a McDonald's. He wanted to prepare for his visit with Ora. He knew she'd probably see right through him. He wanted that, but it was scary too—scary that she would see that he was a failure, a fifty-two-year-old failure.

The sky was oyster gray. Like most small towns, Redwood City had a predictable layout—he quickly spotted golden arches. Johnny stopped smoking in college, but he never stopped loving McDonald's, particularly the french fries. As he savored his food, he thought about Mike's referral to the Pasadena neurologist. He was not going to do that.

Sitting in a booth noshing his food, he watched a small blonde girl and smaller boy playing under a table. A brown-skinned woman sat above them flipping backward though a magazine and twirling the ends of her thick black hair. The children were absorbed in a game. The girl appeared to be making up rules that her little brother was trying to follow. They seemed completely engaged, completely happy. He wondered if he was ever that happy as a kid. He remembered something his favorite Russian writer, Anton Chekhov, once wrote: "In my childhood there was no childhood."

CHAPTER EIGHT

Ora Dillon frowned at Johnny through her retro granny glasses. They were sitting in Ora's office, full of seventies furniture and piles of paperback books. "I've been listening carefully, and I know you're not telling me the true story."

Busted, he dropped his eyes.

"So you're divorced, from that girl we all liked. And now suddenly you don't like caring for rich patients? That's it? No way."

Johnny had been reciting from his McDonald's prep for thirty minutes. Ora's remark knocked him back.

"People get divorced, Johnny. This is California." She pointed to his wrapped hand. "Stick that hand out. Is this why you stopped operating?"

"Is this a medical exam?" he huffed, having lost control.

"No, CSI. Looking for clues. What happened?" She held his hand.

"Hurt it playing racquetball," Johnny said. "Mike's taking care of it. But I stopped operating before I hurt the hand."

"You doing everything you can to fix it?"

He pulled his hand back. "Yes. No, well . . ."

"What do you mean 'yes, no'?" Ora flipped her straight brown hair over her ears in a practiced gesture. "Oh dear! Why are you bullshitting me? Let's reset. You alpha males, brought to your knees by some outside force." She stared hard at Johnny, trying to penetrate. "Biggest thing is *control*. Tax lawyers and surgeons are the worst. But you need to surrender control in here, otherwise we're wasting our time. So talk to me, Johnny. Start with the marriage. Why didn't that work out?"

Johnny dipped his head as if he had been caught cheating. He spoke about how he'd succeeded at everything for thirty years, how he was swept away by that one glorious night at the Polo Lounge—and how he and Lisa never connected emotionally. "I feel like I failed, for the first time in my life——"

Ora interrupted, "How was the sex?"

Johnny gulped. "Uh, great, intense at first. I mean the lady is amazing in bed. Ridiculous. Then it became . . . we had stupid arguments. We'd end up in bed, reconciling, sort of. That wasn't great sex. Then we just stopped, lived our separate lives." His voice caught. "I like Lisa. I have no idea . . ."

"What happened? You don't get women, do you, you big handsome shithead?" She handed him the tissue box. "In college, you never had a real girlfriend. I bet you never had a real conversation with any of those bimbos."

He pulled a tissue. "Some parts of Lisa felt off limits to me."

"Those feelings are not unusual in a second marriage," Ora said. "Pre-owned vehicle. You have to work with that."

Johnny blinked and touched his eyes. "Anyway, new topic. I'm thinking I want to step away from surgery. That's the big lump in my chest."

"Give up surgery? Because you don't like celebrity patients? Or because you're upset about the divorce and you want to punish yourself?"

"It's . . . UC Cedars is a money machine. I didn't know I was so unhappy until Manuel Gomez died on me."

"The Mexican author? I heard he died last year. Was it with you?"

"Yes, he was my patient. I talked him into a heart transplant operation, and then there he was, dead, on my operating table."

Ora raised an eyebrow. "Ooh, that's big, isn't it? Now we're getting somewhere."

Johnny nodded. "I've lost patients. You get over it. This one knocked me out. It was who he was, but also I couldn't figure out what happened. It was like the thing that opened my eyes to what I'd become."

"And what had you become?" Ora asked.

"A very good robot. Good at heart surgery, bad at life. So when this guy died and I didn't know why, it called everything into question."

"Bad at life? Like with Lisa you mean?"

"That's a pretty good example," Johnny said. "Marrying Lisa was *such* a colossal mistake. For her too. Nothing against her—I can't understand how I thought marrying Lisa would be a good thing."

"She's a good woman."

"I know she is. I know she is. Anyway, I need a new start. So I've stopped doing surgery to see how it feels."

"How *does* it feel?"

"Weird, frankly. I'm lost. It's all I know."

"You *are* aware that there are great surgeons who have real lives."

"I guess. I'm thinking of quitting medicine altogether. I've always wanted to be a long-distance truck driver."

Ora laughed. "Shit. Really? Wow, Johnny. Let me ask you. Do you ever think about suicide?"

Johnny was quiet for a long time. "I fantasize about starting a new life in a new place. But not suicide. I hate the idea of killing yourself."

"It won't do any good to start a new life. It never works—the feelings are part of *you*, not your resume, not your location. You have to deal with them straight on." Ora tilted her head. "Now, I need to ask you about your hand, where that fits. When I asked whether you were taking care of it, you said 'yes, no,' which means 'no.' What's *that* about?"

"I don't trust doctors. Mike's an exception—but now he wants me to see a random neurologist. I don't want to do that."

"Why not? You're acting like a teenage girl, cutting herself. If you don't want to practice surgery, take a leave! But don't . . . *harm* yourself to get out of it." She paused a beat and then continued. "Question. You said you don't trust doctors. You're a doctor. Talk to me."

Johnny nodded. "Couple of things. Surgeons are trained to trust only themselves. But . . . yes, I dislike the medical profession. Not only the way it's going, which is straight downhill, but also the way it's always been. I've never told anyone this story. Appreciate you keep it between us?"

"I treat you with *complete* confidentiality," Ora said. "Not even Mike do I talk to about our sessions, if that's what you're worried about."

"You don't?"

"Of *course* not. Which raises another point—you and Mike, and Bo for that matter, you say you're great friends, but you never really *talk* to each other. Each of you has been through a rough patch. I think you guys really do love each other. But why not share what you're really *feeling*?"

"Not that simple."

"Not that hard! Just pick up the goddamn phone. Have lunch or dinner. No agenda. I'm thinking maybe you don't trust *anyone*, Johnny. Not just doctors." She stood up. "Want a cup of tea, Johnny? I do."

"Sure, thanks. Tea would be great. I trust *you*, Ora." Johnny smiled weakly.

"Up to a point. I'll get the tea."

***

By the time Ora returned, Johnny had resolved to share his story. "Okay. So here's me. You ready, girl?" Johnny asked.

"Sure, ready. Go." She delivered Johnny's hot tea and sat.

"This may be hard. I've stuffed a lot of this."

"Fine." Ora cradled her cup in her lap. "There's the tissue box. Go."

Johnny told the story of the horrific deaths of his parents. "I sat there for a day with the bodies. Finally, old Howard showed up half drunk, smelling like a mule. Funny how you remember smells."

Ora nodded, rapt.

"His black pickup was the most welcome sight I've ever seen, to this day. He wrapped the corpses up and said some words over them. The medicine man. We dropped them off at the Indian Health Service in Crow. I never knew what happened to the bodies. I've always felt guilty, dumping them off like that, no ceremony."

Johnny pressed a tissue to his eyes. "Eventually, I resolved to become a doctor, one who drove unpaved roads to help poor Indians. I was so angry at all the doctors in the world, letting my parents die like animals."

"You could even have PTSD from all of that."

Johnny shrugged. "I always felt *safe* as a kid, although frankly I don't remember much. Until that day."

"How'd you get away from the reservation, Johnny? Basketball, right?" She looked at the clock—4:00 p.m. "Mike should be home soon. He was hoping to duck out early."

"I'd like to take you two to a nice restaurant."

"Let's take a break so I can call him. But then keep talking. This is very good stuff."

Ora returned quickly. "He's on his way. I reserved at a place we like in Menlo."

"Great. This's been helpful, lady. I'll answer your question then we can start drinking. Unless you've got something to suggest?"

"I don't prescribe normally, but since you're not from here, I can't milk your account like I usually do with these tech CEOs. I do want to hear the rest of your story."

Johnny nodded. "Okay. So Howard took me in up in Crow, about forty minutes north from Lodge Grass. Sketchy place, but an upgrade for me. Howard's son, Benny, took care of me, steered me to school and basketball. I got the UCLA scholarship. Poor Benny died drunk in his twenties, and then later *his* son, Harry, OD'd on drugs. That's another story."

Johnny stopped talking.

After a minute, Ora spoke, "Maybe not another story at all. That stuff about your parents and uncle and cousins and what you went through as a kid, that's at the heart of this, isn't it? You think if you fail at something . . ."

"That I'll be sent back to the reservation! Yes!" Johnny clapped his hands and laughed. "Sounds stupid, doesn't it?"

"Not at all, baby. We all have a fear like that. We don't always base our life on it, like you maybe did."

After a moment, Johnny spoke, "So what do I do, Ora?"

"Well, nothing dramatic for a while. You've got explosive material inside you. This may be a good time to get back in touch with the wider world. Get around, meet people, read, travel? Part of this is you've been in a bubble for years. Time is your friend. Wasn't it your Coach Wooden who used to say, 'Be quick but don't hurry'?"

Johnny smiled and pushed his floppy black hair off his forehead. "You're pulling out all the stops."

"Here's more advice," Ora said, pointing a finger at Johnny. "Stay away from Lisa. She needs to heal." She paused. "You been dating?"

"No. Should I be?"

"No should about it, is there? It's part of life. Although Lisa would shoot me . . . that is, if you're not put off by women after the divorce."

"Not put off, I just don't get them. I did meet a woman, what, four months ago? Very attractive, young. She gave me her card, wait . . . here." He dug Michaela's card out of the recesses of his wallet and smoothed it out on his knee. He remembered her long soft fingers. He felt a surge of desire.

"Really pretty. An actress. She said don't call until the divorce was final. So the divorce is final. Maybe young thirties? I can't tell women's ages."

"January said you met someone in Cabo. A child, but she sounds sensible," Ora said, her penciled eyebrows high. They heard the garage door opening. "Here's my guy," Ora said.

"Thank you, Ora. Send me a bill." Johnny sipped his cold tea. "Blah!"

"Pour that into the sink. And I *will* send you a bill. Bone doctors don't make what they used to." She winked, stood up, and shouted, "Michael! That you, honey?"

CHAPTER NINE

"Who? Johnny Blood? Oh, Dr. Blood from Cabo. That pushy heart doctor with the broken hand, right?"

"Good memory. That's me."

Michaela's tart recollection of their meeting five months ago filled Johnny's heart. It was a Thursday afternoon, and Johnny had left the hospital early to call her. He sat in the mansion's sunken living room staring at her card and rehearsing his opening before finally punching in her number.

"Let me guess, Dr. Blood, your divorce is final, and you're looking for a little . . . companionship? When was the divorce final? An hour ago?"

"Six weeks ago."

"Oh, I like men who delay gratification—is that how you say it? I don't know many. So what's up, Doc? I'm on location."

"Oh, sorry. Hoping maybe we could have coffee. Where are you?"

Michaela was silent. Johnny could hear muffled conversation.

"Still there?" Johnny asked.

"Let me call you back. I have your number here. I'm filming in Long Beach. It may be tomorrow." She hung up.

Johnny looked at his cell, which flashed CALL ENDED. He thought it was fifty-fifty she'd call back. But at least he tried.

Michaela called early the next morning. She whispered, "Sorry to be so rude yesterday, Doctor. This is crazy here—we're shooting a film. I have a ridiculous suggestion. Can you come down to Long Beach tomorrow, Saturday, about eleven thirty? I'm busy, but I can do lunch tomorrow. Meet at the Long Beach Aquarium? Do you know it? It's amazing. And I won't have to worry whether to sleep with you. I know about you new divorced types."

"Call me Johnny, Michaela. I'll find the Aquarium. Tomorrow eleven thirty?"

"That's right, Doctor."

"It's Johnny," he said.

"I'll know what to call you after I see you. Meet me at the Shark Lagoon. I'll push you in if you come on too fast."

***

Johnny arrived at the Aquarium forty-five minutes early and walked around. He loved the infinite array of nature, but he'd buried his affinity for decades. At the appointed time, he saw Michaela's dark hair and lithe figure approaching. His heart raced.

"Oh, hi, Doctor! Don't you just love this place? How are you? You're so tall!" She offered her hand and a warm smile. She wore a décolleté top and a black wrap. Her skin was ivory. He felt his cheeks flush.

"I'm fine, thanks. Hand's better, see?" He held up his left hand and forced a smile. "And you're right, this is an amazing place," he said.

"Glad you like it. I just have an hour, sorry. Have to reshoot a scene."

"It's okay. You got the Angelina role you wanted?"

"Yes. Good memory." Her eyes were dark and her lips full and ripe.

"Let's eat," she said, looking around. "There's a place to get a decent salad." She stepped off briskly.

"Hasn't a woman smiled at you lately? I saw you blush," she said without turning. He was scrambling to follow and could barely hear. The corridor swarmed with kids.

He pulled even. "Did I blush? I'm not, no, I haven't seen a woman smile at me in quite a while. Not like that."

"Don't you just hate women right now? New divorced guys so hate women in general but so crave the attention of *a* woman. They jump into crazy relationships. My advice, Doctor? Take a break. Give peace a chance."

Johnny was having trouble keeping up with her long athletic stride. "I don't hate women. You've known newly divorced men?"

"Oh, one wanted so bad to marry me. We broke off recently, so I'm still kind of raw about that. It would have been *such* a disaster. I'm flattered you blush when I smile. I shouldn't make fun. I don't see that reaction in the world I work in. It's all about getting me into bed. I hate these people." They had arrived at the salad restaurant. "Here we are. Let's get in line."

Her manner was rapid, high energy, controlled. Johnny was struggling to catch her rhythm.

"Michaela," he said.

She turned to look at him, this time without smiling. "Yes?" Her dark chocolate eyes studied his face.

"Slow down, lady. I told you I'm harmless."

"And I still doubt that." She gazed at him. Her face softened.

"Tell me about your movie. Why Long Beach?" he asked.

She looked away. "This is my shot, Johnny. The film is good, and I'm kicking ass. I need to focus, so we have to put whatever this is on hold."

"No worries. Thanks for . . ."

"I have a lot riding here, is the thing." Her eyes seemed far away.

Salads in hand, they sat at a small table. She grabbed napkins and vigorously rubbed the surface. "The one problem here—they don't clean. Why Long Beach? It's cheap for the producer. And it's good for chase scenes. Wide streets. And the grips can commute. Me, I haven't been home in weeks."

"Franklin Street? That was on your card."

"My little rental house in the flats of Los Feliz. I don't have much money now. I'm hoping this movie will change that. But enough. Let's eat, and I'll tour you around the Aquarium. I'll call in a few weeks. Promise."

They finished lunch, and Michaela walked Johnny around. She stopped at the main exit. Johnny laughed. "I see the fish tour has come to an end."

"Back to work. How old are you, Johnny?"

"Fifty-three. And you?"

"*Never* ask a lady that. Don't you know *anything* about women?"

"Not really. No sisters, mother died early, all-boys high school."

"How long married? You look younger."

"Nearly seven years," Johnny said.

"Uh, oh—seven-year itch kind of guy? Kids?"

"No kids. And it wasn't a seven-year itch."

"So what happened?"

"To the marriage? No idea. It was a bad idea from the start."

"I like your honesty. Most men don't have a clue about women and think they're experts. Divorce can be humbling, so maybe that's it."

"I don't understand women. But I like them. Most of them."

"I can teach you. And I'm only a year younger than Angelina, with better skin."

Johnny showed surprise.

"Good reaction. Anyway, *ciao*, Johnny. Like I said, I'll call when I'm done here." She smiled, rose up on her toes, and kissed him on both cheeks. He could smell her dark hair. She stepped back and surveyed her effect. "There's that blush again. It's cute, so we have that to work with." She winked and pivoted decisively, leaving Johnny to watch her stride away. He rubbed his cheek, remembering her scent.

CHAPTER TEN

Two weeks after the Aquarium, Michaela still had not called. Johnny did, however, hear from Billy Bell, who invited him to Dodger Stadium for opening day 2010. "Giants. And I have messages from my stepmom. And I miss you, Johnny Blood Moon."

Billy had invited Johnny to attend every opening game since 2003. Johnny missed only last year, pleading the divorce blues. He told Billy he still felt blue this year, but Billy pressed, "Get *over* it, Johnny! We can still hang out, can't we?" Johnny gave in. He considered Billy a lonely diamond in the rough, a rare friend whose affection was never confused by interest. He was the only person who called Johnny by his Indian name, and somehow it was okay.

They sat together looking down on the dazzling green field. Dodger Stadium sits in Chavez Ravine, a hollow rimmed by brown hills under a blue limitless sky. The vista remains breathtaking, fifty years on. Dodger baseball was the one activity Billy and his dad, Wild Will, had shared. After Will died and Lisa sold the company, Bell Enterprises moved its headquarters to Chicago. Billy personally acquired the Bell corporate suite at Dodger Stadium. It was his one eccentric asset—and he used it eccentrically. He attended most home games alone and used the space as a writing office when there were no games.

Billy cleared his throat. "You know I live now in that back room in your old Bel Air house. I can get things done in that little den."

"Too dark for me in that den."

"I like it dark when I work. Lisa's usually out at night, but occasionally we eat together. She's been edgy lately. I try to help her just by being around."

"You said you brought a message?" Because of Billy's sharp memory and inability to keep secrets, Lisa and Johnny occasionally used him as a mail drop.

"Messages. The first is, she wanted to see you herself but couldn't do it. Forgive her. That's message one. This divorce is really hard on her."

Johnny shrugged. "She seemed cool enough about it."

"Pure façade. Message two, she wants a good relationship."

"What does *that* mean? Best way is pick up the phone. I have no gripe with Lisa. This whole thing is on me."

"*Please,* Johnny. Message three . . . which I realize cuts against message two. But I promised not to editorialize. She wants no contact for a year. She worries she'll fall backward."

"Backward into what? We haven't been a couple in years!"

"Don't bitch at *me*, chief. Why'd you two ever get married in the first place?" Billy asked.

"God, that's the right question. I guess I felt I was missing something in my life. And I wanted kids, although she . . . ruled that out early on."

"You have me, your gay stepson." Billy laughed.

"Right. Ex-stepson. But to be honest—that was a big dividend from marrying Lisa. Our friendship."

Billy nodded shyly. "Why else?"

"Well, she was a figure in town. At the start, I felt, what, proud that she was on my arm? We were a glamour couple. All the right parties."

"Very West LA," said Billy.

"Yep. That wore off quickly."

"So it was all about you?"

"It wasn't a carefully thought-out plan, if that's what you mean."

"You want to hear Lisa's side?"

"Sure," Johnny looked over at Billy, who was scanning the shimmering green field. "Did she send you here to tell me her side?"

"No, not at all. She'd be appalled at my presumption."

Johnny grunted.

"So Lisa. Similar story," Billy said. "Both of you had rough childhoods. One difference, though, is the factor of my dad. He had sufficient self-esteem for everybody. Dad liked you. He didn't like many guys. She took that as a sanction. Why those two had such a great marriage and you two had such a crappy one, god knows. If people were handicapping those two marriages, money would have changed hands."

"I guess."

Billy kept his eyes on the ball field. "I *like* this Dodger team, Johnny. Ethier, Kemp, Kershaw. These are quality players."

Johnny quietly nodded.

"The owner's the problem," Billy said. "Another thing. Lisa said to remind you, you don't own Benedict Cañon. She said you have what the lawyers call a usufruct interest. She owns the tree, you can eat the fruit."

Johnny shifted in his chair and groaned. "Please! I understand that! She think I'm an idiot?"

"This was last night. She may have had a drink. I can only speculate."

"So speculate," Johnny said, annoyed.

"Well, she doesn't think you're an idiot. But I think . . . that mansion, that's where she and my dad had their happiest years. I think she sees you as maybe prone to rash decisions right now?"

"Not the first person to point that out."

"And like I said she was drinking. Here I am, editorializing."

Johnny stared out at the field. "Pisses me off, her desire to control my affairs. Lisa has a way of making me feel very small."

The game was about to begin. A group started to sing the national anthem. Johnny watched Billy struggle to stand. "Billy, is Lisa angry at me—deep down?"

"Hold on." Billy put his hand over his heart. Johnny stood. They waited for the music to end. The jets roared by. Billy laughed. "Wow! Love that! Sorry, Johnny. You remember Dad was in the army. He liked us to stay silent during the national anthem." Billy eased himself down.

Billy rubbed his face. "Is Lisa angry at you? She's got kind of a generalized rage right now. I'm not sure how she feels about you. She sits and stares out the window, usually with a drink in her hand. She doesn't talk to me about the divorce, except for one strange morning last January."

"What was that?" Johnny asked, still standing.

"It was right before the divorce became final. Out of the blue she asks if I knew your trust ends if you get married again. That you lose the income. I said no, I didn't know the trust. She had this look . . . later I ran into Jack Pettker, her lawyer. I asked whether that clause is standard. He said yes, called it a 'sunset' clause."

Johnny blanched. He sat down.

"Something the matter?" Billy asked, looking at Johnny.

"Forgot about that clause. Never registered. 'Sunset' clause? Normally I like sunsets."

"You have a girlfriend?" Billy asked. "That would be pretty quick. Although Lisa thinks you have a girlfriend."

"Really?" Johnny shook his head. "No, no girlfriend. But I never focused on that clause. Pettker said it's standard?"

"That's what he said. Sure, you're young enough, you might still find another woman. Anyway . . ."

Johnny, recovered now, cut him off. "Okay, so, Billy, I noticed you could hardly get out of your chair for 'The Star-Spangled Banner.' Where's the fifty-pound weight loss? Remember our deal?"

"I . . . you're right. But it wasn't a deal, just a goal, like you said. I'll get on it. How about first I call out for Dodger Dogs?"

"You're hopeless. Come see me. I'll give you a nutrition plan. Don't want you to die, friend, I like these seats."

***

Another week went by—still no call from Michaela. Bo Rathgeber called. "You've been a free man three months now. What's going on with yourself?"

"Trying to scrape up money to pay your bill. That'll take a while."

"Crap. This is the most husband-favorable divorce in history. Worth way more than I charged you. Anyway, your guy already sent me a check."

"He did?" Johnny laughed. "Maybe I'll stop it."

"Too late. January's already spent it. Anyway, reason I'm calling—can you come to dinner a week from Friday? January is having a dinner party," Bo asked.

"Love to, but let me ask you something before I forget. That clause about the trust ending if I get married again, is that normal?"

"Yes. I spoke to you about it. Six months after you get married, it stops. You also lose the use of Benedict Cañon."

"Wow! Went right over my head," Johnny said.

"You're not good with the details. A sunset clause is pretty standard, although this trust is anything but standard. So what about dinner? It's not a big deal if you can't. It's a sizable group she's inviting. Should be some interesting people."

"I'd love to if don't have a date. I'm waiting for a call."

"Is it that actress you met in Cabo?"

"It is. We haven't had a real date yet. I wanted to keep that Friday open. She's making a movie. Can we leave it loose?"

"That's fine. Call me when you know."

CHAPTER ELEVEN

Johnny changed his status with UC Cedars to a formal leave of absence. He told the powers-that-be that six months would probably suffice. The strength in his hand was slowly returning—although he never did visit the lady neurologist—but his passion for surgery at UC Cedars was not.

Johnny was finally, at age fifty-three, building a life. A running friend, a lawyer from the neighborhood, invited him to attend the college basketball championships—the Final Four—in Indianapolis. On the trip, they had long talks about their jobs and lives. Johnny was astonished to hear that politics abounds in large law firms as well as in large hospitals. He was also back to playing racquetball with Gus on Mondays, an ACE bandage protecting his bum hand.

After a match in early April, they soaked in the Jacuzzi. Gus shouted, "Good game, Johnny. How's the hand feeling?"

"Definitely better," Johnny said, flexing his left hand.

"When's the last time you had an ordinary physical?" Gus asked.

"You mean like an annual physical? Can't remember. I'm fine."

"You're at an age where guys should have an annual physical, Johnny. I think it's a hospital rule too."

"I'm on leave."

"Do me a favor? Let me do it. I'm a decent GP."

"I'm not interested."

"What? Takes twenty minutes. I'll take blood and stick my finger up your ass. No charge, not even for the gentle penetration."

"Now I know what you're after," Johnny said. They laughed.

"Tell you what, Johnny. Next week, if you win just one game, I'll not bug you for a while. But if I win two and oh, you submit to my exam."

Johnny quietly rotated his injured hand.

"What do you say, Johnny?" Gus asked. "I'm serious."

"You won't bug me for how long? Say, two years?"

"A year. You're betting against your own interest, dickhead."

"Fine. You win both games, you get to stick your finger up my ass. Long as you don't smoke a cigarette after."

***

Gus won two and oh the following Monday, and Johnny dutifully showed up for an exam the next morning. They joked their way through the twenty minutes. Gus said he would withhold his advice until he saw the blood panel. His eyes showed mild concern, but Johnny ignored it. The next day Gus knocked on Johnny's half-open office door.

"Yah? Come in."

Gus pushed the door open. "Got a sec?"

Johnny saw the papers in Gus's hand. "Sure, sit, Dr. Rogosin. What's up? Do I have cancer?" He smiled and swiveled toward Gus, who closed the door and stood next to Johnny's desk.

"Your PSA's high," Gus said, handing Johnny a sheet of paper.

"What is it?"

"Seven," Gus said. "Look at the report."

Johnny felt the blood leave his face. "There's a lot of false positives, right? Two out of three are wrong, right?"

"True. I'm not a urologist, Johnny, but I can read a blood report. And your prostate has a few bumps. I think you should . . ."

"Get a biopsy? No way. I knew it was a bad idea to do the exam."

"Johnny . . ."—Gus shook his head—"goddamn it!"

"PSA is about the volume of the prostate, right? You put your finger up there, might have inflamed it? This is an area where the cure can be worse than the disease, Gus. Impotence, incontinence." Johnny raised his voice. "I'm *not* going down that path. Doctors are like carpenters. Every problem is a nail. Soon some onc guy will be sizing me up for a bag to wear."

Gus was angry. "Shit! I'm trying to help you! You're treating me like the enemy."

"Sorry, Gus. I'm not very good with doctors. Sorry, calm down. But I don't . . . I'm just not going there. Odds are strongly in my favor. If I begin to feel something . . ."

"You know it's asymptomatic, Johnny. You won't feel anything until you're in trouble. And sure, you may be fine. But there's a chance . . ."

"Life's full of chances. How about the rest of the exam?"

Gus pressed his lips. "Everything else is fine. A few months, I'll bug you again. I can't just ignore it."

"Fine, fine. Now, I've got things to do, Gus."

Gus gathered his papers. As he walked out, he spoke over his shoulder, "Sometimes you're such a fucking jerk, Johnny."

***

On Wednesday night, Johnny's cell buzzed. The caller ID showed UNKNOWN CALLER, and he considered not answering. He pushed the green button and spoke gruffly.

"Hello. Who is this calling?"

"I'm done with my shoot, and I totally love this film! Can we have dinner Friday? It's my first day back in LA, so I'll be totally exhausted!"

Johnny stammered, "Michaela! I'm so happy you called. Where? When?"

She suggested Sofi, a Greek restaurant on Third Street near UC Cedars, seven thirty. She said she could reserve a quiet table.

As he sat savoring his great good fortune, his cell phone rang again. He fumbled it out of his jacket, nearly dropping it. Again, the caller ID showed UNKNOWN CALLER. He punched the button. "Michaela?"

A weak voice answered. "Uncle Johnny? This the wrong number?"

"Who is this?" asked Johnny.

"This is Nicky Bloodman. 'S' is Johnny Blood?"

Nicky was Johnny's young Crow cousin—Howard Blood Moon's great-grandson. Uncle Howard begat Ben; Ben, who had cared for Johnny, begat Harry; Harry begat Nicky. The last Johnny heard, young Nicky was in the army in Afghanistan.

"Nicky, you good, kid? Where are you?"

"I'm here in Crow. Howard's dying. I'm out of the army. It's pretty fucked up, Johnny. This is Johnny Blood, right?"

"It's me. What's the story, Nicky?"

"He's in and out, Johnny. The health service doc thinks he can die anytime. Can you get up here like soon?"

"Maybe Sunday night I can get there. I have, uh, duties until then."

"'K, whatever. He may not last that long. He's asked for you."

"I'll see what I can do, Nicky. But it's probably Sunday. I'll call you." Johnny ended the call. He thought he heard drugs or booze in Nicky's voice.

After a moment, he called Bo.

"Rathgeber. Hey, Johnny."

"Bo, I can't make the dinner Friday. Tell January I'm sorry."

"No worries. Did the girl call?"

"Yes, we have a date. And my nephew Nicky just called with bad news. It's about my uncle Howard?"

"The medicine man."

"Yes. Apparently, on his last legs. I'm driving up early Saturday."

"I'm sorry."

"Thanks. I'm more concerned about Nicky, my nephew."

"I don't know Nicky. Why don't you and I have a boys' dinner when you get back? You can catch me up."

"Good idea, Bo. I should let you go."

"Sure, but before you go. What's the girl's name?"

"The girl? Oh . . . Michelle Powell. Uh, no, it's . . . Michaela. Michaela Powell. Why?"

"I want to check her out. It sounds like you don't know her name."

Johnny laughed. "Protecting me from myself? Like in college?"

"Exactly. You didn't know their names back then either. Call me when you get back."

CHAPTER TWELVE

Johnny arrived at Sofi early. The maître d' led him to a private nook, where he checked his e-mail and watched for Michaela. When she arrived, ten minutes late, Johnny felt his breath catch. She hugged the maître d and chatted for a moment, allowing Johnny time to resume regular breathing. When she finally approached with her dark eyes and bright smile, Johnny stood, fumbling with his napkin. She kissed him on both cheeks. He choked out her name. "Michaela." They sat and looked at each other. She seemed thinner but even more beautiful than he had remembered.

"So! I'm done! And I'm exhausted! I need a wine. Sorry to be late." She waved at a waiter and then studied Johnny's face. "How are you? You look tired. Tell me something I don't know. I'm *so* happy to be finished!"

Johnny gathered himself. "Let me see, something you don't know? So I'm on my way to Montana tomorrow to help with an uncle who's ill."

"Montana?"

"Yes, where I grew up, on the Crow Indian reservation."

"You're an Indian? I thought you were some kind of Hispanic."

"Three-quarters Crow, one-quarter Irish."

Michaela kept her eyes on Johnny's face. Her interest electrified him.

"I know Irish, but I don't know any Indians. Am I supposed to say Native American? So cool! Tell me about your sick uncle."

"Indian's fine. Howard's his name. My father's brother. He raised me, sort of."

The waiter brought a carafe of wine.

"Do you mind if I pour?" she asked. "I love their house red."

"Go for it. How'd the film shoot go?" Johnny asked.

She sipped her wine. "Ugh. Actually, very well. But tell me your story first, your uncle, where you went to college, whatever."

Johnny summarized his life story as the food arrived in waves.

"So your uncle's a real medicine man? That's so cool. What's his illness?"

"The way he's lived his life, I'm sure his body's just grinding to a halt."

She resumed studying his face. "So sad, death. So final. Tell me why you got divorced, Johnny."

The question surprised him. "Like someone once said, that's a personal question. Then I get to ask questions."

She shrugged. "We'll see."

Johnny told Michaela about his marriage, describing his cluelessness about women in general and Lisa in particular. Michaela studied him closely. More food arrived. Michaela had a huge appetite.

"Didn't they feed you in Long Beach?" Johnny asked.

"I didn't eat much there. Trying to stay skinny for the role." She dipped her bread. "But I do like food. Particularly Greek. Keep talking."

"I'm pretty much done. Bottom line, not sure why I got married, not sure why it didn't work out."

"Well, so how does this sound? You say you've never had a normal relationship with a woman. You block out women completely for twenty years, and then in your forties you marry a patient. Kind of impulsive, no? What do they say?—digital? I googled you and saw that *LA Magazine* once called you Dr. Golden Hands." Michaela giggled. "They even put you on the cover I bet because the other doctors were all short and bald. That's during when your marriage was going bad. So you started questioning your life, right? Checking your hairline in the mirror? Bet you bought a fancy car around then too, am I right?"

"Maserati convertible. In 2007. That fancy enough?"

"That's like $140,000!"

"More. That actually was Lisa's doing. You make me feel like an idiot. I never drive with the top down, if that saves me from being a total bozo."

"Not a bozo. Just a normal LA guy with money. So then I bet you had an affair?"

"No, but she did."

"The wife? Really? Trying to get your attention probably. Your ex, she sounds like a nice enough lady, but you were ships floating in the night."

He smiled and raised his glass. "You mean 'passing in the night'?"

They clinked glasses and laughed. "That's exactly what I mean," she said. "I love American sayings, but I mess them up sometimes."

"How did you figure all that out?" Johnny asked.

"Figure what out? Oh, I like to guess people's stories. There's nothing new under the sun. Is that how to say it?"

"Nailed that one. So, Karnak, why did Lisa marry me?" Johnny asked. "That's the mystery for me."

"I'll get back to you on that. I'm out of battery. And I need more facts." She smiled catlike.

"You're just a good guesser." He sipped his wine. "Tell me about you."

"Oh god. Must I?"

"That was the deal."

The food kept coming. Johnny ran out of appetite before Michaela did, but not out of appetite for watching her eyes and listening to her voice.

She started haltingly. She had been born in Athens. Her father abandoned the family years ago; her mother still lived in the old home in Athens. Her eyes filled with tears. He could see there was a lot more to the family story, but he didn't press for details.

She dried her tears with her napkin. "I'm sorry. I'm a little shaky right now. It's easier if I talk about my career. I loved movies as a kid and wanted to become an actor, but I knew I'd never get anywhere in Greece. Greeks are so limited and lazy. They sit around arguing politics and bitching at the system. *They* are the system that needs fixing." She was almost spitting. "These people, the descendants of Aeschylus and Plato, to this day they spend their time avoiding taxes and bribing each other."

She gulped her wine and continued. Working at an Athens television station, she got a small role in an HBO show. She came to America in 2001 on a work visa and had a one-night stand with a producer named Kennedy, the man who eventually got her the Long Beach film role. "The affair with David was one and done—he's happily married, so he's been acting out his guilt to this day by helping me. Thank god! That's all still private, in case you ever meet him."

Then her career stalled. She waitressed to survive. Two years ago, she met a wealthy business executive who wanted to marry her. "He was just divorced, older but good-looking still, looking for a new life. He came on a hundred miles an hour. He had all this money, but I knew I couldn't love him. It would have been a disaster. Although to be fair, I think he loved me in his way." She patted her eyes again with her napkin. "It still hurts to remember. He was a nice man.

"I broke it off, just before you and I met in Cabo. He got angry—he was used to getting his way. Thank god for David Kennedy, who called me just then with the Long Beach role. David thought he had to sell me—I jumped through the phone. It was *perfect*. Although the proof will be with the pudding."

"In the pudding."

She laughed her waterfall laugh and sipped her wine. "I'll be honest, the reason I'm so jumpy and teary—so you're another rich, attractive guy. I feel like I need some space, to figure out . . ."

Michaela dipped her bread and took a deep breath. "Anyway, I got a small advance on the film and a residual if it succeeds. If not, I'm back waiting tables. I used to work here, you know. Don't ever be poor."

She picked up her napkin, leaned back, and scrutinized Johnny's face. "You must think that I'm some kind of a flake."

"No—why would I think that?"

She sat back and flapped her napkin. "Doctor, please don't take me wrong. But we need to go slowly please." She leaned forward, put her hand on his. "I'll be honest. I like you, but I'm still unsettled from my breakup. And I'm very tired. So tonight we go in our separate cars in our separate ways. Then tomorrow, you fly away to Montana. Then . . . who knows?"

"I'm driving. I've never driven up to Montana."

"Oh? Your midlife Maserati?" She managed a smile.

"Not on this trip. I have a Harley bike."

"Really? You're full of surprises. I used to have a bike. A bicycle bike. Wear your helmet. My gentleman friend bought me a Prius. I offered to return it when we . . ." Michaela turned away and emitted a low groan. "Anyway, he said keep it. And I kept it. Is that tacky? So I'm going back to my little house and think about this dinner. Still have to come down from the shoot too. We made a good film . . . well, we'll see. The yucky promotion starts soon. You go help your family. Nicky sounds nice."

"Nicky's the main thing for me. Maybe my chance to . . ." The waiter interrupted him with the check. She pulled her credit card out. He pushed it back. "No, let me pay, Michaela. I'm fine with going slow, but let me pay tonight. It would make me feel better."

"This is a guy thing? I don't know what you're doing, Dr. Johnny."

"Maybe a guy thing. I want to express gratitude for meeting you, for having had such a lovely evening. Simple."

She picked up her credit card. "Thanks. Nothing simple between a man and a woman. Call me when you're back. But—slow, please."

CHAPTER THIRTEEN

The sky was brightening over yellow velvet hills along I-15, as Johnny rocketed north out of the force field of LA, his soul full of purpose. Provo, Utah, was his target tonight. Passing Las Vegas, he shuddered at the ersatz monuments—faux Egypt, faux Paris, faux New York. He turned up his iPod—only the easy sounds of James Taylor and Carole King could soften the sharpness. He felt that he was hearing these lovely lyrics for the first time.

He began fully to relax only when he saw the soft contours and colors of Southern Utah. He was captivated by the endless straight roads, the eternal pink hills, the boulders that had not moved in ten thousand years. He turned off his music and allowed himself to reflect on Michaela and their dinner last night.

She was something entirely new for Johnny—the silken aggressor, warily probing his defenses, parrying his normal cuts and thrusts. Like most surgeons, Johnny was addicted to his own views—not the best listener. Especially with women, Johnny was used to being in control—being on top, as Gus put it. The astonishing thing—he felt that Michaela was right there with him, listening to him, absorbing, evaluating. She had independence, fiber, capacity. What to do with that? How to act?

***

Johnny sped through the sere pastel landscape, mesmerized by the shapes and scale. Rolling north on I-15, he noticed rough roadside shrines made of rocks and found objects: "In loving memory of USA CPL. Hal Maister, our son, Enoch's pride, Helmand 2010"; "God bless Charlie Company 1/6 Semper Fi SSGT Bushnell Smith"; "Bring our boys home with honor." He thought about Nicky. In their last conversation yesterday morning, Nicky said Howard was "real bad." Johnny texted Nicky at rest stops without response. Nicky *always* responded to texts, even if with a bare "K" or "Word."

He remembered Nicky's cute story the other day on the phone. When he joined the army, he combined Blood and Moon together into Bloodmoon, one word, on his application. The recruiter recorded his name as Bloodman, and Nicky let it stand. So his discharge papers read Specialist Nick Bloodman, and that's now his name. He didn't tell Howard, because he remembered how Howard had hated Johnny's name change. They laughed about it. That was their last and best conversation.

Johnny arrived in Provo at dusk and checked into a motel near the university. Nicky was still not responding to calls or texts. In the morning, Johnny called Robert Long, his former teacher and coach, who had also mentored Nicky at Hardin High.

"Johnny! How nice to hear from you! Where are you?"

"Hey, Coach. In Provo, on my way to Crow. I'm about to check out of my room. Howard's dying. And I'm worried about Nicky."

"Oh, I heard about Howard," Coach said. "And Nicky, you *should* worry about Nicky. He may be medicating. Haven't seen him since he came home. He hasn't called me."

"That's what I was afraid of. You know any specifics?"

"No. I hear indirectly. He's a good kid, Johnny. Call me when you get up here. I'd like to help."

Johnny got back on the road, his anxieties sharpened.

***

When Johnny arrived in Crow late Sunday night, he climbed the creaky stairs to Howard's apartment and knocked. No answer. The door was unlocked, so he went in. It was a time capsule—little had changed in forty years, although the space seemed smaller and shabbier. There was Howard's unmade pullout bed, his headdress on the wall, his medicine man bag, the broken furniture, the random kitchen utensils. Above all, there was the distinct smell of Howard— fried food, booze, motor oil.

He opened the small refrigerator—it was empty, except for a can of Dr. Pepper. In the back room were the bed where he and Ben slept forty years ago and Ben's ancient dance trophies. A bed light was on. A book lay on the table: *The Things They Carried*, Tim O'Brien's dark Vietnam novel. On the floor lay two duffel bags stamped with army symbols, one open, spilling clothes, the other sealed. In the closet hung Nicky's army greens with his name tag and rank insignia. Over his name tag were service medals and a badge with a cross and entwined snakes. A medic badge?

Johnny sat on the stool where he had pulled on his socks and shoes in high school. He'd been on the road ten hours, and his eyes were heavy. Stirred by the traces of Benny and Howard and Nicky, he was caught in a spider web of memory. He walked downstairs to secure his motorcycle and fetch his luggage. He undressed and flopped down on Howard's bed, staring at the familiar stained plaster ceiling. He felt anxious. He tried Nicky's cell again. No answer. He fell into a fitful sleep.

At 4:00 a.m. Nicky staggered in. Waking from a dream of his childhood, Johnny first thought it was Howard. Nicky stumbled toward the back bedroom. "Nicky!" Johnny's deep voice startled both of them.

"Wha? Who's 'at? Johnny? God, it's you, Johnny. Oh god." Nicky let out a gasp. "Howard's dead!" He fell to his knees, sobbing into his fists.

Johnny guided him to the back bedroom. Nicky sat on the bed. Johnny removed his shoes. The young man was slender, but strong and nearly as tall as Johnny. His hair was black and floppy like Johnny's, his smooth skin a little darker. His shoulders were broad, his arms and legs long and ropy.

Nicky choked out that Howard had died yesterday evening at the health service and that he himself was "to'lly fucked up, to'lly fucked up." He fell back on the thin pillow and put his brown forearm over his eyes. Suddenly he jerked up, eyes wide open. "Johnny! He said he's your father! Howard said!" Nicky's speech was thick. "Dr. McMahon was sere! Howard woke up and said it! Lass sing he said. That you were his son! With Nola, he said. Then he died. Ass the doctor." Having discharged his critical message, Nicky fell into a deep sleep.

Johnny was stunned. He checked his watch: 4:20 a.m. He decided to walk over to the health service. He scribbled a note for Nicky.

CHAPTER FOURTEEN

Johnny trudged along the rutted road. It was chilly and dark, and he had to watch his step. He could barely make out the low black hills at the eastern horizon. After ten minutes, the road changed from dirt to asphalt, the shoulders from scrub to landscape, and modern streetlights appeared. He was startled to see a gleaming modern building in place of the shabby Quonset hut where he and Howard had dumped Nola's and George's corpses so many years ago.

He approached the shiny building feeling disoriented, even dizzy—the ground of his memory had shifted. He passed through automatic glass and chrome doors. Down the polished corridor, a white-clad doctor was studying a clipboard and chewing on his glasses stem. A nurse in a crisp uniform sat behind the control desk. Monitors glowed behind her. The nurse saw Johnny approach and smiled. "Yes, sir, may I help you?"

"Yes. I'm Dr. John Blood from Los Angeles, here for my uncle . . . or my relative . . . or deceased relative, Howard Blood Moon?"

The doctor raised his head. He was young, sandy haired, of medium build, his Anglo face open and his eyes kind. He stuck out his hand. "Dr. Blood, welcome. I'm Peter McMahon. Sorry about your loss. I was with Howard when he died. Great old guy. Everyone called him Dr. Blood Moon. His body's still here, over in the holding morgue in the auxiliary building."

Johnny, speechless, took his hand.

"You nephew Nicky tells me you walk on water. I also know you by reputation—UC Cedars? Great hospital. You have a minute, perhaps we can talk? My office is right there. Coffee?"

Johnny was reviving. "Coffee'd be great."

"Sure." Dr. McMahon stepped into an alcove. "Help yourself."

The coffee was fresh. "How old is this facility?" Johnny asked.

"It's been, let me see, six years. We're four physicians and a few really sharp nurse practitioners. Here we are, Doctor." He opened his office door, and Johnny passed in. "Have a seat please" he said, waving at the guest chair.

He walked around his desk and sat. "Call me Peter. You want to know about Howard and how he died?"

"And I'm Johnny. Yes. And anything you can tell me about Nicky."

Peter nodded. "Nicky. Nice kid, very capable, but he has issues. He was a medic in Afghanistan. Struggling, like a lot of these young vets."

"So," Peter continued. "Howard died yesterday at, hang on,"—he picked up a piece of paper—"6:38 p.m. Cause of death, pick it: cancer, heart, diabetes, liver. At the end, his lungs filled up, and he couldn't breathe. Well past eighty-five. Back then there were no birth records."

"What kind of cancer?" Johnny asked.

"Prostate. Spread to the bones. Nicky took care of him at home until the pain became unmanageable. They first found the cancer twenty years ago, according to his records. It sat dormant."

Johnny felt the blood run from his face. He cleared his throat. "Don't most men past eighty have prostate cancer?"

"Most do. Like they say, most men die with it, not of it."

Johnny nodded. "I saw Nicky earlier. He said some things . . . let me ask you, if Howard had been hospitalized sooner, could you have . . . ?"

"Saved him? No way. I used to visit Howard in that apartment. It was right to let him stay there. Nicky's like a good RN."

"That's where I grew up," Johnny said.

"Really? Pretty mean quarters over there. Howard was mostly pain-free until the last ten days or so."

"I see," Johnny said.

"Nicky did a fine job. I'm not a cancer specialist, but we do a little of everything here. I called an oncologist friend in Chicago. He said I could remove Howard's testicles and maybe stop the testosterone feeding the bone cancer. That may have bought him a little time."

"How much time?"

"A week? A month?—hard to say. I decided against it. Howard was in pain, he would have had zero quality of life. But my main reason was cultural. Crow men invariably decline to have their manhood cut off, even if it means death. I've seen it before. Nicky agreed."

"Glad I didn't have to make the call—sounds right, though, Peter."

"Did Nicky tell you about Howard's last words, Johnny? About you?"

"Yes, briefly . . . what did *you* hear?"

"Well, he'd been in a coma. We were treating him here just for pain. Then Saturday afternoon, Nicky's reading in there, and I walk in. Suddenly Howard pops up, all alert. 'Tell Johnny! He's my son, with Nola! George took him!' Then he sunk back into sleep and never woke up. Howard had a clear message for you, that he was your natural father."

Johnny sipped his coffee. "I honestly don't know what to say. Nola Ryan Wind-In-The-Trees was my mother. Half Irish, half Crow. We were close—but my childhood was a fog. I thought George Blood Moon was my father. George and Howard were brothers. Why would they switch on me?"

He told Peter the story of Nola's and George's deaths, and that he'd always regretted not knowing how they were buried.

"That was 1967, '68?" Peter asked. "We may have burial records. A lot of effort has gone into reconstructing that sort of thing, so the community has a coherent history. I've done some of the research myself. I'm part Crow in spite of appearances."

"Really? Say, I'd like to see Howard's body. You say it's still here?"

"Over in the other building. The morticians don't come till noon. Come, I'll take you. The sun should be coming up."

***

The quarter-mile walk in the emerging light was on a paved road. A chain-link fence with a razor wire crown ran parallel along their left, the east side. Beyond the fence, I-90 traffic rumbled by. Johnny could see dull ruined shacks and sheds between the fence and the interstate, reminiscent of Lodge Grass.

After a minute, Peter spoke, "I'm very interested in your story, Johnny. I've become deeply immersed in Crow culture. But I can't tell you why Howard handed you over to his brother. It was terrible here during the sixties. You're lucky to have survived, frankly. Lots of kids died."

The sun was at the horizon now, and the tips of the trees were peach gold. The dark-blue sky was cloudless.

"Because of the incredible poverty and the booze, families were, shall we say, fluid. It wasn't unusual for kids to be handed around or just warehoused somewhere. Wives were handed around too. Howard could have been out of commission when you were born—jail, drunk, working at some remote place. There's no telling."

"George was drunk most of the time too, when he was even around," Johnny said. "Not much of a father."

"It was a bad scene. It was hard to be a dad back then."

After a pause, Johnny asked, "Peter, why are you in Crow?"

"Fair question. My wife asks me that regularly. So I grew up in Billings, went to Northwestern for college and medical school. My father, an *Anglo* rancher—not particularly successful—he died when I was thirteen. I always wanted to be a doctor working with Native Americans—that came from my Catholic Crow mother. My uncle, my mother's brother, stepped up and paid for my education."

"Wow. Really?"

"Yes. He made money in mining and had no kids. Here's our utility building." He unlocked the door to a featureless single-story structure. The footprint appeared to be about sixty feet by forty feet. They passed in.

"Welcome to the Taj Mahal. We have the refrigerated holding morgue here in the back, our records, some equipment, and our server center such as it is. Come back to my little office."

As they walked through, Peter continued. "So anyway, after residency at Chicago Medical Center, I practiced internal medicine on the North Shore. But I wanted to come back here. My uncle had set up a foundation. My mother runs it. I talked them into this clinic. The deal was I'd run it, hire the staff. I was pretty young to do all that, but he arranged technical help. It was my dream come true. So here I am."

Johnny nodded. "Can you use a heart surgeon?"

"That would be pretty specialized. You serious?"

"Not really. But like you say, one can dream."

***

Johnny stood alone in the cold room looking down on Howard's ravaged face. He kissed the waxy forehead. Tears fell in a belated baptism. As he wicked up the tears with a tissue, an idea came to him. Johnny walked to Peter's office, drying his eyes. "Excuse me, Peter."

"Hey, Johnny, I think I found Nola and George!" Peter waved at the computer screen. "Says here she had breast cancer. Nothing about cause of death for George. Although there's a couple of interesting notes . . ."

"Like what?"

Peter looked up. "You OK? Your eyes are all red."

"It's getting to me a little. Seeing Howard. Maybe my father." He shrugged. "What was the interesting note?"

"For George, they examined the contents of his stomach."

"And?"

"Full of sleeping pills, it says. Big doses."

Johnny grimaced. "Seriously? So . . ."

"They don't conclude anything. The corpse wasn't fresh."

"So he might have killed himself?"

"Maybe. There's a note in Nola's file too. You ready for this?"

"I guess I don't know till I know."

"She didn't die of the cancer, although it was pretty advanced."

"What did she die of?"

"Blunt force trauma. Her skull was cracked."

Johnny groaned.

"I know. I'm sorry," Peter said.

"So maybe George . . . I remember seeing a fresh blood spot on that shroud thing with my mother. While I was away calling Howard, I bet he took the pills I brought him. All I know, when I came back, he was dead. I sat there for a day, not . . . wow. I thought . . . that's just awful."

"We'll never know exactly what happened."

"I need to absorb this. Would there be police records, or . . . ?"

"The police wouldn't have been involved. It was just Indians."

"Yeah. Shit Indians. We dropped the two bodies off right here. Can you tell how they were buried? Or where?"

"Looks like they're buried in the traditional Crow burial ground, which, if you want, we can bury Howard there. It's over by the Custer area."

Tears trickled down Johnny's face. "Sorry. I've suppressed all this for so long. I've always felt responsible for George's death. Now I know why."

Peter nodded. "If you work with poor people, you realize sometimes that death is not always the worst option. Your mother probably was in a lot of pain. Maybe George loved her more than you thought."

"Enough to kill her?" Johnny shook his head and blew his nose.

"Possibly," Peter said. "It can be a form of love."

"I've always hated death—hard for me to see it as a solution to anything."

"Come work here for a while," Peter said, an edge to his voice. The two men locked eyes.

After an awkward moment, Peter looked away and changed the subject. "So. the traditional Crow burial ceremony, they used to put the bodies on above-ground scaffolds. Some sticks and artifacts from those old platforms, you can still see them over there. It's possible some traditions were honored in 1967. We can go take a look."

Johnny felt a profound sense of relief. Then he remembered the idea he had while wicking up his tears. "OK if I clip a lock of Howard's hair?"

"Oh, shoot. State law . . . oh, go ahead. Be quick. Here's a scissors." He rummaged in a drawer. "This is for DNA so you can check the father thing? You should get follicles for DNA."

"Yes, for DNA. And . . . just to have a lock of his hair. Howard was my father. Whether by blood or not. But you know what's bizarre, Peter?"

"What's that?"

"Just now was the first time I ever kissed him. Ever."

CHAPTER FIFTEEN

It took Johnny two trips to the burial ground to locate the gravesites. Peter went along on the first trip. Nicky helped—he was good with computers, and he was glad to have something useful to do. They arranged to bury Howard nearby.

There was no medicine man left to conduct a traditional Crow burial—Howard was the last acknowledged Crow medicine man, a fact mentioned in the obituary in the local paper. Johnny wrote it—listing himself as sole surviving child. That felt strange. Coach Long knew an Irish Catholic priest who agreed to preside over the burial and to give a homily that incorporated Crow prayer words.

At the grave site on that rainy Thursday stood the old Irish priest, Johnny, Nicky, Dr. Peter McMahon, Howard's best friend Gerald Red Bird, the ageless auto shop proprietor, and Coach Robert Long. That was it. Howard had outlasted all of his friends except for Gerald Red Bird.

***

Four days later, Johnny and Nicky were in a U-Haul truck heading west on I-90, on their way to LA. In the back were Johnny's Harley, Nicky's duffels, and various boxes. Johnny was driving, and Nicky was swaddled in a thin blanket on the back-tilted passenger seat, quietly suffering withdrawal. From drugs and alcohol, and from his former life.

During their conversation in the morgue, Dr. McMahon confirmed Johnny's worst fears about Nicky. "He's in trouble, Johnny. Not only the drugs but also the posttraumatic stress disorder. These Indian kids enlist to get away from the reservation then they get hammered in Iraq or Afghanistan and come back here emotionally devastated. There's a group of them. We don't have jobs or resources here, and they fall into drugs and alcohol. I talked with Nicky when I could. My take is he's a talented boy who wants to do something with his life, but there's nothing here for him."

That did it: Johnny would rescue Nicky. On the night before Howard's burial, Nicky made it easy. "I need help, Johnny. I'm getting hooked on weed. And my head is blasted. Nightmares, can't sleep. Army was good in some ways, but it . . . sorry . . ." He trailed off.

Johnny was firm. "You're coming to Los Angeles. We'll bury Howard, wrap things up, get on the road maybe Monday. I'll rent a truck. I promise it'll be good. Right now, your job is to stop the dope."

Nicky commenced cold turkey that night. Coach Long stood with him at Howard's funeral and then drove back down from Hardin the next day to sit with him. Coach had been a teenage drunk. He sobered up before he started teaching, but he still had street creds. "Forty-five years clean and sober," he'd proudly say. "Still going to meetings."

While Coach sat with Nicky, Johnny tied up Howard's affairs. He disposed of the sticks and rags of furniture, settled a small grocery bill and a larger bar bill, and offered a generous check to old Gerald Red Bird, who had allowed Howard free use of the auto shop apartment for fifty years. Gerald stared blankly—he had just lost his best friend. He didn't take the check. The old Crow mechanic hobbled back into the bowels of the garage. Johnny noticed the rusty basketball hoop over the garage door. He thought about unscrewing it. His first hoop—his ticket to UCLA, Harvard, UC Cedars, and *LA Magazine*. He would let it go. Let it all go.

On Sunday night, Coach Long and Johnny were eating at the local diner. "Coach, thanks for helping with Nicky. I'm taking him down to LA tomorrow. I hope I'm doing the right thing . . ."

Coach waved his fork. "Johnny, he needs you, and you may need him. He needs to get out of Crow like you did. This place'll kill him."

***

Montana is a land without limits including speed limits. As Johnny accelerated out of Crow Monday morning, he savored the thrilling beauty of the vast land. Johnny felt strangely free: he had confronted the ghosts of his past, and his future seemed as limitless as the big sky over his head. Michaela, Nicky, old and new friends, fresh career possibilities.

Back in the Provo motel, Johnny reached to turn off the light between beds. Nicky spoke for the first time all day. "Uncle Johnny?"

"What's up, bud?"

"I know I've been like quiet. A lot of stuff going on inside."

"Not a problem."

"So . . . tomorrow, in the truck, can you tell me your story? I want to hear like your first memory, your growing up, living with Howard and Ben and my dad if you remember. Any stories about them."

Johnny laughed. "Like the story about Howard being my father?"

"You think that's just a story? You wrote it in the obituary. What would that make you and me?"

"I think it's true. People tend to tell the truth on their deathbeds. But it's still hard to absorb. Why did he hide it? Anyway, it makes me your great-uncle, your grandfather Benny's brother."

"We were all Howard's children—that's why I want to hear your stories. I need family." Nicky shuddered. "Need to sleep now."

CHAPTER SIXTEEN

Back on the road before dawn Tuesday, Johnny began his story. "I'll start with Howard. Dr. Blood Moon—his big thing was the Bighorn Medicine Wheel on Medicine Mountain in Wyoming. Ever hear of it?"

"Maybe. What is it?"

"Supposed to be like the tribal Stonehenge. Howard claimed he derived his power as a medicine man from Medicine Mountain. I constantly pestered him to take me up there. One night, he told me be ready early next morning and we'll go. Something came up, and we never made the trip. I doubt if he ever made it up there himself. He lived in his head. As I got older, I came to realize that maybe there wasn't anything up there except a pile of rocks. If that. That the dream is the thing."

"Yeah. Howard said a lot of crazy shit I didn't pay attention to," Nicky said. "Tell me about my grandfather Ben."

"Benny was the real deal. He was five years older—maybe my best friend ever. Built like you. At night we'd talk, over the rumble of the interstate. Howard'd roll in late, drunk. A big stumbly bear, full of sweetness and bad smells. Sometimes he came into our room to talk, that wheezing bad breath. Benny'd steer him back to the pullout, tuck him in, like a dad with a big clumsy kid."

"That was my job too, getting Howard into bed," Nicky said.

"Yeah. Benny was special. He was like my big brother—guess he *was* my big brother. He was so proud I was good at school. Gerald's Auto Repair—the doors rolling up at 7:00 a.m.—was my alarm clock. We'd find food, if Howard had food stamps that week, and off I'd go to school.

"Benny with those shining eyes would show me pictures of the wide world. 'Look here, Johnny. This here's New York. Here's Paris.' He had a thing about LA, the movies, the perpetual sunshine. Especially the Pacific Ocean. He had a picture over our bed with the sun dipping down into it. 'You're going there, Johnny, out to California someday. I'll come visit.' His dream. Southern California was Benny's Medicine Mountain. Benny was handsome, always a girl on his arm. Those old trophies in your room, those were from the powwow festivals for his dancing. And he had an awareness.

"I have no idea how Howard kept us going. In the summer he'd haul trash at the Custer Monument. Winter, he worked in the auto shop. He got free rent out of that, I guess. And he got the food stamps.

"But he was the medicine man. That's how he thought of himself. The old-timers called when they needed some Crow ceremony like at a funeral. He'd grab his bag and headdress. It lit him up more than anything."

"I know. He became a different person, didn't he? Tell me about you, Johnny. How did you get to Hardin High?"

"That was Benny. He insisted I go, and he made me try out for basketball. There was a hoop in the auto shop parking lot, and Ben had a basketball. We'd play horse, in the dark, in the snow. I could shoot, but I never thought I'd make the team. I was skinny and shy. But I did. I learned later the school got funding for Indians on sports teams. Whatever.

"Freshman year I grew six inches. They sent me and another Indian kid to a summer basketball camp in Bozeman. Kid named Steven Silent Fox. He was our center—big and strong. He was more silent than he was a fox.

"Next year the school hired Coach Long. He taught English, got me into reading. He told me his Oglala name: Robert Long Arrow. I asked why he changed it. He said, 'Johnny, you want to amount to anything, you have to put the reservation behind you.' Later, right before UCLA, Coach helped me change my legal name to John Blood.

"In sophomore year, the Hardin Bulldogs contended for the state championship. We made the semis over at Montana State. Stevie made the all-star team—I was honorable mention. That's when I started to peer over the horizon. Until then, I thought I was headed to Little Big Horn College.

"Next summer, Coach found money to send me to a basketball camp at North Dakota State in Fargo. He also gave me novels to read. I played with some good players, learned about nutrition and exercise, read books like *The Great Gatsby, Portrait of the Artist*."

Nicky grunted.

"Coach gave you those books too? I also managed to lose my virginity. Stevie had to work on his father's farm. He put on weight, lost a little quickness. Beginning of junior year I was six four and 180. We went to Bozeman as the six seed. When the statewide all-star team was announced, I was named first-string forward. Stevie was not named. Coach had his hands full.

"We won the championship—I had a good tournament. A UCLA scout offered me a trip to UCLA to work out in front of Coach Wooden. That's when Coach took me to the courthouse to change my name. Howard hated it. I was always Johnny Blood Moon to him.

"I flew to LA that July, and my heart was pounding. My first airplane trip. I'll never forget looking down at LA. A billion toy houses between mountain ranges. The soupy brown smog. But down on the ground, everything was bright and magical, just like Benny said.

"Coach Wooden and I had two long talks, one in the athletic office and one in the gym where he'd sit up in the stands watching practice. He was a fatherly man, seemed to take an interest in me. His assistant told me they'd offer me a full-boat scholarship. You kidding me? I was in heaven.

"We won the state championship again. I was all-state again and tournament MVP. Off I went to UCLA. Stevie Silent Fox went to Montana State. We lost touch. Coach told me he recently died.

"But your grandfather Ben had the worst ending. He had sex with a young Indian girl. She gave birth to your father Harry then she disappeared after dumping Harry at the orphanage. Ben was dead by then, just a kid. Solo auto accident, drunk. I still tear up. Dear Benny. Your dad, Harry, stayed in the orphanage until he was ten, I think. Then Howard took him in. Howard always felt guilty about Ben. By then I was a physician.

"Your dad, Harry, he was a handful, rough on Howard. Like Ben, he got into alcohol. Following the family tradition, he got with an Indian girl, and, surprise, a child was born. That'll be you. Your mom disappeared. Harry tried to be a father, but you spent lots of time at Howard's."

Nicky was silent. They were rolling south on I-15 now, below massive mountains.

"You know the rest, that when you were nine or ten, Harry OD'd and Howard took you in full time.

"I need to pull over here, bud. Too much coffee. Stay tuned."

***

Back in the truck after the pit stop, Johnny glanced over at Nicky, rewrapped in his shroud. "You want to sleep?"

"No. Please keep talking. It takes my mind off how I feel. Tell me about LA. What it was like being an Indian boy there?"

"Hang on." Johnny guided the truck back onto the interstate. "We should be in LA before midnight."

Nicky shifted his weight.

"So, okay, I'm a Bruin. It's hard to remember all the feelings now—high at first then devastated when I learned about Coach Wooden's retirement. I felt abandoned. Then I snapped my Achilles. It was my fault—I stopped stretching.

Never played ball again. Coach Wooden helped me with the scholarships, but, man, I was sure I was on my way back to Crow.

"Without basketball, UCLA was a foreign land. I had trouble making normal friends, although I never had trouble getting the girls. That's a cautionary tale I should tell you someday. Senior year I finally made friends, these two *Anglo* couples. I call them the Final Four. We lived together in Westwood, the UCLA college town."

"What about medical school? Didn't you go to Harvard?"

"I did. When I got in, it was a total shock. I got financial help from these Indian funds. I lived near Fenway Park and had my motorbike, which I won in a card game. Howard taught me two useful skills—poker and fixing car engines. Three, actually, if you count handling guns.

"I was sure I was the dumbest guy in class until first-semester grades came out. I'd worked hard and ended up near the top. It was an incredible rush. I remember walking around Boston in the freezing cold on a cloud. My grades caught the eye of the faculty. Because I'm a minority, they swarmed me, telling me how I could make a ton of money, cure cancer, that the profession needed me, yada yada.

"Second year, I met this girl from Memphis, PhD English program at Harvard. Ruth—tall, long dark hair, beautiful skin, Jewish princess. No idea why she fell for me. I moved in with her on Marlborough Street. I asked her to marry me at a Rolling Stones concert in Boston Garden and she said yes. Right after they played Satisfaction. We'd hang with her literary friends and then screw our brains out. I read the novels she read. That's when I first read Manuel Maria Gomez. Somehow I kept up with my own studies.

"Toward the end of that year, I was starting to feel confined. Ruth's parents didn't like that I wasn't Jewish, much less a frigging Indian who wanted to work with poor Indians. That's also when I started listening to the faculty. Harvard does that—very sly. All these high-powered people. You want to be one. Also I developed a taste for money, living in the brownstone, going to theater, music. I never had any of that before Ruth.

"Anyway, we broke off in June. I was pretty sad. Back to foraging and fast food. I spent a couple of weeks that summer in Crow hauling trash with Howard. I got a job in a cardiac clinic in Boston. I could feel myself selling out. I guess I wanted the Harvard professors to like me, and I wanted not to lose the next Ruth. The other thing—a professor, a black man, he told me that, because I was a minority, if I became a poverty doctor right away, I'd never know if I was any good. The solution, he said, was to go to a good place and outwork everyone and get to where patients sought me out because I was *good*, not because I was an Indian. That made sense to me.

"After Harvard, I was a resident in cardiothoracic surgery at New York Presbyterian. Six years there, including the fellowship. I loved the work—bypasses, transplants, valve replacements, aneurism repair, all the big invasive heart and lung procedures. Very buzzy.

"After that, I returned to LA. I had school debts, and I loved heart surgery. I also had my Final Four friends. So I went to UC Cedars, my Medicine Mountain. Eventually I reached the top. Turns out, I was more interested in the climb than the peak, another bunch of rocks. But I didn't know that until I got there. Then everything started to turn." Johnny stopped talking.

After five minutes, Nicky stirred. "What do you mean by 'turn'?"

"Thought you were asleep."

"Still awake," Nicky said.

"Well, for twenty years I did nothing but heart surgeries—then I got married late, to the wrong woman. I was such an idiot. Then everything fell apart. No more marriage, no more surgery. And recently, I meet this new woman. Bang, bang. So I'm in transition right now, like you. I'm hoping we can help each other get through this next phase."

Nicky mumbled from his cocoon. "I'm down, Johnny. That's an awesome story. Makes me feel better. I'll try to sleep now."

PART TWO

Then wear the gold hat, if it will move her;
If you can bounce high, bounce for her too,
Till she cry "Lover, gold-hatted, high-bouncing lover,
I must have you!"

—F. Scott Fitzgerald, from *The Great Gatsby*

CHAPTER SEVENTEEN

Los Angeles County is unimaginably vast, sprawling over an area larger than Rhode Island and Delaware combined. It contains eighty-eight cities, one of which, Los Angeles, the City of Angels, is the second largest in the United States by population. The county's ten million residents would make it the eighth-largest *state*. It has more manufacturing than Michigan, and its economy is larger than all but fifteen *countries*.

It is also full of *emigrants*, not so much immigrants: people who have fled troubles elsewhere. An emigrant knows more about what she *doesn't* want than what she *does* want. For these probationers, fear often eclipses hope: trepidation trumps aspiration.

Consequently, many Angelinos are in hiding. In the inner city, people of color hide from immigration, creditors, police, school officials, abusive family members, gangbangers. In the tony Santa Monica Mountain communities, the wealthy hide behind hedges from each other, ex-spouses, former lovers, grasping family members, paparazzi, star-gazing tourists, people of a lower class or darker skin (other than help), and, quite often, their own spotty past.

The amount of accumulated wealth in these hills is staggering. When LA's inner city blew up in 1965 and 1992, the tension among the wealthy hill dwellers soared, as did their hedges, fences, and gates. So the grandest houses—such as Johnny's Benedict Cañon —are fortresses, hidden down long driveways, behind locked gates, armed guards, dogs, and razor wire.

Beverly Hills is the capital of this cloistered area—90210, a global brand like Hollywood or Malibu; exclusive, expensive, the most hedged and moated, the least communal community on the planet; a "green zone" where civic spirit comes out only in opposition, to development, to taxes, to difference, to change. Why mess with perfection? To drive west from the city of LA along garish Sunset Strip into Beverly Hills is to pass from cacophony to serenity, from grit to green, from bad air to good, from earth to heaven. Or so it seems.

Arriving back home from Montana Tuesday night, Johnny eased the U-Haul through the security gate and up the long path to the front door of the mansion. Nicky sat low in the passenger seat, observing this strange new world.

Johnny jumped out, unlocked the front door, and turned on the houselights. He rapped his knuckles on the cabin window. "Nicky, come on in. We can unload tomorrow."

He saw Nicky's saucer eyes looking up at the massive facade with its turrets and gargoyles.

"Roll down the window," Johnny said, making a rotation sign. "What's the matter, bud?" Nicky's eyes showed fear.

"Johnny, I can't sleep in that house. It'd make me crazy."

Johnny nodded slowly and looked around. "Grab your bag and come with me." He led Nicky to Billy's former apartment over the garage. It was stale, littered with odd books and candy wrappers. "I think if you open a window, it'll be okay. Is this all right, Nicky?"

"It's fine," Nicky said. "This is fine."

"I'll wake you at seven. We'll grab breakfast and go up to the rehab. Sleep well."

***

Over breakfast in the mansion—daylight made the house less formidable—Nicky reported that he had slept badly. "This is all so crazy. Did you hear that thunderstorm?"

"Slept right through it. Finish up. We should get going."

They put the dishes in the sink, and Johnny backed his Maserati out of the garage—another wide-eyed stunner for Nicky. They headed north over the hills to a rehab facility in North Hollywood called Cri-Help. Nicky was scheduled to stay for thirty days.

While Nicky was processing in, an older man with a kind face approached Johnny in reception. "Excuse me, are you Nicholas Bloodman's father?"

"It's *Nick*, not Nicholas. I'm his uncle. His father's dead."

"Oh, I see," the official said. "His mother?"

"Long gone."

"Oh. Sorry. But he seems ready."

"Ready?" Johnny asked. "For what?"

"To take his medicine. Most these kids, they're still in denial. They fight the program. End up coming back and back."

"Yes, I think Nicky's ready."

"That's excellent. You're the main parent figure?"

"I guess so," Johnny said, feeling the weight of that.

The man offered two brochures, one locating Al-Anon meetings and the other describing the Monday night family codependent sessions.

"Thanks. Who are you, sir?"

"Sorry. I'm the director here. Avasian's the name."

"I see. I'm Johnny Blood." They shook hands.

"I hope you can come here Monday nights, Mr. Blood."

***

Back in the parking lot, Johnny gripped the steering wheel. His stomach was churning. He flipped the visor down and spoke to the mirror: "Your father just died and now you're a father! Mr. Blood, that's you! And you've got responsibilities! Meetings to attend!"

After a moment staring at himself, he flipped the visor back up and pulled out his cell. He ached to see Michaela, but he worried that she wouldn't take his call, that his moment had passed.

She answered on the first ring. "Johnny! You're back!" There was bounce in her voice. "So glad you called. How's your uncle?"

"Howard died. Turns out Howard was . . . my father."

"He was your father? I'm confused."

"Me too. Can you . . . are you busy right now? Can we maybe have coffee?"

"Right now? Um . . . sure! I'm just home, reading a script."

"And the other thing, Michaela, I'm a parent," Johnny said.

"A parent? How . . ."

"Not biologically. I brought my twenty-year-old nephew, Nicky, back with me from Montana. Where can I pick you up?"

After some hesitation, she gave him directions and instructions. He was to park on the street and call her from the car.

Johnny drove the freeways around Griffith Park and pulled up in front of Michaela's pale-blue house. It was a tidy bookmark between two larger houses, one a dormer-window affair surrounded by rose bushes, the other a two-story Monterey with climbing bougainvillea. Johnny was fascinated by the higgledy-piggledy architecture. He called her number.

"Okay, I'll be right out."

He stepped out of the car and opened the passenger door. He studied the front of her tidy powder-blue cottage. The lines were simple—peaked roof, white door between two white-trim windows. Flower boxes in the windows. The lawn, greener than the neighbors', was edged with pansies.

The day was warm and bright. Michaela emerged, waved, and double-locked her door. She was dressed in black jeans, a white tee, and a patterned vest. Her black hair was pulled back into a bun. Johnny was stunned by her simple beauty. She stood on tiptoe to kiss him on both cheeks, one hand on his shoulder. Johnny flushed, not knowing what to do with his hands. Michaela smiled and slipped into the car.

She directed him to an alfresco restaurant on Hillhurst. They ordered lattes and pastries and sat under an umbrella. The sky was hazy. Michaela asked about his trip. When he mentioned Howard, his voice caught. "Sorry. I haven't had a chance to work it through. I got busy with the burial and getting Nicky out. It's pretty confusing. How many times can a guy lose his father?"

"Wow. You're Nicky's what? Uncle?"

"He's my son now. That hit me today at the rehab."

"Rehab?" she asked.

"Yes. Drugs and alcohol. Mainly marijuana. That's why I had to rescue him."

"I have a son," Michaela said. "In Greece when I was a girl I had him. I've never seen him. They took him away at birth. He's seventeen now." She daubed her eyes. "I talk too much. I should be careful."

"Careful of what?" Johnny asked.

"I know it's not fair, but I have to play this close to the vest. Chest?"

"Both work," Johnny said, smiling. "What's the story?"

"I'll tell you someday, promise." Michaela asked Johnny where he lived. "Beverly Hills? Cool! Now that you've seen my little home, Johnny. I want to see your house."

"It's ridiculously over the top. I got it in the divorce. I use about a fifth of it. There's a day staff."

"Let's go! Do you have time? There are people there so you won't jump on me?"

Johnny laughed. "I won't jump on you. Sure, we can go there. I have a meeting at the hospital in the late afternoon. You want to go for a swim, bring a bathing suit. There's a lap pool and a hot tub."

"No, no, no. I just want to see your house. I love looking at big houses—like I said, I've been like a courtesan? That's a dirty word here. In Europe it means survivor. Don't know why I'm telling you my secrets." She giggled.

CHAPTER EIGHTEEN

"It's a magic castle, Johnny," she said, after Johnny's tour of the mansion. "I sort of like it. There's a lot of personality." She had many questions about the house, most of which Johnny couldn't answer.

They sat with soft drinks by the hot tub at the north end of the lap pool. Michaela pointed up the hill. "Is that a trail you can use?"

"Yes. It's a good running trail, if you like that."

"I do," she said. "I run in Griffith Park."

The afternoon flew by. At 5:00 p.m., they were still talking. Johnny glanced at his watch. He jumped up. "God! I completely forgot my meeting!"

"No problem, Johnny, I'll take a cab home."

"C'mon, I'll drop you at a hotel stand. I'm sorry. I'll pay the cab."

"No, no. I can pay," Michaela said. On the ride down, they made a dinner date for Saturday night.

***

On Wednesday, Michaela called Johnny. "This is so embarrassing. I've been . . . I have to leave my house—like right now. My bitch landlady has a tenant who's moving in tomorrow. A friend offered me her couch, but her boyfriend moved back . . . although next week . . . I have another friend who's . . . I can use her house Monday . . ." She sobbed once and stopped speaking.

Johnny struggled to control his excitement. "Hey! Slow down! Not a problem. You saw my house. There are, what, eight bedrooms not being used? I'll call the housekeeper. Just pick an empty room. I won't be there until quite late, and then I have to drive early tomorrow to San Diego."

"I'm so embarrassed. I'm worried you'll take this the wrong way."

"It's not a problem at all. I'll be back Friday. Stay as long as you want."

"Monday. I'll be out Monday. This is awful. I'm homeless! I have three suitcases and three boxes. Just don't get any ideas."

"I can't promise that, Michaela, but I do promise not to jump on you."

"Johnny!" She giggled.

***

Johnny arrived back home Friday afternoon, eager to see his homeless housemate. The housekeeper reported that Michaela was out grocery shopping. "She's nice, Doctor. She loves the kitchen—I've been showing her how everything works—and she's cooking up a meal for you tonight."

Johnny saw the Prius rolling up a half hour later. He felt his body come alive. He rushed downstairs. Michaela walked in with two full brown bags. "Johnny! Can you peel carrots?"

Johnny took the bags. "I peel a wicked carrot." They stored the groceries, and he dragged a stool up to the chopping block. "Could you tell me what the heck you're doing? We have all this help."

"I'm making a nice simple dinner for us. I like to cook. A teeny tiny thank you for taking me in. You're in the people-rescue business lately."

"You really like to cook? I don't know anyone who likes to cook."

"Love it. Italian tonight. We Greeks like to say the Italians learned how to cook from us like they learned how to do sculpture from us."

"But it would be wrong?"

Michaela laughed her cascading laugh, deftly chopping vegetables. Johnny struggled with the peeler.

"Not wrong about the sculpture. After you're done peeling, cut them into half-inch rounds. How was San Diego?"

***

After dinner, they sat over coffee. "Johnny, you're making me feel too comfortable here. So here's my ground rule, like in baseball, right? I still need us to stay separate, go slowly."

"I heard you at Sofi. I'm good with that."

"I could see at Cabo that you like to initiate. Then at Sofi I saw you struggle, not sure what to do with a woman who likes . . ."

"To be in control? I'm a fast learner. Where are you sleeping?"

"Which bedroom? My secret, Johnny, and please don't try to find out. I don't fully trust you. And I don't fully trust me."

***

They ran together up in the hills Saturday morning and arrived back glistening with sweat and laughter. Michaela was in excellent running shape. By the time Johnny came down to the kitchen, she had prepared breakfast. Afterward, she left for a meeting on her new film script. She told Johnny she didn't like the role, but she might have no choice. "I have no leverage, Johnny. I have to follow my agent."

Johnny had made a reservation at upscale Michael's in Santa Monica for their Saturday night date. When she returned from her Burbank meeting in the late afternoon, she fussed about going to famous Michael's. She claimed she had nothing to wear.

"How about a clean pair of jeans? This is LA."

***

Back in the mansion after Michael's, they lingered over a brandy and politely kissed good night. Michaela went off to her secret bedroom, and Johnny climbed up to his suite, full of feeling. An hour later, Johnny, unable to sleep, saw a shape leaning against the frame of the bedroom door. He sat up. "What?"

"Shh." Michaela walked toward the bed, dropping her robe. "Quiet, Doctor. Move over. I'm suspending the ground rules."

Sunday and Monday passed in a borderless, blissful haze. It wasn't merely the sex, which had been missing for both of them—it was the intimate playfulness, the childish abandon. But Michaela held firm about merely *suspending* the ground rules.

He sighed to himself. At least he had her until Thursday.

CHAPTER NINETEEN

Johnny left Michaela alone in the mansion Monday evening while he attended his first family codependent session at Nicky's rehab. North Hollywood—NoHo—is a drab collection of chain retail stores, used car lots, medical marijuana outlets, and small theaters, like much of the eastern San Fernando Valley. Cri-Help, Nicky's lockdown, occupied a two-story brick building between a Chevron station and an LAPD facility, near the hum of the Hollywood Freeway.

Johnny held Nicky by the shoulders. "You look good, bud. How's it going?"

Nicky nodded once. His eyes were clear and his gaze resolute. "Thanks. I've got this, Johnny. Come, sit." They sat on a white vinyl bench facing a wall-sized fish tank under a cottage cheese ceiling, waiting for the family meeting to start. The linoleum floor was worn but clean.

"I like my counselor, Johnny. He was in the first Gulf War. He was a crack addict. Is. Once an addict always an addict, I'm learning."

"What's he telling you? Can you say?"

"He mostly listens. He went through this, the cold turkey, the stress therapy. He says it never goes away completely." They sat silently for a minute. "But he says if you work it, follow the steps, you can get to where you can control it rather than it control you."

Johnny nodded.

"And, Johnny, I want to go to college. My counselor recommends community college. What I don't want to do is apply for disability. I hear guys who do that give up. I don't want to give up."

Johnny watched Nicky study the fish tank. "How old are you, Nicky?"

"Twenty-one next month."

"Right—1989. And you were a medic. I saw the insignia."

"That's the combat medic badge. I'll tell you my stories someday."

"Great," Johnny said. "So I'm gonna get a smaller place for us. Maybe near the ocean? I'm ready for a move. There's a good community college in Santa Monica."

"Totally, Johnny. I can't live in that big house."

***

After the session, Johnny sat in his car and pulled out his cell. He saw that Bo had called. He touched RETURN CALL.

"Rathgeber. Hi, Johnny."

"Bo. What's up? I'm sitting in a parking lot."

"I'll be quick. Your Michelle Powell?"

"Yeah? Michaela is her real name."

"That's half right. Her full real name is Michaela Zoë Poulos."

"Poulos? Seriously?"

"Isn't Poulos the guy at the hospital who used to drive you nuts?"

"Yes, he retired a year ago. Funny coincidence," Johnny said.

"I don't trust coincidences. Anyway, there's nothing on the web about her parents. She's from Greece, like you said, and she has a green card."

"Did you check Arthur Poulos? For any family?"

"I did. He seems to have no family. No info about his early life."

"So it's gotta be a coincidence, right, the name? Pretty sure she said her parents are both still in Greece. Estranged years ago."

"Poulos is a fairly common name in Greece. Maybe like Powell in the United States. So probably a coincidence."

"I'll ask her when I get home. Thanks for checking."

"You should ask the girl more questions than just about her name, Johnny. Don't be a dope."

"Bo, I think this girl may be the real deal. Gotta go."

***

Johnny rode his Harley south along Coldwater Canyon Drive, one earpiece in place, singing with Carly Simon. Crossing Mulholland at the crest of the hill, he stopped to buy two dozen red roses. He could not remember ever buying flowers for a woman. He was nervous as he entered the mansion's garage.

Michaela's Prius was gone. He saw a note on the chopping block in the kitchen: "Johnny, sorry I had to leave. Something popped up on my immigration status. Please don't try to reach me. I'll let you know what's up in a few days. I'm fine. XXXX, Me."

Johnny reread the note several times then ran around the house, looking for her bedroom. He found it in disarray—lights on, clothes scattered on the floor, the bathroom partially cleaned out. She had left in a hurry. He called her cell. He texted. No avail.

After a sleepless night, Johnny asked Bo to lunch. Bo was free, and he suggested Japanese in the Valley. Johnny insisted on Spago in Beverly Hills. "I know it's a trek, but Gary, the bartender, will arrange a quiet table. I really need to talk."

They arrived at the same time and were seated by the bar. While Bo used the restroom, Johnny ordered drinks. When Bo returned, he saw the red wine at his place. "I'm not drinking now, much less at lunch."

"Have a glass of wine with me. Mazel tov," Johnny said, clinking glasses. He slurped his Grey Goose up.

"What's with the hard liquor?" Bo asked. "I remember you drink like you relate to women—badly, and in bunches."

"I'm giving up drinking after today. For Nicky."

"For Nicky? And who's your designated driver today?" Bo asked.

"*Me*," Johnny said sharply. "Tell me about green cards."

"Green cards? What's going on with you? You look off the rails."

"I am. Let's order lunch," Johnny said, waving at the waiter.

Johnny described his trip to Montana and the shocking Blood Moon family revelations. "How do you kill someone you love, Bo? Or yourself?"

"I don't know. Never faced it. Depends, I guess."

Johnny spoke about Michaela's disappearance. His voice caught just as lunch arrived. Johnny ordered a second Grey Goose. "So what kind of 'immigration problem' would make her just . . . walk out on me?"

"You certain she's even legal?" Bo asked. "Maybe it's not immigration at all. You confuse women, Johnny. You come on like a freight train then you get bored. That may work for coeds on the pill, but . . ."

"That's ancient history," Johnny said. "I wasn't bored by Michaela. We were . . . I know she's not a liar."

"How do you know what she is? She already fudged her name with you. There's always some borrowing from the truth in love and politics. Did you get to ask her about Arthur Poulos?"

"No, she disappeared before I could ask."

"Ah. Okay, so let's talk green card." Bo explained permanent visa status. It was not his expertise, but every general lawyer in Southern California knows immigration law. "So if she has a green card, she was probably sponsored by a relative or an employer. Do you know which?"

"No idea."

"Okay. I can't imagine what immigration problem would make Ms. Poulos run off suddenly. Maybe that was code for some other problem."

"Like she got tired of me?"

Bo shook his head impatiently and looked at his watch. "I have a three thirty in Encino. It's already two ten. Should I cancel?"

"Is it really?" Johnny looked at his Rolex. "I'll talk fast." He waved at the waiter and asked for a third Grey Goose and the lunch check. Bo raised his hand to object to both, and Johnny waved him down. He went on to his other topics, his tongue getting thicker in his mouth.

Johnny asked questions about Nick: insurance, adoption, taxes, driver's license, community college. Johnny did not absorb all of Bo's advice—he lacked patience for details, but Bo knew when Johnny had lost his capacity to absorb. Approaching his saturation point, Johnny fiddled with his Rolex. "It's almost three, you should go."

"Soon. But listen to me for one more minute. You were the top heart surgeon at the top hospital, until, what—a year ago? Then you had that one bad experience?"

"Yes, Gomez. And the divorce. And the bad hand. That's why I'm here with you, still trying to sort it out. On the good side, I've got Nicky now. And I have a lot of freedom. And enough money."

"You'll have less money and less freedom if you marry that Greek girl, which sounds to me like you're in danger of, if she ever comes back." Bo tossed his napkin on the table and pushed back, eyes fixed on Johnny. "My point is you need a job that engages you, Johnny."

"I agree, Bo—but for the first time since . . . maybe ever, I'm at a place where I can make a free choice about what to do with my life. Maybe I'll be a poverty doctor, like I wanted years ago. A doctor without borders."

"You a comedian? Poverty doctor? You mean dump all that bling, not to mention the mansion? Just like that?"

"I'm fine with that, seriously. I've got another chapter left. I want to do one more big thing, Bo." Johnny looked around for the waiter. "Maybe I'll just do a lot of drinking."

"You order another drink, I'll hit you over the head," Bo said fiercely.

"Okay, okay. Bo, you're so damn unromantic."

"What do four martinis have to do with romance?"

"I need comfort and counsel, not a cop," Johnny said.

"You have another drink and you'll be talking to a cop. Johnny, you buy me lunch because you want me to tell you what to do. So I'll tell you what to do. Stop the drinking and slow down. And go back to doing what you do best—heart surgery. That's what I think. Now I really gotta go." Bo gathered his things.

Johnny tried one final angle. "I've had this façade, Bo. My Maserati, vanity plate, house in the hills, three Rolexes. My whole life, I've wanted to dazzle. There goes Mr. Perfect, like Mike used to call me. Then I marry Lisa, probably because I thought she would add to my perfectness."

"She was rich. And big boobs. Winning combination. Really gotta go."

"But I didn't *love* her, Bo. What was I doing? She didn't love me either, except maybe when I was weak. That's what women love. Weakness."

"How about cluelessness? What do they think of cluelessness?"

Johnny looked up. "I have no idea, Bo."

"My point exactly. Drive carefully, Johnny. You hear me?"

CHAPTER TWENTY

Johnny stood at the curb peering through the fog of three double vodkas. His Maserati slid up like a green panther, and a grinning valet stepped out. "Oowee, love this car, Señor!" Johnny felt a flush of pleasure as he exchanged a ten-dollar bill for the keys. He ducked into the low car.

Johnny punched the accelerator and surged into northbound Cañon Drive traffic, causing a car to brake. He grimaced when he saw a police cruiser two cars back. He slowed for the red light at little Santa Monica Boulevard. When the light changed, he sped forward. As he did, a small car shot in from the right and smashed into his front, spinning the Maserati around. The driver hopped out and limped toward the sidewalk. A uniformed officer jumped out of the cruiser behind Johnny and tackled the man. His partner flicked on the light bar, maneuvered up to the steaming collision, and stepped out. He gingerly opened Johnny's door. Johnny was sitting with the limp airbag in his lap.

"You all right here, sir?" The tall cop squatted down.

Johnny rotated his head to test his neck. "What?"

The cop started. "Dr. Blood! Is that you? You hurt at all, sir?"

"What? I think I'm fine. Let me . . ." Johnny's speech was thick, and he could smell his own alcoholic breath. He turned his face away from the officer and released his seat belt, trying to sort out what had happened.

"Slowly, Doc. We got the guy. Illegal looks like. Almost killed the best heart doctor in LA. Don't move. I'll shut down the intersection?"

Johnny nodded. The cop moved away, and Johnny rubbed his arms and legs. All seemed normal. He lowered the visor to look at his pale face. He noticed a small cut on his forehead. He sat still, trying to place the cop. He had operated on so many people.

The officer returned. "City Hall's right there, so emergency should be quick. You may not remember me. I'm Capt. William Mir. You operated on my son, Brent. Saved his life. He's an athlete now, community college." The man looked emotional. "Goddamn illegals. How you feeling?"

"Okay. Not hurt," Johnny enunciated carefully. A siren pierced the air.

"You have a little bump there on your head." Mir patted Johnny's arm and left to help his partner with the suspect. A crowd had gathered.

When Mir returned, an EMT was easing Johnny out of the car. "Any pain? Go slow, sir."

"I'm fine. A little dizzy." He put his hand on the car roof for balance. "I'm fine. I'm a physician." He was sure they knew he was drunk.

"You seem fine, Doc," the captain said, glaring at the EMT. "If the tech's okay with it, I'll drive you home. Your car's totaled."

The tech began to protest, but the officer grunted and waved his hand. The tech examined Johnny's forehead, scowling. He wiped it clean and applied a bandage. "Just a bump. Okay, so sign here and you can go."

"Thanks. I can take a cab, Officer. I feel fine."

"No. You may have shock yet. I'll drive you, once we transfer the scumbag into that cage van." A squad of official vehicles had assembled.

***

On the drive up to the mansion, Captain Mir spoke nonstop about his son. As they entered Johnny's driveway, he abruptly changed gears. "Doc, we have a strict DUI law in Beverly Hills. You're drunk. When I opened your car door, the smell about knocked me over. The tech saw it too, which is why he was grumpy. I saw you pull out from Spago, almost bang into that Mercedes. Maybe I'm being a father rather than a cop, but I'm thinking about not writing you up as my thanks for saving my son's life."

The cruiser stopped at Johnny's front steps. The policeman got out and walked around to the passenger door. Johnny stepped out unsteadily.

"I really hate drunk drivers," Mir said. "It's no different than firing a gun into a crowd far as I'm concerned. I need you to convince me you won't drink and drive again, sir."

Johnny nodded. "Made a terrible mistake. I've never done this before. I'm sorry. Is the other guy hurt?"

"A few bruises to go with his tattoos. Probably be in jail for a while. You have a card, Doctor?" The policeman gave him his card: Captain William Mir, Director Community Relations, Beverly Hills Police Department. Mir locked his eyes on Johnny. "You're a pretty famous guy. What on earth would make you get drunk at lunch and drive? Talk to me."

Johnny put his hands on his cheeks. "I feel dizzy. I need to sit." He moved to the steps and sat. Then he spoke slowly. "I have no excuse. Just personal things. My father just died, and I had to put my nephew into rehab, he's a vet and——"

Mir interrupted him. "Bullshit, sir! With all respect, we all have personal things, but that's not a license to kill!" His face was tense. "I'm taking a big chance here, not booking you. That EMT could report me. But I do have one question, Doc. I heard you quit operating. What's that about?"

"Well, I lost a patient I cared about. Still not over it, a year later."

"You talking about the Nobel guy Gomez? You were on that, right?"

"Yes, Manuel Maria Gomez."

"What's the problem? Did you know him personally?" Mir asked.

"Met him once, right before the operation. But I read all his books."

"I read the *Times* article about it. It smelled a little fishy. I made some calls. There was a pending lawsuit, and the hospital basically stiffed me. It was a long shot and I was busy, so I didn't pursue it."

"What was fishy?" Johnny asked.

"Lemme ask you something. Was Gomez political?"

"No. Although . . . his last book was about Mexican drug gangs."

Captain Mir tilted his head. "Seriously? You mind if I take notes?" He took a pad from his back pocket. "Tell me about the surgery, Doc. What went wrong?"

"It was a heart transplant procedure. His body gave out, which . . . I don't know why. Never happened to me before. The whole thing made me . . ." He stopped speaking.

"So it really got to you?"

"I'm not feeling very well. It's why I stopped operating."

Mir looked hard at Johnny. "Probably why you got drunk today too. Listen, Doc, you go take care of yourself. I'll forget the DUI. But I need to ask more questions about this Gomez case when you sober up."

Johnny began to stand. "Why would you care?"

"Maybe I'll tell you when we meet. Can I come by here tomorrow?"

"Sure. After three? I'm sorry again for making trouble."

"I'll be here at three-thirty. And, Doctor, thank you for my son."

                              ***

Captain Mir appeared promptly the next day. Johnny led him to the den off the living room. "This is quite a house, Doctor. The old Bell house, no?"

"Yes."

"I know your ex, Mrs. Bell. Nice lady. She was married to William Bell Senior. I knew him too. Sketchy operator. But I should get to the point," Mir sat and pulled out his notebook. "But before that, you mentioned you had a vet nephew in rehab?"

"Nicky, yes. Nicky Bloodman. Afghanistan."

"I have a suggestion, if I may. My brother Navid's a psychiatrist at the VA in Westwood, specializes in PTSD with these young vets, what your Nicky probably has some of. Right?"

"I think so, yes."

"Navid Mir is the best PTSD therapist in LA, like you're the best heart doctor, which is why you shouldn't get drunk and drive."

Johnny sat quietly, his eyes down.

"Call him. Here's the number. Tell him Captain Bill referred you. There's a big waiting list but he'll take you."

"Thank you. That's very kind. I will do that."

"Now to the point of my visit, Doctor. First, I need you to agree this is absolutely confidential."

"Okay," Johnny said.

"I talked to four people at UC Cedars about this subject matter last year— the CEO, an inside lawyer, a senior physician named McRae, and an Asian woman physician named Irene Chang."

"Stan McRae was my mentor. He retired about a year ago."

"Right after Gomez. I know, he was a good one. He knew everybody and everything, very helpful. Ms. Chang is his successor as chief of staff. A pain in the ass. Anyway . . ."

"So what's the issue, Captain? You've got my attention."

Mir paused, eyeing Johnny. "Issue is possible conspiracy to commit murder."

Captain Mir told a chilling story. Members of the jail-based Mexican Mafia gangs, collectively known as *La eMe*, and the LA street gang called Eighteenth Street, pay hospital professionals to carry out "hits"—assassinations of enemies—through untraceable medical means. The money comes from Mexico. The blame falls on the hospitals, not on the gangs. The hit men are individuals over whom the gangs have leverage—because of dark pasts, vulnerable relatives, drug habits, debts.

"Captain, hang on. You're saying physicians and nurses are killing patients for pay? I don't believe this."

Mir nodded. "That's what I'm saying.'"

Johnny was staggered. "How do you know? How can you tell a 'hit' from medical error?"

"That's what they count on. You usually can't know a crime has been committed until someone comes forward. But you can spot a situation, which is why I was interested in your Gomez case."

After a pause, Mir continued. "Doctor, I think what you're asking, and it's perfectly reasonable, is why this is not a figment of our paranoid police imagination. The answer is we turned a couple of people at County Hospital. First guy came forward voluntarily. A guilty RN who had been down on his luck.

He's in witness protection. The other guy, a physician, is dead. We found out about number two from number one. We looked at number two's bank accounts and saw a big deposit right after an OG mysteriously died in a public hospital."

"What's an OG?"

"Original gangster. Gangbangers rarely live past thirty. An OG is a survivor, a shot caller. Y'know, a gang leader. So this vic was a rival gang leader. And this doc killed him for money. Lately they've targeted higher-value people."

"What do you mean 'higher value'?"

"So some background. It started years ago in inner-city ERs by bribing EMTs. At first it was small potatoes—pulling plugs, pinching IVs. Back then the vics were like snitches, gang rivals, whose murder on the street could have led to retaliation or gang wars. Recently, the vics are, like I say, higher value. Example, several years ago, two gang squad officers died unexpectedly at Good Sam. At Huntington, an FBI agent covering the Mexican drug trade died having his prostate removed. We have reasons to think that was a hit."

"Died during a prostatectomy?" Johnny asked.

"That's the fancy word. And that federal judge we think, at UC Cedars a year plus ago, which is when I visited your four colleagues."

"Was that Judge Freiberg? I remember. Routine hip replacement. He died on the operating table. It was weird."

"Yes. Weird like Gomez, right? So there was a headline, a big funeral, the hospital made a settlement payment to the family, that was it. One of the problems here, the hospital always wants to cover up."

"Surprise deaths hammer hospitals. The lawyers, the press."

"If the homies shoot one of these fancy guys on the street, boom, there's a police crackdown, sweeps, gang injunctions get enforced, everything hits the fan. In hospital deaths, just the hospital gets blamed."

"Smart guys, I guess," Johnny said.

"These guys are plenty smart. In the case of the federal judge, he had just put twenty scumbags in Pelican Hill solitary. So it had all the earmarks, and that's why I spoke to your Cedars colleagues. The big worry is the public finds out and loses confidence in our hospitals."

"Yes, and also the trust among the staff professionals would evaporate if this got out. I could see it literally destroying a hospital. I mean, my trust in *myself* evaporated when Gomez died."

Johnny joined his hands behind his head and leaned back. "Wow! So I'm thinking now maybe Gomez's death wasn't my fault after all."

"Maybe not. When I read that *Times* article about Gomez, I made a note to call McRae. He was gone by then, so I had to deal with Dr. Chang, who stiffed me."

"It was complicated, Captain. There were hospital politics. There was a lawsuit and a big insurance payment. Also, it's quite possible Gomez died naturally, even though I still don't know exactly what happened."

"Let me ask you, Doctor. Did that ever happen to you before? That you didn't know exactly why a patient died on the operating table?"

"I don't think so. He was very sick, like I said, and not a young man. But I always understand why people die. I didn't with Gomez."

"I did a little googling about his Mexican drug cartel book last night. It looks pretty aggressive. So there's a motive. I have to get into this."

"Why you, Captain? What's your role?"

"There's an FBI-DEA task force on drug cartel assassinations in the US. They liaise with local police, and I'm the BHPD liaison. You think I could get you and Dr. McRae to meet with me and my FBI colleague?"

"Sure. Together? Haven't seen Stan in a while."

Mir stood and pocketed his notebook. "Thanks, I'll set it up."

CHAPTER TWENTY-ONE

The interview was set for McRae's condo, a mile north of UC Cedars in West Hollywood. The second-floor flat had been McRae's home for thirty years. The space was full of houseplants, books, pictures of McRae with celebrities and colleagues, and well-worn furniture. A large window faced south along busy San Vicente Boulevard.

Johnny arrived early. The former mentor and mentee greeted each other warmly. A small elderly dog sniffed Johnny's ankle before settling into a wicker basket next to McRae's chair. Johnny tried not to betray his shock over how much Stan had aged. "I like your place, Stan."

"What is this about, Johnny? Can't they leave me in peace?"

"It's about the Gomez situation. I'll leave the details to Captain Mir. His son was my patient, and I had an . . . interaction with him recently."

"Gomez? Oh god." McRae gazed out the big window toward UC Cedars.

"You okay, Stan?"

"I've been better."

Captain Mir and Agent Brill arrived a few minutes late. As they came in, the old dog raised his ears, emitted a low growl, but stayed put. McRae served tea with Johnny's help. The four men sat.

"Sorry, gents, got a little lost." Mir chuckled as he pulled out a notebook. "I thought I knew this area. So to repeat, this matter is highly confidential. We have questions about the death of Mr. Manuel Maria Gomez in 2009."

FBI Agent Brill was a small earnest man in a gray suit and dark tie. He opened a small notebook and spoke without making steady eye contact. "I scanned Gomez's novel about the cartels. I'm sure the goons were not pleased. This could be one of those cases Captain Mir warned you about, Dr. McRae."

McRae shrugged.

"There was a second novel in the works when he died," Johnny said. "Same subject."

"How do you know that?" Brill asked.

"I learned about it when I met Gomez that one time. His last words to me were something like 'I must finish my work about these evil men!'"

Mir and Brill scribbled furiously.

Captain Mir asked Johnny to reprise the Gomez operation. Johnny began with the anonymous call and ended with his meeting with the *amigos* in the family waiting room. Then Mir asked McRae to explain why he chose not to call him about the episode.

"Gomez was a novelist," McRae said, "not a public official. He was moribund when he was admitted. It didn't strike me as a problem."

"I did tell Stan that Gomez was near death," Johnny added. "He had many issues. Although I'd pulled off a miracle or two before."

"Had you read his book about the cartels, Dr. McRae?" Brill asked.

"I wasn't aware of that angle until much later," McRae responded.

Johnny turned to look at McRae, whose eyes stayed fixed on Brill.

Brill squinted at McRae. "Lemme ask you. Were you at all trying to protect the hospital?"

McRae dropped his eyes. "Unconsciously? Anything's possible. But I don't think so. Perhaps I wanted not to retire on a low note."

"I read the old *Times* articles and the complaint," Agent Brill said.

"Yes. Turned out to be a low note after all. But . . . I had a fine career."

Brill turned to Johnny, who was nodding. "Two interesting things you said, Dr. Blood. One was that anonymous call telling you that Gomez was sick, which you then contacted him through his Hollywood agent. Isn't that a little unusual? To reach out after an anonymous call?"

"Yes, but I'd been following his case. He was a personal hero of mine."

"I see. And the other thing you said, that there were unfamiliar guys in the next-of-kin group. Were they the same people at the Gomez condo when you visited him there before the operation?"

"The main guy, with the tattoos, and the older gentleman, I didn't recognize them from the condo. Others I did recognize. The little son I did."

"May we review your phone records from back then to trace the anonymous call?" Brill asked. "Were there any other communications?"

"No, just the one phone call. You can look at anything you want, including my financial records. Remember, I was going through a divorce back then and money was moving around."

"Thank you. That'd be helpful. And Dr. McRae?" Brill said.

"Of course, you may examine my records. You won't find anything."

"Dr. McRae," Brill continued, "was there a video surveillance set up in the OR so we might visually ID the Gomez team?"

"Yes, we installed surveillance cameras after Captain Mir spoke to us about Judge Freiberg. This is all so appalling."

"Dr. McRae, a favor," Mir said, "could you call your successor, Dr. Chang, for us? Pave the way? I remember she's not very . . . cooperative. We'll need those surveillance videos and a list of personnel who may have had access to Gomez.

You gave me those lists from Judge Freiberg's death. I'd like not to have to get a subpoena."

"It would be my preference if you'd call her yourself, Captain," McRae said. "I . . . I can't be dragged into this. I have a lot of anxiety lately."

"Sorry. All right. I bet she makes us get a warrant."

"She may. It's her responsibility to protect the hospital. But I can't be involved. She wouldn't do what I asked anyway."

Brill pocketed his notebook. "I hear you, sir, but my guess is this is not the end of it for you. Thanks for the tea." Everyone stood except Stan McRae, who appeared drained.

"I gotta run too." Johnny stood and shook hands with Mir and Brill. "Call me if I can help, Officers. I still have a few friends at the hospital, but unfortunately, Irene Chang is not one."

CHAPTER TWENTY-TWO

Soaking in the roiling hot tub after racquetball Monday, Johnny shouted above the noise, "Gus, you know anyone at the Westwood VA? I want to check out a psychiatrist there, a PTSD specialist, for Nicky."

"Actually . . . I do, which reminds me, you remember Toby Roberts? Left UC Cedars in 1994?"

"Roberts? Roberts. The oddball with the bushy black beard?"

"Gray now. And much trimmer. He's chief of surgery at the VA."

"Really? So?"

Gus's face hardened. "God*damn* it, Johnny! You're the best heart surgeon in the country! It drives me fucking nuts to see you sitting on your ass month after month!"

Johnny silently studied the bubbling water.

"It's not about the money, it's about *you*! Just do me a favor, dude, call Toby Roberts. Call somebody! Get back to work please! The VA's no UC Cedars, but it's got things going for it. No more ungrateful celebrities, no insurance to fuck with. Toby wants to start a transplant team. You can have joint privileges with Cedars."

"You serious?" Johnny asked.

"I'm damn serious. Call Toby. I told him I'd talk to you."

After a long minute, Johnny nodded. "Thanks, Gus. You're a good pal. I mean it. I'll make the call."

***

Johnny visited Toby Roberts later that week. After a conversation in Roberts's small office, they walked to the cafeteria through drab halls. Toby spoke. "You can see this is not Beverly Hills."

"Toby, I've had my fill of Beverly Hills."

"Grab a tray. They call me Commander here."

Johnny absorbed the mild rebuke and ordered the meatloaf.

Toby Roberts was a large, shambling man with an awkward personality and a dry, intelligent wit. He projected a fussy competence. They sat at an empty common table. Johnny mentioned his vet nephew, Nicky, and asked about Navid Mir.

"Navid? He's good with the kids. Busy man, what with all the stupid wars going on. Might be hard to get on his dance card."

"I know his brother."

"I see. Navid's at the end of this wing. Knock on his office door when we're done. We don't have secretaries."

"I will, thanks," Johnny said. "So, Commander, Gus told you I may be interested in working here? I'm not a veteran, but I can help your minority count. And maybe help with your transplant project."

"Lord be praised! So the leading heart surgeon in California drops in my lap? Wherefore your interest in the Veterans Administration?"

"First, you tell me why *you* came here, and what it's like."

After two hours of conversation—which included a fair amount of Roberts's griping about government overseers—Johnny agreed to apply for a position. Roberts cautioned, "Won't be a problem, but again it's the government, so approvals grind slowly. We can borrow you from UC Cedars while we wait." Johnny began work at the VA the following Friday.

***

The next Monday at Cri-Help, Johnny told Nicky about his plan to work at the VA. "Also, bud, I found a place in Venice Beach for us. It's a stucco box, but it's roomy, has two parts with separate entrances. It sits on a little hill, surrounded by trees. You can actually see the ocean if you know where to look."

"Sounds fine, Johnny. I feel bad making you move."

"Not at all—I actually like it. Say, Nicky, I understand you'll want therapy when you get out. There's a psychiatrist, a PTSD specialist, at the VA in Westwood. I keep forgetting, you don't know where anything is."

"Not a clue."

"I'll bring you a map next time. The guy's name is Navid Mir, Iranian. I made an appointment for the day you leave here. He specializes in guys who fought in Iraq and Afghanistan."

"Sure. Hey, Johnny?"

"Yes?"

"I'm really glad you're going back to work. I've been meaning to say something. And I think your helping vets is awesome."

***

Johnny moved into the Venice house and bought a used Honda Civic for Nicky as a "graduation" gift. On impulse, he also bought tools and spent a weekend taking the engine apart—trying to recall Howard's training from Gerald Red Bird's auto shop. Johnny remembered that his facility with his hands, whether taking apart bicycles or car engines or guns, made Howard's face glow. Now, finally, he understood why—he was his son! When the Civic engine was reassembled, it started without a hiccup. Johnny's eyes filled with tears.

On Nicky's last day at the rehab, Johnny picked him up in the surprise Civic. Nicky was touched. "Gosh . . ."

"You do have a driver's license, right?" Johnny asked.

"Yes. But I've never driven on a freeway. This is crazy traffic, right?"

"It's not that bad."

With Nicky death-gripping the wheel in the slow lane, they headed to the VA. Johnny did office work while Nicky visited with Dr. Mir. When Nicky returned, Johnny looked up. "How'd it go?"

"Fine. Can we go to a McDonald's now? I've been craving a Big Mac for weeks. I'll tell you when we get there. I want to think a little."

Johnny directed Nicky to the large McDonald's on Venice Boulevard near their new home. After ordering, Nicky finally spoke. "So, yes, Dr. Mir's awesome! I think he can help me figure out this new life I have. Did you know he fought in some gnarly war in Iran and had PTSD himself? I have a regular appointment time, and he's got me in a group."

"So glad you liked him. I'm getting to know him a little."

Nicky devoured the rest of his meal and went back for seconds. Johnny sat nibbling french fries. After wiping his mouth, Nicky looked up. "This is an amazing city, Johnny. I want to get to know it."

***

Johnny found a job for Nicky as a tech in a poor clinic in Venice Beach. Then Johnny became immersed at the VA, reverting to his 24/7 mode of working. A couple of weeks in, Toby asked Johnny to join him on a trip to Washington DC to attend a conference and to lobby for funding for the heart transplant unit. They were in DC for a week.

After flying home from DC on the red-eye, Johnny stopped at the Venice Boulevard McDonalds for breakfast. Nicky was at the register. "Nicky! What's this? Where's the clinic?" Cook staff heads turned.

"Sshh. Hang on. I'll take my break and sit with you."

Johnny slid into the booth across from Nicky. "I'm so sorry, kid. This is all my fault. I'm back to my bad old ways."

"Not your fault, man. I'm in charge of my own life. Free, brown, and twenty-one. Ticket to ride in LA town." Nicky smiled his crooked smile. He told Johnny about his relapse. "I biffed. I'm an idiot. I ran to see Dr. Mir and he straightened me out. He said it was the trauma cases at the clinic that threw me off. I thought about you, like what you'd done for me, what a self-indulgent shit I was. But the clinic didn't work for me." He then changed the subject. "So has what's-her-name girlfriend called yet?" He was referring to Michaela.

Suddenly, the building began to shake. The temblor was sharp and short. Nicky turned white and slid under the table. "What the fuck!"

Johnny glanced up to make sure they weren't under something that could fall on their heads. He held his coffee steady. After several seconds, the motion ceased. Johnny spoke, more calmly than he felt.

"Come on up, Nemo."

Nicky peeked up. "Holy shit! Was that an earthquake?"

"That's what they call it."

Nicky resumed his seat, eyes darting around. "Man, I never felt *anything* like that. What is this place? It feels like everything is . . . like the world isn't solid!"

Johnny picked up his burger. "Now what was your question? Michaela? Oh, yes, I told you about her. No, sadly, she . . . no idea where she is . . . but, hold on! You relapsed and I didn't even notice? I feel awful!"

"Wow. Hey, it's all good, man. I know you got my back." Nicky leaned forward and whispered, "I can't believe everyone's so cool about that fucking earthquake."

"You get used to it." Johnny stared at his hands. "So when did that happen? When I was in DC?"

"Yes. Just a couple of nights. Dr. Mir helped me. I'm fine."

"I stayed a few extra days on our heart transplant project . . . I didn't even call you."

"I can't imagine giving someone a new heart." Nicky said.

"But . . . tell me how *you* are, Nicky. I don't even know what to ask."

"I'm fine—clean and sober again. I work here. I play soccer. A guy at the clinic before I quit, he got me on a club soccer team down by the airport. Hispanic guys mostly. They call me *el amigo reservado*—the quiet friend. Because my Spanish is lame. It's now a moniker—'2 Quiet.' Some of the guys may be gangbangers. The team's winning, so it's cool."

"What else are you doing?"

"Small-bore stuff. I read books, go to meetings. Also I signed up for Santa Monica College in January. I'm excited about that."

Johnny looked at Nicky and slowly shook his head. "*None* of that is small-bore. *None* of it. Maybe *I* should go see Dr. Mir."

CHAPTER TWENTY-THREE

Captain Mir called Johnny Saturday, asking to visit him at his new home in Venice. He arrived quickly and came right to the point. "On this Gomez case? I need a nongovernment physician to consult with. My brother says I can trust you, that you're incapable of deception." Mir arched an eyebrow.

"That's a nice compliment, although I don't think it's true."

"Well, it better be true. Navid reads people good. Anyway, I need to ask you some questions. As usual, between us."

Johnny nodded.

"So we got the surveillance videos and saw that Dr. Emilio Hand, the anesthesiologist, was present both at Gomez's and Judge Freiburg's operations. We had to get a warrant—your Dr. Chang is a major pain. So I tried to interview Dr. Hand."

"You tried?"

"I called to set up an appointment, and that's when he bailed for Mexico. Gave no notice."

"Emilio? You're kidding."

"I'm not kidding. I don't kid. His parents were born down there. They changed the family name from Hernandez to Hand after they came north. He's legal, a citizen. Parents are deceased. He apparently took his black nurse with him and abandoned his wife and child."

Johnny was stunned. "Emilio . . . ?"

"Yes. We have his financial and phone records."

"And?" Johnny said.

"Nothing hugely fishy in his US accounts, just some small peaks and valleys, but he probably has Mexico accounts. He made a number of calls to Mexico around the critical time. He was having major financial problems here. He lost money in the market, and he bought a big house in Calabasas just before the crash."

"So you're thinking . . ."

"Pretty obvious. Hand is our lead suspect. We're working with the Mexican authorities, but . . ."

"What's the nurse's name?" Johnny asked.

"Latira Brown is the one who's gone. Worked with Hand, we're told."

"Yes. I know Latira. Quite professional. I can't believe . . . Emilio disappeared. I know his wife."

"He left her holding the bag. And his little kid. Nice guy."

"My lord, why didn't he talk to me?" Johnny asked. "I could have helped him out. I can't believe this."

"The other thing, we ID'd most of that Gomez *amigos* group you talked to, with that son, Juan? Your speech is on tape by the way. Turns out that alpha guy with the tattoos? He's a serious OG from the Eighteenth Street Gang. Here's a still picture."

Johnny took the picture and studied it. "Yes, that's him. OG—that's 'original gangster'?"

"Yes," Captain Mir said. "Good memory."

"Tell me more about the Eighteenth Street Gang," Johnny said.

"It's one of the largest, nastiest gangs in the world. Maybe twenty-five thousand members worldwide, mostly Hispanic. Territory in LA straddles the 10 Freeway between La Cienega on the west to roughly Vermont. Major connections into Mexico and Central America. Dangerous."

"Really? There was that older man . . ."

"We don't know who that older man was. We ID'd the other adults as Gomez's entourage plus the two young boys. That OG with the tatts is in prison now for another crime. Francisco Serrano, his name is. Moniker is Big Talk. We haven't talked to him yet. He's a difficult man. Full of bullshit. Active in Mexican Mafia, the jail gang. We can talk to him whenever we want, he'll be cooking in there for a while."

"I'm blown away by Emilio Hand, Captain. I considered him a friend."

"Call me Bill. Nothing surprises about people under financial pressure."

"Why are you telling me all this?"

"Well, like I said, I need a doctor on my team, and Navid says to trust you. Let me ask you. Am I missing anything?"

"Don't think so. I'm not at Cedars anymore."

"I know, you're at the VA. But you know the players, and you did the surgery. What about Stanley McRae? Anything fishy with him? I saw your look when he said he wasn't familiar with Gomez's novel about the cartels."

"Ah! You're good, Captain. I distinctly remember we talked about Gomez's novel right after Gomez died. Stan told me he'd skimmed it. So I was surprised what he said to you. I dismissed it as a memory lapse. He's getting older. I don't believe Stanley would do anything bad—the only . . . he was close to his deputy Arthur Poulos, who's a different kettle of fish."

"I see. Say more about Arthur Poulos."

"Retired, has a bad heart. In all ways. What do you want to know?"

"I understand he used to have a hard-on for you. Is there anything about Arthur Poulos that should make him a person of interest here?"

Johnny paused. "I don't know. You're right that he hated me. He's always been a dark mystery. You know . . ." Johnny looked out the window.

"What do I know, Doctor?"

"Poulos mentored Emilio Hand when he was starting out. Referred him into cases, including mine. I never understood that relationship. Emilio was so sweet, and Arthur was such a dark guy."

"His background before Cedars is murky, Poulos's is," Mir said. "Not clear how he was even hired, coming out of a black hole in Greece."

"Stan McRae was always his promoter. Arthur was a very effective cardiologist and administrator. If you like hard-ass."

"Anything else, Doctor? Anything else about McRae or Poulos?"

"That's all I can think of."

Mir closed his notebook and stood up. "I may call on you once in a while. Thank you for your help."

"Captain, I'm curious," Johnny said, "is it normal for a local policeman to be working with an FBI task force?"

"Since 9/11, it's not that unusual. I was trained at the FBI Academy at Quantico, but I joined BHPD for personal reasons. My wife wanted to be in Beverly Hills. Family thing."

"I see."

"One last thing, Doctor, before I forget, a word about your Nicky?"

"Yes?"

"Venice Beach is rough, may not be the best for him given his issues. There are a lot of knuckleheads here. There's a Persian cop on the Venice police force, a friend, and . . . well, we talk. Just a word to the wise."

"Oh, gosh. Nicky relapsed once—your brother straightened him out."

"I know from my friend that Nicky was briefly back on the street. Using, maybe dealing. Came close to going to jail. Just keep an eye out. Thank you for your time. Have a nice rest of the summer."

CHAPTER TWENTY-FOUR

On Sunday afternoon of Labor Day weekend, Nicky and Johnny drove the short distance from Venice to Santa Monica to walk on the beach and eat at King's Head Restaurant. The sky was full of wind and puffy clouds. "What an awesome scene!" Nicky exulted as they arrived at the beach, his arms spread wide. "This always reminds me what you said about my grandfather Ben, how he wanted to see the Pacific Ocean."

"Yeah, poor old Benny was a dreamer. He taught me how to dream."

They trudged through the sand toward the waves, shoes in hand. "So you had like a father committee?" Nicky asked.

"George and Howard didn't do much more than warehouse me."

"But Ben taught you how to dream? That's being a father, right?"

"True," Johnny said. "Dreaming's the most important thing a father can teach. Benny qualifies. There were others, Coach Long, Coach Wooden, even Manuel Gomez—which is one reason his death hit me so hard. A doctor named Stanley McRae was a father figure for me professionally."

"So, Johnny, you're on my father committee for sure. Is that cool?

"Absolutely cool," Johnny said.

They reached the hard sand and stood together looking at the vast arc of sky and sea. The beach was full of kids and dogs. Two gulls squabbled over a bit of seaweed. The ocean glittered with sunlight.

"There's nothing like this scene, Nicky. Your grandfather was right. This is the only place where I can forget all the nonsense, even just for a minute. It makes everything else small."

Nicky squinted at the horizon. "I love the blues. The different blues."

"Fabulous," Johnny said, nodding slowly, as if seeing a truth that had been elusive. "So let's keep walking." They turned right toward Malibu.

After a few minutes, Nicky spoke, "You know, when I graduated from high school, Howard told me the army would put hair on my chest. But Mr. Long was opposed. He said he was worried about the drugs. He said I should go to college. Anyway, I enlisted and took off for basic training. Then I got orders to Fort Sam Houston in Texas for medic training. I was good there, actually kicked ass. That's why I know what you do is so awesome. Giving new hearts."

Chatting away, they crossed the beach toward the restaurant and went inside. The pub crowd was young and noisy. Nicky nodded toward the pool players, who turned away. "Those are the dudes I got tangled up with when I relapsed," Nicky whispered.

They sat away from the loud music and made a dinner of bar food and soft drinks. Over coffee, Johnny's cell buzzed. He nearly missed it because of the din. Caller ID read S. MCRAE. "Excuse me, Nicky." Johnny spoke into the phone, plugging his other ear, "Blood. Hello?" The voice was faint. "Hold on please."

He stood and shouted, "Be right back, bud." Nicky gave a thumbs-up. Johnny walked out and turned left toward the beach.

"Stan?"

"Yes, Johnny. I have an enormous favor to ask of you. I'm here at UC Cedars with Arthur Poulos, who's gravely ill. I just saw Gus, who, I understand, became director of the Heart Institute when you moved over to the VA."

"Yes, but I still have privileges at UC Cedars."

"So I understand. You know Arthur suffers from irreversible cardiomyopathy. He's been on a transplant list for months. He had a bad episode last night—I was with him. But we were lucky—a donor heart turned up with his unusual blood type. Gus says this is Arthur's shot. I'd appreciate it if you would do this, Johnny." McRae emitted a nervous chuckle.

Johnny swallowed hard. "I'm maybe thirty-five minutes away."

"Gus *said* you would. I'm so grateful. Call him on his cell."

"I'm on my way. Tell Gus I'll call him in two minutes."

Johnny closed his phone and raced back to the pub. Passing in, he saw Nicky at the center of a tense group of young men. He pushed his way through and used his most authoritative voice. "Excuse me, I'm a doctor and I've got a medical emergency. Bloodman, I need you to come with me."

The startled group backed off. Johnny grabbed Nicky's arm and steered him toward the front door. Johnny handed the greeter a fifty-dollar bill. "This is for our bill and the rest for the waitress."

Nicky spoke so the greeter could hear. "She'll never see a cent."

On the sidewalk, Johnny broke into a trot. "Let's jog to the car. What the hell was that about?"

Nicky, jogging alongside, ignored the question. "Where're we going?"

"To the hospital. I actually do have an emergency. In the car, you can tell me about that scene in there. Have to make a quick call now."

Slowing to a brisk walk, Johnny pulled out his cell. "Hey, Gus, I'll be there in a half hour. What's up?"

"Sure, Johnny. Poulos is in bad shape. They're prepping the new heart. Glad you're coming, Johnny. That takes big balls."

***

In the car, Johnny swung east onto Santa Monica Boulevard. "I'll get out at the hospital, Nicky. You drive back. I'll get a cab home. Now tell me what was going on in the bar."

"I'm trying to understand this place, LA, where I fit in. It's like a different planet from what I'm used to."

Johnny looked over at Nicky and saw tears streaming down his face.

"Nicky, what's up?"

"It was dumb to go in there again. The owner thinks I'm a snitch. He's a big dealer, and he thinks I ratted on him when I went clean."

"Did you?"

Nicky raised his voice. "Of course not! Pisses me off. I just wanted to get sober. So I disappeared on those guys after I saw Dr. Mir when you were in Washington. Then I show up with you tonight. They probably think you're a fucking narc or something. Venice is gnarly for me, I don't fit in. It was way easier in Crow. I knew everyone, knew the rules."

"I had a big fitting-in problem here when I was your age," Johnny said. "For three years in college, I felt lost. I envied the black students—at least they had each other. I had no one."

"So maybe it isn't just me?"

"It's not just you. It takes time. Being an Indian boy in a white man's world is very hard. I *still* feel isolated, truth be told."

"Johnny, has anyone you know ever hated you? I mean, personally?"

"Yes."

"Really? That's hard for me to . . . Who? Can you say?"

Johnny hesitated. "The guy I'm about to operate on."

"Really? And you're gonna help him?"

"Yes, really. I'm gonna help him. I'm a physician."

Nicky paused for a minute, thinking. "That's fucking awesome!"

"What about your soccer buddies, Nicky? You get along?"

"I'm not in their tribe. I have one good friend there, guy named Paco. He's been trying to live normal. He says they're leaning on him to get jumped in."

"Jumped in?"

"Yeah, that means join the gang. Paco tells me some of the players are Eighteenth Street but from rival subgroups. I should understand tribal. But, man, it is confusing."

"Eighteenth Street? That's a nasty bunch, right? Shouldn't you quit?"

"No, not yet. It's cool. I'm good. I need to handle it by myself. And thank you for helping me in the restaurant, Johnny. That move was rad."

***

The transplant operation took over six hours. Poulos was wheeled away at 3:30 a.m. Johnny, Gus, and Stanley McRae sat together in the OR nurses' station looking down at the floor.

"I'm beat. If I had a cigarette I'd smoke it," Gus said.

Johnny rubbed his face. "Stan, tell me what happened."

McRae's face started quivering. He had been famous for controlling his emotions. "Turning into a weepy old man." He rubbed his eyes.

"No problem. Been a long day."

McRae took a deep breath. "We were having dinner at his place in Century City. I've been trying to help Arthur find a consulting position. He was acting stubborn, like he does. He slumped over. I did CPR, and his cook called 911. Johnny, you handled his first bypass, didn't you?"

"Yes. 1995? I heard he's had episodes since then."

"Many episodes, yes."

"We were friendly until I operated on him," Johnny said. "Then he dropped me like a hot rock. That was long before the director thing. He's always been a mystery to me."

McRae shook his head. "I was sure we'd lost him. They put him on the heart-lung machine then Gus found this miracle blood match."

Gus yawned. "Absolutely a miracle. Motorcycle accident. Arthur was a dead duck. I'm tapped out. Good night." He stood up.

"Let me say something first, gentlemen," McRae's voice was tight, "Arthur was the engine of our medical staff operation. Sure, he has peculiarities. Johnny, he still sees you as the source of his . . . frustrations. I've broken my pick on that."

"Old news," Johnny said.

"Yes, of course. But we'll have that issue when he sees you."

"Not before late Tuesday afternoon. Sorry, I have surgeries lined up."

"Can you and I meet here, say at ten to five Tuesday?" McRae asked.

"Sure. I never did anything to hurt Arthur, Stan. You know that. I never gave a shit about him personally."

"I know you didn't intend to hurt him," McRae said. "That's not your nature. Let's get to bed, boys. Johnny, I'll see you Tuesday ten to five."

***

McRae seemed nearly his old self when Johnny met him Tuesday outside the transplant step-down unit. "The intensivist reports Arthur's stable, Johnny. I'll go in ahead of you. A minute ago he was asleep."

"Stan, a question," Johnny said, "Poulos has no family, right? You have his power of attorney?"

"Yes, I have his power." McRae looked nervous.

The examination went forward without incident. Poulos was on the ventilator, eyes closed. McRae hovered while Johnny listened to Poulos's chest. The new heart sounded strong. As Johnny stepped back, Poulos's watery eyes blinked open. McRae moved into Poulos's field of vision. "Can you hear me, Arthur? You're doing fine." Poulos's eyes closed, and he sunk back into sleep.

***

Johnny arrived at the recovery unit at noon Thursday. McRae was waiting outside. "Hi, Johnny. We had a talk, Arthur and I did. He knows you're involved. Just go in there and be your normal self. He should be fine."

McRae shuffled off, and Johnny entered the unit. Poulos, off the ventilator now, lay sleeping in a nest of wires and tubes. Johnny asked the nurse about meds. While they were talking, Poulos opened his eyes. Johnny stepped forward. "Arthur? It's Johnny Blood. How you feeling?"

Poulos looked away.

"Stanley just left. You must be good friends."

Poulos flicked a look at Johnny.

"You know you had a transplant?"

Poulos looked up at the ceiling. "Mm. You did it."

"I did it, yes, sir," Johnny said, looking at his charts. "You seem to be doing well so far. I adjusted the drip. Nothing dramatic, need to build your strength. Your job is to rest, take your meds, let us know about any pain, discomfort." Johnny reached for Poulos's wrist. Poulos recoiled slightly. Johnny ignored the movement.

"Pulse is good. No infection so far. I'm going to examine you now."

The exam was quick. At the end, Johnny stepped back. "I'm done. I'll be back over the weekend. Any questions?"

"Why you here?" Poulos said in a deep voice. "You're the last . . ."

"Take it easy. I'm here because I'm a physician and you're a sick man. And because our common friend Stanley McRae asked. How about a truce? Once you're well, we can talk about the past. I'd appreciate a chance to do that."

Poulos lowered his chaotic eyebrows. "Goo' for you," he growled.

CHAPTER TWENTY-FIVE

Johnny returned to UC Cedars early Sunday morning. Poulos had been transferred to a private room, and they were alone. Poulos's bleary eyes followed Johnny as he worked. "You know my feelings about you."

Johnny nodded. "I ignore that. Last two times I let feelings get ahead of patient duty, I got in trouble. Married the first one, and that turned out poorly. Next one was Gomez. So I ignore feelings—you're my patient, that's it. We can talk about our feelings when you get better." He walked over to the bed. "Tell me how you're feeling today. I mean physically."

"I feel like shit. You know I won't get better."

"I don't know that at all. Lift your arm."

Poulos lifted his arm. Johnny pulled his stethoscope and listened to Poulos's chest. "Sit forward. Can you?"

"Help me."

Johnny raised the bed. He gently helped Poulos lean forward and listened to his chest from the back. "The incisions are healing nicely."

"That Gomez who you admitted for free, that started everything going downhill for me," Poulos said.

"Maybe so—for me too, I guess. That may be literally true, but I never intended to hurt you, Arthur. Not then, not ever. Breathe deeply."

Poulos took a deep breath.

"Sounds good. Listen, Arthur, let's stop squabbling. I screwed up—I got emotionally involved with Gomez. His death changed my . . . well, you don't need to hear about my problems."

"No, I certainly don't," Poulos said. "Stan tells me . . . you did a fine job on the transplant. But someone else can take over now."

"I'd like to see it through if you don't mind. Your recovery is hardly a slam dunk, and I think I'm in the best position to help you. But if you want me out, tell Stanley and I'll get out." Johnny began to write.

"Maybe I don't want the best position."

"Whatever, sir. Can I lower the bed back down for you?"

"No." Poulos tried to look gruff. He looked confused instead.

Johnny stared down at Poulos. He pushed the button to lower the bed. As the bed was descending, he spoke, "My parents died in front of me when I was a child. No doctors would come. No one cared about poor Indians. That's why I decided to become a physician. Because everyone should have access to decent medical help. Even Indians. Even guys who hate me. You want to fire me, fire me. But don't do it because you think I tried to screw you. I used to gripe about you because you tried to manage me, and I don't like being managed. Never anything personal. So unless you fire me, you're going to have to put up with my smiling face."

Poulos narrowed his eyes. Johnny nodded once and walked out.

***

Billy Bell called Johnny later that morning to invite him and Nicky to the afternoon Dodgers game. "Late notice, Johnny. Any chance?"

Johnny hadn't seen Billy in months. "I'd like to see you. Been working nonstop. Tell you what, I'll call Nicky. Depends on his schedule." Nicky was available and was excited to go to his first Dodgers game. He swung by UC Cedars to pick up Johnny. On the way downtown, Johnny encouraged Nicky to continue his army story. He needed a distraction from dark Poulos.

"So from medic training in Texas, I went to the NATO base in Rota, Spain, for advanced training in battlefield medicine. That was the most fun ten weeks ever. My high-school Spanish got way better because of this girl I met. I got orders to join a hospital in Kandahar, secondary care, for wounded soldiers mostly from IED explosions. I made two good friends, medics, who I learned later both were killed. It's always a mistake."

"What's a mistake?"

"To make friends with people that close to death. I think I need to stop there, Johnny. More later."

"Is it hard to speak about that stuff?"

"Very hard," Nicky whispered. "But Dr. Mir tells me I should do it. It'll help me, he says, get over the survivor's guilt."

***

Billy and Nicky sat in the back of the suite in animated conversation. They paused only to stand for "The Star-Spangled Banner," after which Billy gave Nicky a short history of the national anthem. The first inning came and went, and they were still in the back looking at Billy's computer and laughing.

Johnny was sitting up front. "You guys having fun bonding back there? So I have to watch this game alone?"

After some whispering, they joined Johnny in the spectator seats. "Sorry, chief. We were having fun talking," Billy said.

"Johnny, you have to see Billy's black hole simulation thing!" Nicky exclaimed.

Billy chuckled. "This kid so reminds me of you, Johnny. Except he's smarter and more interested in my stuff!"

"Aren't those the same thing?" Johnny asked, eyebrows dancing.

Billy laughed his deep basso laugh.

Nicky looked down at the ball field. "What an epic ballpark!"

***

On Saturday, Johnny was in a staff meeting at the VA when his cell rang. Caller ID read GUS ROGOSIN.

"What's up?" he whispered, cupping his phone. "I'm in a meeting."

"Your friend Poulos. He's got an infection, we had to move him back to the CCU. I've got antibiotics going. Looks serious."

"I can get there maybe forty-five minutes," Johnny said.

"Nothing you can do. Come in the morning if you can."

"I can. How's his spirits?"

"He's Poulos," Gus said. "What can I say? He's still a dick. You becoming best friends after all the screwing he's done to you?"

"I don't know. Call me if anything happens."

CHAPTER TWENTY-SIX

Arthur Poulos's infection did not bend to treatment this time. By Sunday morning he was battling pneumonia. Johnny could only stand by while the infection team scrambled to stabilize him. That was the day Nicky's club soccer team was scheduled to play their first playoff game—at Exposition Park in downtown LA. Johnny hated to miss it.

In the early afternoon, a Greek Orthodox priest visited Poulos. Later, a lawyer arrived to document Poulos's intentions. Poulos was adamant that no one, not even McRae, should know about his estate plan. Because of medical stops and starts, the legal work dragged on into the evening.

After the lawyers left, Johnny stood with McRae at the foot of the bed. Poulos was sleeping and back on the ventilator. "Boy, Stan. Look at him. I hope we didn't kill him by letting him work with the lawyer."

"He insisted. You know Arthur." Stan turned his head away.

"I'd be surprised if he lasts two days. Not much starch left. Was he alert today through the will thing?"

"He seemed fairly engaged," McRae replied.

"You don't look good, Stan. Go home, get some sleep."

"Yes. What time do you plan be back here tomorrow, Johnny?"

"I can be here at ten. Unless there's a crisis."

"I'll see you here then. I'll get that night's sleep."

***

Johnny left the hospital and rode his Harley south along La Cienega Boulevard toward Venice Beach under a dark sky. He loved the warm soft desert air that blanketed LA in September. The Santa Ana desert wind soothes, but it also burns up hillsides and homes and makes people crazy, or so they say. On the final lap to the condo, he felt his cell phone buzz twice against his thigh. When he arrived home, he saw multiple calls from CAPT MIR. As he held the phone, it buzzed again. He pushed PWR.

"Blood."

"This is Bill Mir. Where you been?"

"At the hospital and just now on my motorcycle . . ."

"Were you with Poulos? I need to see him ASAP."

"Poulos? Not a chance, Captain. He's on his deathbed. I give him twenty-four hours max."

"Oh jeez! I *have* to talk with him."

"He can't talk with anybody. What's up?"

"I can't say on the phone. But it's very important. I have a subpoena."

Johnny raised his voice. "I don't care if you have ten subpoenas, you can't see him!"

"Ach!" Mir exclaimed. He paused for a moment. "What it is, I finally could look at Poulos's financials and phone records."

"What did you find?"

"I can't say on the phone. You know the word 'bingo'?"

"What about bingo?"

"Doctor, Poulos is a murder suspect. I need to ask him questions."

"Well, like I said . . . it's impossible. You could kill him."

Mir stopped talking. Johnny waited.

"Do me a favor, Doctor. If there's a moment, ask him what he knows about Emilio Hand and Latira Brown, and what they did to your author friend Gomez. And keep that confidential between us. Not a peep to anyone else. Just in case he wakes up for a minute and you're alone."

"You mean *I* should ask him? I doubt I'll have the chance."

"Just do it if you can. That's all I can say. A big favor."

"Very unlikely. But . . . we'll see. God!"

***

When Johnny stepped off the elevator Monday morning at ten, he was met by an agitated Stan McRae.

"What's up?" Johnny asked. "Poulos okay?"

"Oh, Johnny! Arthur's rallied a little. He's in there with his daughter."

"Daughter? I thought you said he had no family. Funny how people come out of the woodwork when the will comes out of the drawer."

McRae rubbed his beard and sighed. "I never said he had no family. I said I had his power of attorney. He has a wife back in Athens and a grown daughter. I met the daughter for the first time last night. Mika."

"Mika?" Johnny glared at McRae. "Michaela? God, no! Is my Michaela here?"

"Please, Johnny," Stan said, holding Johnny's arm. "Yes, it's your Michaela. And she is here." Stan summarized what he knew. "She told me she ran off to London after a meeting with her father."

"But why?"

"You'll have to ask her. But the thing is, Arthur's now concluded you're not a monster. Now that he's facing death, he's come to his senses. We took him off the ventilator. He apologized to Mika, he wants to apologize to you. He wants to see you together."

"God! You say he rallied? He was toast last night. What a crazy mess!"

"Yes, rallied, a little. Still critical. He gave me a number and told me to call his daughter after the will. She's been in LA just a few days. She came right over. She's lovely. Arthur perked up. She's in there now."

"What on earth turned him around?"

"About you? I don't remember *ever* seeing Arthur change his mind about another human being. Maybe he got a feel for you while you were treating him. He spoke to that priest."

"So what happens next?" Johnny asked, shaking his head.

"I'll go get Mika to come out. Come back in together when you're ready."

"This is nuts." Johnny paused. "So Arthur Poulos! A deathbed conversion? He wants forgiveness?"

"Not forgiveness, Johnny. He says he just wants a chance to say he's sorry. He apologized to me too."

"Apologized to you? For what?" Johnny asked.

"Wait here." McRae turned on his heel and walked down the hall. Johnny watched him enter the CCU.

***

The next few minutes were an eternity. Finally, Michaela emerged. Seeing Johnny, she broke into a run and fell into his arms. They sat on a bench, holding each other.

After a minute, she eased away, squared her shoulders against the wall. "Give me a sec." She pulled a tissue and wiped her face.

"Sit there. I'll get you a glass of water," Johnny said.

She nodded.

Johnny returned with the water. "How's your father right now?"

"I'm *so* glad to see you, Johnny!" She sipped the water and took a breath. "Daddy's very bad. He looks like a little raisin, all tiny and wrinkled."

"Are you okay? Your father . . . he's the reason you left?"

"Yes." She sobbed once.

"And now he wants us together?"

"Yes. To apologize, he says."

"What does he want to apologize *for*?"

"Not sure. He has a lot to apologize for." Michaela's red eyes drifted away. She stood. "I'm going to the loo. When I get back, we'll go in."

She strode off. Johnny watched her, his head swimming.

After a brief moment, Michaela returned refreshed and looking lovely. Johnny tried to smile. "How'd you do that?"

"I'm an actor, remember? Let's go do this."

They walked down holding hands. As they turned into the room, Johnny dropped her hand and whispered, "I'm still the attending physician." Nodding at Stan McRae, Johnny moved to Poulos's side. "How we doing today, Arthur? Understand we have a visitor."

Poulos opened his eyes and nodded once. Michaela stood at the foot of the bed. Poulos waved a crooked finger in her direction. He said in a hoarse whisper, "Next to Dr. Blood please."

Michaela moved next to Johnny and grasped his hand.

Poulos nodded again. "Good." He took several deep breaths. "I owe you both . . . an apology." He cleared his throat twice. "Stanley always said you were a good man. I'm sorry . . ." He cleared his throat again. "You two have my blessing . . . what it's worth. Not much. Sorry . . ." He gasped for air.

"Daddy," Michaela said, stepping forward and touching his cheek, "please rest now. We hear you. And we really appreciate it. I owe you an apology too. None of us is without sin."

Johnny looked at Michaela, a question in his eyes.

Michaela grasped her father's hand. "Just sleep. We'll talk later."

Just then, white-jacketed Gus Rogosin strode into the room. He scanned the scene with wide eyes and nodded toward Johnny. "So, Dr. Blood, the plot thickens. Or at least the crowd thickens."

"Michaela, meet my friend Gus Rogosin. Gus, this is Michaela, Arthur's daughter."

Gus arched an eyebrow and put out his hand. "We-ell. Hello, Ms. . . . Poulos? I think . . . didn't I just see your face on a billboard on Robertson? The name was different."

"Michelle Powell maybe? Nice to meet you, Dr. Rogosin."

Gus rubbed the back of his neck. "Gus works fine. I don't get all this, but, hey, I'm just the plumber. So can you nice folks give me a moment with the patient?" He looked at Poulos, who lay still, his eyes closed. Gus whispered to Johnny, "Our patient looks blue around the gills."

Johnny nodded. "Stan, Michaela, I'll meet you outside. I'll brief Gus."

Michaela walked out, and McRae followed, looking back over his shoulder at Johnny. Johnny's eyes followed McRae out the door and shifted to meet Gus's deeply skeptical look. "Shit. I know, I know, Gus. I owe you an apology. But let's focus on Poulos. I thought we lost him yesterday, but I guess he had a little surge when Michaela came last night . . ."

Gus grabbed Johnny's arm and steered him into a corner. He seemed angry. "*Wait* a goddamn minute, Johnny. I decided not to ask until you were ready to tell me. Is this Michaela . . . the rumored girlfriend? You're dating frigging Poulos's daughter? Shitting me? And she's also this movie star babe Michelle Powell? What am I, chopped liver? And maybe fucking crazy?"

"All the above, I guess. Calm down—I should have told you months ago, but I was sure it wouldn't last. I didn't want the embarrassment. Then she left me, and, well . . . but I didn't know Poulos was her father until just now. Honestly. Let's play racquetball tomorrow night? I'm having dinner tonight with Michaela. I'll tell you what I know then. He's had his little rally, but he's had a big morning repenting—don't ask."

"Repenting? So all is forgiven?" Gus was astonished.

Johnny put his palms up and half smiled. "Guess so."

"Un . . . believable! Greeks never forgive! I'm a Slav, I know my Greeks!"

Suddenly, Poulos noisily cleared his throat and opened his eyes. He wiggled his finger toward Johnny.

"Looks like the patient wants to talk to you," Gus said.

Johnny approached the bed. "Yes, Arthur?"

"'Portant. Bend down." Johnny put his ear to Poulos's mouth. "Tell Mika, Alexis Farakos is dead, her first husband. Dead two years. Sorry, I . . ." He closed his eyes.

"I think I got it. So her first husband, named Farakos? He's been dead two years? You want me to tell her that?"

Poulos nodded once and looked up at Johnny. He wheezed: "Sorry. And . . . sorry about Gomez."

"Gomez? Is that what you said?"

Poulos squinted. Johnny remembered Captain Mir's request. He took the plunge. "Arthur, you know anything about Emilio Hand and Gomez?"

Poulos opened his rheumy eyes as wide as Johnny had ever seen them opened. "Ah!" he said. Then the fleshy lids slowly dropped.

Johnny backed away, watching Arthur Poulos lose consciousness.

CHAPTER TWENTY-SEVEN

Late that evening, Johnny and Michaela met for dinner in the coffee shop of the Beverly Wilshire Hotel. They were spinning from the day's events. Johnny said he was on call at the VA and might have to run at any time. "Staffing's tight at the VA—not like at Cedars."

She tried to smile. "There's so much to say. We still have to go slow, Johnny, in spite of . . . all these feelings. I'm still jet-lagged, and I have to start publicity tomorrow. I feel so . . ." Her voice broke.

Johnny glared at her. "Why did you leave me, Michaela? What did your father threaten to do? I need to understand."

She bowed her head. "When you went to see your Nicky that night, he called my cell, told me to meet him. We met at the Century Plaza. He threatened me, ordered me to leave you. I . . . had no choice." She sobbed into her napkin.

The waiter came up and saw the tears. "Oh, I can come back."

"No, no, hang on," Johnny said. He ordered for both, and the waiter fluttered away.

"How did he threaten you?"

She whispered, "To expose me. To deport me. He didn't say it, but . . . it's a long story, Johnny. Can't I tell you later? I don't have the strength."

"Deport you? Sure, well, I guess you're back now, no rush."

She took a breath. "Sorry. Yes, I'm back now."

He smiled at her. "Are you really back? You're so beautiful. What do I call you? Mika? Michelle?"

She smiled through her tears and reached for his hand. "Yes, I'm really back. Back with you. For good." She took a breath. "I love to hear you say Michaela. Mika makes me feel twelve years old." She sipped her water. "You moved to the beach, Johnny?"

"I did. We did. You'll meet Nicky. He had problems in the big house. We have a rental in Venice."

"That gorgeous mansion, sitting empty?"

"For now. Before I forget—after you and Stan McRae stepped out this morning, your father told me to tell you . . . your first husband, Farakos?"

"God!"

"He's dead. Been dead two years. Your father said he was sorry, I guess because he didn't tell you."

Michaela appeared stunned. She reached for her napkin. "Alex Farakos. Pure evil. My god, Daddy! What on earth . . . ?"

"He wanted you to know. He's not gonna live much longer."

She pressed the napkin to her eyes. "I have such mixed-up feelings about my father. Best would be if he just died quietly." Her voice took on an edge. "At least he showed some positive human quality today. First time ever. He is my father, but he was *so awful* . . . There are things . . . I can never forgive."

"Your mother, is she well?" Johnny asked.

"Yes. Dear Maria. She'll never leave Athens. I call once a week. I flew there from London. I've no idea what to tell her now."

"And your son?"

"Pavlos. Seventeen now. Older than me when he was born. My mother said Pavlos knows he has a birth mother somewhere."

Johnny watched Michaela's sparkling eyes.

"My goal was when he turned eighteen I'd step up. Maybe help with university expenses. That's why I'm working in this awful business. I have a picture. May I show you?"

Johnny nodded. "Please."

Michaela dove into her large black purse. The waiter brought the salads and scurried away. She found a small photo. "He's sixteen here." Her moist eyes flitted between the photo and Johnny's face.

"Handsome boy," Johnny said. "He has your eyes."

"Isn't he gorgeous? Greek men are totally fucked up, excuse me. But they're sweet and beautiful when they're boys. What's your Nicky like?"

"Two steps forward, one step back. I'm not supposed to probe into his life. Parenthood's hard." Johnny looked up and smiled. "He knows about you. Knows almost as much as I do."

"I know. I'm so sorry." She stabbed at her salad. "So the evil Farakos is dead. *God.* Would you believe, I'm still not sure whether I was ever legally married? In Greece you're supposed to get court permission if you're under eighteen. Then Farakos threw me out, literally. Right after my mother threw my father out. Welcome to Greece."

"Well, Farakos is gone now, so no more worries," Johnny said.

"*If* he's gone. I don't trust my father far as I can throw him." Michaela peeked to see if her idiom worked.

Johnny smiled. "Dying people usually don't lie. I googled Alexis Farakos. Two names came up. One was a government minister? A Socialist? I can't read Greek, but this guy was born in 1938 and died in 2008."

Michaela slowly shook her head, staring at Johnny. "Probably him. I'll ask my mother to confirm he's dead. That'll make her day."

Johnny looked at his watch. "I should go, Michaela."

"Okay, I'll put this on my room." Michaela looked at Johnny and smiled. "There's that blush again."

"You do make me blush. I was thinking of seeing an allergist."

"Johnny . . . " Michaela tossed her napkin on the table and reached for Johnny's hand. "Can you come up to my room now?"

"We may be interrupted."

"I'll take the chance."

***

Johnny and Gus played vigorous racquetball Tuesday night. Settling into the Jacuzzi, Gus bunched his brows and gave Johnny his most annoyed look. "I'm really mad at you, asshole. I thought we were friends."

"I apologize. I should have told you about Michaela, but like I said, I never thought it would last. When she walked out on me after like the perfect weekend, that confirmed my suspicion, so I just buried it. But like I said, I had no idea that Arthur . . ."

"Johnny, you're telling me this *femme fatale* you were secretly banging and falling for, she neglected to tell you that her father was your nemesis at UC Cedars?"

"I never mentioned work matters. Anyway, they had a falling out years ago."

"Oh? And now they're holding hands? Doesn't add up. Did you know she has a stage name and that her face is plastered all over Sunset Strip?"

"I knew the stage name. I never look at billboards."

"Johnny, jeez! Your head is so far up your ass when it comes to women! Plus, these European babes, everything's always a little off center. Plus, she's an actress, a paid professional phony. What else can I say? How can you trust her about anything if she doesn't tell you that her father worked in the same place you did?"

Johnny was silent.

Gus sighed. "When it comes to women, you are so . . . It's like you were born without natural sensors, except for your dick."

"There's something special about her."

"There sure is—she's gorgeous! You better keep your dukes up, pal."

***

Johnny looked in on Poulos after racquetball. The gray-faced patient slept through the visit. Next morning, Wednesday, Johnny was buried in paperwork at the VA when his cell phone rang. It was Gus. "Johnny, Poulos just died. Had a massive stroke. Lights out. Nothing we could do."

"Oh, shoot!" Johnny took a breath. "*Hate* to lose a patient."

"Not your fault. Also a world-class asshole, but may he rest in peace. Call your girlfriend. Her pop just died. She needs to hear from you."

***

Johnny called Captain Mir that afternoon to report on Poulos's death.

"I heard," Mir said. "Did you get a chance to ask him my question?"

"About Emilio Hand? I did. He didn't . . . actually, he looked surprised, and he said 'ah!' and then he fell asleep. He never woke up again."

"'Ah'? That's it? Hmm."

"Oh, but right before that, he said he was 'sorry about Gomez.' That's when I asked him about Emilio Hand."

"He said he was sorry about Gomez? How do you read that, Doctor?"

"He was apologizing for a lot of things right then. Could have been an apology for the way he tried to throw me under the bus."

"Or, way more likely, an admission of guilt."

"You know things I don't know, Captain. Those were his last words."

"It was a deathbed confession. The bastard."

PART THREE

Heav'n has no Rage, like Love to Hatred turn'd,
Nor Hell a Fury, like a Woman scorn'd.
—William Congreve, from *The Mourning Bride*

CHAPTER TWENTY-EIGHT

It was late October. Autumn—subtle in Los Angeles—was in the air. Nights a little cooler, mornings darker, trees dusty after endless dry days. A lifetime had passed since Johnny told Ora Dillon in Redwood City about his desire to reinvent himself as a truck driver. His future had arrived—the Gomez funk was gone; he was back doing surgery, learning new skills, building something, battling the system--now the US government, not UC Cedars management. And thanks to Michaela and Nicky, a life was taking shape outside the OR.

In the weeks following Arthur Poulos's death, Johnny and Michaela worked hard in their separate worlds. At Poulos's thinly attended memorial service in the UC Cedars chapel, Johnny had whispered to her, "Next couple of months until the film premiere, we'll both be busy—let's just live separately, trust each other, grab coffee when we can." Michaela leaned her head on his shoulder. Like a veteran professional married couple, they would graze on whatever their days served up until the film release December 10, after which they would feast.

Johnny started peeking at the Hollywood trades. The buzz about *Why We Love* and Michelle Powell was growing. *Variety* reported that the film had serious box-office potential and a shot at technical Oscars. On the phone, Michaela deflected his questions. "I talk all day about it. Ask me something else."

"I do have a question about your father. Do you know how he found out we were dating?"

"I'm not sure you want to know."

"Why not?"

"He told me it was your ex-wife who told him."

"Lisa? That doesn't make any sense."

"It makes sense to me. I'm a woman."

"But how . . . ?"

"He told me in the hospital. He said to watch out for her."

***

Late one evening, Michaela's studio limo passed by Nicky's McDonalds on Venice Boulevard. She told her driver to stop—she wanted to meet Nicky. She had been charmed by Johnny's iPhone video, displaying Nicky's warm, crooked smile as he asked whether he "could take your order." When she walked into the store, she saw the Blood Moon face behind the counter.

She stage-whispered, "Nicky! You're gorgeous, just like your uncle! Got a minute? Oh, sorry—I'm Michaela." She stuck her hand out.

Nicky took a break, and they huddled in a booth. After twenty minutes, Nicky extended his hand. "Thanks for dropping by. Gotta get back to work." Michaela ignored the hand and stood. "Okay, but first a lesson in European kissing. Stand up, Nicky Bloodman. Look right here at me." She touched her nose. "Now kiss me twice, here and here." She touched her cheeks. He complied, blushing deeply. His blush was the coup de grâce. Nicky became a valued member of her universe, and she of his.

***

In early November, Johnny and Michaela met for lunch at the In-N-Out Burger near Hollywood High School. Johnny asked whether *she* had a shot at an Oscar. She smiled and looked out at busy Hollywood Boulevard. "Not really. But every actor has her eye on award season. *Every* actor. I do like my work in this film."

Johnny nodded. "Reminds me. I'd like you to meet my UCLA friends. We watched a lot of movies in senior year and used to bet on who would win Oscars. Then we had a big party. You've not had lifetime friends?"

"Hard to when you're hiding out all your life. Let's get to know each *other* before I meet your lifetime friends."

Johnny nodded. "Fair enough."

"Johnny, I don't think I've ever had a real adult friend," Michaela said.

"Not ever? Maybe I can step into that role."

"Impossible. No such thing as friendship between a man and a woman, unless one of them is gay. Even that can get weird. The hardwiring—is that the term?—makes them always want to jump on each other. That's how the world is."

"My plan is to change the world." Johnny reached for her hand.

***

Some days later, Michaela called Johnny, who was in the Venice house eating fast food and watching Sports Center. "Johnny, something amazing happened. I can't tell you over the phone. Can we have a late dinner tomorrow? But no funny business, yet." She giggled. "Soon enough. Four weeks."

"Three and a half till the premiere. I'm crossing days off on my calendar to December 10. Yes, I can do tomorrow night. Any hints?"

"No, but I do have something else. I can get tickets for a screening of *Why We Love* for next Friday. Would your UCLA friends want to come? I know it's short notice. It's at three thirty at CAA in Century City."

"My UCLA friends? I thought you . . . well, sure! I'll call. Will you join us for dinner if they come? That will get them here for sure."

"*That's* a little scary. But Nicky *said* you'd ask. Nicky really wants to meet them. He's pushing this."

"Nicky is? I see. You're very . . ." Johnny hesitated.

"Fickle. Foolhardy? Stupid? The two women will look at me as a pretender for Lisa's place. The men will look at me as a piece of meat."

"For a minute. Then you'll all be friends. They're good people, Michaela, and your natural charm will kick in, eventually."

"I'm the age of their kids," Michaela said. "But Nicky wants to, so . . ."

"It'll be great. Gotta go. See you for dinner tomorrow, 9:00 p.m.?"

***

Johnny arrived a few minutes late the next night at the Beverly Wilshire. He saw Michaela waving. "I beat you, Johnny! First time ever. Let's order quick. Then I'll tell you my news." She waved down the waiter, and they ordered. "But, first, are your friends coming to the screening?"

"Yes! They're all coming. Screening and dinner. They're excited."

"Lovely," Michaela said, rolling her eyes. "I'll try to behave."

"I'm sure you'll behave. Here's the wine."

The waiter poured, and they clinked glasses.

"So my lifelong good behavior came home to roost this week," Michaela said, smiling, "like chickens from another world."

"What do you mean?"

"My father's will. He left me *$3 million.*"

"You serious? Arthur? That's *crazy!*" Johnny was watching Michaela closely. His mind flashed to Captain Mir and the Gomez investigation.

"Could be more—lawyer says there's no estate tax this year, which is weird. Anyway, I have all this money, Johnny."

"But what . . . ?"

"For his, let me read it, 'Lovely daughter Mika, who he hopes will not despise him for all eternity as he deserves.' A bunch has already been wired to my account."

"Unbelievable. Does that make you feel different about him?"

"Never. Money has nothing to do with feelings. This is just part of his deathbed conversion craziness. So thought you'd like to know that your girlfriend wants to take you to Sofi's, where *she* will pick up the check."

"Deal."

Michaela's eyes filled up. "Now I can help Pavlos. All my life, I've had no money. Maybe I can even get out of movies now?"

"Just when I'm getting interested?"

"Don't waste your time."

CHAPTER TWENTY-NINE

"I want to pay you for this, Ora. Turn on your meter."

Lisa Bell said this to her friend Ora Dillon, who was settling into the guest chair in Lisa's lush, capacious office, high above Century City. It was 9:30 a.m. on Friday, the day of Michaela's CAA screening. Ora had flown down early to visit Lisa. No one, not even her husband, Dr. Mike, knew her plan. He would fly down later today.

"Why pay?" Ora asked. "I called you. And you know I see Johnny professionally."

"'Cause I want to talk to you, and I want it to be confidential, without worrying about the others . . ." Lisa's words were slightly slurred.

"Hon, I promise I won't talk about this with the others. You don't need to pay me for that. Excuse me, dear, have you been drinking?"

Lisa winced. "Just some wine."

Ora watched Lisa self-consciously rearrange herself in her massive desk chair. Her thick makeup failed to hide the cracks in her once-smooth facade. It struck Ora that the large Picasso up behind Lisa's chair, a woman deconstructed into colorful parts, aptly mirrored Lisa's chaos.

"What I want, Ora, is for you to ask me questions so I don't ramble."

Ora tried to comprehend Lisa's need. "Before I do, let me be clear—I wouldn't be comfortable with you as a paying client."

"Fine, no pay. Whatever. But it *must* remain absolutely private!"

Ora bristled. "Sure, sister, I *said* it would. Now tell me what's going on."

"I wanna murder Johnny Blood and his girlfriend."

"Lisa! If this were formal therapy, I'd have to report you!"

"Not literally murder—calm down. Manner of speaking. Anyway, that Greek bitch girl is the one I hate. I still don't know what to think of Johnny. And, yes, I drink too much." Lisa's eyes were slits. "I lie awake at night thinking of ways to hurt her. That's how I go to sleep."

"Hurt Michaela? Why?"

"Oh, I *hate* the sound of that name!" Lisa's eyes filled with tears.

Ora slid a Kleenex box across the broad desktop. "Good god, girl! What's going on with you?"

Lisa softened her tone. "Sorry. I'm really messed up."

Ora was trying to follow Lisa's mood swings. "I can see that. You don't really mean physical harm, do you?"

"'Cause you'd have to turn me in? No. Haven't you ever hated someone? Michaela Poulos. Michelle Powell. She didn't even tell Johnny her real name. The phony bitch destroyed my marriage." Lisa spit this out.

"Not to argue, but I believe they met *after* you signed the divorce."

"That's just her bullshit story!" Lisa was close to shouting.

Ora put her hands up. "Whoa, okay! New subject. Can you talk a little about your family background? We have time, and I don't know anything."

"Turning this around into a deep shrink session?"

"I can see why you'd think that. I'd like to understand you better."

***

At 2:00 p.m. that day, the Final Four sat in the vast sunken living room at Benedict Cañon. Johnny was pacing back and forth. "I love this! It's like being back at Veteran! The five of us together! It's been too long."

After an awkward pause, January spoke, "So what's the plan today, Johnny dear?"

"Forty-five minutes we leave for the screening in a van. Tonight we'll have a catered dinner here. Michaela and Nicky will join us. I'm pretty pumped."

"You sure are," Mike said. "Haven't seen you this hopped up in a long time! Can we help pay for something?"

"No, no. All on me. I'm celebrating being with my friends. And please, please be nice to Michaela. You can be a tough crowd."

"Oh, we'll love her to death, poor thing," January said. "She's probably nervous as a cat, prospect of facing this bunch."

Johnny pointed at himself. "Not as nervous as this cat." He smiled at Ora, who was looking at him with narrowed eyes. She looked away.

***

January and Ora sat together in a guest powder room combing their hair. Jan spoke first, "You're awfully somber today, honey."

"I'm sorry. I saw Lisa Bell this morning."

"You saw Lisa, today? In person?"

"Yes. I'm *so* worried about her."

"She called me last night," Jan said. "I wasn't going to say. She was drunk. Couldn't make out half of what she said."

"Last night?"

Jan shrugged. "It was maybe nine o'clock. She rambled on for, I don't know, ten minutes. Then she just hung up."

"Can you tell me what she said?"

"To the extent I understood it. I didn't promise secrecy."

"I did. Sorry."

"If I may, Ora, aren't you walking close to an ethical line, seeing Johnny professionally while you're having a session with Lisa?"

Ora groaned. "I worry about that. It wasn't a paid session. I told her she couldn't be my patient. They both know I talk to the other."

"She was sloppy drunk on the phone," Jan said. "Went on about Johnny's bitch girlfriend. So annoying."

"Unhinged. We get to meet the girlfriend today, don't we?"

"Michaela? Yes. I'm looking forward to that."

"I have mixed feelings," Ora said. "It puts us more in the middle. Jan, you and I have to be careful. Lisa has no outlet except us. She's not in good shape." She stood up. "I should go find my husband. We leave soon, right? This ridiculous house is so big I get lost."

Ora walked down the hall and ducked into a small unoccupied room. She closed the door and sat in the dark, her head in her hands. She shuddered, recalling the horrific story Lisa told her this morning about her girlhood. Ora's day-nightmare about Lisa dissolved when Johnny burst into the room. "Ora, what are you doing? C'mon, we're gonna be late to the screening."

CHAPTER THIRTY

The CAA mega-palace—known locally as the Death Star—sits across the Avenue of the Stars from the Century Plaza Hotel, site of the Poulos father-daughter meeting in May. Michaela and Nicky greeted the van as it slid up to the curb. Johnny made introductions, and the group followed Michaela into the massive building and its plush red screening room. All seats were filled.

After the show, the Final Four, buzzing about the film, reboarded the van for the ride back up to the mansion. Nicky, Michaela, and Johnny followed in Nicky's Civic. A light rain fell. Johnny talked about his friends. He could see Michaela was fidgety.

The elaborate Chinese dinner was catered by Wolfgang Puck's people. When the caterers arrived with their white coats and bamboo containers, Bo whispered to Johnny, "Who you trying to impress?"

"You. Commemorating my DUI fiasco after Spago, Puck's first restaurant. The day that turned my life around."

"You should have been thrown in jail, not turned around."

"True. Funny how things work out."

The group settled into the big living room with drinks and nibbles. Michaela was radiant. Johnny could see the men trying not to stare at her and the women trying not to stare at Nicky, who was busy stuffing his face. Breaking the awkward silence, January exclaimed, "We *loved* the movie, Michaela! Bet it gets some award nominations. Can you talk about the filming and everything? I love the stories—my son's a filmmaker."

Michaela talked about the shoot and the personalities. She had a charming shyness when she spoke at length, still not fully confident in her English. Johnny was intrigued by how she held the group in her hand.

As they moved to the dining room, she spoke about the film business generally. "It's awful, so day to day. I'm fine right now, but it can disappear any minute. For so many years I had to scratch for a living, Johnny knows. Then you get a random phone call. It's so much luck."

Everyone nodded, rapt. Michaela looked around. "I'm doing all the talking. Somebody else should . . . ?"

This was met by a chorus of objections. Ora held her hand up. "Hang on, Michaela's right. Let's have more of a group conversation. Nicky, you're eating half the food here. Why don't you tell us what you're up to?"

Nicky drew the back of his hand across his smiling mouth. "I'm up to eating! Is this food epic or what? You're right, I shouldn't eat all of it." He wiped his mouth again, this time using a napkin. He looked around. "You're Ora, the shrink, right? When Johnny brought me here, I thought my head would explode. I never saw a house like this except on *Rich and Famous*. Whoa!" Nicky speared a dumpling with his chopstick. "Don't know how to use these dumb chopsticks. So I went into rehab."

"One of our kids went through that," Dr. Mike said. "Looks like you're doing pretty well."

"So far so good," Nicky said, his mouth stuffed. "'Scuse me. No manners." He swallowed and smiled. "My main problem was the panic and the bad dreams. You know, you think you're back in it—you wake up sweating and everything. I'm pretty over the panic attacks, thanks to my therapist. So I love shrinks." He offered a high five to Ora, sitting next to him. Ora hit his hand with gusto and a smile.

"I still got work to do. But, like, my Uncle Johnny's been totally awesome. In front of your friends, Johnny, I'd like to say thank you for taking care of me like you do. I know I'm a handful."

"Well! You are a handful, bud, but it's nice of you to say that."

Johnny studied Nicky's face with fresh eyes. The young man was freely discussing intimate subjects with these strangers, displaying a new dimension. Nicky had expressive dark eyes that didn't quite match, thick black hair, smooth latté skin, full lips. His two-day stubble and black T-shirt were LA *à la mode*. His long nose was off center like his smile—oddly enhancing the appeal of his face. He moved like a leopard. Like Johnny, he colored easily. When he spoke passionately, Johnny saw a dreamy look on the ladies' faces. A feeling of warm breathless pride welled up in Johnny's chest.

Meanwhile, Michaela had receded. Johnny detected a coolness between her and Ora, but he wasn't sure. The conversation ranged over many subjects. Encouraged by Dr. Mike, Nicky talked about his Afghanistan experience. Everyone was riveted.

As dessert was served, Johnny's cell buzzed—GUS ROGOSIN. Johnny excused himself and walked out of the room.

"Gus, what's up?"

"Where are you, Johnny? Are you sober?"

"With my UCLA friends. Haven't had a drink. Why?"

"Your ex is here with me, she wants to talk with you."

"Lisa? Where is she?" Johnny asked.

"We're at the Medical Center. Hold on."

"Johnny?" It was Lisa. Her voice was tense.

"Lisa, what's going on?"

"It's just that . . . Billy had chest pains, and Gus says he needs multiple bypass surgery immediately. I didn't know you left here. Why didn't you tell me?"

"You didn't want to . . . we can discuss that later. So Billy needs bypass surgery? Was it a heart attack?"

"I think Gus said so. I just want you to do the operation."

Johnny thought of pushing back, telling her that Billy was his friend, that there were excellent heart surgeons who could handle it. He checked himself. "Okay, be right over. Let me talk to Gus again."

Gus came back on. "Small MI, I don't think too much damage. I did an exam, and he needs a multiple bypass. I can't fix it. He's obese, so there's that. Your ex wants you to do it yesterday."

"Fine. Who's there?"

"Kim."

"Max? Can you ask him to take the lead? Don't tell Lisa."

"Sure. Your ex is quite attractive when she's upset."

"Maybe. Anyway, I've got a house full of guests. I'll be there soon as I can."

"We can work with that. See ya."

***

Johnny apologized to his friends for having to run, citing a patient emergency. Nicky walked him out and asked him to call when he had a chance.

"What's up?" Johnny spoke with a parent's alertness.

"Nothin'. Just give me a call when you can."

Wrapped in an old poncho, Johnny rode his Harley down the hill through a steady shower. He changed clothes in Gus's suite and ran to the OR. Lisa greeted him in the waiting room with a verbal punch. "I can't get over that you quit here!"

"Billy knew. He said you didn't want to talk to me. Let's put that off for now, Lisa. What happened to Billy?"

"He was alone in the back part of the house. I was at the golf club. I guess he had chest pains and told Ernest. Ernest dialed 911 then called me. I got there just as the paramedics were taking him away. I was sure they'd bring him to some public hospital." She started to cry.

"I'm sorry. Where's Gus?"

She waved toward the OR.

Johnny nodded. "We'll talk later."

***

Billy's surgery was uneventful. Johnny looked for Lisa afterward. She had left a note for him. "Johnny, call me when you finish, any time. Lisa." Johnny looked at his watch. It was 2:00 a.m. He called.

"Is Billy okay?" Her voice was slurred.

"He's fine, Lisa. Surgery went well. Heart attack was small."

"When can I visit him?"

"Tomorrow. Probably afternoon is best—he'll still be in the cardiac care unit. He'll be groggy. But he should be home in a few days."

"Oh god! Well. I'm going to bed," she said curtly.

"Lisa, I should be here maybe five o'clock tomorrow. My colleague Dr. Kim will be his primary."

"I don't know a Dr. Kim," she said.

"He's very good. I trained him."

"Well . . . can't be as good as you."

"Don't be so sure. Good night."

CHAPTER THIRTY-ONE

The next day, Johnny saw Lisa sitting outside the CCU radiating tension. "Lisa, hi. Saw that article in *Philanthropy Today* about you and your foundation."

"Johnny! They kicked me out again! That Dr. Kim you like so much!"

"You should be proud of that article. You're a great manager." Johnny was hoping to deflect her anxieties. He failed.

"Billy's got all these tubes! It's very upsetting!"

"Should be clear tomorrow. Problem is he's so fat."

"I'm sure he's addicted to food. You're his one friend, you should see him more often!"

"You're right, but . . ."

"And so you're working at the *Veterans* Hospital now?"

"Yes, Lisa." Johnny pressed his lips together. "Slow down. I need to check on Billy. Can we have a quick dinner? If I'm back on your talking list?"

The suggestion startled Lisa. "Where?"

"The Salud Café under the other tower is quiet," Johnny said.

"I don't have *any* time."

"Let's meet here at six. It's a quick walk over."

She hesitated for a moment. "All right."

***

Johnny went into the CCU. He saw Max Kim leaning over Billy with a nurse at his elbow. "How we doing, Max?"

Kim twisted around, holding his stethoscope. "Hey, Johnny. Mr. Bell here's doing fine. We're still a bit groggy."

Johnny walked around and squeezed Billy's meaty hand. "Billy?"

"'S'at the famous Dr. Blood Moon?" Billy rasped. His face seemed fat and gaunt at the same time.

"It's me, friend. I was with you during the operation."

"Heard that. I didn't lose fifty pounds. Don't be mad. Think progress."

140

Kim straightened up. "You're doing fine, Mr. Bell. Should be home by the weekend."

"Home," Billy spoke in a flat tone.

"Heart damage was minor," Kim said. "But you need to lose weight."

"That's *his* line." Billy tilted his head toward Johnny.

"Needs to be your line too, sir. I'll take off now." Kim nodded at Johnny and walked out.

Billy sagged. "Lisa still here?"

"Outside in the corridor. We're having dinner. She looked . . . surprised when I asked."

"Shoot, yes, surprised! 'F I had any energy I'd laugh."

"I'd like to have a decent, you know, relationship with her."

"You don't try you don't get." Billy's eyes drooped.

Johnny stroked Billy's head. "Curious what you mean by 'progress.'"

Billy smiled, his eyes closed now, tears tangled in the lashes. "Mos' important product." He sank into sleep.

Johnny walked back out to the waiting area. He told Lisa that Billy was sleeping. She glared at him and strode toward the CCU. He spoke to her disappearing back, "See you here at six."

***

Johnny walked through familiar bright corridors toward the Bell Wing. As he emerged from the elevator, he nearly knocked Gus over. "Hey, dude!" Gus exclaimed. "You left your dirty skivvies on the bathroom floor! Were you raised by wolves?"

"I actually may have been. Can I make some calls in there? I'll clean up my mess."

"Sure. Lisa's old bean counter Tom Schultz's in there. He's retiring soon, did you know that? Hey, how 'bout racquetball later tonight?"

"Tonight?" Johnny thought for a second. "Why not, I need the money—eight o'clock? I'm having dinner with my ex."

"You're having dinner with the gorgeous Lisa? That'll be a source of rich discussion. See you at eight."

***

When Johnny entered Gus's suite, he saw Tom Schultz hunched over a laptop. After a minute, Schultz raised his eyes, started, and sat back. "Oh!

Johnny! Thought you were Gus." Schultz was a long beanpole with a narrow, nervous face and a high forehead. He fiddled with his wire glasses.

"Hi, Tom." Johnny sprawled on the leather sofa and looked around. "Nothing's changed, I see. So you're retiring?"

Schultz fluttered his fingers over his thin hair. "Um, yes, end of the year, which . . . Johnny . . . " He closed his laptop and stood. Facing Johnny, he removed his glasses. "I was going to call you. Can we . . . would you have time to talk, soon?"

"About?"

"Mrs. Bell. But please don't say anything."

"I'm having dinner with Mrs. Bell tonight."

"Oh god. Please don't tell her that you saw me."

Johnny shrugged. "Okay. Big mystery. How about lunch tomorrow?"

"Yes? Could we possibly go off campus?"

"California Pizza Kitchen, eleven thirty? Too early?"

"No, fine. That should be fine." Schultz put on his glasses, bowed awkwardly, picked up his laptop, and walked out the door.

***

Johnny surveyed the familiar space. Gus had not altered Lisa's Polo Lounge look. He retrieved his dirty clothes from the shower room and sat on the couch again. He glanced up at Matisse's dark-eyed woman. Looks just like Michaela, he thought. He pulled out his cell, took a picture, and fiddled with the settings to make the image his wallpaper. He dialed Toby Roberts at the VA. Toby had asked Johnny to assist on a lung operation early tomorrow. Toby didn't answer, so Johnny left a message confirming that he'd scrub in by 7:30 a.m. Then he called Nicky.

"Johnny."

"Hey, Nicky. You had something you wanted to talk about?"

"Yes. Got a little *problemo*. You remember that playoff game in Exposition Park?"

"Yes. Hated to miss it."

"That was you being lucky. When we lost, the guys started fighting each other. There's some gang rival shit they like suppressed while we were winning. Anyway, cops were there, grabbed a couple of them. Me and my friend Paco walked away when the fight started, although not before I caught a punch from the main guy."

"I thought I saw a bruise after that game."

"Yes. I got in over my head. Paco tells me I need to get away from the beach now. I'm on their shit list, and they know where I live. I been sleeping on Michaela's couch. I'm really sorry, but we should . . ."

"Nicky, slow down. So we have to move out of the beach house? Are you okay in the garage apartment until we figure this out?"

"For sure. Sorry to be such a drag."

"No worries. The lease is almost over. I'll get our stuff moved back to Benedict Cañon. Let's meet up there tonight. I can get there by ten thirty."

"Yeah, I should clear out of this hotel. Michaela's leaving any day now, she keeps saying. She lives a crazy life."

"I know."

"She told me about her son, Pavlos, in Greece. You know what you're getting yourself into, Johnny?"

"Not really, Nicky. But you know what? I'm ready."

CHAPTER THIRTY-TWO

At 6:00 p.m., Johnny arrived at the CCU to meet Lisa for dinner. He found her sitting by Billy's bed, staring into space. When she saw him, she leaped up.

Johnny whispered, "Sorry. How's Billy?"

Lisa reached down for her purse. "Oh! . . . Better. Sleeping."

"Can I have a second to check him? Don't know what your time is."

Lisa regarded Johnny with cold eyes. "I'll visit the ladies' room. Meet me outside in five minutes. I have to be in Santa Monica by eight."

"I'll be quick."

When Lisa walked out, Billy half opened one eye. "Dr. Blood Moon," he rasped, "how nice of you to visit."

"Thought you were asleep, Billy."

"I was faking."

"Ah. Just so you know, you should gain strength fairly rapidly. Can I open your shirt?"

"Anytime."

Johnny stepped up. "Feeling okay?"

"Right now, sure, given all. If you mean cosmically, I've been pretty depressed." Billy's eyelids fluttered. "Sorry. I'm normally a half-full guy."

Johnny listened to Billy's chest. "Happens to the best of us. I've not been much of a friend. Your heart sounds fine."

Billy squeezed his eyes shut. "Not your fault."

"When you're out of here, we'll talk it over." Johnny said. "Got a heavy date right now."

"With an angel," Billy's eyes stayed shut. "Lucifer was an angel once."

***

Johnny silently led Lisa through the brilliant underground maze to the café. Johnny ordered water, white wine for Lisa, Caesar salads for both. Johnny played with his napkin. "Glad we're talking, Lisa. I've been floundering. It took me quite a while to restart my life."

"I don't care about your restarted life."

"I know I was a lousy husband."

She closed her eyes and shook her head. "No shit. Fine. Why did you quit UC Cedars?"

"Got fed up. It's all about money and ego."

"So you prefer veterans better than . . . ?"

"Celebrities. Yes, I do. You may remember—I went to med school to help poor Indians. Then I got swept up in the power and glory and money."

"Nonsense. Life *is* power and money."

The waiter served the salads. Lisa ordered a second glass of wine. "I don't know why I agreed to have this dinner."

Johnny watched Lisa's eyes, scanning everything in the room except Johnny's face. She was pale, talking through clenched teeth. "I'm sorry," Johnny said.

"I hate that about you!" Lisa hissed, peering at Johnny through narrowed eyes. "You're always apologizing! Maybe you *are* sorry, but you never respected me. For who I am. Is that what you're sorry about? It *should* be."

"I *totally* respected you, Lisa," he said. "How could I not respect you? The work you do . . ."

"As a *woman*, Johnny. As a woman! Maybe the word is 'regard.' I never felt your regard, your warmth. Dare I say *love*? Yes, I know my work is good. Will would have been proud of me. But that's about respect, not regard. He had plenty of regard for me."

Johnny was lost.

Lisa looked past Johnny, chin forward. "There are still feelings. Frustration. Anger. Now, this girlfriend."

"I was frustrated too. But I'm trying to move on. And I do have a girlfriend. Just trying to move on."

Lisa gulped her wine. "Benedict Cañon is sitting empty!"

"I moved out because my nephew who's with me now had stress trauma. He's doing better. We're moving back this week."

Lisa betrayed a bit of interest. "I heard the boy's a vet. I know something about PTSD."

"I remember you funded research."

"Do you plan to move back permanently?"

"I doubt it. I'd like to downsize my life . . ."

Liz's face suddenly hardened. "Let me ask you something. Billy needs a place to live. I have to go to London for a while. I so worry about Billy. I've been awful—I don't know how he puts up with me."

"He just told me he's been depressed."

Lisa looked sideways. "No wonder. I'd like Billy to live with you for a while. He'll need a nurse and a driver. I'll pay for it all. He's almost an invalid. He can't drive anymore. Hardly can walk."

"It doesn't help, Lisa, that he's two hundred pounds overweight."

"He promised me he'd go to Weight Watchers. But . . . the other thing, I just started construction at Bel Air. It'll be noisy. So . . ."

"It will be my total pleasure. Nicky and Billy like each other."

Lisa looked down at her hands. After a few seconds, she spoke softly, "Do you love her?"

He sipped his water, trying to follow her shifts. "Do I love . . . Michaela? I don't know. There are things about her I still don't know. I've made a mess of my relationships with women. I'd like one to work out."

Her voice shot up. "*Really*? And now you've finally got your son."

"I respected your choices, Lisa."

"No choice," Lisa muttered. "I couldn't have had kids even if I wanted to."

Johnny's mouth gaped open as he watched her drain her wine glass. She spoke as if she were wrapping up a meeting. "So then you'll take Billy?"

Johnny struggled for composure. "Uh . . . sure. Happy to. He'll be getting out of here, maybe Saturday. I'll set it up."

"Good." Lisa stood up, her moist eyes drilling down on Johnny. Twisting her face, she sobbed once and strode away.

CHAPTER THIRTY-THREE

Johnny and Gus played vigorous racquetball that night. They split games and agreed to defer the tiebreaker. The Jacuzzi soak chat was the key part of their friendship ritual. Gus gingerly lowered himself into the hot water. "So—how was the dinner with your ex-old lady?"

"Crazy. Tears, anger, calm talk, crazy talk. I told her the divorce made me rethink my life. She doesn't give a shit about my rethinking my life."

"I agree with her. I don't think anyone can 'rethink their life.'" His hands formed air quotes. "Life just comes at you. What's wrong with that?"

"Just once in my life I'd like to have control over my future. Or at least reshuffle the deck."

Gus shook his head. "Can't be done. Life just happens, dude. Plans fall apart once the first shot is fired, like Napoleon said. How do you make a life plan with a girlfriend like that in your bed? A stiff dick has but one plan."

Johnny laughed. "Women do have an effect."

"No shit, Sherlock. You recall I'm in LA 'cause of a woman. You know my pathetic story. That she up and left my ass, and here I sit, fifteen years later, soaking it in hot water with you."

"Why don't you date? You're not *that* much of an asshole."

"Hey, we're talking about *you*, not me! I *like* my life, though I'd like to get laid a little more often."

Gus asked questions about Lisa. Johnny was vague, distracted—after a few minutes, he glanced up at the clock. "Oops. Sorry. Gotta go meet my nephew up at the mansion. I guess we're moving back in." He reached for a towel. "Next week, let's play the tiebreaker."

"You got it, bro. Have a good week with our nation's finest."

***

After assisting on the lung surgery Tuesday morning, Johnny finally called his internist at the VA, Dr. David Minting, about the results from his government-required physical. Minting insisted Johnny come to his office ASAP. Johnny dressed and walked over.

"You've not been returning my calls."

"I know, David. Sorry, been busy."

"We're all busy. You have a high PSA, 9.3. You need a biopsy. This won't affect your employment here. It's not contagious, obviously. But you do need to take care of this."

Johnny's mouth went dry. He knew the increasing PSA reading indicated possible prostate cancer. Gus had said his prostate felt "rough." In Montana he learned that his father—the DNA match was positive—had metastatic prostate cancer. Johnny's heart sank. Most treatments impacted sexual performance.

"I'll take care of it, Dave. What do you think is going on?"

"PSA's a rough gauge. But if you ignore it, you may turn a manageable situation into an unmanageable one. Any cancer in your family?"

"My father had prostate cancer. He recently died. He was over eighty."

"Well, there you go. I'm sorry about your father."

***

Johnny jumped on his Harley to have lunch with Lisa's accountant, Tom Schultz, at CPK. He saw Schultz in a back booth and slid in.

"Tom, hi. I'm really interested to hear your story."

"Oh. Hi, Johnny. Let's order first." Schultz waved at a waiter.

Johnny ordered a cheese pizza and Schultz a salad. "So . . . ?"

"Oh. This is mainly a confession." Schultz's eyes sightlessly surveyed the room. "She had me snoop on you for years, Johnny. She was convinced you were seeing other women. That's the thing. She had me review your charge slips for hotels, meals, gifts."

"Lisa did? Seriously? Starting when?"

"In 2005. First, I felt awful, but I was sure you never saw other women or did anything secretive—that's how I justified it."

"So . . . go on."

"Oh. This is so uncomfortable. When that writer Gomez died, there was a written hospital report. Lisa learned about it I'm pretty sure from Dr. Poulos. He had told her you were seeing other women, and she believed it. She told me to get a copy of the report. You left one on your desk. I made a copy and gave it to her."

"Really? And then she leaked it to the *Times*! So it was Lisa!"

"She wanted to strike at you. She hated your passion for your work. Kept saying she felt abandoned. Her divorce threat was originally just to get your attention. And then one thing led to another."

"Kidding. She seemed so determined. I'm such an idiot!"

"She was livid you were so passive about the divorce. It confirmed you were seeing other women. Me and Pettker—she'd drink and rant at us. Then she'd put on her CEO face for the rest of the world, including you."

"How on earth did I miss all that?"

"Oh, you just assume the best of people, Johnny. She kept pushing me to 'dig up dirt.' I went through your wallet when you were in the gym once. I found the card for Michelle Powell. Michaela was written in."

Schultz was silent while lunch was served.

"When she saw the card, she flipped out, hired a private investigator. The PI found her real name—Poulos. She pushed the PI to find a connection with Arthur, which he did, somehow."

"God!" Johnny muttered. "Sorry. Go on."

"Oh, when the divorce become final, she started drinking to get drunk. In May, the PI told her you and Michaela were together at Benedict Cañon. She told Poulos, and Poulos called Michaela. Lisa was thrilled—she'd gotten rid of your girlfriend. There was still hope for her."

"Hope for Lisa? This is insane!"

"She and Poulos were working together now. I told her I was quitting--with the PI she didn't need me. She offered money if I'd sign a confidentiality agreement. I took the money. I'm violating that agreement today."

Johnny nodded.

Schultz's eyes were down. "I feel awful." He stirred his salad.

"Anything else, Tom?" Johnny had eaten two bites of pizza.

"Oh, yes. The main thing. I want to apologize to you, Johnny, for the snooping. By the way, I think Lisa's PI may have dug up something tricky about Michaela. That's the best I can offer, Johnny, a little heads-up. I don't think you've seen the end of this."

"Dug up what tricky something?" Johnny asked.

"Oh, Lisa mentioned a phony green card application."

***

After lunch, Johnny walked over to UC Cedars. His head was spinning, between his high PSA number and Schultz's disclosures. He needed the comfort of seeing Billy, who was sitting up in recovery, pink-cheeked, watching the History Channel. Johnny told Billy about the cancer diagnosis but not about the Schultz disclosures. Not yet.

"Why are you delaying, Johnny? Get the biopsy. What are you waiting for? Death?"

"No. I'd hoped . . ."

"Hoped for what?" When Billy mused about large concepts, his eyes had a gauzy, faraway aspect. When he dealt with earth-bound problems—other than his own—they had Wild Will's eagle aspect. "Use your common sense, Doctor!"

"I guess," mumbled Johnny.

"You know, Johnny, you always bring your problems to me just before you've pulled the trigger. My role, I guess, is to switch the safety off." Billy smiled and settled his head back into his pillow. "But what do I know about guns? I hate guns."

He closed his eyes tight. "I don't expect to live very long, Dr. Blood Moon. And that's just fine. But while I'm still here, I need you in my life. Please get the biopsy."

CHAPTER THIRTY-FOUR

Thanksgiving morning dawned bright and crisp in Beverly Hills—thin clouds drifted high in a pale-blue sky; the temperature promised to touch seventy before Michaela would remove the turkey from the oven.

Thus begins so-called winter in Los Angeles—the best weather months of the year. The days tend to be clear and cool unless the winds reverse and blow hot desert air west toward the ocean. Billy was explaining to Johnny that these were the "Santa Anas"—a corruption of the Spanish word for Satan—the devil winds, the crazy-making winds. The two friends sat together in the kitchen looking out the window at the brilliant day. Billy was waiting for Michaela to arrive to begin cooking dinner. Johnny was about to run over to the VA for a couple of hours.

It poured rain yesterday. The storms that roll down in waves from the northwest are another feature of LA's winter. But even rain carries a dividend: the *very* best days of the year are those that follow the scouring rain. The snowy peaks edging the LA basin become sharply visible, the air crystalline, the sky deeply blue—all transitory, startling, like human moods.

Billy's mood was improving. Discharged from the hospital eight days ago, he was living in the Wild Will Bell wing of the mansion, attended by his lively new bodyguard-cum-chauffeur, Antonio. Billy was using a motorized wheelchair—he had trouble walking because of his weight and atrophied leg muscles. As Johnny stood to leave, he asked Billy whether he was comfortable living in his father's former rooms.

Billy pondered. "I love being here with you and Nicky, but—you're right, this house is full of ghosts for me."

After Johnny departed, Billy and Antonio organized pots, pans, bowls, and condiments per Michaela's instructions taped to the fridge. Billy excitedly described today's dinner group for Antonio: Billy, Nicky, Michaela, Johnny, and Nicky's soccer friend Paco. Last Sunday, Nicky impulsively brought Paco up to the mansion. Billy, smitten with the young man, toured him through the house and impulsively invited him to Thanksgiving dinner.

***

Michaela's turkey came out of the oven golden and glistening at three thirty, to the applause of her all-male audience. Dinner was soon on the table. Michaela had added accent to every item. Over coffee, baklava, pumpkin pie, and contented smiles, Billy announced the verdict from his wheelchair, "A Greek success—truly delicious, Michaela."

She salaamed in thanks. Nicky laughed. "So Christmas decorations are already up on the light poles on Sunset. What a crazy place LA is. I looked at the weather channel—it's already snowing in Montana."

"We don't have Thanksgiving or snowflakes on lampposts in Greece," Michaela said. "LA *is* a crazy place. It's all about making you think you're someone else somewhere else doing something else. Who said 'there's no there, there'? It describes LA on a tee. I complain about Greece, but at least there's some there there."

"'To a tee, Michaela." Johnny whispered. "And that 'there there' thing was about Oakland." She shrugged.

Billy turned to Paco. "What about you, Paco? Any Thanksgiving traditions where you live?"

Paco was a small young man, with cropped black hair, brown skin, and coarse athletic good looks—he looked like a lightweight boxer. He seemed tense and sat away from the table. "Where I live? Not really. I've never had a meal like this. Where I live we really don't celebrate holidays." He picked up his napkin. "Maybe Christmas if there's a family. Don't mean to be rude, but I should go. My sister, she's getting off work soon, and it's just the two of us."

Michaela spoke, "Take some leftovers, Paco."

"Thanks, but I don't . . ."

"No, absolutely, dude!" Nicky said, standing up. "We'll give you a doggie bag for Teresa. You can have another Thanksgiving with her."

Paco stood. "Really? You're really nice people. I give thanks for that."

The boys went into the kitchen.

"He never knew his parents," Billy whispered to Johnny and Michaela. "He's a good bright kid. I'd like to help him out somehow. They live in a horrible part of the city."

The boys returned. Paco carried a brown paper bag. "Thank you all, so much." He seemed emotional.

"Johnny," Nicky said, "Paco has a question. Go ahead, ask him."

"Well . . . so, Doctor, I saw you have these books by Manuel Maria Gomez. Did you ever read those books?"

"Every one."

"Did you know him or anything?"

"I met him one time. He was my patient when he died."

"Seriously?" Paco looked startled.

"Why do you ask, Paco? Do you like his books?"

"Totally. I read his books over and over. I should go. Thank you again." He backed up toward the door.

"I'll walk you out," Nicky said. Billy, Michaela, and Johnny sat silent for a long moment after the boys left.

Johnny finally spoke, "Wow! What was *that* about?"

Michaela stood. "Wow is right. He's sweet, but he's so nervous he makes *me* nervous, like a dog that's . . . what's that word, Johnny?"

"You mean feral?"

"Yes. Like a feral dog. Can I pour coffee?"

Nicky returned. "He's fine, don't worry about Paco." He resumed his seat. "I'll have coffee, Michaela." He softly tapped the table. "Can I, uh . . . so I need to tell you a story. I wanted to wait till Paco left."

Johnny sat back, thinking about Paco and feeling a sense of dread.

CHAPTER THIRTY-FIVE

"This is why I have nightmares, still," Nicky said. "My last gig in the army was at an FOB near Pakistan on this road called A-Zero-One. It runs from Jalalabad over to Peshawar--the most dangerous road in the world, they say."

Johnny saw Nicky slip deeper into himself as he spoke. "My unit was on a steep hill we called 'No Booze' after Nabuz—a Pashtun village we leveled. Night before Thanksgiving we'd been up there three weeks. Weather sucked—cold and wet. There were fingers that ran off north and south. Otherwise it was straight down granite.

"Just before dawn, it's snowing, totally dark—boom! Rockets come in. Our guns shoot back—this goes on, back and forth. Loud, loud. They lob in mortar rounds. *Krump!* Those are nasty. Rockets are mostly noise."

"I hear mortars are insidious," Billy was fully engaged.

Nicky ignored Billy's comment. "Sappers come along the fingers to probe our perimeter. They're like totally mowed down. Now it's lighter, but there's still a cold fog. I can hear our air support, but it's zero visibility. We take casualties. One guy's hurt real bad. I bring him to my bunker. He hands me a picture of his family. I keep moving around, looking for wounded guys. A rocket knocks me ass backward. I check my eyes, my nuts—I'm fine."

Michaela's face tightened. "God!"

"More probes come—they get wiped out again, then it's quiet, then more incoming, more probes. Goes on like that for hours. I'm hunkered in the bunker. My badly wounded guy dies—I was away. When I come back and find him dead, I close his eyes and sit him up. I needed the company.

"It's Thanksgiving. I look at my dead hole mate, I wonder what Thanksgiving was like at *his* home in Alabama. I look at his family, his mother. I'm the only person on earth who knows he's dead. Bobby was his name. I feel hugely responsible. All of a sudden I'm crying."

Nicky stopped to settle himself. He put his hands to his cheeks, took a breath, and blew it out slowly. He continued softly. "I vowed then—I said to Bobby—'Dude, if I get out of this shithole alive, I promise to tell our story next Thanksgiving.' So here I am, doing my duty to Bobby.

154

"So suddenly these jerks are running around in our camp. I hear the sergeant shouting and then pop, pop—gunfire. Somehow a few Taliban climbed up the sides of the fucking rock—impossible. They run around shouting '*Allahu Akbar*'and shit. Then it just stops. I peek up out of my hole, and there's this, like, tall Osama Bin Laden guy walking toward me with his Kalashnikov hanging from his shoulder. All I have is this old .45 I bought on the black market. I slip the safety off."

Nicky reached for his apple cider. His hands trembled, and he spilled a few drops. Johnny quietly wicked them up with his napkin.

"Thanks. So . . . so this guy in his robe and turban and doggy little beard, he's standing there, maybe ten meters away. His AK's still down by his side. I can see he's scared shitless. His buddies are all dead, so he's lost. There's this big lump under his robe.

"We look at each other for a long time, and he half turns like he's going to leave. I shoot him, and it spins him around. He, like, stares at me, holding his shoulder, angry, like I let him down. I shoot again, he falls over. After a minute, I creep over to him, thinking I'll find explosives. Instead, I find an aid pack like mine. He's a fucking medic!

"I start to treat his wounds. He has these big brown eyes. He shakes his head. He doesn't want me to fix him. His collarbone is shattered, but I've seen worse. There's this metal tag on his aid bag, which I rip off—still have it, keep it with my own dog tags.

"It's all over. We find out later that hundreds of them got hung up climbing the cliff. Only a few made it up to the top, including my medic."

Nicky eyes drifted off into space.

"So what happened to your medic, Nicky?" Billy asked.

"Oh. So the choppers come in. Captain and I, we're the last to leave. My medic's barely alive. Captain's like, 'what the hell, bring him.' I carry him to the chopper, and he's in my lap bleeding. As I carry him down the ramp at base camp, he just—dies. Never forget it—he goes slack in my arms and his bowels let go. This deep sadness runs through me. Still does when I remember."

Nicky touched his eyes with his napkin.

"Look at me, I'm all teary again. When I hand the body over to the navy doctor, I try to hide my crying, but he sees it. He just nods. I could see in his eyes, he understood I was like 'it coulda been me.'"

"My god. I don't get it, Nicky," Billy said, looking drained. "What would possess a young man like that to climb a cliff to go to his certain death? It can't be just ideology." Michaela, mesmerized, was shaking her head back and forth. Nicky vigorously rubbed his face.

"Whuf! No, not ideology at all. It's all about your buddies. You do crazy shit in war because you don't want to let your buddies down. That's why that guy went slack when he saw his buddies were all dead. He was alone with his god. Alone, it makes no sense."

"Peer pressure, peer regard, that's what makes people do crazy things," Billy said. "Plenty of books about how soldiers—gang members too, I'm thinking of the world poor Paco faces—will do most *anything* to earn the respect of their comrades. Even Weight Watchers, how that works, at the risk of trivializing the subject, that's all based on peer pressure. You don't want to step up on that scale and lose face in front of everyone. The Japanese built a civilization around face—peer pressure."

Nicky's composure was returning. "Same with AA. The fact you're part of a group, it's very powerful. By the way, Paco's not a gang member."

"I heard him say that," Billy said. "He's very courageous. But he worries if he keeps turning them down, they'll mess with his sister. I'd really like to help them get out."

After a pause, Johnny spoke, "That's what messed me up too," Johnny said. "Peer pressure. When I was in med school, becoming a poverty doc was not cool. What *was* cool was to get a prestigious residency. Then to get hired by a place like UC Cedars. The applause! The peer group kept changing, but my craving for peer respect never ceased. Until Gomez. Suddenly I didn't care what people thought."

"Yes, same thing, Johnny, in Afghanistan." Nicky was animated. "Units kept changing. Didn't matter. I wanted to be respected by my buddies, whoever they were, my best friend or the guy who reported in yesterday."

"Maybe not an external thing at all," said Billy. "Maybe something innate. A craving for respect, like we have for food or sex."

"May I raise an example of what you're saying?" Michaela asked.

"Please do," Billy said. They were spaced around Lisa's elegant dinner table, designed for twenty people. The candles were fizzling and smoking. Johnny stood to brighten the room lights and pour water.

"Celebrity." Michaela paused to let Johnny pour. "Thanks. Celebrity's an addiction too. I've seen nice people turn into monsters, maybe like your nice army friends who turn into killers, Nicky. It's like people recognize me on the street. I feel high when it happens. I used to worry about publicity because of my crazy past, now I worry about it messing up my future. I'm probably saying too much."

"Not at all!" Billy exclaimed. Conversations like this were his elixir. "I don't know about your past, Michaela, but I do understand your concern about your future. How on earth can a, say, a George Clooney or an Angelina Jolie, how do they have a normal life while everyone's telling them they hung the moon?"

"I'd like to try it out," Nicky said with a sly smile. "Being driven around in a limo and everything. I'd be down for that."

"You're down for it, Nicky, because of the girls throwing their room keys at you," Michaela said tartly.

"Busted!" Nicky said, throwing his napkin in the air and catching it.

"Great subject, though," Billy said. "I love the comparison of celebrity with a kid charging a machine gun nest to impress his buddies—a kid who wouldn't hurt a fly back home. I imagine, Michaela, you can't believe what anyone tells you now that you're on billboards. You're no longer a human being—you're a confection, a divinity, a font of opportunity and redemption. Everyone wants to touch your hem. Beware, though. Some day, the worst may happen—when you look in the mirror and see *yourself* as divine. Your real self goes away. That's when you're dead."

"That is not going to happen to me. I'm getting out." She glanced at Johnny, who shrugged. "I want to be like Johnny—not caring about what other people think. Except maybe friends like you."

"I cared for years," Johnny said, looking at Michaela. "Cared deeply. I wasn't a Hollywood star, but I was a local celebrity. Addicted to myself. I dressed the part, drove the car, craved the applause, looked in the mirror, saw the halo. I married Lisa to feed my craving. Then I got lucky—life slapped me. And then I met you, Michaela."

After a moment, Billy muttered, "Lisa, poor stepmom, sitting in a hotel room all by herself on Thanksgiving. I feel bad."

Johnny raised his eyebrows. Michaela studied the smoking candle. Billy clasped his hands on his huge stomach and leaned back. "So, okay, here we all sit, lady and gentlemen. Johnny, what I meant in the hospital by 'progress'? That was about me getting slapped by life. I hereby announce I am no longer in denial about my food addiction."

Nicky clapped his hands. "Yo, Billy! You're on your way, big guy!"

"And there's little old me," Michaela said. "Facing the *prospect* of addiction—because of a stupid film. I think it's gonna be a hit, boys."

"So do I, Mika," Nicky said. "Mega hit. Get ready for rehab."

The house phone rang. Billy and Johnny looked at each other. Very few people had the house number. "I'd better get that." Johnny ran up the steps into the kitchen.

"Hello?"

"Johnny?" It was a woman's voice.

Johnny whispered, "Yes, this is Johnny. Who's this?"

A man spoke, "Johnny, it's Mike and Ora! You're not answering your cell. What's the whisper for? You dealing drugs on Thanksgiving?"

Johnny spoke with relief, "I just thought . . ."

"I know what you thought, Johnny," Ora said. "She just called me from London. Dead drunk. Middle of the night there. I had to talk her out of calling you. Anyway, it reminded me we hadn't properly thanked you and Michaela for the lovely movie and dinner. So here we are giving thanks on Thanksgiving."

CHAPTER THIRTY-SIX

Friday morning was cool and fragrant in Beverly Hills. Nicky and Michaela rose early to run up in the hills. Johnny passed, saying he needed to talk with Billy. He had been secretly relieved when Michaela had begged off lovemaking last night. Still passing blood from the biopsy Wednesday, he was worried about his ability to perform.

Over breakfast, Billy told Johnny about his latest book project. He waggled a fat finger in the air. "*God's Progress*. That's the working title. It's a concept that's been very much on my mind. It's about how our universe progressed, if you will, from a singularity at the Big Bang, an infinitesimal speck, to a vast, uniform cloud of expanding gas, eventually developing wrinkles, which became stars and galaxies and planets, which then bred organic life forms including roses and cheetahs and Ludwig van Beethoven and Jerry Seinfeld. Isn't that a history of positive *progress* . . . ? So how does blind randomness produce positive progress?"

"Well, let me know when you figure it all out. Maybe it'll shed light on my own random life."

"Ah, yes, cases. It always comes down to cases, Johnny. As it should. As it should."

***

The next day, Saturday, dawned overcast. The cooling marine layer had crept in from the ocean. Johnny and Michaela were waking up in the upstairs master bed, arms and legs tangled in silky nakedness. Tomorrow she would fly to Las Vegas to film promotional videos.

Michaela smiled catlike, and Johnny kissed her nose.

"Morning," he whispered, absorbing her animal smell. He loved the contrast between her white skin and black hair.

Stretching, she gently withdrew from Johnny's arms to prop herself on an elbow. "Morning, you."

158

"Where you going?"

She gazed down at him. "Just here. You've been so patient with me. I'm not a very easy girlfriend."

"Oh? Say more. I reserve my rebuttal time until I hear the full prosecution case."

"Oh, stop," she said, touching his lips with her finger. "Be serious. I want to talk about something serious."

"Okay."

"It's just . . . that I don't do well with men who come on strong. I know I'm not what you're used to. You like to initiate, like in Cabo."

"Is there a reason? For your needing to be in control?" Johnny looked up at the wainscoting. "Look at that ceiling."

"What about it?"

"The trim up there looks like little eyeballs. I learned recently Lisa spied on me for years. She thought I was cheating and hired a detective."

"That's totally creepy!"

"That's how she learned Arthur was your dad. Through her PI."

Michaela was silent.

Johnny rolled over to face her. "I had dinner with Lisa in the hospital after Billy's bypass. I was trying to mend fences. She's a mess."

"She still loves you," Michaela said sourly. "I have a rival. I went through that business with my retired executive boyfriend. His ex-wife still loved him. I felt her bitterness, even though I never met her."

"You don't have a rival, Michaela. She doesn't love me, she hates me. Because I abandoned her, unquote. Is love the same thing as hate?"

"They're related." Michaela said. "Why are we talking about Lisa?"

"Those eyeballs up there. Sorry. I need to call Bo about the detective. Jan and Bo usually have a sense of what Lisa's up to."

"January and Lisa are friends?"

"Jan stays in touch with her. Lisa doesn't have normal lady friends."

"She's like me. I hope someday I can have normal lady friends. I'd like to be a Valley wife, like January, with kids and a garden club."

They lay silent for a few seconds.

"Sorry to go off on Lisa," Johnny said. "My timing's not always the best. You were saying earlier about your need to control?"

"I'm getting used to your poor timing. Yes, I want to explain why I need to control things. Now don't interrupt."

Michaela half rolled away from Johnny toward the bedside table. She spoke rapidly, as if trying not to lose courage. "Farakos saw me when I was fifteen. I was pretty. He told my father he wanted me. My father resisted at first. But Farakos threatened to reveal what he did for the colonels as a young doctor. Farakos was the Socialist interior minister. He used to call my father Mengele."

She sighed. "This is so hard. So my father gave me to Farakos like a piece of meat when I was fifteen. I wanted to die but didn't know how. Then Farakos threw me out on the street. He found out . . . I wasn't a virgin, and he beat me, wanting to know who I'd been with. He raped me and beat me again. Over and over."

"That's awful! Turn toward me." Johnny gently touched her shoulder.

Tears fell sideways out of Michaela's eyes.

"You weren't a virgin at fifteen?" Johnny asked.

Michaela turned toward Johnny. "I had sex once with another teenager. Stupid. Doesn't matter. But that's not what I told Farakos."

Michaela's voice caught. She reached for a tissue and touched her eyes. "What I told him . . . was that my *father* had raped me. I lied. I hated my father so much. That's when Farakos threw me out. Then he went after my father. Forced him out of Greece. My father never knew I said that about raping me."

Johnny was up on his elbow now. "My god! No wonder . . ." He saw the little girl peeking up, wanting comfort. He touched her hair. "Hey, don't hide. You were just an angry kid. That's all the weapon you had. Not sure if I deserve to know all this."

"I *want* you to know, Johnny Blood. It's part of me. These are the things . . . can you understand now . . . ?" She sobbed into her pillow.

Johnny sat up against the headboard. "And now I get why you apologized to your father that day in the hospital."

"Yes. Do you also get why I've lived my life like a refugee, feeling there was no safe place for me on earth?"

"I do. Can . . . do you think . . . ?" He was searching for the right question.

Michaela choked out her words. "Johnny, don't say anything . . . please. I need to move away from my father and Farakos . . . even poor Lisa Bell . . . and Hollywood too. All the ghosts, all the crazy people who want to hurt me, to use me. I want *so much* to get away, with you. To a safe place . . ."

She froze for a moment. Suddenly she kicked the bedclothes off the bed and pulled him on top of her. Her determined strength surprised him. His compliant gentleness surprised her. They made sweet love.

***

Johnny had to fly to Oakland early Sunday on VA business. Gus's call caught him at Burbank airport. Gus apologized for bothering him on a Sunday. "Knowing you, you probably got to the airport two hours early."

Johnny laughed. "Not that early. But go ahead. What's up?"

"Tell me what happened with your biopsy? I don't trust you on this."

"The follow-up meeting is tomorrow afternoon."

"What's up with that? I told the guy to set it up for Friday!"

"I moved it to Monday. A day or two doesn't matter, Gus."

"Fuck! Aren't you curious if you have cancer? Jeez!"

Johnny was annoyed. "I'm on it, Gus! What else? That's not why you called."

Gus was quiet for a long moment.

"You still there, Gus? Hello?"

"Still here. Would you mind if I asked Lisa out on a date? Your Lisa Bell?"

Johnny scrambled to organize his thoughts and feelings. "Hold on—picking myself up off the floor. That may actually be cool, Gus. But it's *real* complicated."

"She gets back from London today. I'm supposed to see her tonight at a fund-raiser, and I was gonna ask her out. I figure she'll be jet-lagged, so she just might say yes. I wanted to ask you before I did it. I could delay it."

Johnny felt confused. "No, don't delay it, go ahead. I appreciate your asking, but she's not my Lisa Bell anymore. She likes you. She'll say yes."

"More me liking her, I suspect. So I'm single, she's single . . . oops, hospital call coming in. Let's talk tomorrow. Racquetball?"

"Still healing from the biopsy. I'll watch you take a Jacuzzi bath."

"I'll call you." Gus hung up abruptly.

Johnny, full of feeling, pondered the message on his cell: CALL ENDED.

CHAPTER THIRTY-SEVEN

On Sunday night, with Michaela off to her Vegas shoot and Nicky off with friends, Johnny sat with Billy in the mansion's kitchen nibbling leftover turkey. Johnny had decided to tell Billy about Lisa's spying program. Billy listened quietly, head down. When Johnny finished talking, Billy backed his wheelchair away from the table. "Why'd you tell me this? So that I'd tell Lisa?" After a moment, Billy looked up. His face had softened. "Thank you for one thing, though. For taking me in here with all that's going on in your life."

"Nicky loves that you're around."

"He's so great. I envy you having a son. Maybe I'll adopt Paco."

"So why do you like Paco so much?"

"He's a beautiful kid who needs a break." He rotated his wheelchair a half turn. "Time for bed."

As Billy rolled away, Johnny pulled out his cell. He needed to tell Bo about Lisa's snooping program. Bo asked questions about Michaela's past, and Johnny reluctantly told him about her youthful marriage and child.

"Johnny, it's very common for people running away from their past to omit things on their visa application. Probably Arthur was her sponsor and made her lie. I have a law school friend, we're very close, director of the immigration service—ICE—in DC. I can talk with him."

"Don't . . ."

"Hold on. Hear me out. He can check her file on his computer. I've been through this before, and he owes me—I've done him favors."

"Michaela will kill me . . ."

"Then don't tell her! You *gotta* fix this. Here's the problem. The movie's a hit, Michaela's a star, Lisa gets drunk and calls the ICE hotline or the press. You just told me Lisa has a history of anonymous leaking."

"I don't like operating behind Michaela's back," Johnny said.

"Don't worry about it. This guy's my close friend. If he gives his blessing like I expect—the marriage was illegal, the kid was given up at birth—I'll sit down with Michaela and go over it."

"So just one more secret I'm sitting on. What about Lisa?"

"We'll talk to her about the PI—not so P anymore. I can scare her—these guys skirt the law all the time. Let's focus on immigration right now."

***

Gus and Johnny met at the Jacuzzi Monday night. Johnny sat on the ledge. Gus shouted over the jets, "What's up? How went the biopsy?"

"Not good. I have prostate cancer."

"Shit. How bad?"

"Not bad. Gleason score is low. The plan is watchful waiting."

"Are you okay, friend?"

"I don't know. Maybe a little scared. I've never been sick, except for broken bones. I'm a surgeon, so I know to stay away from surgeons. Now I have to tell Michaela. But not right away. And Nicky."

"Will she be pissed if she finds out you sat on your cancer?"

Johnny smiled. "You have the absolute worst sense of humor. I think she'll be fine. I'm sitting on a *lot* of nasty secrets right now."

Gus cupped his ear. "Anything juicy?"

"You might ask your girlfriend, Lisa. How'd *that* go last night?"

"Went fine, we have a date. Can't call her my girlfriend yet. You have things to tell me about her?"

Johnny rubbed his cheek. "You trust *me*, right, Gus?"

"Trust you? You're incapable of deceit. One of your problems."

"Lisa thought I was seeing other women before the divorce. When I started seeing Michaela, she hired a PI to dig up dirt on her."

"Oh, *that's* annoying. Why would she want this dirt?"

"Take a guess. When is your date with Lisa?" Johnny asked.

"Saturday the eleventh—she has to go to London this week. Dinner up at your old house in Bel Air. Fancy, fancy."

"That's the day after the movie premiere. Michaela wants me to walk with her down the red carpet. I'm thinking I'll slip in a side door."

"Why the side door, Johnny? Don't you want to be on the front page of *Variety*? Leonardo di Blood. Pop, pop, go the flashbulbs."

"Exactly what I *don't* want."

"Because of Lisa?"

"In part. Also, what's the point? I think I should shut up now."

Gus's face took on a soulful look. "You mean there's more? The older I get, the more bizarre life is. I just want a little female companionship, and now there's all this crap. Secrets, conspiracy, spies, obsessions."

"Lisa has a good heart. Maybe you can help her."

"I just want a girlfriend. I don't want a stealth mission. Oh lordy."

***

When Johnny returned to the mansion that night, he found an agitated Nicky. They sat in the kitchen with soft drinks. "It's about Paco, Johnny. He's good with you knowing this, but only you."

"What is it?"

"So Paco's half-brother is a big gangbanger. Dude's in prison now, but he keeps calling Paco. I guess they can get cell phones. He wants Paco to join his gang. Paco's worried about his half sister, who's not related to the half brother, what they might do to her."

"That's awful."

"Apparently normal gang shit. But that's not the main thing. I remember when Manuel Gomez died, you were totally bummed. So much so you stopped operating? Then later, you got your mojo back? I guess something happened. Can you say what it was?"

"It was . . . I learned it wasn't necessarily my fault that Gomez died. I have to be careful. Why do you ask?"

"Well, so Paco wants to get out of the 'hood. The half brother hates it that Paco's smart, reads books and everything, that he wants out of the life. He knows how he loves Manuel Gomez."

"Yes?"

"So he told Paco that Manuel Gomez was murdered. Can that be?"

Johnny was stunned. "Uh, theoretically possible. What else?"

"That's all I know. Paco thinks there's something to it. He knows more, but . . . it's death in that world to snitch."

"I need to talk to Paco," Johnny said.

"I thought you'd say that. I'm thinking maybe if Billy would help them relocate to where the homeboys can't find them, you know? Maybe there's a chance Paco would talk to you once he felt safe. He trusts you, Johnny."

"Because of our Gomez connection?"

"Maybe. Maybe because of what I tell him about you."

"What do you tell him about me?"

"Don't worry about it."

Johnny grimaced. "So do I just sit on this information?"

"Why not?"

"Well . . . let's say that someone did get to Gomez. I'm not saying it happened. So that hypothetical person is still out there, maybe getting ready to do someone else."

"I hear you, Johnny. I'll get moving with Billy and Paco."

CHAPTER THIRTY-EIGHT

Michaela, back from Vegas, was uncharacteristically tense about the approaching film premiere. She strongly opposed Johnny's side-door entry plan for the premiere. It was her big moment, she said, and she wanted him on the red carpet with her. Johnny dug in. It was their first serious quarrel, and they didn't have the time or tools to resolve it. Michaela called the night before the event with an ultimatum. She sounded half hysterical. "I don't have time to argue! I want you with me! Forget the trip north if you don't come." She hung up.

That night, Johnny decided to give in. He was afraid of losing her. He called first thing in the morning. "Michaela, I . . ."

"It's all about Lisa, isn't that it, Johnny? I've been *so* good! I don't want to be good anymore. This is our time. I want you with me!"

"I hear you—you're right—I'll do it." He cautioned that he had a surgery at noon that he couldn't move. He thought he could get to her hotel lobby by no later than five thirty.

Michaela was silent for a long minute. Then she said, "Thank you. I'm sorry. I just need you with me. I'm a little scared, that's all."

***

Michaela had pressed the studio to hire Nicky as her body person. Nicky was pumped. "Woo-hoo! Sign me up, Mika!" His duties were to drive her and Johnny in a studio limo from the hotel to the theater—Nicky was ignorant of the lovers' quarrel—then to shepherd them down the red carpet into the theater, get them seated on time, and finally, drive the getaway SUV after the premiere, shed of the swarming paparazzi. Nicky claimed he hadn't had so much fun since Spain.

***

166

After his noon surgery at the VA, Johnny found himself facing an emergency. A colleague, a young navy doctor he had been mentoring, had a heart attack of his own and needed emergency surgery. Johnny had to do it. He called and texted Michaela, but she had turned her phone off. He finally called Nicky. "Nicky, I can't reach Michaela. I have a patient emergency here, and I won't be able to meet Michaela at the hotel like I said. Can you get word to her? She's gonna be pissed."

"Why is she gonna be pissed if you have an emergency?"

"Long story. Just let her know—tell her I'll get there soon as I can."

***

Iconic Grauman's Chinese Theater is a hideous horned dragon of a building sitting on sleazy, mixed-use Hollywood Boulevard. If not for the celebrity handprints and footprints pressed into the concrete, the theater would have been razed long ago.

When Michaela's limo slid up to the curb at 7:00 p.m., Nicky emerged first. The crowd pressed in as he handed Michaela out of the vehicle. As she arranged her sleek dress and her smile, she whispered to him, "Get me through this, dude." These were the first words she'd uttered since Nicky gave her Johnny's message in the hotel lobby.

Nicky cleared a path like a down lineman. "Stand clear please. Thank you." He was astonished at the crowd's breathless response. He peeked back. She was radiant, floating through the flashes—her smile had never been sweeter, but her eyes were elsewhere.

***

The 1920s lobby, a pastiche of geegaws and faded colors, was packed with men wearing women's scarves and women wearing men's hats. Johnny arrived just as the film was about to begin. He saw Nicky's shining eyes. Johnny grabbed his arm. "Nicky! Where's Michaela?"

"Hey, Johnny. Is this epic or what? I met Adam Sandler and Owen Wilson and the guys who wrote *The Double* . . ."

"Where's Michaela?" Johnny's voice was husky with emotion.

"Over there, middle of that crowd. So I have to get you two guys seated in five minutes. Come with me." He dove into the scrum.

"Johnny!" Michaela reached for him. Her eyes were smiling. "I want you to meet David, my friend that I've told you so much about."

He shook hands with a stocky bald man whose bright blue eyes crinkled warmly. "Hey, Dr. Blood. Some madhouse, huh?"

Before Johnny could respond, Nicky grabbed their arms. "Sorry, time to go to our seats." He marched them through light applause to the front of the theater. Michaela smiled and waved. Nicky sat between them.

"I'm so sorry I'm late," Johnny said to Michaela, behind Nicky's head. "A colleague got very sick . . ."

She reached across and touched his arm. "It's fine. I know you tried. You okay? You seem grumpy."

"Just hate to be late. He's a kid I'm close to . . . and this thing is . . . *insane!*"

"Totally," she whispered, smiling to someone behind him. She waved down the row. She turned toward Johnny and stage-whispered, "Most of these people are nice, but they turn into werewolves at things like this. Like I did last night with you. Over there is the lead and his mother. Sweet old lady."

Johnny, feeling relieved, turned to look. "She looks familiar."

The lights dimmed.

***

After the film, the audience stood and applauded, all eyes on Michaela. She stood and shyly bowed. As the applause subsided, Johnny turned to Nicky. "So . . . ?"

"Michaela has to hang minimum a half hour. Then she'll hit the john. There's a secret exit door. We'll join you at the car. Then home. Zip, zip."

"So it's home now?" Michaela asked archly, looking at a small mirror.

Nicky grinned. "More home than your sofa, Mika. Guy needs a home. You said you were moving out of that big ass hotel weeks ago."

"Have to be flexible in Hollywood." People were converging on her. "Here we go again." She stood and started shaking hands.

Nicky held out keys to Johnny. "You can go to the car—black Escalade, northeast corner of the lot. We'll be forty minutes with luck."

***

Their luck was poor—an hour passed before they emerged. Johnny had gone out to the car after chatting briefly with the lead's mother, a baffled blue-haired lady who was once his patient. Outside, Johnny sat in the vehicle, scrolling through his e-mails. His sick colleague managed to send one saying that he was out of the woods and that he hoped Johnny enjoyed the film. How did he do that? He felt a profound sense of gratitude.

He saw them approaching, swarmed by photographers. Nicky drove the SUV slowly through the flashes. In spite of efforts to divert the frantic photographers, two full SUVs followed them out. As Nicky sped through sketchy sections of Hollywood trying to shake them, Johnny and Michaela sat in the back, eyes closed, holding hands. They had dissolved their differences with a few simple words and an easy kiss. Johnny was amazed at the strength of their reconciliation. It told him that the fundamentals were solidly in place.

It was a ragged troupe that arrived at the mansion early Saturday morning.

***

On Sunday afternoon, Bo called Johnny with news about Michaela's green card situation. His ICE friend had reviewed her 2002 application and said the omissions were a nonissue. Her green card was solid. Johnny promised Bo he'd tell all this to Michaela as soon as he could. "She's been off doing interviews. What about Lisa?"

"Ach! Not so good. January spoke with her. She now knows you know about her PI. I guess Billy told her too. She . . . kinda lost it on the phone with Jan. Now she's not returning our calls."

***

Johnny performed three demanding surgeries Monday at the VA. Googling on his breaks, he saw that *Why We Love* had dominated the weekend box office. At the end of the day, feeling energized, Johnny rode his Harley to UC Cedars for a cafeteria dinner with Gus in lieu of racquetball. Gus reported that he had strained his back over the weekend. They went through the line and sat in a corner.

"You tell Michaela yet about your cancer?" Gus asked.

"We're driving north Wednesday. I'll tell her tomorrow."

"It's so unlike you to delay. You been through this a thousand times."

"Different when it's about yourself. It's . . . she's not had an easy life. She doesn't need a husband who can't have sex."

"That's just a tiny possibility. Show a little vulnerability. They like that."

Johnny tossed his head. "Truth be told, Gus, there's not a great track record at this table on the subject of handling ladies in stressful situations."

"I resemble that remark! But—hey, you way underestimate yourself, dude. You do, you know. You're . . . better now. You've progressed. Anyway, she either loves you or she doesn't. Time to call her hand."

"This is not poker," Johnny said. "But I am feeling a little more confident that this is gonna work."

"Never in doubt. Now, new subject. Tell me about the premiere. Your girlfriend is sure photogenic. It was fun seeing Nicky running interference."

"Nicky was in hog heaven. Me, I hated every minute of it. We had our first fight—I didn't want to walk on the red carpet. I gave in, but then I ended up being late anyway because of an emergency. She was totally great about it, thank god. But at the premiere, I've never been so out of my element. All these suits jerking each other off."

Gus laughed. "Always wondered what that world was like. So it's just as much bullshit as anything else?"

"Way more. Now tell me about your date with Miss Lisa."

Gus's face became solemn. "So I show up Saturday at your old house on the golf course, all cleaned up, roses in my hand. Lisa was lovely. She didn't drink at all. Okay, whatever. She didn't mention the premiere—the press coverage wasn't till Sunday morning. So except for a strange phone call last night, which I'll talk about in a minute, I don't have much to report."

"Putting on her best face for her new boyfriend."

"Her best face is very good, as you well know. We had a lovely, civilized evening. She spoke about a heart research project in the UK. She wants to involve UC Cedars—so there was a business angle—she'll finance it if we opt in, which I'm thinking, why the hell not?"

"She's very sharp when she's not being weird."

"Not weird at all. Didn't take a drink, didn't ask about you, which I half suspected she'd drill me about you."

"That's good, I guess."

"So . . . we have this nice candlelight dinner, retire to the den, then a little canoodle, and she—I hope this is okay to tell you, Johnny—she takes me by the hand, and we . . . uh . . . ."

Johnny laughed. "Retire to the bedroom, where you plank her."

"Exactly. Or she planks me. Let's say . . . she was enthused. Afterward, I fall asleep in the hoary tradition of older gentlemen postcoitus."

Johnny laughed. "Is that how you strained your back?"

"That'll be my secret. Anyway, I had to get out early. She got up with me, fixed breakfast, all wifeylike."

"You're way ahead of me. Didn't know till just now she could cook."

"The coffee was thin."

Johnny laughed again. "You're used to that hospital mud. But you said she called you last night?"

"Oh, boy! She was tired or maybe a touch tipsy. Or both."

"She mention the film?" Johnny asked.

"No, but she was sure honked off about something. She needed to tell me what a torment her life is, how her friends have abandoned her. A different Lisa. It was pretty unsettling. This is one lonely woman."

"I think that's at the heart of it. Loneliness."

"Maybe. Don't have a clue what's next. I really like her, Johnny. I hope that's okay. And now, there's this research proposal. This is an attractive project she's putting in my lap."

"Not the only thing she's putting in your lap, I warrant."

Gus slapped the table. "Definitely! *Not* to be understated! Say, does she know we talk like this?"

"Not from me. Lisa seems to have a selective handle on reality."

"So she doesn't know we're gossip girls? Shit. It's probably the end of my fledgling sex life once she finds out."

"She won't find that out from me, Gus."

Gus hesitated, searching for words. "I *do* . . . I do have something to tell you, though . . ."

Johnny closed his eyes. "You're gonna tell me she's amazing in bed?"

"You devil! How'd you know I was gonna say that?"

"Uh . . . experience maybe?"

Chapter Thirty-Nine

Johnny told Michaela about his cancer diagnosis Tuesday morning. "There's no good time for this, but . . ." He spoke haltingly, watching her face.

She blanched and listened stiffly, trying to comprehend. "I don't know anything about cancer. Are you going to die?"

"Not gonna die. They caught it early. It could be dormant for years. They're very good at managing it."

She asked him how *he* felt about it. Her question surprised him—he had been focusing on the feelings of others. He said he didn't know how he felt; he wasn't used to being a patient. Johnny picked up his coffee cup.

"I'm so sorry, Johnny. I really don't know what to say. This all feels so, you know, formal, so like out-of-body." After a pause, she said she wanted to go for a walk alone. "Up the hill. Just to think."

He touched her cheek. "Go walk. I need to tell Nicky, and then I have to go to work. I'll be home later." She glanced at him once and strode out.

***

Johnny sat quietly for a few minutes. Then he stood and walked back to Nicky's bedroom. Nicky was on his bed pulling on his socks for a run. "Johnny, I hope it's cool that Brent and I are looking for an apartment together for when I start at Santa Monica College in January. I'm sure I'll be back here a lot."

"Yes, of course, it's fine. But I have something else to talk to you about." He sat. "I'll dive right in. I've been diagnosed with prostate cancer."

In contrast to Michaela, Nicky groaned, fell backward on the bed, thrashed, and struggled not to cry. "Wow, cancer!"

"Yes, but it's under control, Nicky. They're very good at managing this particular kind."

"But, still . . ." Tears trickled down his cheeks. "I can't lose you, Johnny. I'm not ready for that."

"You're not going to lose me. Not for a long time." After ten minutes of fitful conversation, Johnny said he had to go to work. "I told Billy. He can talk to you about the technical side, if you're interested. I'll be home tonight. I just told Michaela too."

**

Nicky decided to run after all, hoping it would clear his head. A scant fifty yards out, he saw Michaela coming down the hill. She didn't see him until he said, "Hey." She froze like a deer. Her face was wet with tears. She stared at him with wide eyes, as if he were a threat. He thought she was never more beautiful. "Johnny told you," Nicky said, offering a small towel.

Michaela accepted the towel and dried her face, nodding. As she handed the towel back to Nicky, she collapsed into his arms, sobbing.

**

In December 2010, the Benedict Cañon mansion was a massive horseshoe with its open end north toward the hills. The main house closed the horseshoe on the south. The two wings bracketed a long lap pool culminating in a circular hot tub at the north end. The running trail began north of the hot tub across a hedge at the base of the hills and climbed rapidly uphill.

At this time, Billy Bell was living in the east wing. His suite consisted of a large bedroom, a bathroom, and a den. Nicky's smaller bedroom was at the tip of the west wing. He had recently moved out of the apartment over the garage. Johnny and Michaela's vast bedroom suite was on the second floor of the main house.

The pool furniture had been pulled back to accommodate Billy's morning walks around the lap pool, prescribed by Gus to strengthen his leg muscles. He was passing around the south end of the pool when he saw Nicky and Michaela coming down the hill trail, leaning on each other. As they stepped around the hedge, Billy raised his cane in a Lear-like gesture. His voice boomed. "Welcome, warriors! I spy an excuse to cease this stupid walking I'm supposed to do. Confusion to all doctors!"

Ignoring Billy's flourish, Nicky led Michaela to a chaise by the hot tub. She sat, sighed, and put her fists to her eyes. Nicky hovered. Billy approached along the west side of the pool. "You kids okay? You look like you just survived a car crash. Can I do anything?"

"Billy, do me a big favor." Nicky stood. "Stop cracking jokes and wait here with Michaela while I go get water." He ran off.

"Let me guess what happened," Billy said, sitting. "I bet Johnny finally told you about his cancer. And you went for a walk to clear your head. And you ran into Nicky, who was probably doing the same thing. And it's hitting you both pretty hard."

Michaela squeezed an eye open and nodded twice. Color had drained from her face. Nicky ran up with cold water bottles and a towel for Michaela. He sat and twisted the bottles open. "What were you saying, Billy?"

"I said I see that Johnny finally got around to telling you. He's been so worried how you'd react. I've read a lot about prostate cancer since he told me he was going in for the biopsy. I think I can offer you both some comfort. If you don't mind the facts."

Michaela stared at Billy. She swung her legs to the ground, sat forward, and toweled off her wet face. "Okay." Her voice was hoarse. "What are the facts?"

Billy held forth for fifteen minutes. At the end, Michaela spoke, "So just to be clear. Nothing will happen soon, but . . . if Johnny has to have that thing removed, he may lose his sexual, what . . . ?"

"Yes, some of his sexual function. Possibly, if he has a prostatectomy—that is, his prostate gets removed. He'd lose his ability to create semen, to have babies. But it's highly probable he'd still be able to get an erection and have sex. And enjoy sex."

"Okay, I can deal with that," said Michaela, standing and tossing her towel on the chaise. "Billy, there are times that your candor puts me off. This is not one of those times. Thank you."

"Michaela, please sit down again," Billy said. "Just for a minute. I want to tell you and Nicky a personal story I've never told to anyone. I'm thinking it may be helpful."

Michaela sat back down, intrigued.

Billy spoke slowly, "I was in love once, believe it or not. And I was loved. Yes, this big, broken-down fat man, in a romantic relationship once. Long time ago. A beautiful young man. We loved each other deeply."

Nicky glanced back and forth between Billy and Michaela. Billy raised a finger. "If you repeat this story to anyone else, I will have to kill you both. Or something." He took a breath and continued. "It was in college. There were reasons that this wonderful relationship had to end. Reasons we couldn't fight or control. A lot of it was just the attitude of the time. Back then, hostility toward gays was overwhelming.

"So what we did, my lover and I, we made up our minds to savor every day together, in spite of this horrible overhanging external thing. I am so glad we chose to do that, rather than fight it. We enjoyed the days we had, and when time came we went our separate ways, cold turkey. I can't say without regrets, but we did it. What we did, how we lived those days fully and lovingly, has left me with a lot of spiritual capital, frankly, that has sustained me for a long time. I haven't seen nor do I know anything about my former lover, not a word since then, but I'm comforted that his life is better too simply because we decided to savor those days together. That's my story."

***

Michaela went upstairs to lie down. Nicky restarted his run up the hill, and Billy resumed his walking. When Nicky returned to his bedroom, he found a thick book on his pillow, *The Emperor of All Maladies*, and a note. "It's about the history of cancer. Knowledge is helpful. Billy."

Nicky thumbed through the table of contents. He spoke out to himself, "Awesome. Thanks, man." He would finish it in two days.

That afternoon, Billy texted Johnny. "Michaela and Nicky are doing fine, Dr. Blood Moon. Just stay close to them. They need you."

CHAPTER FORTY

Johnny and Michaela left Wednesday morning in her studio limo, still at her command. They were headed to Post Ranch Inn in Big Sur, a resort on California's Central Coast. Exhausted by events of recent days, Michaela fell asleep; Johnny watched the swelling golden hills glide by with their dark spots of live oaks. After a fast five hours, they arrived at a cluster of cottages on a high bluff overlooking the shimmering Pacific Ocean.

Entering their cottage, they saw red roses, a bottle in a bucket, and a folded note, arrayed on a carved wooden table in front of a live fireplace. Michaela breathed in the fragrance and picked up the note. "So sweet." She was sure it was from her producer friend David Kennedy. The roses were from Kennedy, but the champagne and note were from the studio.

When Michaela read the note, she burst into tears, ran into the bedroom, and threw herself on the massive bed. Johnny followed, rubbing his cheek. He sat on the edge of the bed. Michaela's face was buried in a pillow, and her back was heaving.

"Michaela?"

Without turning, she thrust the note at him. Michaela had been nominated for a Golden Globe in the category of best supporting actress. After elaborate congratulations, the note apologized for its more challenging message: early tomorrow, a helicopter would fly Michaela back to LA. The note explained that the nomination triggered two small-print clauses in her contract: a drop-everything obligation to be available for two days of interviews—reduced to one day, given the circumstances—and a fat cash bonus. The helicopter would deliver her back Friday morning. And if she liked, their stay could be extended a day at studio expense.

Johnny read the note and moved a box of tissues from the side table to the bed. She turned her wet face toward Johnny.

"Oh, Johnny! It's all so, so upsetting!"

"You're so beautiful when you cry. May I offer my congratulations?"

This triggered a fresh burst of sobs. She pulled tissues.

Johnny suppressed a smile. "I know I'm clumsy, but this is *wonderful* news! You've reached the top of your profession!"

"I was *so* looking forward . . ."

"To shutting down? Me too. We can still do that. We'll extend, maybe even for a few days. But—wait a minute. Sit the hell up, lady."

His tone got her attention. She sat up, rearranged the pillows, sat back, folded her arms, and glared at him, chin tucked in. Seeing his joy, she didn't know whether to laugh or cry. She emitted something in between.

"Now *stop* it! All of a sudden, you're *somebody*. No one can take this away from you."

"It's all frightening!" she breathed. "And I'm *so* exhausted. And now I have to get up in the dark and do another——"

Johnny interrupted her. "Wait. You're not hearing me, Michaela. This is different. This is about, *you, your* accomplishment. I'll be fine here alone for a day. You do the interviews then you're back, and we can relax, talk . . ."

Michaela nuzzled up to Johnny's chest. He draped his long arms down her back. She took a deep breath and rasped into his neck: "Oh, Johnny! You can't *imagine* how tired I am of talking to these same stupid people . . . and not talking to *you*. But . . . okay!"

She sat up and blew her nose. She whispered, "When I saw this sweet cottage hanging over the ocean, I wanted to be here with you forever. Then that note. Ugh. Sam can drive me to the helicopter in the morning, I guess?"

"Atta girl. I'll let Sam know."

***

Johnny rose with Michaela before dawn. After she left, he found a running trail on the uphill side of Coast Highway. Big Sur consists of muscular green hills rising dramatically up and away from the roiling ocean. Fog and mist swirl in the folds of the hills. Post Ranch occupies a narrow ledge on the ocean side of the highway. Johnny's trail followed the contours of the hills. He loped through the dark trees as the sky brightened, remembering his boyhood runs and listening to Fleetwood Mac.

After the run, he called Nicky, catching him in the Civic. Nicky whooped about Michaela's award. "So *sweet*! She must be totally amped!"

Johnny said she was on her way to LA in a helicopter.

"*A helicopter! Awesome!*"

"You're enjoying this way more than she is. You doing okay?"

Nicky's voice dropped an octave. "Yes, I'm good. Sorry about my breakdown yesterday, Johnny. I ran into Michaela, and we talked with Billy. He was amazingly helpful. He gave me this book about cancer. I read half of it last night. I called Dr. Mir too. So I'm good, and I'm totally down for you."

"That means a lot, Nicky. Cancer's a scary word, but like I said, this is a version they're getting pretty good at, so chin up, both of us. I'm about to start the Llosa book you gave me."

"Love Llosa, Johnny. He's up there with Gomez."

Johnny started the novel after breakfast. It was dense, and his mind drifted as anxieties pressed in. He worried about how Lisa would react to the award nomination. He resolved to call Gus. Then he thought better of it.

After a massage and a shower, he walked out to the highway. Stopping at a small stand, he ordered a cheeseburger and picked up a TV listing. His heart jumped when he saw that UCLA was playing Cal at 7:00 p.m. tonight. He would forget about Lisa and Gus at least for this one day.

***

Michaela returned at ten thirty Friday morning and went straight to bed. They had a late lunch on the patio and decided to hike. As they stepped off, Michaela told Johnny she'd been invited to Greece next month, after the Golden Globes dinner. The Greek consul had called to report that she was a hero in Athens. "He said my visit could help national morale. Can you imagine? I can visit my mother and go see Pavlos. And maybe help my people a little. But when I travel I always worry about my visa——"

Johnny interrupted. "Which reminds me . . ."

Michaela raised her hand. "Hold on, let me say one more thing. I want Pavlos to come to the US, maybe for college. I can afford it now."

"Absolutely, Michaela. We'll have these two boys. I'd love that."

"Nicky and Pavlos? Maybe they'll be friends."

"Yes. Are we ready for serious subjects yet?"

Michaela turned her eyes toward the ocean. "Why not? Nothing can hurt us here, right? Look at the different blues and that pink and silver at the horizon."

"Reminds me of Cabo. So anyway . . . I figured out what your father threatened you with—your green card. I've been talking with Bo about it. I told him about your Greek husband and baby. He guessed maybe you didn't disclose those things on your visa application . . ."

"He's right! I didn't disclose those things. My father wouldn't let me."

"That's what he guessed. Turns out, Bo is close friends with the head of immigration in DC. He called him. He asked him about not disclosing your husband and child."

"Oh, Johnny! What have you done! The head of immigration knows about my case? Why . . . ?"

"Calm down, Michaela, it's fine, all under control. The guy said that, given your circumstances, it's not a problem. He put a note in your file that it's all fine. Your green card is fine. We had to anticipate what Lisa might do, and now maybe the press will be sniffing around after this Golden Globe nomination."

"Oh god! That makes me crazy! What could Lisa do?"

"We know that your father talked to her. And Lisa's PI . . ."

"Maybe read my visa file? Like it's public?"

"We know he found your real name, Poulos, and your relationship with Arthur, so apparently he got into it somehow. Bo wants to preempt Lisa or any other busybody—with your new celebrity, who knows? The fact is, anybody can write anything."

"Oh, Johnny! I guess have to trust you. But you look worried."

"I was worried you might think I got out ahead of you."

"You sure did, but I understand. And I like Bo. He seems sensible."

"He's careful, and he cares. He needs to talk with you."

"So my visa is really okay, you're saying? I can't believe it! And you're saying this award nomination changes things? David Kennedy told me if we went to San Francisco, we would have been mobbed. The film was released there Saturday, and I guess it's crazy, which is why he steered us here."

"Yes, it's a brand-new ball game. But there's no reason you can't go to Greece. Your visa is perfectly fine."

They walked silently for a minute, heads down. Michaela lifted her eyes. "The only solution is for you to marry me, Johnny Blood."

"What . . . ?"

"Wouldn't that solve all our problems?" Her eyes sparkled.

Johnny stopped walking. He stammered, "Yes, but . . . I was . . . I wasn't . . . I love you, Michaela Poulos. Will you . . . marry me?"

Michaela smiled. "You're so darn smooth, Johnny Blood. No, I won't marry you, not yet. But when we do marry, I'll be Michaela Blood. No more Poulos, no more Powell, no more Michelle. That's my deal. There's that blush again!"

Johnny spread his arms like a supplicant. "Do you really love me? Can we talk about our feelings now?" Johnny dropped his arms. They stood gazing at each other, on an impossibly high cliff overlooking the vast gleaming sea.

"This makes me dizzy, Johnny."

"What makes you dizzy?"

"Everything. This. You. Marriage. The sky is so blue. Like in Greece."

She took his arm and turned him toward the cottage. "Let's walk back before I fall in the ocean." She leaned into him. "Yes. We'll get married. Of course, I love you, silly . . . more than I've ever loved anyone . . . but we need things to settle down."

"What things do you mean?"

"Like my life. Your life. This crazy response to *Why We Love*. What do I do with that? My trip to Greece. Lisa. The press. Meeting my son—maybe he's coming to the US? My poor old mother. She actually took my father's death hard. It's like a bunch of earthquakes. Yes, and your cancer too. I talked with Billy and did my own research."

"So you know? I don't want to commit you . . ."

"*Don't* even think it. I want you to *listen* to me, Johnny. That's *not* important. We *will* get married, and we'll do whatever it takes to make you as well as you can be. But whatever happens, I'm always with you."

Johnny was speechless.

"You should know, Johnny, I may have my own problem with having children. I may have had damage out of that marriage to that animal in Greece. My ob-gyn said I'll get pregnant or I won't."

"So we're both maybe damaged goods? I don't think there's anything you could say——"

"Marriage doesn't matter," she interrupted. "A piece of paper."

They went on silently, thinking their own thoughts.

"Johnny, you once told me you were 'feral' as a kid. I had to look that word up. It means like a wild animal?"

"Yes. Hiding out. Trying to survive."

"Well, I think feral described me too, until I met you. Can you understand that's how I felt?"

Johnny nodded. "I can. Billy tells me I never really left the reservation. That I'm still that feral kid. Still hiding out, scrounging."

"You were for sure that way when I met you. Billy and I have talked about this. But you've changed. Or, I should say, you're changing. Me, I want to change too. To slow down, focus, eliminate what's not needed. Decide who I am, who I want to be. With you. Plenty of time to get married."

"No rush, I agree. Not on marriage or on anything. You've taught me."

They walked on, heads down.

"Maybe Gus was right," Johnny said. "A person can't control things."

Michaela perked up. "What? Gus said that? I meant to ask. I heard Gus's dating Lisa Bell. Little bird told me."

"Bird named Billy?"

"Yes. He is the *nicest* man."

"Billy *is*, but he *cannot* keep a secret. Here's the cottage."

"It's so pretty. So what did Gus say about not controlling things? You know I'm interested in control."

"He thinks people can't control their future. That things just happen."

"*We* can!" Michaela exclaimed. "Well, even if we can't, let's enjoy it, enjoy the ride. We're together, Johnny. That's all that matters."

"Absolutely."

"And then there's Lisa still." Michaela unlocked the cottage door. "I'm glad she and Gus are seeing each other. Poor girl, I still feel for her. I understand lonely. Does Bo have a plan if she does ballistic?"

"Goes ballistic." Johnny smiled, closing the door behind them.

"Fine, *goes* ballistic, bananas, bonkers, bullshit, whatever she does, around the bend. Does Bo have a plan?"

"Bo has a plan, yes, if Lisa goes ballistic. Or if the press picks it up. Like I said, Bo wants to talk with you soon."

"Fine. And, Johnny? Maybe I'd like to move away from Lisa's eyeballs. That bedroom creeps me up."

CHAPTER FORTY-ONE

Back in LA, Michaela drove to Encino to see Bo in his office. He explained how her personal backstory had shifted from an existential threat to a manageable PR challenge, perhaps even an opportunity. With Bo's coaching, her publicist drafted multiple press plans in anticipation of various events. Each involved telling her life story, or versions of it—her publicist said her emergent fan base would love the rags-to-riches part.

To Michaela's surprise, telling her story to strangers and especially revealing her deepest secrets to Johnny produced a profound sense of release. She was slowly putting her father, first husband, and chronic personal shame behind her. The upcoming trip to Greece and visit with Pavlos felt like a new beginning.

Johnny could see her emerging from chrysalis to butterfly. He also sensed the steady deepening of their relationship. She pressed him to come along with her. "Don't just *watch* me, Johnny. *Be* with me. *Change* with me. The Golden Globes dinner. You *have* to come." Johnny dug out his tux.

***

Christmas season came without ceremony in the mansion. No decorations, no tree—traditional Greeks and Crow Indians didn't do Christmas trees, and it never occurred to Billy, buried in his back rooms. Michaela had quietly moved back in, returning her scant belongings to Lisa's capacious closets. She sold her Prius and bought a small Lexus. Johnny commuted to the VA on his Harley. Meanwhile, *Why We Love* was soaring, and Johnny's friends were making plans.

Nicky and Brent Mir found an apartment in Westwood. Johnny smiled when he saw how close their apartment was to where the Final Four had lived years earlier. It was a drive to Santa Monica College, but they decided it would be worth it. Brent was shooting for UCLA in the fall, and they loved the energy and the coeds of Westwood.

Billy told Johnny that he planned to move back in with Lisa. They were sitting in the mansion's vast kitchen. "She can't be alone," Billy said.

"I'm worried what she'll do to *you*, Billy. You're not recovered yet."

"I'm much better. Going to Weight Watchers again. Down twenty pounds." He patted his belly, still huge. "Approaching my fighting weight. No more wheelchair. I had a nice chat with Lisa the other day. And you guys are moving soon!"

"Not soon, Billy. And you can live with us at our new place."

"No, I'd feel like a fifth wheel. Or a third, if you drive a motorcycle. My place is with my stepmom. I have high hopes for her in the new year."

***

Gus was puzzled by Lisa's silence about Michaela's Golden Globe nomination. She didn't mention it, but he sensed a growing tension. She was due to fly to London to meet with the Royal Brompton research team on her foundation's major project. Gus worried that she was not in shape to be alone, and not in shape to negotiate. She insisted she'd be fine and took off, arriving on a cold and rainy Christmas Eve.

Elegant Claridge's had been Wild Will Bell's favorite London haunt, and he and Lisa had enjoyed good times there. She had told the Royal Brompton people that she wouldn't arrive until Boxing Day, the day after Christmas. So Lisa would be alone on Christmas Day for the first time in her life.

After ordering a room service dinner, she called Gus in LA. It was noon, his time, and he was in his director's suite. He told her he'd be working through until Christmas morning. "No one here except me and a couple of grumpy residents. God help anyone who has heart problems tonight. Tomorrow I visit my pop. But I'm really glad you called, Lisa."

The chat was good, but for Lisa the effect dissipated quickly. After room service arrived—a Caesar salad and a quart bottle of Southern Comfort—she shut off her cell phone and settled in to brood over her growing collection of magazine clippings about Michelle Powell.

One picture in *People* magazine particularly galled her. It was a grainy half profile of Michaela with her hand on a man's lower back, standing on the front steps of Benedict Cañon. To Lisa's deep distress, the story noted that the house deed listed the owner as "The William and Elizabeth Bell Trust." The man was indistinct; the caption called him "Michelle's Unidentified Male Escort." To Lisa he was quite distinctly Johnny Blood. That picture went up on the mirror.

Christmas had always been Lisa's favorite holiday. It was the one day when her rough-cob father might smile at her. In spite of his disappearance when she was fourteen, the memory of that smile permanently infused her feeling for Christmas. Tonight, however, alone, blue, sinking into drink, Lisa fixed the hot point of her feelings on Michaela Poulos, the evil architect of her decline. Everything was on Michaela—the divorce, her depression, this terrible boozing, her hostile friends, Billy's bad heart—all of it! The illegal alien bitch, living in her house, sleeping in her bed with her husband, living off her trust. Johnny, she reasoned—or concluded without much reason—was merely a guileless fool who let himself be manipulated for sex or god knows what.

In the small hours of Christmas morning, Lisa, chaotically drunk, composed a rambling e-mail directive to her PI, still on retainer. She told him to prepare a letter to the head of US immigration to "reveal the truth" about this "illegal immigrant bitch" who was getting all these Hollywood plaudits. He was to disclose her Greek marriage and abandoned child. He was to say that these critical facts had been illegally omitted from Michaela's 2002 permanent resident visa application. Therefore, he was to conclude, her 2007 visa was invalid and this woman who was "all the rage in Hollywood" now was ripe for deportation.

Lisa directed the investigator to conclude with an account of Michaela's immoral lifestyle. The bare bones of this story came from the PI's investigations, but the flesh came from Lisa's imagination—the sleeping around, the wild Hollywood parties, the association with drug users and dealers, the serial stealing of other women's husbands.

The PI didn't reply to Lisa's e-mail for two days. When his response came, it was formal and sharp. He would *not* write such a letter—it was *not* how he operated—and it raised serious legal and ethical issues. He requested that their retainer arrangement be terminated.

After her apologies and a generous retainer increase, the PI agreed to suggest language for a letter *she* might choose to send, although he required complete deniability. He would send language in time for her arrival back in LA in January. She was offended by his final words, that he respectfully hoped she would "cool her jets" between now and then.

Lisa was scheduled to arrive home on January 6. Billy planned to move back to Bel Air on January 9. So she'd have those few days to work on the ICE letter. She rummaged through the clippings scattered around her suite—the Golden Globes dinner was the evening of January 11. Maybe she should wait to see how *that* went before sending anything to anyone.

***

Back home in Bel Air, Lisa watched the Golden Globes alone with her Southern Comfort. Michaela was resplendent, a special target of TV cameras. Johnny was a handsome escort in the glittering ballroom of the Beverly Hilton

Hotel. In an instant audience survey, he and George Clooney were voted the two men most likely born wearing black tie.

After the supporting actress award presentation—not to Michaela, although the camera lingered on her as a gracious and gorgeous loser—Lisa, trembling with rage, scrawled an address on an envelope and stuffed the letter she had prepared into the envelope. She staggered out the front door into the chilly fog and placed the envelope in the mailbox for pickup in the morning. Then she fell into bed, besotted and spent.

***

Billy had returned as promised to Bel Air to be with Lisa. They had gotten along in the few days since his return. He had set boundaries—doctor's orders. For one, he insisted he could not live with her drinking. He knew she'd ignore his injunction at night. So in these first days, Billy retired to his rooms after dinner, tense about their shaky armistice.

While Lisa was watching the Golden Globes in the front living room, Billy watched in the back den. He snuck forward just once, to score a quart of chocolate ice cream from the kitchen fridge. Lisa didn't notice.

***

For most of their lives together, Billy had slept late, while Lisa rose early. In recent times, the pattern had flipped. As Billy was enjoying his tea in the Bel Air kitchen early the next morning, the doorbell rang. It was the mailman, a diminutive Japanese, holding out Lisa's letter. "Sorry to bother you so early, Mr. Bell. Who addressed this letter left off the last name, and there's no return address, I thought you should see. It's not sealed, and PO box is blotted. Postal system bad now. Laying people off left and right."

Billy took the envelope. The scrawl was barely coherent: Director John M. [blank], Immigration and Customs Enforcement, over a PO Box number. The POB number was obscured by a splash of amber liquid. He felt a jolt of anger, a rare emotion for him.

"Wow, we must have been tired last night. I'll take care of it. Thanks." Billy would normally ask the postman about his family, but not today. He knew exactly what kind of a bomb he had in his hand. He had to think.

CHAPTER FORTY-TWO

Billy was paralyzed by indecision. He knew Lisa would explode if she knew he had her letter. He thought about destroying it, but that was not Billy, not how he operated. The letter sat unread in his desk drawer for days. He stewed and lost sleep.

The Oscar nominations were announced a week after the Golden Globes gala—Michaela was nominated for supporting actress. Unlike the quirky Golden Globes, an Oscar nomination was serious business. Johnny called Billy with a heads-up. With difficulty, Billy just listened.

But the news spurred him into action. He went back to his den and read the letter, his heart pounding. He knew Michaela's family history was sketchy, so those allegations didn't bother him—it was Lisa's hateful *purpose* that got him. Every word was tipped with venom, aimed to kill. It was wrong, unbalanced, evil, Gestapo tactics. He had to deal with it. But he was not good at confrontation, and he had no one to lean on for help. Billy decided to wait on events.

***

On the morning after the Oscar nominations, Billy was alone at Bel Air. Lisa had been away for days. The loud ring startled Billy. He picked up the extension. "Yes?" Billy assumed it was a junk call.

"May I speak with Lisa Bell, please?"

"Who's calling please?"

"Meg Connell, *People* magazine. Mrs. Bell available please?"

"She's not . . . home. Don't know where exactly she is."

"I have an old cell number. Who are you?"

"I'm Billy Bell, her stepson."

"You know Dr. John Blood, Mr. Bell? My story's actually about him."

"I know him. But . . ."

"Can you just tell me where he is? Is he with Michelle in Europe?"

186

"Sorry, it's not my place to say. I'll give Lisa your message." He hung up. The phone rang again. He let it ring.

Forty-five minutes later, Billy still had not moved. This time his cell phone rang. Caller ID said LISA.

"Lisa, where are you?"

"Can we have lunch, Billy, just the two of us? At the house?"

"Today? You had . . ." Billy caught himself. "Where you been?"

"Gus and I went to Palm Springs. I should have told you. I'll be home in an hour. Tell Ernest to lay out salads. That okay? Just want to talk."

"Sure. I'd like to talk too, Lisa. You sound good."

"Just want to have a little chat. Need to take care of my stepson."

***

Ernest laid out an elegant lunch for two in the formal dining room. The nice Lisa arrived, sober, smartly dressed, and coiffed. Over lunch she spoke airily about her trip and her work. She asked Billy about his writing and glided by his uncharacteristically curt answer, "Going all right."

Billy was confused. He felt his heart, his damaged heart, going out to her—she was trying *so* hard. But he sensed her inner turmoil. Making conversation, she asked whether he liked the house remodel. Billy mumbled something about his bedroom seeming brighter.

"Yes, we cut back the olive trees and painted the walls lighter."

She shifted tone. "Billy, I'm sorry I've been gone so much. Gus is so busy, we grab time when we can. And my heart research project is at a critical stage. It involves people in London and now UC Cedars." She said something else, but Billy wasn't listening. He was fingering her letter in his pocket, afraid he'd run out of courage before the lunch ended.

Lisa placed her napkin on the table. "Something on your mind, Billy? You seem distracted."

"Sorry. Guess you heard about Johnny's cancer diagnosis?"

It was if he'd hit her with a stick. "Johnny Blood? Has cancer?"

"Oh . . . I assumed you knew. Gus didn't tell you? Prostate cancer. They think they can manage it, so there's no radical treatment yet."

"Cancer? I can't believe it." Her eyes filled up, and her voice became scratchy. "Must say, this Oscar thing about the girlfriend . . . now, cancer?"

"I assumed you knew." He fingered the letter again.

She touched her eyes with her napkin and mumbled, "She'll soon be getting hers."

"Lisa, you had a call from *People* magazine today. A Meg Connell." He was holding her letter against his leg.

Lisa had a sardonic smile on her face. "Oh, Meg, yes. She reached me. She was writing about Johnny. I got her pointed in another direction."

"Is this the direction?" Plunging into the abyss, Billy slid the envelope across the polished table.

***

Johnny welcomed Michaela home from Greece Wednesday evening. The woman in Johnny's arms in the mansion foyer was full of joy. Her visit to Athens had triggered a celebration that had warmed her heart. She was salve for her beleaguered homeland. Her celebrity actually, astonishingly, *helped* people, lifted their spirits. She was, for the first time in her life, proud to be a Greek.

She was also proud to be a *mother*.

After Athens, she flew to Crete to meet Pavlos. She said that her son was a delightful young man, shy, but so happy to be meeting his real mother. Yes, he'd love to come to the United States for school. He spoke perfect English, was bright and motivated and—to her great relief—was unaffected by her celebrity status. She was just *mother*.

While in Crete, she learned about her Oscar nomination by e-mail from Johnny. She said it was like reading about an earthquake on Mars. She quickly forgot about it.

"We talked for hours. He's a bright boy full of curiosity." Johnny had never seen her so animated. "We went for a morning run through the olive groves. It's so beautiful there. We'll try to Skype once a week. His job is to work hard in school, and my job is to clear his path to America. Maybe next fall he could come?"

"Why not?" Johnny said. "Nicky's all set to be a big brother."

Her eyes were misty. "Johnny, I'm so happy!"

Leading Michaela down the carpeted steps into the living room, Johnny pointed to a stack of phone slips on the coffee table. "You get an Oscar nomination, I guess the phone rings." It seemed half the calls were from Meg Connell. They listened to her latest voice message. "This is Meg Connell, *People* magazine. We have information that you omitted information about having a husband and a child on your green card application. Please call me ASAP—my deadline is tomorrow."

Johnny shook his head. "That's Lisa's work. Probably lost it with the Oscar nomination. So, sweetheart, let's call Bo, see what he says."

"Call the reporter," Bo said after they explained the situation. "Tell her three things and write this down. First, that her information is wrong. Second, that your lawyer wants to talk to her before you'll say anything, and that she'll understand why when I speak to her. Writing this down?"

Johnny spoke, "I am."

"Me too, Bo." Michaela giggled. "Together we're as good as half a lawyer."

"That's a stretch. Third thing, tell her you'll give her an exclusive but only if she agrees to your ground rule. Write this down. Ground rule is that she will not name any of your family, including Johnny, in her reporting. If she agrees, you'll meet with her and give her the full story you worked out with your PR person. You do that, Ms. Connell will be your biggest fan. 'Pregnant teen cast out on the streets of Athens nominated for an Oscar.' The American dream. These reporters are people."

"I'd like a ground rule that she doesn't embarrass Lisa."

"That's a nice thought, Michaela. Tell her to keep Lisa out of it too."

"What do you Americans call this?" Michaela asked. "Hanging it all out?"

"Letting it all hang out." Bo chuckled. "It's definitely an American thing. You'll do fine."

And Michaela did do fine. Meg Connell was both a mom and a grandmom. She agreed to the ground rules. Michaela gave her a short telephone interview Thursday and a sit-down exclusive and photo shoot at the mansion Sunday. *People* published a teaser story the following week and a full-length, highly favorable cover story the week before Oscar night.

***

Seated next to Johnny in the Kodak Theater at the Oscars in February, once again glittering, glowing, gorgeous Michaela did not get the award, but she did get a standing ovation when her nomination was announced. She later told Johnny that it was this bizarre evening that finally convinced her that she must terminate her film career as soon as possible.

CHAPTER FORTY-THREE

When Billy slid the letter across the table, Lisa's eyes locked on him. Brows bunched, lips puckered, she resembled a disapproving schoolteacher. He squirmed under her gaze, his moist face and bald dome alternating between blanch and blush. The letter sat between them. He rambled on about the mailman. "He brought it to me. What was I supposed to do? It wasn't even sealed. I didn't read it for a week."

Her face quivered. "I'm so not good for you."

Her shift startled him.

"I'm two people, Billy. Sometimes I can't control . . . especially when I drink."

"Then stop drinking if that's what it is!" Billy's voice rose.

She started. Her eyes filled. "I *can't* stop, Billy. I have this *pain*, about the divorce, Johnny, especially this woman. I hate her. Johnny couldn't do this to me. It's not his nature."

"Do . . . what to you?"

"Abandon me! Cast me aside!"

"But . . ."

"Let me finish my fucking sentence!" Lisa hissed. Billy recoiled.

"Sorry." She tried to collect herself. "I know about the fraud, the lies on her visa, the sleeping around, the drugs . . ."

"Lisa, slow down. You're way off base. Bo called immigration and they said that her visa was not a problem, if that's what you're driving at. She was never legally married. She never knew her child. Didn't your investigator tell you?"

"What? How could they . . . with all that . . ."

"Apparently, Bo has a friend high up in immigration. Her visa status is all cleared up. But you said something else, Lisa. I know for a fact Johnny didn't date Michaela until after the divorce . . ."

"She's an evil woman," Lisa hissed. "I'm just sorry the letter was so badly . . ."

"Wouldn't have worked anyway. You're not listening, Lisa."

"When . . . ?" She stopped talking.

"When what? When did they talk with immigration? I think it was back in December when Bo called his friend."

"Bo did? January should have told me! She only said Johnny knew about my investigator . . . oh god! I gave that *People* reporter all that story! Now she'll write about the jealous ex-wife, suicide-bombing everything! And she'll fall in love with Michelle Powell and do a puff piece!"

***

It was a puff piece indeed, and it led to the standing ovation on Oscar night. Lisa drank herself unconscious during the broadcast. Waking Monday morning on her bedroom carpet, TV still on, she realized that she had made a complete and utter fool of herself.

She had to regroup, and to do that she had to withdraw from the field of battle, so clearly arrayed against her. She booked an immediate flight to London and called Gus. He was busy, so she sent a text asking him to call her. Gus, her one remaining ally, was busy and missed the message.

On her way out, she taped a note on the fridge for Billy, apologizing for her abrupt departure, hoping he'd understand. Of course, she wrote, he could stay at Bel Air or move back to Benedict Cañon, his choice.

Lisa called Gus's cell from LAX. Until now she had managed to wall him off from the "bad Lisa," but the wall was developing big cracks.

Gus picked up and whispered, "Lisa, what's up? Can't talk long."

"I'm boarding a plane to London in ten minutes. Someday, I'll . . ."

Gus was upset. "London? Lisa! Goddamn it!"

"I . . . I," she stammered.

Gus interrupted, "Don't answer. My response was inappropriate. Maybe I'm crazy, but I'll miss you."

"I . . . I'll miss you too. But I have to get out of here." She shifted to business mode. "For one thing, I'm fed up with the Royal Brompton people. The Brits are *so* difficult. You should come to London to lean on them."

"But that can't be the reason you're leaving so suddenly! Well . . . call me when you get there. Haven't been to London since Margaret Thatcher. Maybe it was Elizabeth I. Gotta go."

***

When Billy read Lisa's fridge note, his chest tightened, his knees buckled, and he awkwardly slid down the refrigerator door onto the floor. Ernest and

Antonio were away. Close to fainting, he dug out his cell and called Johnny. Johnny, at the mansion, directed 911 to take Billy from Bel Air to UC Cedars. He then called Gus and jumped on his Harley.

Meeting Gus at the ER entrance, Johnny asked about Lisa's sudden departure. Billy had choked out the essence of the note. "What the hell is she doing? I'll bet it was the standing ovation Michaela got."

"No idea. She called me from the airport," Gus said, his eyes down. "I'm dealing with . . . I don't know what I'm dealing with anymore."

Johnny nodded. His feelings were complicated. "I know, man. That's why Billy collapsed. He can't handle her zigs and zags. He takes it personally, like I used to. She should have known he would . . ."

"Shit, I take it personally too! Why doesn't she come to me if she feels fucked up? How do you think I feel . . ."

Johnny was silent.

Gus shook his head vigorously. "I'm sorry, dude. I have no one else to yell at. The Lisa I know has been totally cool, Johnny. Then, bang, this crazy call—Cheerio, I'm off to London! Fuck me!"

"We need to talk, Gus. How about an emergency racquetball game tonight? I've missed playing. If your back's okay."

"Brilliant idea! I need so badly to hit something!" He closed his eyes and paused for a short moment. "Lisa did say she might fly me over to London to help with the Brits on her research project. Lean on Royal Brompton, she said."

"There you go." Johnny said. "But that sounds like more denial. She'll probably keep you captive in that big suite at Claridge's. All the more reason we have to talk."

"You've been protecting me?"

Johnny squinted at his friend. "You know I have. I was naively hoping that the redemptive power of love would kick in and make her well. But it's apparently not working. So we need a new plan."

They saw the ambulance pulling into the ER *porte cochere*.

"Here comes big Billy," Gus said. "How about eight tonight, Johnny?"

"You're on."

***

Johnny dominated the match. They settled into the hot tub. Gus nodded absently. "So she's literally killing him—killing herself too!"

"You mean Billy? How is he?"

"He's fine. He basically just fainted. I'm keeping him overnight for observation. Fundamentally he's not very well."

Johnny nodded, and Gus studied his hand floating on the water. He spoke slowly, "I wondered why Michaela got that ovation at the Oscars. It was that *People* article, and that was Lisa's handiwork. Wow. I can imagine how she felt when she saw it." Gus nodded at Johnny. "So, chief, what's the plan?"

"I've been talking to people, Gus. Lisa's mother, she called me out of the blue. And Tom Schultz, who's back temporarily at her foundation. Schultz tells me his board and Royal Brompton are ready to can Lisa."

"If Royal Brompton's unhappy, my funding's in trouble."

"I'm sure it is. Everything's about to blow up. What we have to work with is your relationship—that's number one—Lisa's position with the foundation, her girlfriends, maybe Billy, maybe her mother. That's the leverage. She's pretty much shredded everything else."

"Leverage? What do you mean?"

"Have you ever been through an intervention meeting?"

"Really? Is that where things are headed? Shit."

Johnny nodded.

"That's where everyone gets in a room?"

"Right. And we tell her she has to stop drinking or she loses her job, her boyfriend—that would be you—her family, friends, everything."

"And I lose the grant and the sex. Johnny, I don't want to do that until I personally try with her. I need to form my own conclusions."

"I understand that. If you want coaching help, I have a friend who's orchestrated a lot of interventions. You remember my mentioning Ora Dillon from Redwood City? Wife of Dr. Mike?"

"Let me ask you something, Johnny. Why are you so active on this? I don't know how to feel about that, frankly."

"Well, you know, Michaela and Billy are impacted, and I . . ."

"What else?"

"I'm a physician. She's sick. I took an oath."

"And . . . ?"

"Gus, Lisa's been in my life a long time. She was my wife. Maybe I feel a little . . . responsible."

"Responsible? For what?"

"Dunno. Michaela's been teaching me about what Lisa's going through. Rejection. Loneliness. I had no idea. She thinks I can do some good. It would help me, frankly, if I could. Even better if it would help you. But . . . you want me to back off, I'll back off."

"You're not responsible for anything, dude. But I hear you, friend. Let me think about it. Give me Ora's cell number."

Chapter Forty-Four

On Wednesday morning, Gus called Ora Dillon. "Ms. Dillon, we haven't met, but my name is Gus Rogosin, and . . ."

"Gus! You're Johnny's best friend. Call me Ora. Let me get rid of the airline on the other line. I think I know why you're calling. Hang on."

"Uh . . ." Gus was both impressed and nonplussed.

Ora came back on. "Sorry, that was pretty rude. I'm here in Encino with my girlfriend January. Can you and I have lunch?"

"Like today? The two of us?"

"Yes." Ora chuckled. "Just me. One of us is bad enough."

***

They met at a steak house near UC Cedars. Gus loved his beef. Ora came right to the point. "Lisa's sinking fast. There was this kamikaze *People* magazine thing she did. She's been humiliated, which may be good. Her theory about Michaela . . ."

"That she caused the divorce?"

"Exactly. She's starting to understand that she had it wrong."

At first, Gus was reluctant to open up, but Ora's command of the subject and her obvious concern for Lisa drew him out. Little was left unsaid. Ora's parting advice was "Don't confront her. I know you have a nice bubble relationship. Believe me, the bubble will burst. But don't overreact. She's a good girl. It's worth it. But we need your leverage."

Gus groaned. "Like Johnny said, now I'm leverage."

"I know. Feels cold. Your warm heart is the best thing Lisa has going for her. In a few weeks, Lisa's due to fly back here for her mother's eightieth birthday. Mrs. Phillips is on the team now. Her health is okay except for the scoliosis, but she's torn up about her Lisa."

Gus thoughtfully sipped his Arnold Palmer.

"Interventions mostly fail because of denial," Ora continued. "Lisa won't deny she's a drunk. She talks about it to us all the time."

"Not to me," Gus said.

Ora said that the planned intervention would involve the Final Four, Lisa's mother, Tom Schultz and the vice chairman of the Bell Foundation, Billy Bell, if he's up to it, and maybe Johnny. Gus's eyebrows went up.

"Johnny?"

"He's still a player in her world. The idea is surround her with the people she cares about, give her an ultimatum with no exit. We'll have a plane waiting to take her to Betty Ford. For what's called the Gold Standard program—ninety days lockdown."

Gus played with his fork. "What happens after ninety days?"

"Hopefully you can be with her, help her find a good local therapist who specializes in addictive behavior."

Gus grimaced.

"Gus, you are *the* key. I can tell you're *almost* there. She really is a good girl. Call any time. You've done a lot of heart procedures, I've done a lot of interventions."

Gus nodded and waved for the check.

***

Lisa called Gus the next day to discuss his London visit. She sounded sober and corporate on the phone. "The Royal Brompton people are eager to meet you. You'll stay here at Claridge's. Come a few days early." He cleared his schedule, hitched up his jeans, and headed for the red-eye.

Gus's first days in London were a dream. The weather was unseasonably sunny and warm. The good Lisa and he popped into museums, attended live theater, enjoyed late, lingering dinners. They laughed, held hands, made love like honeymooners.

At room-service breakfast on Wednesday, Lisa wore a white silk robe, and Gus a suit and tie. He was due at Royal Brompton at eleven. "Don't think I've ever seen you with a tie, Gus," Lisa said, smiling. "Cute. So I'm ready to pull the plug on Brompton. If they don't want our funding, screw them. They're blaming the NHS. Such nonsense. The NHS has no money—they crave outside funding. Maybe you can find out what's going on."

Rain had returned to London. When Gus arrived at Royal Brompton, he was greeted by Dr. Nigel Cooper, the elegant director of research. After small talk, Dr. Cooper got to the point. "Mrs. Bell is quite impossible, Dr. Rogosin. That's the sum and substance."

"Please, it's Gus."

"Right, and I'm Nigel. I'm being direct with you, Gus. We want this funding, but we need a steady hand at the tiller, and Mrs. Bell is not that hand."

***

At the end of the two days, Gus sat for tea and a summing up with Dr. Cooper. Gus liked Brits. He enjoyed their erudition, their manner, their understatement. He had come to like Nigel Cooper, who seemed less waspish than the typical British professional.

"Thank you for your time here, Gus," Dr. Cooper said, his half-glasses clinging to the end of his long Norman nose. "We wanted to communicate two points: first, that this research project *must* be done, for the good of medicine. We are clearly the right partners. The second thing, the delicate thing, is Mrs. Bell's role. I will not presume anything about your personal relationship—forgive me."

"I do have a relationship, but please let's talk candidly."

"Right. There's a great deal at stake. Mrs. Bell cannot be involved. This is a showstopper, as you Americans say. Her behavior has declined from barely acceptable to appalling."

"I understand, Nigel. My friend Lisa is in trouble. Due primarily to alcohol, I'm sure you're aware."

Dr. Cooper crossed and recrossed his legs. "Yes, I *am* aware. So sad. My dear wife was a quiet alcoholic before she died years ago . . ."

"I'm sorry."

"Right. So I know something of what you're dealing with. I think we have . . . I'd say perhaps six weeks to save this. The Bell Foundation are quite capable—although they've lost good people lately because of Mrs. Bell. And I fully understand the need for foundation engagement, the legal requirement, expenditure responsibility under your revenue law. I'm pleading for your active help. I don't know where else to turn."

***

At dinner with the good Lisa that night, Gus said that Royal Brompton was essential and the project was salvageable, but they had work to do on the oversight structure. He deflected her anxious questions and urged her to forget business so they could enjoy this last evening. Lisa bowed to the shift of power. Extracting Gus's promise that he'd call her after his return, she drank more than one glass of wine and barely hung on. Next day, Gus rose before dawn and flew home.

***

With Gus in the air Friday, Lisa wandered past a Chelsea newsstand. She saw the tabloid headline: "MICHELLE POWELL PREGNANT." She tore the newspaper off the newsstand and fumbled for coins. The story below the headline was less dramatic: Michelle Powell had taken a film role as a pregnant woman. However—as her erstwhile PI later confirmed—the headline reflected reality. Michaela was indeed pregnant. Lisa was devastated. She hunkered down in her suite with her Southern Comfort. That night she called Gus's voice mail with an angry, teary, incoherent message. As Ora had predicted, the bubble had burst.

***

In late March, Lisa quietly flew home for her mother's eightieth birthday. Gus picked her up at LAX and drove her to Bel Air. As she entered her living room, she was startled to see her friends and colleagues, Johnny, Billy, and her mother. Everyone stood except Mrs. Phillips, bent over on a settee, eyes down. Lisa glanced back at Gus and burst into tears. Ora came forward and led her to a bathroom. Lisa returned with moist nervous eyes and sat next to Gus on the sofa.

She looked over at her mother, her face tight. "I have to ask a question before you all start. Then I'll do what you all tell me. Mother, what happened with Daddy? Why did Cindy die? I need everyone to hear this."

The room froze. Johnny looked at Ora, who shrugged. Ora, poised to rescue Mrs. Phillips, watched the old lady's face twitch and then settle. "Why in front of all these people?" Mrs. Phillips spoke in a tremulous voice. She waved her lowered head back and forth. "I did everything I could to protect you, dear. He was impossible. He walked out because . . ."

"Say why he walked out! That's what killed her!" Lisa's voice was tinged with desperation.

"This is so long ago. Because . . . I couldn't protect *you* anymore. You know that." Her voice was barely audible. "You were getting too pretty. I told him I'd kill him. And I would have. You were all I had left. My Cindy was gone by then. I couldn't protect her from herself."

Ora was ready to intervene. The old lady's voice became a whisper. "*That's* why he walked out. Because I made him. I couldn't . . . you were all I had left . . ." She seemed to shrivel under the pressure of memory.

Ora spoke up in a firm tone, "Lisa, honey, we're all here to say we love you, but it's time to get sober. You'll fly to Betty Ford for a ninety-day stay. Gus'll drive you to Van Nuys where there's a plane waiting."

Gus touched Lisa's hand. Lisa looked at him blankly. He stood. "Lisa, we need to go, but I want to say, in front of everybody here, I'm sure you're concerned about your research project. Me and the Bell Foundation staff will carry it on. It's all set up, so you won't need to be involved."

Lisa sat like a zombie, eyes down, absorbing the blows. Gus gently helped her stand. As she shuffled toward the door on Gus's arm, everyone stood except her mother. As Lisa passed by her mother's small bent figure, she leaned down and whispered, "Sorry, Mother. Next year I'll make sure you have a nice birthday. I guess now I have work to do." Mrs. Phillips nodded at the floor.

Lisa never looked at Johnny, who stayed silent, or at unkempt Billy, rubbing his beard in the back of the room. Dr. Mike Dillon and Bo Rathgeber sat together on the sill of the bay window. The foundation people leaned against the back wall. Ora and January waited near the door. "I'm *so* sorry," Lisa said in a throaty voice as she approached the two ladies, "to put you through all this."

Ora hugged limp Lisa. "We love you, babe. Get better." Gus, holding her purse and suitcase, waited while the ladies stroked her.

Before leaving, Lisa turned around. "Thank you all. I will try my best. I promise."

PART FOUR

God, it would be good to be a fake somebody rather than a real nobody.

—Mike Tyson

CHAPTER FORTY-FIVE

In early May, Johnny performed his first lung surgery in twenty-five years. As he strode along the dim hall in search of a celebratory cup of coffee, he felt his cell phone hum. It was NICKY.

"Johnny! Just got my grades. All As." Johnny heard bounce in Nicky's voice.

"Nicky! That is so great! Congratulations!"

"And our SMC volleyball team made the playoffs. First playoff game is Saturday noon at Glendale College. You said you might come to a game? That's mainly why I'm calling."

"Saturday? I think I can make that."

"And, Johnny? Sunday, is Michaela gonna cook dinner again? I can bring a couple of my teammates, and my new girlfriend."

"New girlfriend? Sure. Say, Nicky, how's your friend Paco? I haven't heard anything in months?"

Nicky paused. When he spoke, his voice had lost its bounce. "I definitely need to talk to you about that. Paco chilled for a while, but . . . he told me some gnarly things recently. How about . . . can we have dinner, like, tomorrow?"

"Tomorrow, Friday? Sure, if it can be late, like eight thirty. You like Greek?"

"Don't know Greek."

"It's a little like Italian. Hey, Nicky, so *great* about those grades!"

***

Nicky arrived a half hour late at Sofi's. "Sorry I'm late, Johnny. Paco's outside, down the block. Is it okay to bring him in here?"

"Oh, I see. Sure. I'll get a more private table if that would be better." He pointed to the nook where he and Michaela sat a year ago.

"That's good. I'll get him. Give me a minute."

***

"I'm glad to see you, Paco," Johnny said. "Sit there. I'll order if that's okay, then we can talk."

Paco was wearing a hoodie. Johnny was shocked by his gaunt face. His hollow eyes scanned the restaurant as he spoke. "So I'm in a situation, Doctor. Nicky said we could talk."

"Of course. Are you okay?"

Paco ignored the question. "Nicky told you about my half brother?"

"The one in prison?"

Paco nodded. "He's a fucking crazy madman, excuse me." He looked around again. "I don't know why I'm trusting the two of you."

"Maybe you have to trust somebody," Nicky said.

"What's your last name, Paco?" Johnny asked.

"My last name? Whoa! Why . . . oh. So Señor Gomez was for sure murdered, Dr. Johnny?"

"Possible."

"That's on my half brother. The name is Serrano."

Johnny nodded. "Your half brother is Francisco? Big Talk?"

Paco nodded once and ducked further into his hoodie. The waiter arrived with starters and soft drinks.

"So Frankie's dead meat," Paco said. "But I don't care anymore. You're in touch with the cops?"

"Months ago a Beverly Hills police officer and the FBI talked to me about the death of Señor Gomez. Nothing lately."

"The FBI? So they're on it? So that's good. Homies follow Teresa to and from work now. She works around the city, rides the bus all hours. I need to get her out. That's why I'm here."

Johnny nodded.

"Nicky says Billy Bell still wants to help us move. I will absolutely pay him back someday. Once we move, I'll tell you about Frankie and his homeboy with the kill tattoo. You know what I'm saying?"

"I think so."

Johnny asked for permission to talk to his police contact about the relocation. "They know how to do it. The FBI does. I don't have a clue."

Paco hesitantly agreed. "If you have to. But Dr. Johnny, I will never talk directly to any cop. It's gotta be all through you. That's my deal."

***

Next day at 11:30 a.m., Johnny arrived at the Glendale College gym for Nicky's volleyball game. Families sat in clusters on wooden bleachers. He saw a familiar face and climbed up. "Captain Mir? You by yourself?"

"Dr. Blood! Long time no see. You're here for your Nicky? Come sit. I like your Nicky. Brent's doing better in his grades 'cause he's got better friends this year. Looks like he'll get into a four-year college. Knock on wood." He knuckled the bench.

Johnny sat. "I hear Brent's the go-to spiker."

"Yeah, he's pretty good. But that doesn't get you a job. You're the one who gave him his health back. I'll never forget that."

"Captain, I'm glad I ran into you. I was gonna call."

"Call me Bill here, please."

"So I haven't heard anything from you in a while."

"Ah—FBI agent Brill was detailed to Texas. He's back now. There hasn't been a hospital assassination since Gomez. We're thinking they know we're on to them. We don't have anything new on Gomez since the Arthur Poulos stuff came out."

"What Arthur Poulos stuff?" Johnny asked.

"Oh, didn't I tell you the rest? You still dating the daughter, right?"

"Right. We're engaged."

"Oh? Well—congrats. Michaela. She's sure a looker. I saw that movie with the funny name, love something. My wife dragged me. Not too bad. Michaela didn't like her father, I recall. Although he left her money?"

"Michaela's thinking about other things now. Tell me about Poulos."

"Poulos—so we got a warrant and found big spikes in his accounts around when Gomez died. That's when I called you in the hospital, to talk with him? He was hammered in the stock market in early 2009 like a lot of people. He panicked, sold everything at the wrong time. The first spike after that was an inbound 300K, which came in before Gomez died. We traced that to your ex-wife. Poulos had these valuable Greek coins that she bought. She said they were friends and she wanted to help him out. Billy Bell, I guess, is a coin collector, and she was looking for a birthday present. We bought her story—she had judgment issues, but we didn't figure her for an accessory to murder.

"The day Gomez died 100K went out. We couldn't trace where it ultimately ended up. We think Emilio Hand, his Mexican account. And then a big amount came in a few weeks after Gomez died. Probably laundry money from Mexico where they do a lot of laundry. And the other is that the FBI traced your anonymous phone call about Gomez. You remember that?"

"Of course."

"They traced that call to the vicinity of Poulos's apartment in Century City. Don't ask how they do that. And they found other calls between Poulos and sketchy people, or people in sketchy places, including Mexico. So Poulos was involved in Gomez's death along with Dr. Hand. That's what we know, but there hasn't been anything new in a while. Emilio Hand and that black nurse are still missing."

"Did you talk to Francisco Serrano about any of this?"

"Big Talk? If you pull a Mex mafia guy into a law enforcement interview, the other bangers often as not waste him as soon as he gets back to his cell. Serrano isn't going anywhere."

"He was in the hospital that day," Johnny said.

"Right, but we need more leverage. He would deny everything, and then we probably lose him. We need a link to the shot caller. We don't think Big Talk is a shot caller. Too dumb."

"I may have a link," Johnny said. "I was about to call you. But I promised my source I'd speak in general terms until we had a deal."

"Deal?"

"Yes. Let me explain."

Johnny described the Paco situation. "So that's all I can say now. We need to do the relocation before he'll give us more. But I need help on the move. We'll pay for it. My friend Billy Bell will."

"I know Billy. You say the kid is not willing to talk directly with law enforcement?"

"Nope. Has to go through me."

"Okay. Just be careful, Doctor. These guys play for keeps."

"I'd like to help this kid."

"A lotta kids need help. So on a one-to-ten scale, what's the value of the information we get if we help, ten being guaranteed conviction?"

"Seven or eight?" Johnny said. "Hard to say."

"That's impressive. I'll call Brill. FBI knows how to relocate people."

"Sooner's better than later." Johnny looked down at the court. "Here they come. There's my Nicky. Your Brent, he's the tall kid? I wish he'd come to our house for dinner Sundays."

"So it's your house they go up to on Sundays? I did not know that." Mir pointed toward the players. "Look how they all look alike. Indian, Persian, Mexican. Murray, the black kid. Different shades of coffee." He laughed at his own joke. "My Brent, he's six five. Your Nicky, he's what, six three? Great setter. They call him Gold Fingers."

After a short silence, Mir spoke again, "Johnny, I want to tell you something. Just as a friend. It's about your ex. She's a person we worry about."

"Lisa Bell? Why do you worry about her?"

"I'm sure you know she, uh, drinks a lot lately. Not just one-off bingeing, like you did that time. Beverly Hills PD has this secret unit called Citizen Rescue Service, the CRUSH unit—I'm the head, in my spare time, as community relations chief. Don't tell the press." Mir chuckled to himself.

"Our mission is to keep our leading residents out of jail—like you that time—and prevent accidents. We keep a list of what we call 'citizens' who like to get drunk in bars. Some big people—actors, CEOs, politicians. Mrs. Bell's one. The bartenders call me when a citizen shows up to get drunk. Martinez at the Polo Lounge, he and I started this years ago."

"I know Martinez. Sounds like a good idea."

"Anyway, a while ago Gary at Spago calls me. Mrs. Bell is there getting drunk. I go over, take her up to your old house in Bel Air. Not the first time, so she knows me. We actually get Christmas presents. What I want to say, in the cruiser she went on about how you left her high and dry, how your girlfriend was evil. Tears. Real bitter. Just saying."

"You should know, Bill, Mrs. Bell is at Betty Ford right now."

"Oh, she is? That is really good news. She's a nice lady."

"Since March. Anyway, thanks. I think it's under control."

"I'm so glad to hear that," Mir said.

CHAPTER FORTY-SIX

SMC won the playoff match. Sunday night, Johnny and Michaela hosted Nicky, his new girlfriend, and half the volleyball team for a celebratory dinner. Brent Mir showed up, and Johnny greeted him warmly. "Good game, Brent. I saw your father yesterday. Glad you came."

"My father. He's cool but pretty controlling. We don't drink alcohol at home. That's Mother. Father worries I like to party, which I do. He found out this was your house and you don't serve alcohol, so here I am. By the way, thanks for saving my life that time."

The dinner in the mahogany dining room was spirited. With Nicky's help, Billy gave a brilliant, simple lecture about the history of money, using PowerPoint and actual rare coins. The young people loved it.

***

The next afternoon, Monday, Johnny met Nicky for coffee in the VA cafeteria after Nicky's weekly session with Dr. Mir. "Nice to talk with your friend Brent. He told me things about you."

"Like what?"

"Like that you've been elected team captain and how you met your girlfriend. Like that you're an AA sponsor for some of your friends. And you want to be a physician."

Nicky shrugged.

"You don't tell me much, do you?"

"Guess not. I saw you in the stands with Captain Mir Saturday."

"Yes. I asked him to help with Paco's relocation."

"Will they help? Paco's been calling."

"I think so. Captain Mir needed to make some calls."

"It needs to happen soon."

"I got that. Nicky, can you tell me about your girlfriend? Michaela will ask me. She's a cute girl—Avila?"

"We sleep together," Nicky's eyes twinkled with mischief. "And it won't last."

"I remember those things from my college days, but I think I'll leave that part out. Where's she from? What's her last name?"

"Don't remember her last name. She's from East LA. She's seriously heterosexual. She's smart, majors in English at Cal State. That's all I know. Her last name is Sanchez—now I remember."

"You seem to remember more as we talk."

Nicky spoke glumly, "Johnny, I'm really worried about Paco. He's hanging by a thread down there."

"Keep your distance."

"I'm not good at keeping my distance. I'm used to helping people."

"That's good, but this is dangerous stuff."

"I just hope we can do it soon. You should see where they live."

"Soon as I can. By the way, Nicky, your girlfriend, who you say you're sleeping with and that it won't last?"

"Yeah?"

"I've been meaning to tell you *my* story someday—my sex life when I was your age and why you shouldn't do what I did."

Nicked flashed his crooked grin. "Do what I say, not what I do?"

Johnny smiled. "Exactly. Because it screwed me up royally about women. I'm still digging out. I'd like you not to have that problem."

"Well . . . let's have that conversation soon."

***

After Nicky left, Johnny's cell buzzed. It was CAPT MIR.

"Yes, sir. What's the word?"

"We have an apartment set up in a safe place, near a community college. I have the keys. Jobs should be available for the girl."

"Great. They're eager to move. Can we meet? I'd like to bring Nicky along. He has the contact."

"I have lunch with Navid tomorrow, so I could drop by your office."

"Say one thirty?"

"Perfect, Johnny."

***

Later that evening, Johnny and Michaela sat together in the bedroom suite of the mansion sipping fizzy water. Michaela, visibly pregnant now, was packed and ready to leave for her shoot in Vegas tomorrow. Her role came with a substantial upfront payment—the award nominations had propelled her to a new level of compensation and control. But what most interested her was an opportunity to promote a perfume, *à la* Catherine Deneuve. "I'm hoping it's my way out of Hollywood," she said.

Johnny sensed that something was weighing on her. After a minute he asked, "Something on your mind, sweetheart?"

She smiled. "You're starting to learn how to read me. So when I told you I was pregnant last month, I was so nervous. I stopped taking the pill because of your cancer. I didn't tell you. I really wanted to have your child."

Johnny shook his head. "I told you I was thrilled."

"I need to hear that over and over. I felt so guilty not telling you. I do worry about your prostate thing. You never talk about it."

Johnny's eyes dropped. He had not been faithful to his watchful-waiting appointment schedule.

"Be careful, Johnny. For *us.* You have a family now. We need you healthy. I just couldn't live without you."

He reached for her hand. "You're amazing. Truly amazing. I promise I'll take care of myself."

She studied his face.

"So did you like Nicky's girlfriend?" he asked.

"You're changing the subject . . . so I will too. I'm ready to get married, Johnny. And I want to move to a real *home*. Not this crazy big Lisa house anymore. Maybe even away from LA?"

Johnny's eyebrows went up.

She patted her belly. "I want this baby to be born into a marriage. And Pavlos, when he comes here, I'd like us to be a traditional family."

"You know what you're walking into?"

"That's up to me, isn't it? Oh, you mean Lisa?"

"I wasn't thinking about her . . . but she's halfway through Betty Ford."

Michaela seemed irritated. "I have a baby in my belly. You don't want to get married, just let me know. But don't let Lisa control it."

"Of course not. Let me . . . I'll be seeing Gus tomorrow."

"I like Gus. He's very down-on-earth. Down-to-earth?"

"He may be less down-to-earth now. I think he's in love."

"That's a good thing, no? Is Lisa in love too?" Michaela asked.

"Lord knows where her head is."

"It's not her head, it's her heart we're talking about."

"Even more confusing. So what's the timing for getting married?"

"The shoot's maybe eight weeks. August? I've been good about Lisa. But at some point we have to live our own life."

Chapter Forty-Seven

Michaela left for Vegas Tuesday morning. After lunch, Johnny and Nicky greeted the Mir brothers in Johnny's office at the VA.

Captain Mir spoke, "I asked Navid to join us—I hope it's okay. He told me he met this kid Paco once with Nicky. Navid reads people good."

Johnny nodded toward Navid.

"Here's the deal," Captain Mir continued. "The apartment's up in Santa Clarita. It's pretty clean up there. There's a community college called something like Canyons College. The landlord lives on the ground floor. Retired cop. Two bedrooms, it's nice. I checked it out personally. They can move in whenever. He'll need a deposit and one month's rent." He handed Nicky the keys.

"Billy set up a debit account," Nicky said. "They'll move ASAP."

"ASAP? Reminds me, you were in the service, weren't you, young man?" Captain Mir asked. "My Brent tells me you're pretty squared away."

"Brent's a good dude."

"He *is* a good dude." Captain Mir looked at Johnny and smiled. "He liked the dinner up in your house, Johnny. He told me all about Billy Bell's talking about money and showing Poulos's old Greek coins." He winked and rubbed his hands together. "This whole relocation-for-information thing makes me nervous, because I'm dealing through intermediaries. So I needed to ask Navid in front of you two. Are we okay? You met this kid."

"Like I told you, Bill," Dr. Mir said, "he's solid, although he's got issues. How could he not have issues, living in that kill zone his whole life? He's as much PTSD as my vets. The relocation is good. Although there'll be an adjustment. Always is with these big changes."

"That's what I wanted all of us to hear," Captain Mir said. "Good kid, but not going to be simple. So, Doctor,"—he looked at Johnny—"when can you tell me about the bad guys?"

"When they get settled, I guess. Maybe week after next?" Johnny looked at Nicky, who shrugged.

"ASAP," Captain Mir said. He winked at Nicky. "Navid, let's go."

The Mir brothers left, and Nicky closed the door. "It's been a rough week, Johnny—Teresa had to stop working. They're waiting for my call."

"Okay. Get it done. You have the keys."

"I do. I will."

"Be careful, Nicky."

***

That night, Gus began their Jacuzzi chat with a bellow. "Johnny! What's up with your constantly whipping my ass? I've been writing it off to stress and jet lag. But maybe I'm just turning permanently to crap!"

"You have a lot on your plate."

"*Really?* You mean like Lisa out at Betty Ford? And running the Heart Institute and keeping her Brompton project on life support? And my day job, seeing patients? And keeping the Heart Group afloat without your revenues? And my father with Alzheimer's who doesn't know who I am? Not to mention my sex life on hold once again. Why would you say that?"

"That's some of it," Johnny smiled. "How *is* your dad?"

"God, it's so sad, Johnny. He was so vigorous—now he just sits there." Gus took a deep breath and exhaled slowly. "Let's talk about something pleasant. Your Nicky asked me to lunch. He's *such* a good kid. He's got these big plans, college, med school . . ."

"I'm the last to know," Johnny said.

"I love to gas with him," Gus shouted. "He'd make a good doc. I toured him through the Medical Center. He wanted to know what you did, where you did it."

"I'm sure you dazzled him, like McRae did me in 1985 when he stole my soul."

"What's up with Stan McCrae, Johnny? He totally dropped out after Poulos died. Doesn't return his calls. You were pretty tight with him."

"I talked with him a few months ago. I feel guilty not staying close. He was very good to me."

Gus nodded absentmindedly and played with the hot water. "It's damn perverse. I think about her all the time. She can't call out—but I listen for the phone. I really miss her."

"Well . . . ahem." Johnny moved closer to Gus and lowered his voice. "Speaking of Lisa, here's a new challenge for you. Michaela says she wants to get married before the baby is born."

"Uh-oh. When's the due date?"

"October. You know, Gus, if I get married, I lose the mansion and my trust income. And the Bell Heart Institute gets $50 million."

"What? No shit! Is that really how it works? Your Lisa trust ends if you get married, and that's where the money goes?"

"Yep, I think six months later. You mean you didn't know that?"

"Nobody told me. Who would tell me? Holy shit! That makes me an interested party!"

"Yes, Mr. Director of the Heart Institute, your career soars if I get married. Build a building, pay yourself a big bonus!" They looked at each other and laughed out loud. Then the laughter subsided. They both slid lower in the hot water.

Gus spoke, his mouth just above water level, "Shit. So let me get this straight. Lisa emerges from Betty Ford walking on eggshells. She finds out you two are about to get married, goes fucking crazy. Then fifty mill goes over to the institute, which advances my career. So while my career is advanced, I've got this crazed woman in my bed. If I'm lucky. Maybe she's back in Betty Ford. Do they have a returns policy down there?"

"Well, wait a minute. Michaela wants to be married when the baby arrives," Johnny said, "which I get."

"And when does Michaela want to get married?"

"After her shoot, maybe August. We could go to Mexico."

"Mexico?" Gus jumped up. "Jesus Christ, Johnny! Where you and Lisa had your honeymoon? Give me a fucking break!"

"You're right—I'm an idiot. We can't go to Mexico."

"And August! What's the fucking rush? Lisa gets out of Betty Ford at the end of July. C'mon! The kid isn't due until October!"

"Her second kid. Second kids come early. She thinks you're practical."

Gus was irritated. "What the fuck does *that* mean! Listen, chief, I want everybody to be happy, but you can't blow Lisa away day one."

"You're right. I wasn't thinking. I'll fix it."

Gus dunked his head for a few seconds. When he came up, he spoke with his eyes closed tight. "It's all so totally screwball. This woman I'm falling for, her bitter obsession is with my best friend's girlfriend. But you and I know her problem is way deeper. I wouldn't be in this if I thought she was merely jealous. That she still loved her ex. That's just a proxy for something else, maybe her sister or her missing father or her dog, who the fuck knows? There's an open wound."

"Which led to the drinking."

"Yes, exactly, the pain medication."

Johnny sat on the ledge and reached for a towel. "So how about September? Vegas? Low key."

"If it has to happen. I just need time to work it."

"I hear you." Johnny stood and started to towel off. "New subject, Gus: Billy Bell."

"My hyper-obese heart patient. Lisa will insist I stay as his doctor. He's so fucked. Not only the heart."

Johnny nodded gravely. "We have these amazing Sunday evenings with Nicky's friends. Michaela cooks, Billy salons. I've never seen him so happy. But he's been talking about returning to Bel Air with Lisa."

"Good god! Lisa's so bad for him! And he's not good for Lisa either. He reminds her of Wild Will and Johnny Blood." Gus rose out of the hot tub. "Oh, hey, I've got something else. If we've solved Lisa and Billy."

Johnny threw Gus a towel. "So what's your something else?"

"What it is, I'd like to hire Nicky for pay, to help me with the Brompton project. I need a reliable gofer. He'll see the inside of a major research project, and he might save me a trip to London."

"He might get to go to London? Can I do it? I've only been to London once. Rained the whole time."

"I'm sure your European fiancée will drag you through London."

Johnny smiled. "Sure, go for it. Thanks for the heads-up. At least I'll know one thing about Nicky's life."

***

A week later, Nicky and Johnny had dinner in Westwood. Nicky reported that Paco and Teresa liked their new place in Santa Clarita. "So far so good. Paco's got a job in a bakery. He'll start school in the Fall. Teresa connected with a home health care agency. Paco's still pretty jumpy."

"Can I call him for the Gomez details? Captain Mir's bugging me."

"I asked him yesterday. I think the answer's yes, soon, but like I said, he's really jumpy. And sad. Almost a sure death penalty for his brother."

"I thought he hated his brother."

"Still his brother."

"I guess."

The next day, Johnny called Paco. Then he met with Captain Mir.

***

In the last week of July, Lisa called Gus from Betty Ford. It was the night before her discharge. She caught him early in the morning in London. She reported that she'd passed her "finals" and was packing, filling out forms, squaring her shoulders. She was buoyed by Gus's soothing baritone voice but was upset that he was so far away.

Lisa had always been attracted to Gus. Like Wild Will, he was from the Midwest, grounded, comfortable in his skin—the opposite of Johnny Blood, running so hard from his past, apologizing for everything.

The long-distance conversation brought home how isolated she was, how far away from human warmth she'd drifted, how removed she was from her life's work. When she hung up, she felt weepy, liquid, afraid. Then—the sharp craving for a drink. She went through her mental drill. Gus had clearly been happy to hear from her—that was lovely—something to hold on to. He said he'd try to cut his London trip short. They might even see each other tomorrow night.

***

The next evening, Lisa's limo slid up to the Bel Air house. The sun was arcing west, and the blue shadows from the cedar trees were creeping up the white stucco wall. A red-tailed hawk rode soft currents high above the golf course. Lisa had been away for three months, and the familiar scene had an alien quality to it. It unnerved her that no one was there to greet her, to welcome her, to ease her homecoming—not even her longtime retainer, Ernest, whom she had called from the car with a salad order.

Her hand shook as she unlocked the house door. Ernest was in the foyer, on the phone. He waved, bowed, and handed her the phone. "Welcome home, Mrs. Bell. It's Billy. Here, I'll get the luggage."

She took the phone and stepped into the living room.

"Billy?"

"My dear, how are you doing?"

"I'm tired. Glad to be back. I think."

"Well, I'm *very* glad you're back, Lisa, and I'm looking forward to seeing you, maybe even moving back in there with you. In due course."

"You'd move back here?"

"Yes. Home is where the heart is and all that. And you're my family. Johnny and Michaela are planning to move out of Benedict Cañon to a new home. I guess they have to move out if they're married."

Lisa could feel her rage rising.

"You know she's having her baby in the fall," Billy chattered on.

Lisa blurted out, "Are they married?"

"No, not yet . . . not sure about timing . . ." Billy seemed finally to focus on what he was saying. "Soon. Anyway. Welcome home."

"That they'll get married soon, you're saying, Billy?"

"They didn't . . ." Billy stammered. "I think so . . . but I'm just guessing . . ." Michaela had told him confidentially they'd get married before the baby arrived. But Billy was incapable of intrigue. "Well, yes, they'll probably go to Mexico soon. Johnny asked me to keep it quiet, but . . ."

"Mexico? To get married?"

"That Johnny . . . yes, I suppose . . . I'm sorry . . . but you have to . . . this is not the right way, but, my dear . . ."

"I have to get over it! That's what you want to say, right?" Lisa's voice was rising. "My literal first minute home? Ohh!"

She hung up and burst into tears. After a stop in the bathroom, she went to the kitchen to ask Ernest to pull her Jaguar out of the garage. He'd prepared the salad she'd requested. She said she wanted to pop down to the Polo Lounge for dinner. "I'm hoping to meet Dr. Rogosin later. Call Martinez and reserve a quiet table for two indoors. Eight o'clock."

Ernest was used to her mood swings. "Yes, of course. I'll put this salad in the fridge, Mrs. Bell. I haven't dressed it yet. Luggage is in your bedroom."

CHAPTER FORTY-EIGHT

The maître d' at the Polo Lounge was alarmed by Ernest's call. Martinez had known Mrs. Bell since Wild Will days. He was there when Johnny Blood proposed to her at table thirteen—he was the first person they told. They seemed so happy then. Since the divorce, he knew not to put her at table thirteen. He also knew about Betty Ford. After thirty years on the job, Martinez knew many secrets—Beverly Hills land mines. Luckily, secluded booth eight was available for Mrs. Bell—he walked over and put a RESERVED sign down. Then he called Captain Mir.

"Mir," the officer barked into his cell. "Yes, Martinez, what's up?"

"It's Mrs. Bell. She's on her way here. I think she just got back from Betty Ford. Do I serve her if she asks for a drink?"

"Oh god. I guess you have to, unless she becomes a danger."

"If she has one, she'll be a danger to herself. She reserved a table for two. Maybe she won't ask, maybe——"

Mir interrupted. "First thing they teach you is don't go near where you used to get drunk. I need to make a call. If she starts drinking, call me and I'll come over. Let's hope that doesn't happen. Betty Ford's expensive. You would think it would work better."

***

Johnny Blood and Michaela were sitting at the kitchen table in the mansion finishing dinner when Johnny's cell phone rang. They were celebrating her return home today from Vegas.

"Sorry, I should take this. It's that Beverly Hills cop."

He touched PWR. "Bill? What's up?"

"Martinez at the Polo Lounge just called. Your ex, Mrs. Bell, is on her way there. Just fresh back from Betty Ford."

Johnny was horrified. Collecting himself, he told Mir that he wanted to call his colleague Dr. Gus Rogosin. "He has . . . they have a relationship. That's the best bet. Oh gosh, I think Gus may still be in London . . ."

"Whatever you say, Johnny. Martinez will call me if she starts."

"I'll call you right back." Johnny hung up and looked at Michaela, who was clearing dishes. "Sorry, hang on, sweetheart. A bit of a crisis."

"Lisa's back?"

"Just back from Betty Ford and on her way to the bar. I need to find Gus." He called Gus's cell. He got voice mail and left a message. Then he thought to call Nicky, who was traveling with Gus.

"'Lo?" Nicky sounded half asleep.

"Nicky, where are you?"

"'Sis Johnny?"

"Yes."

"I'm in London. Friggin' 4:00 a.m. here. Whassup?"

"I need to find Gus."

"Hold on. Lemme get out of bed." Nicky came back on yawning. "'Scuse me. Gus left for LA last night. Left me in charge." He chuckled. "Looking for his flight. Oh, here's . . . his arrival time is, uh, LAX, 9:20 p.m., your time. But he has to change planes in San Francisco."

"Okay, bud, thanks. I'll call you when I can. You good?"

"Yeah. It's awesome here! Just like in the movies."

"Right, gotta go. Talk later."

Johnny turned to Michaela. "My cop friend has this warning system with the bartenders around town. Lisa's on her way to the Polo Lounge. Gus is on a plane."

"*You* go rescue her," Michaela said. "*You* do it. Right now. It's just down the street. Use the Lexus." She dove into her purse for the keys.

Just then his phone rang. It was GUS ROGOSIN. "Gus? Thank god!"

Michaela nodded, still digging in her bag.

"What's up?" Gus asked. "You sounded hot in the voice mail, dude."

"It's Lisa." He told Gus the story.

"Bad. Bad. Bad. I'm in San Fran, waiting for my connection. So I won't get there until, like ten-ish."

"That's too late. Michaela is telling me I need to get down there right now. I think she's right."

"You would make me eternally grateful if you would do that."

"I'm on my way."

Michaela handed him the car keys, still nodding.

"You're the best," Gus said. "Give Michaela a big kiss for me. Go scoop Lisa up, get her up to Bel Air. Expect me there around ten unless I call. Tell her . . .

it's over with me if she takes one fucking sip. You hear me, dude? It's not easy for me to say that."

"I hear you, Gus. I'll tell her."

"I think I hear my plane being called. Here we go, bro!"

Gus hung up.

"Just go help her," Michaela said. "Run!"

He kissed her. "That's from Gus. Mine comes later." He ran to the Lexus. As he drove down the hill, he called Captain Mir. "I'm on my way, Bill. Should be there in five minutes."

"Good plan. Martinez hasn't called. So far so good."

***

Johnny threw the keys at the valet and ran through the lobby of the Beverly Hills Hotel into the Polo Lounge. Martinez grasped his hand and vigorously shook it. "Dr. Blood, I'm so glad you're here. Mrs. Bell, she arrived a few minutes ago and ordered a drink. The bartender, he made it up, but I couldn't . . . so thank god!"

"I'll take it to her. Where is she?"

Martinez led him to the bar where the tawny sweaty double Southern Comfort over ice sat glistening on a white napkin. Johnny was startled by its beauty. He picked it up and sniffed it.

Martinez raised his finger to his lips and tilted his head sideways. Johnny saw Lisa's lowered head half hidden behind a powder-blue pillar. He walked over and placed the drink in front of her. "Lisa, I just spoke with Gus. He's on his way. He told me to tell you that it's this drink or him."

Lisa tried to comprehend through wet eyes. "What? Johnny!" She whispered hoarsely. She buried her face in her dinner napkin. Heads turned in their direction. He slid in next to her.

"He's on a plane," Johnny whispered. "Couple of hours away still. He asked me to come here. Actually . . . Michaela told me to come here, and Gus agreed. Looks like just in time."

Lisa started to sob. After a few seconds, she leaned against his shoulder, still sobbing into her napkin.

Johnny put his arm around her. They sat that way for a long time. Finally, she sat back and took a deep breath. "I'm going to the ladies' room. Then let's leave." She stood and looked down at the sparkling cut crystal glass filled to the brim with bourbon. "God! Get rid of that."

***

Silence reigned during the ten-minute trip along Sunset to the Bel Air house. Johnny drove the Lexus, and Lisa composed herself in the visor mirror. Johnny was trying to figure out how to get through the next hour.

When they arrived, Ernest greeted them as if they were expected. The tall, elegant butler asked if he could fix something to eat. Johnny responded, "No, thanks. I've eaten."

Lisa asked Ernest to dress the salad he'd prepared. He nodded and stepped off toward the kitchen. They moved into the living room, and Johnny sat on an ottoman. Lisa stood with her back to Johnny.

"Do you want me to leave, Lisa?" Johnny asked.

"No, I need you to stay. Please. I can't be alone. I know this is horribly awkward, but I need someone with me now. Even if it's . . . you." She paused, still facing away from Johnny. "I'm supposed to apologize to the people I've harmed. But you're the last person . . . or maybe the first person . . . I'm so confused!"

"I'm glad to stay if you want until Gus gets here," Johnny said.

"Yes. Please. I'll be right back." Lisa left the room.

Ernest brought her salad and opened a tray. He set a glass of water in front of Johnny. "Nice to see you, Doctor. It's been quite a while."

"Yes. Thanks, Ernest."

Lisa returned, her eyes puffy and red. She sat and silently stirred the salad with her fork. Johnny looked around, trying to find something to say. "You've changed this room, Lisa. It's nice."

"Yes."

After a minute, she spoke in a low voice, staring at her salad, "When I came back here tonight, Billy was on the phone telling me you're getting married in Mexico. She told you to help me tonight, you said?"

"Michaela? Yes. But we're not getting married in Mexico."

"Why would she want to help me?" She resumed stirring.

"Michaela gets . . . she was abandoned by her father too," Johnny said. "She's a good person."

Lisa looked Johnny in the eye for the first time all evening. "I heard that story from a different angle once."

"From Arthur?" Johnny asked.

She played with the salad. "Arthur did a lot of . . . lying, I found out. Anyway, when I came in through *that* door." She waved at the front door. "Billy was on the phone . . ." She gasped. "I *must* get a hold of myself . . ."

"It's okay."

"No! It's not!" Lisa put her fork down and raised her voice. "You're trying so hard!—but I still *abhor* you, Johnny Blood! I can't believe you're sitting there!

And at the Polo Lounge! You *abandoned* me. I felt so . . . *abandoned*!" Johnny watched her try to control her breathing. "Our marriage was awful, but you shouldn't have just *left* me! Not that way!"

"I . . ." Johnny was searching for words.

"*Don't* say anything," she hissed. "I want . . . I need to say some things, Johnny. Don't worry, I'll calm down. There are things I should have told you when we got married. But not those, not yet. Tonight I need to tell you about Arthur Poulos. What he tried to do to you, through me."

She settled herself and ate a bit of salad.

"I hated your medical practice. It felt like there was no room for me. Then Arthur told me you had other women. I believed him. So I hired . . ."

"Wait, Lisa. I know about the PI, what he did, about the leak to the *Times*, your getting Arthur to drive Michaela off to London—I know all those things. You don't have to repeat it, you don't have to apologize. It's past. I had no other women before the divorce. I did not mean to abandon you. I know now that it felt that way to you, but I had no idea."

Lisa seemed startled. After a minute, she continued in a level tone. "I've never known you to lie. You really aren't a bad person, Johnny, you're just a fool sometimes. A holy fool, Stanley McRae once said about you."

"I am. I can be. I don't pick up everything. But I don't lie. Like I told you at that dinner, I'm trying to change how I am. Trying to——"

Lisa interrupted, "I need to say one more thing. When your author died, I just knew Poulos was responsible. He so hated you. And you so loved that writer. And you hated when patients died. You had a horror of death. I felt awful, complicit. I just . . . let it happen."

"Lisa, you had nothing to do with it. But I need for you to listen to me. You and I had a great, lovely moment once upon a time. No one can take that away from us. But we were not cut out to be marriage partners. I know that now, and so do you. We made a mistake getting married. We tried, we failed. We've both suffered. But it's time to turn the page. Maybe I am a fool, but I know that you've got a great guy in your life—the best guy I know on this earth. And I've got a great girl. It's time . . ."

Johnny's cell buzzed. It was GUS ROGOSIN. "Excuse me, Lisa."

"Gus, where are you?" Johnny watched Lisa's eyes, which were fixed on his cell phone.

"I'm ten minutes away. You gettin' along, dude?"

"Splendidly. Here, talk to your lady. She loves you, Gus." Lisa sobbed and reached for the phone.

***

The following Monday night, six days after Lisa's Polo Lounge close call, Johnny and Gus played racquetball. Gus won, barely. He was elated as he stepped into the Jacuzzi. "Woo-hoo! I *can* play this game. And I have lunch money for tomorrow! Life is good."

Johnny feigned a frown. "Fifteen yards for excessive celebration."

"Accepted. Hey, Johnny, seriously, I can't thank you enough for helping Lisa last week. That was frigging huge."

Johnny's face softened. "You're welcome. Now tell me about how the rest of the week went up there. I'm dying to know."

"Well, right after you left, she fell into bed. Alone. Next morning she was still pretty shaky, but we had breakfast and talked. Or she talked. And talked. Gradually she pulled herself together, like 80 percent, by the afternoon. We visited a shrink lady recommended by Betty Ford. She likes her and will go three times a week. Then we returned to the house, and she did a little weeping and craving for a drink."

"Sounds like you've been a trooper, Gus."

"I'm her structure. That's apparently the key to sobriety. I've moved in. Meanwhile, we've rescued her Royal Brompton project. We close over there in late August. I'm secretly hoping to bring her over to London for it. Getting back to her work is important for her."

"You're amazing, Gus."

"Not been much of a love affair. More like home health care."

"No, It's totally good, Gus. The love part will follow."

"I sincerely hope so. Oh, by the way, Johnny . . . Johnny, Johnny . . . how to say this? Michaela and you, I think you're off the piñata hook. Give me notice, but September should be fine for getting married." Gus held up dripping crossed fingers. "Billy's big mouth strangely prepared her."

"Michaela's fine with September and Vegas. But, wow, that's incredible work on your part, Gus. Six days in Bel Air. The creation."

"She was *so* fragile when she arrived home Tuesday. So when Billy throws his grenade, boom, she runs down to the Polo Lounge like it's her bomb shelter! That's why what you did for her was so critical."

"How *is* Billy, by the way?"

"Billy is . . . I'm very worried about Billy," Gus said. "He's mortified about his fuck-up. He doesn't know about her Polo Lounge flyby—don't tell him. Lisa's been good with him. She forgave him."

"He's not returning my calls," Johnny said. "He's hiding out, he does that."

"I'm worried he's given up. All the weight is back and more. I'm gonna hand him off to someone else, Johnny."

"Lisa's good with that?"

"Yes, she's fine. She gets that Billy's health issues are his issues, not hers. More important for you, she gets that Michaela's not the devil. Betty Ford went deep. And her shrink seems effective. And she and I are getting pretty tight again, Johnny. Still a work in process, don't get me wrong."

"What isn't?" Johnny said.

"Exactly. She's starting to come back to earth, which is why that Polo Lounge episode was so scary. Five minutes later . . ."

CHAPTER FORTY-NINE

Nicky met Johnny for an early dinner on Tuesday at Tanino's Italian restaurant in Westwood. "So, Johnny, I have this little office on the top floor of the Bell Wing—Gus put my name on the door!"

"For some reason Gus likes you." Johnny smiled at his young charge.

"Johnny,"—Nicky looked up at his uncle—"while I got you, uh, captive here, you were gonna tell me about your experience with women?"

"Right. You still dating Avila?"

"No. I have a new girlfriend now."

"Oh? What's *her* story?"

"Works in a bookstore, trying to make it as a writer."

"Name?"

"Uh, Meg something. Wait, it's on my hand. Muller. Or maybe Miller."

"On your hand? Maybe we do need to talk."

Johnny spoke about his youthful, serial, sex-centered relationships in college. How he loved the chase and especially the win. "I enjoyed the conquest, Nicky, that first time, entering her the first time, always the best moment. They're all different, the way they smell, the little noises they make, the way they resist and then yield."

Nicky smiled. "You're making me horny."

"I'm forgetting you're twenty-two. I didn't know their last names either, nothing except their bodies. After a few times, I'd lose interest."

"Sounds familiar," Nicky said. "I like the ones who fight a little."

"I did too, but then what happens? You get a reputation. As kind of a sleazeball sex addict. You're not invited to parties. You get snubbed by other ladies because they talk to each other. But the worst thing, Nicky, you start feeling dirty. Sex is part of a total program. It's to make babies, but it's also for social stability. Relationships, family. It's how men and women fit together. Intimacy. It strips all the nonsense away, if you do it right. I'm fifty-five years old, and I'm just now getting this."

"Random sex *can* be an addiction. Is that what you're worried about with me?"

"You know addiction better than I do. I just don't want you to end up like me."

"What exactly do you mean?"

"You remember the story about Ruth in med school? For years after, with a few forgettable exceptions. I was a monk. Until I met Lisa Bell."

"I remember. What happened then?" Nicky asked.

"After Lisa's first husband passed, it was like the back of my mind telling the front of my mind, so here's this beautiful, connected, not to mention wealthy woman, a chance to get married, have a real life. So I proposed. It was stupid."

"Why stupid? Why didn't it, like, work out? Okay to ask you that?"

"I'd never learned how to relate to a woman as a person. To talk, to listen, to appreciate how they feel about things, what their needs are. How to let them talk without jumping in and trying to solve their problems."

"Lisa's a little nuts, isn't she?" Nicky asked. "I hear things from Billy. I may meet her on this London project."

"She's been struggling. Booze. But she's doing much better."

"So I hear Gus and Lisa are an item?"

"Yes. Gus is very good for her. And she's a good person."

"He's good for me too. He's awesome. So how about Michaela? You got it all figured out now?" Nicky tilted his head. "About women?"

Johnny laughed. "Michaela has taken me to school."

"Ni-ice!"

"It's very nice. I'm very lucky. We're getting married."

"Awesome! When? Why?"

"Why? Good question. Because we're ready. And we love each other."

"You ready to graduate from Michaela school?"

"Something like that. Michaela's expecting in October. And her son is coming here soon. Her Greek son."

"Pavlos," Nicky said. "I'll take care of Pavlos. Like Benny took care of you. We're the same age difference."

"Well, that's . . . what can I say? She wants us all to be a real family. So do I. Our three sons."

"What happens to Billy? Omigod, he's so fat again! Hardly can walk."

"Yes, not good. But Sunday night dinners start again this weekend. Get your friends. Bring Meg. Talk with her first. Find out what her last name is before Sunday."

"Uh-oh. Homework."

***

In early August, Captain Mir knocked on Johnny's office door at the VA.

"Sorry to bother you, Johnny. You got a minute?"

"Come on in, Bill. What's up?"

"I was just here seeing Navid. Thought I'd swing by."

"Any news?"

"We picked up that Eighteenth Street shot caller with the Gomez kill tattoo, and we finally spoke with Big Talk at Pelican Bay. He didn't tell us anything, but he was dead within two days like we thought he might be."

"God! Does Paco know?"

"I'm sure he knows."

"Jeez. Poor kid. Are you getting anywhere with the shot caller?"

"Yes. Moving toward indictment. He's got priors. We think he may plead. The fact they advertise who they kill with tattoos—what is a jury going to do with a tattoo that says 'Gomez' with a big K over it? And a moniker like Death Moon?"

"Death Moon?" Johnny asked.

"They call him Dee Moon, but it's short for Death Moon."

"Gang monikers are like Indian names. Mine was Blood Moon."

"You're an Indian?"

"Yep. Crow."

"Always thought you were some kind of Middle East derivation."

"You're not alone. So, Bill, you solve the Gomez murder?"

"Not totally. Dee Moon was the guy who called you about Gomez and got the two doctors paid. We don't have the deep Mexico connections yet. Those guys have a short half-life. Your anesthesiologist Hand is dead. We still don't know where the black nurse is. Probably dead too."

"Emilio's dead? God, what a tragedy."

"Turned up in a morgue in Mexico City. Whacked."

Johnny put his hands to his cheeks. "God!"

Mir's voice dropped. "I do have a warning for you, Johnny, which is mainly why I'm here. And for Billy Bell and your nephew."

"Which is?" Johnny asked.

"Stay away from Paco and his sister for a while. The mob is deep and ruthless. I have nothing specific except—stay away."

"I hear you. Should I talk to Billy and Nicky?"

"Absolutely. Soon. Please." He put out his hand. "Gotta go."

***

That night, Johnny found Billy reading in the back wing of the mansion. Billy's broad face brightened when he saw Johnny. He pulled off his glasses. "Johnny boy! Come on in here. To what do I owe this pleasure?"

"Hi, Billy. I, uh, I learned a few things, about your friend Paco. His half brother's been killed." Johnny sat heavily in an overstuffed chair.

Billy's face darkened. "He told me. At dinner last night."

"You had dinner with Paco?"

"We do that once a week up there, like you and Nicky used to."

"Billy, wait a sec. Captain Mir came to see me today. He said we've got to stop seeing Paco and his sister. Was Nicky with you last night?"

"No, he doesn't come. Just me and Antonio, my driver. He's packing a pistol now. That was Lisa's requirement." Billy rumbled his deep laugh. "Antonio was military police. I told Lisa about my pal Paco—she made me promise Antonio would carry a weapon. I also told her a lie, that I'd stop seeing these kids. But I'm not going to, Johnny."

"You're taking a terrible chance. These people are ruthless."

Billy spoke sharply, "Paco's my family. And Teresa. I love these kids, and I'm going to stand with them."

"Billy, maybe I need to tell you more of the story behind why the cops were so interested in Paco. We all agreed not to because . . ."

"Because I can't keep a secret?" Billy smiled. "I don't blame you. I have a big mouth, like Frankie Big Talk did. I still feel awful how I ambushed Lisa on her first day home. But I know everything anyway. Maybe even more than you do, maybe even more than the cops, about Manuel Maria Gomez, Arthur Poulos, Emilio Hand, the killer tattoo, the Juarez cartels, Gomez's book, which I've read. Pretty good read. Little long."

"Really?" Johnny was appalled. "Is this all from Paco?"

"Johnny, listen. You know I don't have long to live. I'm not going to abandon these kids. It's the only thing I care about. These two good kids. I've put something in my will for them. They know that. Maybe that wasn't smart to tell them."

"Jesus, Billy!"

"I know, dumb. But if something happens to me, I wanted them to know they'll be taken care of. They're my kids now."

"Did you say Lisa knows the Paco story?"

"Not all of it. Some of it. You'd be pleased to know I'm more discreet in my dotage. But don't worry, she's got distractions of her own. I'm proud of her, how she's working to fix herself. Gus has been so enormous for her."

"Yes."

"So I'm not going to back off, Johnny. I'm just not."

"Keep Nicky out of it."

"I will. I've been doing that. I've talked it through with Nicky and Paco. These are clever young people."

Johnny pondered Billy's broad benignant face. "God bless, my friend."

***

The next night, Johnny and Michaela had their long-delayed dinner at Sofi, the one Michaela wanted to pay for. They sat in their old nook, where Johnny, Nicky, and Paco had met earlier. Michaela was floating.

As the wine and food started coming, she exulted, "I've never been so happy, Johnny. Our baby boy, we have to talk about names. We get married in six weeks? My Pavlos is coming, I have my new perfume steady job, no more movies—I didn't tell you, I turned down a big film role last week. My agent was going to kill me. It was written for me."

"Really? Well, if that's what you want. Hard for me to criticize quitting a job you're good at."

"That's what I want. No more films. I never want to do anything besides be a mom and a wife."

"Never say never."

"Never! There, I said it! I mean, really, never!" She laughed her charming tinkling laugh. Johnny hadn't heard it in a while.

"You've got two movies in the can. What about those?"

"*King Henry* comes out in November. I got a little check there. And a bigger one for the pregnant mom role. Maybe some back-end if they do well. With the will money, the film money, the perfume contract money, I'm pretty set for life even if you kick me out, Doctor."

"This doctor won't kick you out. But that reminds me."

She reached across the table and touched his lips. "I don't want to hear any sad stories tonight, Johnny. This is our happy night."

"Sorry, you need to know this one thing—that your father orchestrated the death of Manuel Maria Gomez. He got the anesthesiologist to . . ."

"Stop! I don't want to hear anymore. I know . . . I knew he did something like that. Is the money he gave me . . . ?

"Tainted? Don't worry about it. They're not going to ask for it back."

"I feel okay if I use it for Pavlos, his grandson, for his education. It's not like I'm buying a yacht."

"Not a problem. There are other parts to the story . . ."

"I don't want to hear other parts to the story! I just want to be in my safe little world. Just with my kids and my husband, and this nice dinner and this lovely red wine." She lifted her glass and studied it. "Johnny, shouldn't we move out of LA?"

Johnny was silent.

"It doesn't feel safe here anymore. Not that it ever has. And now there's nothing holding us. No more films. Billy's going back to Bel Air. Nicky's applying to colleges around the country, he says. You seem frustrated working for the government. Don't answer. Just digging a seed."

Johnny smiled.

Michaela returned his smile. "Planting a seed?" She sipped her wine. "Tell me, how is your cancer?"

"It's fine. I've been going for regular checkups. I have another checkup next week."

"It's just because you never talk about it."

"You got my serious attention when you got pregnant. I'm taking care of myself like you told me to. Under control."

She looked into his eyes, fork poised. "Okay, I believe you this time."

Johnny watched Michaela attack the food, now arriving in waves. "Eating for two," she half apologized. She was even more beautiful, he thought, now that she was pregnant. He had planned to tell her about Paco, Billy, the gangsters, the Gomez investigation. Not tonight. He would just enjoy her enjoying her life.

CHAPTER FIFTY

In mid-August, Johnny called Gus. "So the wedding is set for Labor Day weekend in Vegas. Then we drive up to Utah. This is your notice."

Gus groaned. "The shoe droppeth. I'll talk to her nibs. If you feel the earth move under your feet, you'll know why. How's 'bout a bachelor racquetball party Monday?"

***

The match was close—each won a game. They decided to stop, tied. Sliding into the Jacuzzi, Gus seemed jaunty. "That was fun—we both played well. And . . . Lisa's cool about your wedding. Stirred but not shaken."

"That's really good news," Johnny shouted. "Gus, I'm nervous. All of a sudden, Michaela's so serious. She wants out of LA."

"Girls get serious when they get married and have babies. That's the Lord's design."

"I guess. What am I in for?"

"Well, if you believe the words of my first wife as she walked out the door, you're in for increasingly routine sex and suffocating compromise. Doesn't have to be that way, though, but you *do* have to work at it. Consider that advice my wedding present. Anyway, back to Lisa, speaking of working at it—so I cleverly packaged your tough news with my happy news, that Dr. Cooper at Royal Brompton has graciously, after my pleading and begging, invited her to the closing in London. She's stoked."

"I'm so impressed with your handling of all this," Johnny said.

"I have an incentive. I'm in love. There, I said it. And your old Bel Air pad is a great house. Way better than that Disneyland castle you live in. Not to mention my condo shithole."

"We'll be moving out of Disneyland after the baby arrives."

"You're leaving LA that soon?" Gus asked.

"No, not yet anyway. Something local probably."

"That's good. So has big Billy decided what he's gonna do then? He's at Bel Air today, working in that creepy back den. I think he keeps a sex slave back there."

"Now that you're taking care of Lisa, I'm guessing Billy's lost his purpose. Although he really does care about those two kids he's helping." Johnny had told Gus the Paco story.

"World's sweetest masochist. Sad. If I were a life insurance company, I'd pass on him. New subject: your Nicky. He's doing a fabulous job. It's so much fun to work with him. He's a sponge."

"The job is perfect. He loves it. We had a talk the other day about women, relationships. I shared my deep expertise how to mess up. I saw him doing what I did at his age—jumping from one flower to the next."

"One pussy willow to the next." Gus smiled. "But give him some slack, for Pete's sake. What was it St. Augustine said? Give me chastity, Lord, but not right now? Nicky's going to London to set up the closing."

"He'll be there with Lisa? That'll be fun to watch."

"Yes, it will," Gus said. "I bet they end up liking each other."

***

In late August, Lisa and Gus and, separately, Nicky, flew to London for the Brompton closing. Lisa arranged rooms at Claridge's. Except for a shy handshake in the lobby, she and Nicky didn't interact until the night before the closing. Gus booked a dinner for the three of them at an Indian restaurant.

Settling in, Gus saw from their body language that he'd have to initiate conversation. "Hope you guys like Indian. Whoops, no offense." He winked at Nicky.

Nicky laughed. "You mean they don't have bison burgers?"

Gus laughed, and Lisa smiled.

"So, Nicky," Gus said, "I have a couple of admin questions. First, when's your flight home?"

"Red-eye tomorrow night. I'll miss the closing dinner. Sorry. Back to school Monday."

Lisa spoke in a polite tone, "What are you majoring in?"

"No major yet, but I like English and science. I want to transfer to a four-year college if I can get in and then like maybe go to medical school."

"Like your uncle Johnny?" she asked.

"Guess so." Nicky broke off a piece of naan, dipped it in sauce, and stuffed it in his mouth. "Mmm!"

After a pause, Gus asked Nicky his admin questions. Nicky gave concise answers. Lisa seemed impressed.

Lisa and Nicky warmed up as the evening progressed. Gus could see Lisa responding as a woman to Nicky's effortless animal energy. When the dessert menu arrived, Nicky looked at his watch. "Oh, shoot! Hate to be rude, but there's a meeting I promised I'd lead tonight, so I should run."

Gus nodded and gave Lisa a furtive look. "Can we all go?"

"Well," Lisa said, calculating, "why not? I haven't been to an AA meeting since I arrived. Is this one where everyone has to speak?"

"No, it's, uh, a big group. And it's open, so you *can* come, Gus."

Gus waved for the check. "Can we walk, Nicky?"

"If we hustle," Nicky said, processing the idea that Lisa and Gus would join him at an AA meeting where he would share his story. "Brits run it . . . but you'd be welcome. I'd actually . . . it'd be cool!"

***

"I'm Nicky, and I'm an alcoholic."

"Hi, Nicky."

Preliminaries done, Nicky started his share. Two dozen people sat in a circle. From their dress, most seemed to be city professionals.

"So I grew up on an Indian reservation in Montana where there was a lot of crime and drinking. I did my share of both." After talking about his youth, he shifted to his army experience. "Afghanistan was where I started to get loaded regularly. I was an army medic. Everything was cheap and available, and the pressures were humongous, from the clinical work I did, which I don't have the time to tell you as much as I'd like."

Everyone was mesmerized, no one more than Lisa Bell.

"I didn't hit bottom till I got back home to Montana when I was discharged early because my great-grandfather who raised me was dying, and I was his main support. Howard was way over eighty. I got home, and he was dying, and I was . . . I got lucky. Just as I was going around the bend, my uncle Johnny, who was Howard's son—but he didn't know it—he came up from LA and rescued me essentially. He's a big-time heart surgeon. First thing he did, he made me promise to go cold turkey and go into a rehab facility. Then he took me in like a son and helped me get started in college, and his girlfriend who's an actress helped me too, like became my older sister, they're both awesome."

Nicky stopped to take a breath. He looked over at Lisa, sitting next to him. Tears trickled down her cheeks. Nicky looked at Gus, sitting next to Lisa. Gus lifted his chin, bidding him to continue.

"On top of going through withdrawal, I had combat stress too, PTSD they call it, like so many guys, which makes the craving worse because you have nightmares and panic attacks during the day—it's so hard to like adjust when you get home, you need something for the pain basically. Everyone I know who was over there had it to some degree, including two awesome British guys I got to know, and we stay in touch through e-mail.

"I never would have made it without Johnny and Michaela, but . . . so I finished rehab and went off to community college, and I go into these rooms as much as I can, and I have an amazing therapist in the Veterans Hospital in LA. I've relapsed once, but I've been clean and sober for almost a full year now. I'm in school, and I hope to become a physician. That's about it. I'm a very lucky dude."

The group sat mute, stunned by Nicky's story. One person clapped, and the others picked it up. People stood, and the applause became general. Then they sat and were quiet.

Nicky broke the awkward silence. "Well . . . thanks."

Two others shared, but their stories were flat after Nicky's, which was still in the air. The meeting threatened to end prematurely. Nicky looked around. "C'mon. Anyone else like to share?"

After a moment of shuffling silence, Lisa waved her handkerchief. "I'll go. Uh, my name is Lisa, and I'm an alcoholic."

"Hi, Lisa."

Gus and Nicky looked at each other.

"I'm pretty new to meetings. I didn't know about this one until Nicky told me at dinner. Told us." She tilted her head toward Gus, who had settled back and crossed his legs. Lisa, gathering strength, took a breath and plunged on.

"Hearing Nicky tell his story, which I did not know, it touched me, the fact that he would tell it so bravely. It made me want to tell my story too. Nicky's uncle, the doctor who rescued him, he's my former husband. The divorce was hard on me, and I started drinking heavily. I had a propensity—my father was a drunk. He left the family when I was fourteen. A few years later, my twin sister, who never got over his leaving, she killed herself. I had to quit college, get a job to support me and my mother.

"But there's this one thing I've never told anybody, except for two women psychologists. Not even the man I love, who's sitting here on my right." Lisa kept her focus on the shoes of the people across from her. Nicky saw Gus's face twitch imperceptibly.

Lisa's voice dropped to a whisper. "Never told Johnny either. I guess he'll find out now." She stole a glance at Nicky, who shook his head.

One of the British regulars spoke, "Lisa, madam, could you speak up please? Hard to hear in this awkward space."

Lisa sat up straight. "Yes, sorry. So my mother, she never knew this story either. She thought I was just a business genius. I *think* I can tell my story here today. The anonymous part of AA helps, although . . . well, who knows? This is the shame and anger at the heart of my life, why I have trouble with disagreeable things. Probably why I became a drunk.

"My first marriage . . . well, back up. I was a pretty girl at nineteen. When I dropped out of college, I needed to find a job. I became an actress in pornographic movies. This is the thing. I drove every day to Encino in the Valley, which is still the porn film capital, and did that. It was high pay—mother was an invalid, and we had no money. I hated it, hated myself, still do, but I had no other skills. I was scared we'd starve.

"So I did that, for three years. I reached the top of that so-called profession quickly. I was smart enough, had a certain 'talent,' I guess." She used air quotes for emphasis.

"So the owner of the business, and I want to be careful, I caught his eye. We connected, more than just sexually. Long story short, we got married, had one good, almost a normal year together. Then we became, essentially, business partners. I ran his businesses including the porn films. Then he died. I sold the business top of the market. Made a lot of money, and I've been trying to use it to help . . . well, I'm rambling. But . . . anyway, that's what I did. At least now I said it."

The group was mesmerized by Lisa's story. She looked down at her clenched hands. "I'll say again, I love this guy next to me and hope he doesn't hate me because of that mortifying story.

"Oh, sorry! I'm supposed to talk about my alcoholism and recovery!" Lisa exclaimed, clapping her hands. "Okay! Briefly. I didn't drink much until the divorce. I bottomed out six months ago. I was drunk almost every night, tried to hurt someone I believed, and it was all my boozy imagination, that she ruined my life. My ex's girlfriend, now his fiancée. Instead of hurting her, I actually helped her career, and I completely embarrassed myself. I ran away to London. My few remaining friends pulled me back and shipped me off to the Betty Ford Clinic. That was rough, but good and helpful—but if it wasn't for this guy here, I wouldn't have made it. I've been clean and sober now for little over seven months. Some of that was Betty Ford, so I'm still pretty new. I confess, every day I crave a drink. But it's getting better. I'll never take another drink. That's a promise, and that's my story."

Again, there was stunned silence, followed by a standing ovation.

One of the British regulars spoke, "Well, hmm, quite so! How to top the Americans? Well, um, I suppose we should end now."

He recited the AA closing patter. "Thank you all for sharing. Very good, very good. Thank you, Lisa. Quite powerful and, may I say, courageous? I wish you the best. And, Nicky, thank you for your service."

CHAPTER FIFTY-ONE

The late September day was sunny and hot. Lawyer Jack Pettker trudged up the steps of the Bel Air house to meet with Billy Bell. Pettker's briefcase was packed with superseded will codicils and trust amendments. Billy was an inveterate reviser. He was Pettker's favorite client, not because of the fees, which did flow, but because of his sweet, generous nature.

Billy still lived at Benedict Cañon with Johnny and Michaela, who were away getting married in Las Vegas. But he kept a key to Lisa's Bel Air house, where he was working today in the back den on his estate plan. Lisa and Gus were up in Santa Barbara.

Billy's Antonio welcomed Pettker and led him to the back den. Billy smiled and waved but made no move to rise from his desk chair. Pettker was shocked by Billy's enormity and deshabille. His hair was long and greasy and his beard a hircine mat that crawled down to merge with his wild chest hair. His face and head were blotched with vague yellows, browns, and reds. He waved at the cracked leather guest chair. Pettker recognized it as Wild Will's desk chair.

Billy pulled off his smudged glasses. "So nice to see you, Jack. Yes, that's Dad's old chair. Sorry, I can't get up. I'm not going to last long with this fluttery heart. So I want to finish at least this one project."

Pettker interrupted, "I . . . you could outlive me, Billy!"

"I don't think so, not with . . . how I feel. I find myself . . . what's the point? I like food. Not many pleasures left." Billy smiled and pulled on his glasses. "But let's not debate. Here's what I want to do."

***

After Pettker left, Billy called Nicky Bloodman.

"Hey, Billy, what's up?"

"Nicky, I hoped you still might be around. School started?"

"Oh, yes. I'm here in the mansion trying to read ahead while Johnny and Michaela are away. I can graduate in June if I push hard."

"That's great. Say, can I interest you in helping me celebrate Paco's twenty-first birthday? It's on Monday."

"His birthday's on Labor Day? Twenty-one? That's big. Johnny doesn't want me hanging with Paco, because, you know . . ."

"I do know, but it's just this one time. We'll have a quick pizza, sing happy birthday, and be back home by nine. Paco and Teresa would so love to see you. They talk about you all the time. Antonio will drive us."

"I haven't seen Paco in months. Is he doing okay?"

"Yes, starting college like you. His sister's working pretty steadily. So it's all good so far."

"That's awesome." Nicky thought for a moment. "I think I'd like to do that. I could use a break. What time on Monday?"

"Antonio and I could pick you up at four thirty. Would that work? Antonio packs a weapon, you know. He was an MP in Iraq."

"I know. We exchanged our stories. He's a good dude. Sure, four thirty, Monday. See you then."

***

The restaurant was tiny Pizza del Sardo in Santa Clarita, Paco and Teresa's favorite. Paco and Nicky were excited to see each other. Billy glowed with happiness.

Nicky saw the two hunched hooded men enter, their dark eyes searching the restaurant. He recognized the older man and lunged toward Teresa, shouting, "Everybody get down!"

The older man exclaimed as he aimed his weapon, "Quiet, you dead!"

Antonio, eating at the bar, spun and drew his pistol. An off-duty police officer pushed his wife to the floor and pulled out his piece. The small space exploded with noise, which stopped as suddenly as it started, except for groans and whimpers.

Both gunmen were down, the older dead, the other severely wounded. Paco and Teresa were unhurt. Billy was dead, shot twice in the head. He had caught rounds meant for Paco. Nicky was writhing on the floor with a shattered left shoulder. A lady at the next table had been shot in the ankle. The police report said that dozens of shots had been fired, and it was a miracle that only one bystander was hurt.

The patrons had cleared out, except for the off-duty policeman and a male nurse. The nurse was attending to the wounded lady and to Nicky, who was conscious but bleeding heavily. Antonio crouched by Billy's body, covered with a red checkered tablecloth. The off-duty cop had disarmed the wounded gunmen and was tying him up with a rope. The bartender was standing by the bar, waving a red napkin, muttering, "What the fuck? What the fuck?"

The police were there in force in two minutes.

***

A week after the shooting, Johnny sat on the leather couch in Gus's director's office, gazing down at Beverly Boulevard. "What a world, Gus. I just left Nicky with the orthopods. They'll have to rebuild his shoulder, but they're good at that. Nicky's right-handed. They say six, eight months, he should be good as new."

"I think so. Lisa may take longer to heal from losing Billy," Gus said. "Still hanging in clean and sober, though. I'm proud of her."

"Billy was her last link to Wild Will. Plus, he was Billy."

Gus nodded. "That he was."

"Yeah. It's so sad. Suicide by gangbangers. I'm sure he died smiling, taking bullets meant for Paco. I wish he hadn't dragged Nicky up there. Do you know he set up a life endowment for Paco and his sister? And he left Nicky a college fund, and his books and his coin collection."

"Where are those two kids now?" Gus asked.

"Who knows? Iowa? Miami? South America? The FBI took over. A full-bore witness protection deal. What a way to start life. Probably never see them again."

"Will that wounded shooter live?"

"The young guy, he's hanging on," Johnny said. "Just a boy getting jumped in the cops think. The dead guy was the serious OG."

"What's 'jumped in'? And what's an OG?"

"Jumped in is gang initiation. OG is original gangster. A pro. I'm learning the language."

"That's a bad sign."

"I know, I know."

"How's Michaela? Hey, dude, congratulations on your wedding, by the way. Not to mention!"

"She's fine, thanks. Big as a house, but more gorgeous than ever. This thing really shook her up. Especially Billy's death. She didn't know about the gang stuff. Didn't want to know. She's trying to change her life—like me, only in the opposite direction. I'm trying to join the human race, she's trying to resign."

"You're both fucking nuts," Gus said, pressing his index finger to his temple.

"I know your views. We never did make it to Bryce. Someday. Maybe a family outing. Her two sons are due next month, Pavlos from Crete and our little Billy Ben."

"Seriously? Billy Ben? Sounds like a redneck from Texas."

"We may move to Texas. Or somewhere in the South."

"You're getting closer to moving?"

"After this shooting episode, Michaela wants out of LA. I'm ready. I like the vets, but I'm fed up fighting the government."

"You worried about retaliation of some kind?"

"I suppose a little. But it's more than that. There's nothing here for us anymore."

"That would be sad for me," Gus said. "Speaking of sad news, I heard in the corridors of power that your former father figure . . . Stan McRae?"

Johnny looked up. "Stanley? What about him?"

"Not sure, nobody can get any information. Rumor is he had a stroke. He's at home, in hospice maybe?"

"Really? God, not a great week for the people I care about."

"I'm doing fine, thank you very much. Although my father passed last week."

"Oh, I'm so sorry. I didn't know. Was he . . ."

"It was fine. Peaceful. He . . ." Gus's voice broke.

Johnny stood, stepped around the desk, and put his hands on Gus's shoulders. Gus leaned his head against Johnny's arm. They held that pose for a long minute. Gus broke the silence. "Okay, thanks, pal. I'm good."

Johnny returned to the leather couch and sat hard. "That's tough. I hadn't heard that. Hadn't heard about Stanley either. I should go see him."

"Stan was a good leader. Even though . . . I could never figure out why he was so tight with Poulos."

"I think there's a story we don't know," Johnny said.

"Like what?"

"Not sure . . . I shouldn't talk . . ."

"You speak in tongues. Does it connect to the Gomez deal?"

Johnny hesitated. "That's a good guess. There's still a lot I don't know about the Gomez deal. They're still trying to fit things together. This shooting in Santa Clarita . . ."

"Relates to Gomez? No shit!"

"Don't jump to conclusions just because I can't keep my mouth shut. Maybe Stanley could shed some light if I can get in and see him. And maybe then I can get on with my life. Move south. Change my name to Johnny Jack. But we didn't have this conversation, Gus."

"No problem. You sure got my attention, though, dude."

***

Johnny called McRae's home number that afternoon. The woman who answered said that McRae couldn't come to the phone. "He mentions your name, but he's very weak, Dr. Blood. I'll tell him you called."

The next morning, Johnny's cell buzzed. As it did a year earlier, the caller ID showed S. MCRAE.

"Blood. Is this Stanley?"

A thin whisper rasped, "Johnny."

"Stan, you're sick, I hear. Can I visit? I'd like to see you."

"Tomorrow morning, early as you can."

"I will. Seven okay?"

"Seven. Yes. You know where I live. Please."

CHAPTER FIFTY-TWO

Johnny had to miss an important meeting to see McRae. VA officials were in town for go-no-go meetings on Toby Roberts's heart-transplant project. The signs were not encouraging.

But he had to see Stanley. And he didn't care anymore about Toby Roberts's dreams. He had his own dreams.

Johnny drove the short distance from the mansion to West Hollywood. Arriving before 7:00 a.m., he was buzzed up to McRae's condo. He sat in the kitchen and sipped a cup of thin coffee while the hospice nurse fluttered around. "This is not a good idea, sir. He's terribly weak."

"He called me. I want to see him."

"You'll have to wait for Doctor to finish."

After ten minutes, a man emerged from McRae's bedroom and offered his hand. "I'm Dr. Farbstein. He'll see you, Dr. Blood. Be careful. He's quite fragile."

"Thanks." Johnny stood. "What's he suffering from?"

"You'll have to ask him."

The nurse opened the bedroom door. Johnny stood in the doorframe, his eyes adjusting to the dimness. The familiar scent was of old age and death. He stepped in and approached the bed. He was shocked to see the gaunt mummy that was once his vigorous mentor. McRae's skin was parchment, and his mouth was ringed by sores. Only his eyes were alive.

McRae pointed toward a wooden chair. "Sit, Johnny." His thin voice had surprising fiber. "I'm glad you came. I have more energy than these dreadful people know." He paused. "What are they telling you?"

Johnny pulled the chair up to the bed. "Stanley! Well! I'm glad to see you. They say you're very sick. They won't tell me what the problem is."

"AIDS." He paused. "Just look at me. An aggressive version, on top of immune system issues I've been battling all my life. I'm gay, you see." He studied Johnny's face. "No reaction?" Half of his mouth smiled. "And I guess I had a small stroke two weeks ago. My left side is weak. You're the only outside person who knows all this." He stopped to catch his breath. "The worst is my lungs are failing. I won't go to the hospital, Johnny. I need your help." His coal-black eyes fixed on Johnny.

"God, Stan! Of course, whatever you need, but I have some questions if you have enough energy. I'll try to make them yes-or-no questions so you won't have to talk too much."

"I know what your questions are. I can talk as much as you want." He paused. "If you can be patient. My breath is short. But I want to start with my request."

Johnny nodded. "Please."

"Open the drawer there and take out the gloves." McRae rolled his right thumb toward the bedside table. Johnny opened the drawer and picked out a pair of surgical gloves.

"Put the gloves on. They're your size. I got them from your OR."

Johnny did as he was told.

"Now, pick up the false bottom. Take the key out. And the note."

Johnny found a small brass key and an envelope.

"Suicide note," McRae said, twisting his lips. "Give it here."

Johnny handed him the envelope. "That's what I was afraid of, Stan."

"Yes. Okay now, over there, that long narrow drawer at the bottom of the bureau?" McRae waved toward the other side of the room. "Unlock it please." He cleared his throat. "There's a box in a blue pouch."

Johnny crossed the room, bent down, and put the key in the keyhole.

"I haven't tried that lock since Arthur died," McRae rasped.

After a few attempts, Johnny managed to open the drawer. He removed a blue silk pouch containing a heavy box. He suspected the box contained a weapon; he was familiar with weapons from his adolescent years in Crow Agency. "What do you want me to do with this?"

"Bring it here. Open it. Tell me what's in it."

"I think I know what's in it."

Johnny returned to his chair and slid the box out of the pouch. It was made of dark rich wood. Ornate gold letters read: Stamitos Makarazos. He opened the box and beheld a blue metal pistol in a plastic bag, sitting in a crimson velvet bed. He removed the pistol from the plastic bag and weighed the gun in his gloved hands. He was struck by its simple beauty.

"Haven't held one of these in years. Decades. It's a Browning M1911, a .45-caliber service pistol, semiautomatic action—a World War II officer's sidearm. Looks pretty clean. Safety's on." He ejected the magazine and examined the chamber. "Full magazine, live rounds, don't know how old. There's nothing in the chamber. My father, Howard, he had one of these. I took care of it. We used it for target practice when I was a kid. I remember the big kick."

"Good," McRae said. "From what you told me years ago, I thought you might know how to chamber a round."

"What are you driving at, Stan?"

McRae's eyes narrowed. He spoke with a bitter intensity. "These people want me to die in as much misery as they can arrange. Deaden me with steroids and morphine and let me drown in my own mucous. I don't want that death, Johnny."

"You want me to shoot you?" Johnny cocked an eyebrow.

"Of course not." Stan started coughing. When he finally caught his breath, he shook his head and waved his good hand back and forth. "My grandfather, my mother's father, he gave me that pistol over fifty years ago." His eyes drifted. "He was a Greek army officer in the First World War, fought with the French in Serbia. That pistol was a gift from an American officer. He wore it in the victory parade through the *Arc de Triomphe* in 1919."

"You're Greek? McRae?"

"My real name is Stamitos Makarazos, like on that box. My grandfather had it made for my twenty-first birthday. I became Stanley McRae when my father sent me from Athens to my aunt McRae in Baltimore in 1950." He stopped to breathe. "He found out I was homosexual, yes, and that wouldn't do for the son of an ambitious Greek army officer. So he exported me to America." A minute went by. "I lived with my widowed aunt and my grandfather in Baltimore, went to school there through medical school. Lovely city. My father, Col. Nikolas Makarazos, was finance minister in the 1967 Junta." He paused again. "When the colonels were forced out, he went into exile. Died at ninety. I have little memory of him."

McRae coughed. "Could you refill my water glass, Johnny? From the bathroom tap? I need to catch my breath a minute."

Johnny set the gun parts on the bed and got the water. As he sat, he asked, as casually as he could, "Is there a connection here with Arthur Poulos?" He picked up the gun parts and re-settled them in his lap.

"*Now* we're on to your agenda," McRae said. There was an edge in his voice. His eyes wandered. "Yes, of course, there is. Arthur loved that gun. Whenever he came to visit, he'd take it out, clean it, oil it. Those bullets are from him." He stopped for breath. "I never touched it, I don't think twice in fifty years.

"But to answer your question. My father supervised Arthur's work in Greece during the Colonels' Junta. Arthur was a prodigy. He had started out as a heart surgeon—that's important. You didn't know that."

"Really?"

"Yes, which is one reason he was so jealous of you. When the Socialists forced him out of Greece years later, Arthur came directly to me at Cedars. He had almost nothing except my father's story about me and compromising pictures." McRae raised a handkerchief to his face.

"Can I do that for you, Stan?"

"No, I can do it." He wiped his face. "Arthur also had a portfolio of professional credentials, letters of recommendation, most of them phony. I made sure we hired him. As a cardiologist, not as a surgeon. I took a chance, pulled in a lot of favors."

"So he blackmailed you? I thought there was something like that."

"Yes. I know you suspected something. But he turned out to be a fine cardiologist, didn't he? And administrator? Perversely, we became friends. Two exiles, helping each other hide our stories. Vipers in a bottle."

"Did you know about Arthur's role in the Gomez death?"

McRae paused again to wipe his face. "I knew."

"What did you know?"

"I learned about the gang hospital killings from that Iranian police officer after Judge Freiberg's death. Then out of the blue, Arthur asked me to loan him half a million. He'd suffered badly in the stock market crash in 2009, and he needed cash. I didn't have that kind of money, and he knew it. I wasn't going to borrow for him. That was a tense time. I found out later he got money from your ex-wife. Sold her old coins. I think he used it for Emilio Hand, who was desperate. Arthur mentored Emilio, and I think he had something on him too. I heard poor Emilio died recently in Mexico."

"That's what I heard. The bad guys probably didn't want Emilio alive, knowing what he knew."

"Yes. Arthur told me on his deathbed what Emilio did." He took a breath. "Not the first time. And what *he* did. Unforgivable. They both received money out of the Gomez settlement, which Arthur railroaded through the insurance." McRae seemed emotional. He wiped his face again. "So, yes, I knew. I'm sorry, Johnny. I know how it impacted you. But Arthur . . . he would have . . .

"After his heart transplant." McRae was losing his voice. "Arthur felt remorse. You remember that priest? And then he apologized to all of us? Crazy. I guess even with the worst people, there's always a spark." He closed his eyes. "His killing Gomez was about you, Johnny. Arthur was terribly sick, he had just lost half his net worth. Emilio was an even worse mess, close to bankruptcy and his marriage failing. Arthur was desperate to take you down before he retired. You were everything he was not."

"He came very close to taking me down," Johnny said. "Lisa told me she bought those rare coins from him to help him out."

"Yes. Well . . . I'm sure she didn't know Arthur's evil plan. I knew Mrs. Bell. She's a good person, a little . . . confused?" He paused again. "Those two little coins . . . Arthur had them in his mouth when he came through customs in 1992. Fifth-century Sicily, mint condition. Beauties. That was all the value he had when he showed up on my doorstep. Plus the dirty pictures. Mrs. Bell's money enabled Arthur to bring Emilio into the game."

Johnny listened quietly, his gloved hands absently caressing the weapon.

McRae peered at Johnny. "Tell me about Mrs. Bell, Johnny. Is she still . . . ?"

"She's better, sober, trying to get her life together. She and Gus . . ."

"I heard that about Gus. Gus is a good man." McRae reached for his water glass with his trembling right hand. Johnny helped him take a sip. "Thanks. It's been my life's work to prevent people knowing I'm gay. That's all I care about anymore."

"Why, Stan? It's not a big issue anymore."

"It certainly was a big issue in Greece in the late 1940s! A big issue with my father! It was a big deal here too, until . . ."

"Maybe fifteen years ago. But now it's not such a big deal."

"I'm an old man, Johnny, locked into an image of myself. See those pictures on the wall?" McRae waved his good hand. "I'd never be in those pictures with those estimable people. It's still a big deal to me, a weakness."

"Being gay? It's not a weakness, Stan, for god's sake! It's the stupid world that's weak."

"My weakness is not that I'm gay, it's that I can't change." He stopped to even out his breathing. "That I can't come out of the closet on my deathbed. Except here, today, with you, but for a specific purpose, which, even that is not easy." He fumbled with his handkerchief. Johnny helped him wipe his brow.

"Thank you. I've been imagining this day for a long time. My hope is that you will keep all this private. I must make that assumption." He paused. "I want to die thinking that the world regards me in a certain way. That does not include gay or AIDS or foolish or that I was a fraud, complicit in a murder. That I lied to everyone from the board of the medical center to law enforcement agents. A criminal!"

Johnny put the gun and magazine on the floor. He stood up, moved to the window, and cracked the curtain. The view was south, down busy San Vicente Boulevard. The sky was gray, and rush hour was beginning. Across the street, someone was unlocking a shop door, preparing for the new day.

"You're not a fraud as far as I'm concerned, Stan. You were my rock. I would never have made it without you. We all have things in our background."

McRae coughed. "Thank you. Your opinion matters. I am telling you all this so that you will do what I'm requesting."

"What are you requesting?" Johnny said, returning to the chair and picking up the gun parts.

"Right after Arthur died, I went into a gay bar here in West Hollywood. It had been many years. I don't know what possessed me—I guess I was depressed that my friend had died."

"Some friend, Stan."

"He *was* my friend! He was the only person who knew the real me! When he died, *nobody* knew me. Do you know how that feels?

"I had a right to be depressed, a right to do something stupid when I lost him!"

"If you say so."

"I do say so! Please respect that!" McRae was agitated. Tears pooled in his eyes.

"Okay, sorry—I've done some stupid things too."

"Yes, indeed you have.

"So I contracted AIDS. Right here in this bed with some cute young gentleman I never saw again. He wore a red sweatband on his head, and that was all he wore. I had to pay him. I don't want the world to know that." He paused for a long time.

"I don't want to die a miserable death, Johnny. When I die, at the moment I die, I want to believe that I'll be remembered in a certain way." He had another coughing fit. Johnny sat patiently.

"You're the only one alive who knows my real story, Johnny. So you have a special responsibility.

"Help me work the gun there." His eyes glowed.

"Stan, even if I wanted to, which, I have big trouble, there's a law . . ."

"I know the law. It's my gun, not yours. Just chamber the round then you can leave, as long as the safety's on when you leave—that is not killing me or assisting my death. You'll have time before I . . ."

"But . . ."

"Johnny, *please*. I'm running out of gas. One other thing. I think you do respect me. I think you love me, if I may. I want to think that. That's why I called you. Why you came. Why I told you these things." His breathing rattled now. He tried to clear his throat. "Arthur knew I loved you, not just like a son, although there was that. He hated my feelings for you. You were so beautiful then and so simple in your bubble. You never wanted anything except to do surgery. Everything else was in the way." Johnny wiped his brow again.

"Arthur didn't understand that. You weren't a very good director anyway. But you were a great surgeon. A genius."

Johnny smiled. "No, I'm not a good manager. Gus is so much better. Even Arthur would have been better. And all of this might have been avoided, if Wild Will Bell hadn't . . ."

"Probably *not* the case." McRae spoke sharply. "Arthur had such a hard heart. He would have found a way . . ."

"To bring us all down? Your friend Arthur?"

"My friend Arthur. Yes! It was just a matter of time before he unraveled. Before he couldn't bear it anymore. But the fact is I *am* gay, I *did* go into the bars. And you *are* more talented than he was. And he *did* try to sell his daughter. And he *did* do monstrous things. And I *did* love you! That was a world he could not accept."

"He wanted to destroy that world?"

"Until the very end anyway. Whatever *that* was about, the deathbed apologies. People are so strange." He paused. "One more question, Johnny, before I lose all my energy. I worry about you, your prostate cancer. I hear you're not taking care of it."

"I decided just this week to have it removed. The numbers are getting worse. I haven't told Michaela yet, she . . ."

"That's a good decision."

"You love her, of course. She's very beautiful. Arthur's daughter. Life is so strange. She's pregnant?"

Johnny smiled. "Yes, she's pregnant. We're married now. I think she'll be all right with it. She's been through a lot, but she's tough. She's been teaching me things, Stan, from how to love a woman to little Greek phrases. She wants us to move away from LA."

"Where would you go?"

"Anywhere. The Midwest? Back to Montana, Medicine Mountain?"

"Medicine Mountain?"

"My father's imaginary holy place. Doesn't matter."

"I see. Whatever would you do? You told me once you wanted to care for Indians. Is that it?"

"Did I? I don't think I'll ever be complete until I do that."

"Is that your father's holy place?" McRae embarked on a two-minute coughing fit. Johnny, hovering, worrying, handed him tissues. After a while, McRae resumed normal breathing. He spoke in a whisper, "I like Michaela, that one time I met her. It's good that you're married. I didn't know."

McRae lay silent for a minute, his eyes shut tight. Johnny let him rest. He whispered, "Now help me work the gun."

"I . . ." Johnny raised his gloved right hand in protest.

"Don't say no!" Stan's eyes blazed, and he tried to sit up. "It's wrong to let me suffer! I don't want to die that kind of death!"

Johnny stared at McRae, whose fiery burst seemed to consume his last bit of strength. He sunk back into his pillow and closed his eyes again, his face ashen. The pistol sat in Johnny's lap.

After a long moment, McRae whispered, "*Please* help me, Johnny. I can't do it alone. I beg you." He paused, his eyes closed. "Just give me the option."

"I'm not in your will, am I?"

"No. Everything goes to UC Cedars. That's my guilt."

Johnny's face firmed. He had made a decision.

"Okay, Stanley. Open your eyes. Watch this." He lifted the weapon to the level of his head. An image of Howard rose in his mind's eye. With effort, he brought himself back to the present moment.

"Loading the magazine." He pushed the magazine into the stock with a click. "Chambering a round." Johnny moved the slide back and forth along the barrel, seating a round in the chamber. "Now here's how you release the safety." He flipped the safety to the off position. He placed the primed weapon on the bed next to McRae's right hand. "Okay, Stanley, now it's ready to fire. Go ahead, shoot yourself!" He moved the box and pouch from the floor to the night table and dropped the little brass key on top. "God!"

McCrae sighed. "Thank you, Johnny. It matters that you care. Now, put the safety back on, and you should go."

Johnny re-engaged the safety. He snapped off his gloves, stuffed them in his pocket, and stood. "What's the best way out of here?"

McRae put his right hand over his heart. "Fine, so, safety's on. Now you're not responsible. Lock the door there so they can't come in easily. Go out the back door here behind the curtain." He waved toward the curtain on the back wall. "It goes down to the lobby. Check out with the guard. There's a security camera, which will record you leaving and the time."

Johnny stood and walked across the room to lock the door. As he did he noticed a wicker basket in the corner. "Stan, where's your little dog?"

"Ah. Sweet Buddy. Dead. Last week. So sad." Long pause. McRae's eyes were squeezed tight. "You'll have at least ten minutes before I do anything. If I do anything."

Johnny stood by the bed. "Good-bye, Stanley. Stamitos—may I? *Yia sou.*" Johnny bent over and kissed him on the forehead. "My Greek is not so good yet."

McRae's closed eyes were leaking tears. "Of course, you may call me by my real name. My dearest Johnny Blood Moon." Pause. "*Yia Sou.*"

THE END

ACKNOWLEDGMENTS

This is always dicey because it risks leaving people out and misstatement. Suffice it to say, I am deeply grateful to those friends and advisors who read drafts of this book and especially for their candid feedback—always valuable, always welcome. It's the only way to grow and learn.

But I must single out a few especially long-suffering folks. I am not a physician, so my polymathic pal Dr. Mark Farbstein was my Virgil on this journey through the medical world. I think he read three drafts, and his counsel about the idiom and culture of doctors and hospitals, as well as his astute literary observations, were incredibly useful. Nor am I an immigration expert, so the advice of my lawyer pal Eric Avasian about Michaela's visa challenges was indispensible. And, of course, my long-suffering wife, Belinda, read *beaucoup* drafts and listened to innumerable laments. What a blessing to have her around. As we, shall I say, mature together, the gloves come off, and I really learn from her sharp, sensitive, loving reading and deep thinking. And thank you sis-in-law Susie for the lovely front cover image. Finally, thanks to my editor, Meghan Pinson, for fearless efforts to get me to squeeze the water out.

The usual bailout at this point is to say that any remaining errors are all on me, which is true. I did finesse or ignore some advice—it sure seemed like a good idea at the time. If any of my adds or omissions did not advance character or story, then I should be taken out and shot. Or something.

CPSIA information can be obtained at www.ICGtesting.com
Printed in the USA
LVOW11*2020311014

411431LV00002B/45/P